A life above the line – just!

C. P. (Charles Pierre) Altmann

authorHOUSE

AuthorHouse™ UK
1663 Liberty Drive
Bloomington, IN 47403 USA
www.authorhouse.co.uk
Phone: UK TFN: 0800 0148641 (Toll Free inside the UK)
UK Local: 02036 956322 (+44 20 3695 6322 from outside the UK)

© 2020 C. P. (Charles Pierre) Altmann. All rights reserved.

No part of this book may be reproduced, stored in a retrieval system, or transmitted by any means without the written permission of the author.

Published by AuthorHouse 10/23/2020

ISBN: 978-1-7283-5675-4 (sc)
ISBN: 978-1-7283-5674-7 (e)

Print information available on the last page.

Any people depicted in stock imagery provided by Getty Images are models, and such images are being used for illustrative purposes only.
Certain stock imagery © Getty Images.

This book is printed on acid-free paper.

Because of the dynamic nature of the Internet, any web addresses or links contained in this book may have changed since publication and may no longer be valid. The views expressed in this work are solely those of the author and do not necessarily reflect the views of the publisher, and the publisher hereby disclaims any responsibility for them.

This book is a fictional life of a character in advertising with some true, real life events and accurate anecdotes, which are deliberate, to demonstrate what advertising was really like in those halcyon days of the last quarter of the 20th Century, and a bit beyond. All of the other stories could have happened, and in many cases did, in one way or another, but they have been fictionalised to protect the identity of companies and personnel. There is no attempt in these fictionalised stories to base the people on anyone known to be living or dead. Any notion that these people are real is purely coincidental and in no way intentional.

CONTENTS

Chapter 1	"Failed at everything else"	1
Chapter 2	'A horse, a horse, my kingdom for a horse'	14
Chapter 3	'Never underestimate the power of a woman'	44
Chapter 4	'Go West Young Man – To The Land Of Opportunity'	82
Chapter 5	'International White Trash in New Markets'	119
Chapter 6	Internationalism – 'The way of the world'	161
Chapter 7	A Game of Chance	190
Chapter 8	'The Risk Taker'	216
Chapter 9	Be the difference & do it differently	246
Chapter 10	Beyond Control	273
Chapter 11	The Final Curtain Call?	299

CHAPTER 1

"Failed at everything else"

Christoph Aitkins always denied his foreign origins. For this reason he was only too happy when people abbreviated his name simply to Chris. Physically he was not ugly, but nor could he be described as handsome. What he had was charm in abundance, a really positive outlook on life with a pretty well permanent smiling countenance and a mischievous sense of humour as well as a quick mind with rapier sharp repartee. His behaviour and demeanour was truly more English than the English. For someone exuding such confidence it was surprising that he walked with a stoop, which apparently came from a time when he had grown very quickly and was conscious that aged 13 and 6ft 2ins(in old money) he stood out, towering over his age group. Green eyed and fair haired he was somewhat unfairly described by a disapproving Anglican parent, of an early love and girlfriend, as 'a blonde bull-necked German Papist'. True he had played rugby up to county level and this had not enhanced his looks giving him two broken noses and at the time a solid 19 inch neck. It was also factually correct that he had been brought up a Catholic and after expulsion by the Jesuits aged 12, having held the beating record there with a ferula, across his hands, for unruly behaviour, he had then gone on to the Benedictines. Here he also held the record for beating but this time with the cane across his rump, before in 1966 corporal punishment was finally abandoned and made illegal. However, his origins were decidedly not German but from a longstanding Swiss family who had been given their coat-of-arms, for fighting, as a mercenary, alongside Louis V11, in the disastrous Second Crusade (1147-1150).

Chris was very much his own man and led his life totally on his own terms. He 'played' the game of life to his rules or, at the very least, to his interpretation of these rules. He didn't go to University - out of choice - but then, back in 1969, when he left school, only around 7% of pupils went on to further education. Instead, on leaving school, he became a hippy and went off travelling around Europe, at the same time pursuing his passion for writing – seeking as he put it 'to get that out of his system'. Somewhat high on dope he wrote a book about his views and observations on the Italian Renaissance – which, even he, on reflection, believed was worthy of doing nothing with. He then scribed a novella love story, which was lost by the woman he gave it to type – perhaps fortuitously, he would wryly remark.

Eventually, when the air and his head had cleared but still somewhat the worst for wear he took refuge in the Channel Islands and laid low on Alderney. Chris took a job as a kitchen porter, graduating to second chef status, in a popular compact marine hotel, situated close to the harbour. Quality was not at a premium and certainly refined dining was neither called-for nor even on the menu. He made the most of his time off even finding time for an afternoon romance, between shifts, with one of the waitresses, who curiously had never ever left the island.

Once his health had been fully restored and with some meagre savings not so much from his long hours in the hotel kitchen but from bets taken over the bar, as no betting shop existed on Alderney, he headed back to the mainland, the metropolis and home. Starting with mobile discotheques, slightly impeded by his inability to drive, and party management; he even organised a black and white cat themed ball for the Lord Mayor of London. However, he soon realised his company, Allegro Entertainments, was not going to earn him a proper crust, never mind make him a fortune. So followed a spate of distinctly 'uninteresting' jobs in the City of London, including working for the National Westminster Bank ('our roots are our branches') – curtailed by glandular fever ('the kissing disease') and Lloyds of London in a clerical roll where his only real claim to fame was being photographed and featured in their recruitment advertising. He was however amused that the risks accepted even included insuring the Norwegian model, Julie Ege's (1947-2008) legs for over a million pounds; while another policy insured an actress from 'an eagle picking up a tortoise and dropping it on her head' - a somewhat unlikely event given the filming was at Elstree Studios.

Having always loved his holiday jobs in retail with Harrods it was not surprising that he found his way back over the counter. At the same time he continued to write articles, observations, letters and poems and even embarked on a romantic novel, based on his luckless encounters with other more worthy suitors for the attention of a 'femme fatale'. Unfortunately, for Christoph, this too got mislaid in one of his various domicile moves – probably a blessing in hindsight, especially as he comprehensively failed to win the lady's heart.

In the early days of the 1970s the Army & Navy store in Victoria was a crusty old fashioned retail emporium, with its Victorian (1874) soot blackened exterior, based in a largely residential area. It had seen, and had, better days when the British Empire was at its height and when it had both the reputation and capability to supply and ship, literally, anything from a pin to an elephant to and even from the colonial 'masters'. Curiously, Christoph, despite its dated image and appearance, found the place his metier. It seemed to play to his strengths. He quickly established himself as a charming, patient, adept and deft salesman in the Men's Department. When a depth of sale was required, or there was a need for a little gentle persuasion to clinch the sale, or even the need for a persuasive argument, Christoph was their man. He served Royalty, such as Princess Margaret and her flunkies, who carried the money, as easily and comfortably as he did little wizened old ladies, or fearsome matriarchs. Even flashy young blades seeking to impress at a ball, party or event and wanting the right advice as to the best and most appropriate, shirt to accompany their dinner jacket, sought out Christoph's opinion. The till receipts rolled up and his reputation grew accordingly.

Indeed, progress was only impaired and somewhat blighted by three events. The first was affection of the heart where Chris discovered the beautifully made up and striking ladies in the next room's Cosmetics Department. These dalliances included a tall, slim, raven haired, dark eyed East ender, who was Manageress of the department. Managing his romances, through the various echelons of the department, took new found skills of subtlety, poise, and dexterity – or, in effect, deviousness. Christoph knew that the key was to keep the fine looking mature beautiful manageress on side, which he accomplished with aplomb.

The second event that affected his status quo was actually within the Men's Department and came somewhat unexpectedly from an Iranian born colleague. Amir had teamed up with Christoph to try to drive the sales of men's shirts and so while Chris employed his unhurried charm and gentle humour to woo the sales, Amir took the quick sales, especially at lunchtime. One week, after a series of record sales week-on-week, Amir simply did not appear and had gone absent without permission. His departure remained unannounced and unexplained. It later transpired that security had been watching both Christoph and Amir for some time with utmost discretion. They had discovered that there had been a series of incidences of petty pilfering which over time had increased in frequency and involved the higher priced items from the shop floor and stock room. These items included tiepins, cufflinks and studs most of which was recovered when a raid was carried out on Amir's premises. One evening, as Christoph made his way out, from the staff entrance, and down Howick Place he was alarmingly pulled into a side doorway and found a stiletto blade from a flick knife pointed at his throat. His assailant was a menacingly threatening looking Amir. Amir was certain that Christoph had 'grassed him up' reporting his activities to security. It took all of Chris's calmness and persuasive powers, under considerable pressure, to convince Amir that it was hardly him as he had been under scrutiny and investigated as well. Furthermore, he had had no knowledge of what had happened or that anyone else beyond himself was under surveillance. Fortunately, as Amir reflected on this, he appreciated that Christoph had no cause or reason to suspect him, and certainly he had not taken Chris into his confidence and as such he had no knowledge on which 'to shop' him.

A life above the line – just!

Just as suddenly as he had appeared Amir then disappeared into the night leaving Christoph somewhat shaken but unharmed.

The third factor had much more serious consequences for Christoph. It was decided that after the Amir affair that the stock rooms in the basement should be sorted and cleaned out. It seemed, on initial observation, highly unlikely that any cleaning had taken place possibly for over a century. By the time Christoph had finished the task he had developed a persistent cough which gradually developed into a fever. Day-by-day Chris's health gradually deteriorated and when in a private moment, in the office of the Cosmetic Manageress, he started to cough up blood she had him sent home to bed. By the time Chris got home he could barely breathe. He called the doctor, who on hearing of his symptoms, immediately called an ambulance. Lying close to the open door into the flat, to facilitate ease of access for the ambulance crew, they found Chris only semi-conscious. Fixing an oxygen mask over his face they stretchered him out and carted him off to St. George's Hospital in those days located at Hyde Park Corner, now the site of the Lanesborough Hotel. It proved to be a very long slow recovery from what was diagnosed to be viral pneumonia. This event did mean that his estranged parents met for the last time over Christoph's fractured and wrecked body, as his mother read the racing results much to the disapproval and disgust of his father. He was fortunately well enough to sit up in the communal lounge and watch the 1973 Grand National when agonisingly Red Rum got up in, the shadows of the post, to beat Crisp, the Champion 2 mile chaser, bred in New Zealand, whom had boldly and bravely led from start to finish, carrying top weight. It was Red Rum's first Aintree experience and he would go on to win the race 3 times and be second twice before retiring, as the greatest Grand National horse in the history of the race.

Shortly afterwards Christoph finally got back to work but was advised by the hospital medical team to start slowly and take it relatively easy, as he sought to rebuild his strength. This meant he was given light duties and paperwork in the office, which he both loathed and resented. He was, after all, a natural born front man and salesman. Christoph throughout his life was always most dangerous and unpredictable when not fully or properly occupied and when he wasn't kept really busy. Too much time on his hands gave him far too much time to think. This was such an occasion and circumstance. As he studied the environs of the Army & Navy store he recognised that their in-store communications and external advertising in the National and local press was stylistically outmoded, definitely dated and distinctly unremarkable. Accordingly, Christoph decided to approach the Marketing Department, then quaintly known as The Press Office – more like depressed – & Public Relations Department (note no mention of advertising!) and was eventually called up to go and see Mrs Passmore. When he got there he was confronted by a frosty, slim, draconian, clipped woman in her late 40s, with tightly curled dark hair and pillar box red lipstick, dressed in a tightly fitting knee length grey checked pencil skirt and matching bolero jacket. The meeting did not go well. Mrs Passmore was not a woman to be challenged and least of all by a 22year old upstart. Christoph became more and more animated when it came to a discussion over the communication and advertising of the store and its consumer offerings. Perhaps describing this as being antiquated with black and white line drawings, from a by-gone age, which failed to bring the products to life or engage the reader or viewer was maybe not the most tactful approach to take. As he went on to talk about the need not merely to show but to persuade and sell he saw Mrs Passmore's hackles rise and her sour face gradually turned red with white blotches. When he had finished he was finished. She described him as an arrogant, unknowing, outspoken and offensive young man. He was dismissed literally and metaphorically.

Quite undeterred Christoph then wrote to the Vice Chairman, Doug Skidman, and outlined to him his views about the style of the store's communications internally and externally. He also expressed his disappointment that no Personnel representative nor member of Management had been involved in this interview process with Mrs Passmore. A few days passed and then Chris received a call from Mr. Skidman's office requesting for him to go over and see him there and then. The Management offices were situated in a separate building facing the store on Howick Place and involved crossing the road and walking up to the 4th floor. Arriving there he was soon ushered into a large oak panelled room where seated behind a sizeable dark wood desk was a short stoutly built man with a slightly ruddy complexion and flat glossy Brylcreemed hair immaculately dressed in a plain charcoal double breasted grey suit. Here sat a person exuding an air of authority and confidence. He peered at Christoph, after asking him to sit down, rather as a cat might study a cornered mouse before pouncing. Then somewhat flamboyantly waving Christoph's letter in one hand he barked, "And so Mr. Aitkin where do you think a letter like this is going to get you?", in a gruff sonorous South London accent. Christoph smiled mischievously and responded sprightly "Exactly here, Sir, and now I can tell you what I feel I can do for you…" He continued to outline his views and Doug Skidman listened attentively, gradually relaxing back into his Chesterfield studded chair, but still never taking his pale blue eyes off the prey before him. Christoph went on to outline his criticisms of the retailer's communication and how, in his humble opinion, it could be changed, and arguably improved, at no risk to the reputation of this emporium, or indeed the group, as a whole. Mr Skidman started to make notes as this impassioned pitch progressed and when it ended there was a brief silence, during which he tapped his fingers on the desk top, as he perused his notes, and then a slight smile crossed his face as he stated "Well you have certainly managed to make an enemy out of Mrs Passmore, so I can't really have you imposed on her. However," he continued, "I do have a job that needs to be done and that is to bring greater unity and consistency in promotions and communications across the stores in our newly expanded group (they had recently acquired the South London group of retail outlets, Chiesmans), particularly in the Southern half of the country."

And so it was Christoph virtually overnight became the Group Promotions Manager and travelled extensively through the Midlands to Birmingham, Warwick and Stratford right down to Dorchester in the South West and around London and the Home Counties with Bromley, Romford, Streatham and Ilford. This truly was living the high life! Through discussions with Senior Management members of the individual stores and their buyers locally and centrally Christoph established where there was common ground and which areas of the business could and should be supported unilaterally. Christoph demonstrated how a uniform look and style could be achieved both internally and externally for these joint promotions maximising impact and budgets. A yearlong plan was put in place and the cost-effectiveness of this centrally controlled activity programme quickly became clear. The results followed and the new look and style was acknowledged as being a positive key factor despite the doubts initially expressed. Christoph was always on the move and so even though he had a desk in Mrs Passmore's domain he was largely able to escape her looks of disdain, distrust and deep dislike.

But then suddenly it all started to unravel for Christoph as he sought to extend the remit of his 'job spec'. It began to go wrong when he decided to trial a weekly Newsletter to be given out to customers as they came into the flagship Victoria store. If successful he believed he had the format to do this in all the stores with slightly different versions. The idea was simply to promote offers from different departments on every floor. The Vice-Chairman was so taken with the idea that he asked Christoph to present the draft of the likely content and general look to the full Board. At the meeting the chairman, Mr Billing, a crusty, grey-haired, urbane gentleman was so enamoured with the concept that he suggested that every week there should be included a special tip, that could be highlighted. Oh dear, the wrong language to use with Christoph present as given his passion for horseracing this he took to mean a betting tip. It so happened that The Great Metropolitan Handicap (one of two major handicaps in those days run in the Spring at Epsom; the other being The City & Suburban) was being run that week at Epsom. Christoph's selection Quarrymaster duly obliged at the rewarding odds of 14/1 in the 20 runner race. However despite this favourable result the Chairman was in a state of high-dudgeon and demanded an explanation as to why suddenly his store was providing racing tips. Even when the mix-up over the word 'tip' was explained this failed to pacify him and he did not see the funny side of this situation – possibly because he hadn't taken the tip and 'got-on' at a good price?

A life above the line – just!

However, Christoph's position was about to get even more untenable when once again his entrepreneurial streak rather got the better of him. He had spotted a business opportunity in a small Men's outlet, owned by the Army & Navy, in Artillery Row, just a block down from the main store on Victoria Street. At that time this was a rather dowdy, dark and uninspiring shop with limited trade and a poor sales record. Using his old contact, Mr Sexton, from the Men's Department, Christoph proposed the idea of galvanising the business in this off-shoot through selling reduced priced items. In the discussion that ensued Mr Sexton felt he could lay his hands on some heavily discounted Ben Sherman shirts, providing Christoph could modify the outlet. Overnight the Bromley fitters were brought up to London and wooden rack containers were erected with green felt stapled to the front, draped down long enough to hide the additional stock of shirts beneath the racks. Bright strip lighting replaced the dull overhead lamps. An initial 6,000 shirts were purchased and these were priced at just £3.95 each or three for a tenner. They literally took off, selling like hot-cakes, so much so that a further order of 4,000 was placed and within 6 weeks these too had virtually sold out. Mr. Sexton was over the moon but regrettably not everyone on the main Board was as ecstatic or exuberant.

Christoph felt there was a real opportunity to drive sales from discounted products that had proven to be slow movers in the main store, through this small outlet. He felt that this could be done just as easily for cosmetics, toiletries, records, shoes and even arguably for pre-packed sandwiches – a relatively new concept at that time. With the business results on the shirt sales behind him Chris went to see his 'champion' Doug Skidman and in enthusiastic tones, informed him what had been achieved over such a short time and outlined his proposed blue print for the future – in what in today's world would probably be called a 'pop-up' outlet. Mr. Skidman put up his hand, smiled ruefully and remarked," Stop, stop. I know all about the success of the shirt venture as Mr Sexton has already reported the results to the Board with obvious delight while acknowledging your part in this. However, this activity has seriously put out the nose of a Senior Board

Member whom had been requested to look into what could and should be done with this outlet, below Artillery Mansions, and had concluded that really nothing was viable for this place. There is a feeling among some of the Board Members that you are an uncontrollable young upstart and a 'Jonny come lately', and that you fail to follow the correct procedures or toe-the-line and that, in the end, your rashness will cost the Company money and could even put the very reputation of the store at risk. I should state that this is not a view shared by me, nor indeed by Mr. Sexton." Chris tried to defend his actions and to protest at these accusations as well as seeking to justify what he had done but to no avail. Eventually, Doug Skidman smiled at Christoph across the table and stated, "Christoph, I have to thank you for giving me a real sense of excitement and adventure. I have appreciated your 'can-do' attitude and get up and go approach. Your positive enthusiasm and drive to make things better and different are truly admirable and infectious. But genuinely I believe you are in the wrong business. You are a true entrepreneur." With that he threw a large bundle of notes wrapped up tightly by a thick rubber band and said, "Please accept this, as a small gesture of appreciation and by way of my personal thanks. But take my advice and go into Advertising." And with that he got up and shook Christoph warmly by the hand and escorted him to the door. Indeed, that was that and Christoph's sortie into retail was over.

However, getting into advertising while it sounded right was by no means going to be easy to achieve. Christoph had no degree, no contacts and had had a somewhat chequered career since leaving school in the summer of 1969 – little of which experiences, if any, could be considered relatable directly to advertising. The one advantage he perceived was that many conversations around the dinner table revolved around the advertising on air at the time, which was considered far more interesting than the programmes that surrounded the commercial breaks. Inevitably, by networking, he encountered a number of people from advertising agencies. Christoph was struck by their level of confidence, self-assuredness and the glamourous lifestyle they seemed to enjoy, be they secretaries or account people. His appetite had been fuelled by his views of the work done for the Army & Navy and he had really enjoyed doing the window bills for the Artillery Row outlet and the slogans and materials that advertised the joint stores activities in sales promotions. Christoph, with his love of writing, not surprisingly saw himself as a copywriter – but just how could that dream be fulfilled?

And then as luck would have it his big break came. Joining a dinner party and Bridge evening at his mother's he met an American working, during his summer recess, in London, in the Library/Intelligence Centre at Gris Advertising. Louis Freshman, was a professor in Speed reading and Rhetoric at Columbia State University. He had been able to get his summer posting through a close friend of his, Glynn Midlark, who held the position of Head of Research and Planning, at Gris and respected Louis's mind, intellect, observations and level of industry. In the inevitable discussion that ensued Christoph outlined what he wanted to do. Louis suggested it might be prudent to take any position he could get and then seek to move into the Creative Department, once he had got into an agency. By the end of the evening Louis had agreed he would talk to Glynn Midlark on Christoph's behalf. This he duly did and a few days later Christoph met with Glynn, who turned out also to know his mother through bridge and horse racing, two popular pursuits they had in common. Glynn agreed to take on Christoph as he put it, "Simply for the sake of your dear mother. I'll put you on 6 weeks trial and pay you £23 a week out of petty cash. You will be based in the Library and act as Messenger Boy for my Research Department. Oh and you start on Monday. Let's just see how it goes."

There were a number of immediate and long term outcomes and ramifications from this offer, which, of course, Christoph accepted without hesitation. The first thing was that Christoph had to give up going to Glorious Goodwood (held in the last week of July and during the first week in August), as he could hardly take off the first week in his new job, even though he knew his new boss would be going. The second outcome was that his mother while clearly delighted that he had found proper and hopefully gainful employment was horrified that he was going into advertising and remarked to him, "Whatever am I going to tell my friends?" It made it sound as though he was being sent to borstal, or prison, or alternatively he had joined some shady or lascivious profession. Maybe he had? Such was the poor regard that advertising was held in amongst the conservative older generation at that time - unless one actually owned 'the shop'. The longer term ramification of this decision was that Christoph remained on 6 weeks trial for some 8 years. This was due to external factors early on and then political circumstances, largely beyond his control, later on and then finally he was quite happy not to have a contract.

In the early months everything was fine but by October there was the Oil Crisis, caused by the Arab OPEC countries creating an embargo on oil. This affected the US and UK particularly, as they had supported Israel, against the invasion of their country by Egypt supported by Syria, during the Yom Kippur War. This embargo lasted until March 1974. At the same time back home relations with the Coal Board and the Conservative Prime Minister, Ted Heath, had broken down completely over pay and conditions, which led to strikes and resultant shortages of coal needed to generate electricity, through the coal fired power stations, nationwide. Ultimately, Mr Heath declared, at the end of December 1973 that as from January 1st 1974 there would be a 3 day working week to conserve energy during the winter months. This continued until the 7th March 1974 by which time the Prime Minister had called a General Election, confidently believing that people would vote him in again, with an even bigger majority, rather than the Labour supporting Unionists who had just held the country to ransom. Rather like Theresa May, in May 2017, he had read the electorate completely wrong, but unlike her, also without a majority, he was unable to form a coalition with other parties to form a Government. There is an old saying that 'if you've got a mandate to govern - then govern'.

Throughout these difficult and turbulent times Christoph did not dare raise his head over the parapet, or even submit the petty cash forms for encashment, by the Finance Department, for fear of being a casualty of the expression 'last one in first one out'. He walked to work and gambled what money he had been given over Christmas and for his Birthday back in December. If he won he ate and if he lost he had to rely on the largesse of friends. Many years later when people asked Christoph why he had gone into advertising he would smile with a twinkle in his eye and respond by saying "because I had failed at everything else". Given his perilous position at the very start of his career in advertising he very nearly failed there too. However, hidden away in a small side room, off the library, the size of a broom cupboard, or small stock room, but with a small window, where no one came in, he busied himself, working in his coat and using a small Calor Gaz Camping Lamp as a source of light, once it got dark. He survived not just his first 8 weeks trial but his first 8 months. He was truly a fire risk at all levels!

CHAPTER 2

'A horse, a horse, my kingdom for a horse' – William Shakespeare, Richard 111

Christoph had always believed that his way of living could be broken down into four compartments where he believed at least one of these had to be going well at any given time. These four elements were Finance, Work, Gambling (primarily but not exclusively horse racing) and Love (read women). These aspects of his life were, of course, not mutually exclusive and indeed often they were closely associated. It was not totally surprising that Christoph viewed his whole life as something of a gamble, with the opportunity to engage in chances, to live on the edge, take risks and hope for the best, after all he was born a Sagittarian – the gamblers astrological sign – half horse half archer, which he deemed to be satisfactory justification. It could also be argued that his early influences led him in this direction.

Sent to Boarding School, from the age of 7, Christoph found, in his later years there, that if he played tennis (which he did fairly well being in the First V1, for his whole 5 years at Senior School), given the unpredictable nature of the English weather, this could free up considerable time in the summer to follow his passion for horse racing. It had even been suggested that he had selected his Secondary School, breaking with a long family tradition, on the basis of its close proximity to Lingfield Park and Brighton race courses and also being in

A life above the line – just!

reasonably close proximity to Sandown Park, Kempton Park and Ascot. Given that he had been a bookies runner for his grandmother from the age of 12 this was not entirely implausible. His maternal grandmother and his own mother had instilled in Christoph a fascination for the turf and the Sport of Kings and in particular for the Flat, where there were no obstacles to impede the horse's progress. The colour of the silks, the speed, tactics and position in the race, plus the sound of galloping hooves flared Christoph's own nostrils with excitement. Even his mother's brother 'Uncle Billo' provided him with the Annual edition of Raceform the content of which reflected on the previous year's results, which they would mull over, discuss and debate at great length. With this pedigree it was hardly surprising that Christoph would bunk off from school and head to Brighton Races, arguably one of the most difficult courses, built, as it is, on the side of the Sussex Downs where the straight is a sheer drop, making it one of the fastest 5 furlong courses, along with Epsom, in the racing world. Many an unbalanced horse and inexperienced jockey has come to grief on this racecourse. But at the same time many good horses have excelled there including the one eyed Belper and most recently Pour La Victoire with 10 victories here. At the time Christoph was there as a schoolboy there was the flashy, lengthy, deep-bodied grey, Raffingora, who had started his career there in 1968 and held the course record before going on to bigger and better things. In fact, in 1970, he broke the course record for 5 furlongs at Epsom, when ridden by Lester Piggott and was good enough to win prestigious races at both Sandown Park (The Temple Stakes) and then at Goodwood (the King George Stakes), trained, like another grey favourite of Christoph's, My Swanee, by Bill Marshall.

Christoph loved his 'illegal' race course outings but in his final year he was lucky not to have been expelled. Having been given a 'fag' (a junior boy allocated to the individuals in the senior year to do menial tasks) for which he had no use. Christoph decided rather than having him make his bed, or polish his shoes, he would get Robert to put the bets on for the syndicate he was running at school. This entailed visits by Robert to Three Bridges, Crawley or East Grinstead. Unfortunately, on one of these missions, Robert was spotted by a master as he emerged from one of these betting establishments. To his credit the 'fag' did not welch on his prefect but took full responsibility. However, as soon as Christoph found out what had happened he immediately owned up, took the rap and accepted that this particular avenue of betting and financial remuneration would cease forthwith. Nevertheless, this in no way dimmed his enthusiasm for the track which had been heightened when Jim Joel's magnificent horse Royal Palace won the 1967 Derby in spectacular fashion (he would go on to have a record of 9 wins in his 11 races, trained by Noel Murless). But not only did Christoph have the winner he had the second, Ribocco, and the third, Dart Board, in the right order in his Tricast, which made him a tidy sum. The following year saw one of Christoph's favourite horses of all time, Sir Ivor, owned by the American Ambassador, Raymond Guest (who as a wealthy business man had rather fortuitously won the race with Larkspur in 1962, at 22/1, when the favourite Hethersett was brought down in a melee that finished with one horse being destroyed and four jockeys injured) won the Derby with an electrifying turn of foot, coming late on the wide outside, showing similar speed to that he had shown in the 2000 Guineas. Only Vaguely Noble who beat him comfortably in the Prix de L'Arc de Triomphe and Royal Palace were rated higher than him, in 1968. He was a truly game horse running 13 times winning 8 times and being placed on 4 other occasions in races in Ireland, England, France and even America. Racing was truly in Christoph's blood.

Even in the early summer of 1969 as he was sitting his A-Levels Christoph demonstrated his sense of priority. As he was going down on the Saturday morning to sit his last paper, the S-Level in English, in early July, he was stopped on the back staircase to answer a call that had come through to the public phone situated on this stairwell landing. It was his grandmother, who simply stated, "You are coming to Sandown this afternoon, after all it is The Eclipse (Sandown's premier flat race) and it is Saturday". Christoph replied "Sorry Gran I can't make it as I have a 3 hour scholarship paper in English starting at 9am, in just a few minutes, and so I won't be able to get to Sandown in time." Undeterred Granny responded "Don't be so ridiculous darling, just finish the exam early, do it in 2 hours and then you'll be here on time and I'll give you lunch." And so it was. Christoph left the examination hall early, handing in his paper, with the excuse that he had a bad migraine. He did get to the racecourse on time and though he didn't get Distinction in this paper he was happy enough with a Merit so all in all it proved to be a satisfactory result. More particularly as he was delighted to be there to see Wolver Hollow win the big race, which proved to be the first of many Group 1's for the emerging talent that was Henry Cecil (later Sir). Sir Henry would go on to train 25 Classic winners, 75 Royal Ascot winners, be Champion Trainer 10 times and end up training perhaps the greatest of them all, Frankel, before sadly succumbing to cancer, aged 70, in 2013. Christoph was particularly pleased that Wolver Hollow won that day, with Lester Piggott 'up', as he, like Raffingora and another of his favourite horses, Negus, was grey and his grandsire was Grey Sovereign.

Shortly, before The Eclipse, in mid-June, Christoph had snuck off to Royal Ascot to meet his mother, who had arrived in Car Park 3, with a hired Morning Suit and Top Hat for him to change into. Imagine his surprise and abject horror when walking down from the Parade Ring to the Paddock he found himself strolling directly towards two senior masters from school. Realising the potential awkwardness of the situation, let alone the ramifications, he decided to confront these masters with supreme self-assurance, "Good afternoon gentlemen, I hope that you are having a fortunate day on the horses?" The two masters looked at each other rather edgily and then one spoke rather nervously, "Christoph, how nice to see you, though we would be very grateful if you could ignore the fact that you ever encountered us here, when back at school." Christoph smiled knowingly and nodding his head sympathetically replied "Absolutely – your secret is safe with me. Good day gentlemen" and with that he doffed his 'topper' and walked on greatly relieved and chuckling to himself.

However, Christoph was not inherently lucky when it came to gambling generally and horses specifically. He firmly believed that, as with everything in life, he had to make his own luck. In this regard Christoph differed from his mother whom always had the uncanny knack of picking outsiders, even pacemakers, who would run out of their skins, and way above their previous form, when they were carrying her wagers. One pacemaker, he recalled, slipped his field in a race at Ascot and won at 50/1. Christoph was actually with her in 1986 when 'Mrs. H', jointly held the record for a Dual Forecast (now known as an Exacta). This happened in the Wokingham, one of the big handicaps of the week, then run on the Friday but now on the Saturday of the Royal Meeting, but still over the straight 6 furlongs. Touch of Grey at 20/1 fought out the finish with Manimstar at 33/1. There were only three winning tickets and The Horseracing Totalisator Board (The Tote) paid out by cheque the princely sum of £3,414.70. All around the betting shops, for weeks later, were posters with the headline 'Woman in Hammersmith wins record pay-out on the Dual Forecast'. What was particularly fortunate in this case was that 3year olds seldom win this highly competitive race and Touch of Grey and Bel Bayou in 1987 were the only two horses to achieve this in the last 30years!

But Christoph genuinely did believe he could make his own luck and when it came to horse racing this meant studying the form, developing a system that could increase his odds, beyond that of simply betting on the favourites, which was around 33% of the time. Christoph selected horses of interest and then rated them by distance, going, jockey, trainer and track. In the end he had increased his chances of winning to around 42%. During his 'resting period' between working at The Army & Navy stores and commencing his job at Gris Advertising he would spend upwards of 4 hours studying tomorrow's race card, the night before, and often would not find a bet at all. During this fallow period he would also go to the local racecourses and bet on the close finishes. Standing on the winning line he would position himself to assess which horse in the photo-finish had won and then rush to the bookies, put his bet on based on his view, before the official result was called and then await the judge's verdict. In nearly a year, in numerous races betting on his eyesight he only lost one photo-finish and that was on Diamond Edge at Sandown, when he was standing on the wrong finishing line – the first one being for chasers and the second for hurdlers – a costly mistake!

Christoph made his investments from the £1,000 his grandfather had left him and then from the dole money he collected weekly at the Job Centre in Hythe House on Shepherds Bush Road. He would collect his money and then 'invest' this in Corals situated then on Hammersmith Roundabout. Chris kept a meticulous record, for a year, and by the end of this time he had turned £1,000 into £26,000, enabling him to live the good life. This was spent at La Val bonne and The Saddle Room nightclubs, as well as at the Playboy Club and other gambling venues such as The Knightsbridge Sporting Club and The Cromwellian. Even at the tables Christoph employed a method, only playing Black Jack (Vingt-et-Un) and only increasing his stake as he got on a winning run and then taking it back to the base ante when the run ended. Christoph would sometimes play for hours just to win £100 in the course of the night but his system seldom failed him. He had learnt never to chase his losses and only carried the amount of cash he was prepared to lose and never carried credit or debit cards, to tempt him further.

But it was horses not tables that were really his game. He read and studied the form daily and continued to do so throughout his life. Chris loved the thrill of the gamble and betting on his judgement. He was a good sport and never minded losing, but he became quite excited and animated when he won as for him it vindicated his good judgement and 'informed' selection. Yes, of course, 'lady luck' still had to play her part but to Christoph there was something truly enthralling about being right.

However, even Christoph had no idea how significant horse racing would prove to be throughout his advertising career. In the early days in order to supplement his meagre petty cash emoluments at Gris Advertising he bet the horses around the corner at Ladbrokes. When he won everything was fine but when he lost he walked to and from work. His reputation quickly spread and by the time he had moved into Account Management in 1976 the agency's van driver 'Wardie' knew to bring him the copy of The Sporting Life, first thing in the morning. Both were in the office by 7am and over coffee and marmalade toast Chris would peruse the form. It was Chris's responsibility to get the papers back on the Media Director's desk before 9am, by which time the day's selections would have been made.

During those early days in Account Management Christoph had the reputation of being a 'bit of a hot-head' and expressing his views most vehemently and passionately. Occasionally this would boil over into frustration and exasperation and Christoph would habitually resign. Indeed to some he was amusingly known as 'The Serial Resigner'. One of the Deputy Managing Director's, John E Goldman, came up with an elegant solution for dealing with these moments of crisis. He would call Chris to an early morning meeting and after listening to and seeking to answer his concerns they would reach a compromise (and even sometimes a conclusion or resolution). Lunch would then be proposed followed by an afternoon's racing at a local course. This became a fairly regular occurrence between early 1976 and the late summer of 1978. It proved to be the perfect remedy and Christoph not only calmed down as he felt he was being listened to, but he relaxed as he appreciated the rest from his work and his efforts which bordered on being compulsive. Undoubtedly many of his outbursts were born out of his long working hours and from sheer fatigue.

In this same time period Christoph was moved around accounts and eventually having proven himself on toys, cosmetics and industrial accounts, with the departure of some of the team on Thomas Healey, he was surprisingly put on to their business – the highly prestigious, number one account in the agency. This was truly the big leagues as Thomas Healey was a major FMCG (fast moving consumer goods) Company. At that time, at Gris Advertising, Thomas Healey's media budget was the biggest account in the agency and its production budget was the second largest.

There had been some nervousness and trepidation expressed internally, within the agency, about appointing Christoph to this account. He had built up a reputation for being outspoken, direct and not always the most diplomatic, to either clients or agency personnel alike. He was certainly no 'Yes Man' and was seldom overawed. At the briefing before joining the team, John Goldman, affectionately known as the 'nervy one' had made it quite clear that no one at Thomas Healey

A life above the line – just!

must ever know of your enjoyment of 'having a flutter', as they might think you, or through you, the agency is gambling with their money.' Imagine then, with this message still ringing in his ears, the surprise when Christoph's first actual encounter with Thomas Healey came over racing tips! One morning, at 8am, Chris was sitting in his office – where the sun most definitely did not shine - when he heard someone crashing about in the outer office. On investigation he was confronted by a short, stout, dark-haired man with a slightly flustered manner, who on encountering Chris stated in a deep Canadian burr "You, Christoph? I'm Brian Prence, Associate Director at Thomas Healey." Chris took a deep breath shook hands and replied, "Yes, I'm Christoph, though I also answer to Chris." Brian looked Chris up and down and then somewhat surprisingly asked, "So Christoph what have you got going this afternoon?" Chris quickly, getting his thoughts together, responded, "Well Mr Prence, I am in the process of doing a shipment and share report and then I shall be embarking on a competitive media and copy review," ignoring deliberately the possible suggestion that this gentleman could be referring to racing selections. Unsuccessfully, however, as Brian Prence persisted, "Chris, I have it on good authority from your recently departed predecessor, that you'll bet on two flies going up a wall, or, at a cricket game, you'll wager on how long before the next run is scored; so I'll ask you again 'what have you got going this afternoon' and if we are going to get along don't bullshit me?" Realising that the game was up and he was cornered, Chris hesitantly replied, "Well Mr. Prence, I have heard there are three horses running 'over the sticks' – Gin Top, Trio-J and Cedarwood." "Okay", pushed Brian speedily, "How do I bet 'em?" – getting Christoph ever deeper into the mire. "Mr. Prence, I gather there is a bet termed a Patent, which is 7 bets – three singles, three doubles and a treble." "Right then Chris here's £70, go place the bet for me." Chris duly obliged, as did all three horses, Gin Top at 6/4; Trio-J at 7/2 and Cedarwood 6/1. Christoph made money and Mr Prence cleaned up, making over 'a gorilla' (£1,000). No further words were expressed about that day but there were to be many more subsequent occasions. In some cases, Brian Prence would even stop meetings, always held in the basement – known as 'the dungeons' – to state that he would like to have a quiet word with Christoph outside. The Gris Management would look at each other with dismay wondering what trouble Chris was in or what problems he had caused this time! In fact, Brian Prence simply wanted to know whether the conditions were suitable, or had changed, to favour a particular selection, since the early morning. Once, Chris had told Brian Prence, at their 8am 'meeting', that there was a good horse running at Ascot, but Shuffling needed rain and soft ground. Shortly after noon the meeting was stopped and the two of them left the room and headed up to street level, where they were found, in good spirits, standing in the doorway watching the rain teeming down from a dull leaden sky. The bet was on and Shuffling romped home at 7/1. So it was that Chris's career on Thomas Healey became firmly established. This recognition clearly had nothing to do with his Account Managing abilities, nor his insightful and challenging skills, but simply down to successful tipping. Christoph realised that on such strange events and fortune can careers be made and even lost!

Indeed, his reputation for horseracing became further enhanced when Christoph was invited to Thomas Healey, based in the North of the country for the Friday night's racing at Gosforth Park (Newcastle) and then to stay over and go to 'The Pitman's Derby' otherwise known as The Northumberland Plate. It was here that Chris met Mark Jones, for the first time, a Brand Manager. Mark would become a client of Chris's three times in his advertising career and become a lifelong friend. Racing was proving a fruitful, if not always profitable, ally.

When in the autumn of 1978 Christoph was sent to Gris Advertising in New York, having fallen out spectacularly with the UK Management, when the strategic and creative work he had been working on studiously was changed at the 11th hour, by his returning, from holiday, boss. Chris was instructed to present this adapted and revised work but refused, on principle, as he did not believe in it. This intransigence led to his being sent by his Chairman to the USA. Knowing no one there meant Chris found himself travelling by subway to Belmont Park at the weekends. Chris was there when Spectacular Bid was beaten by the locally trained Coastal in the Belmont Stakes. The grey, Spectacular Bid, then ran up

A life above the line – just!

a sequence of 17 straight successes and he was finally syndicated for US$22m in 1980, having won 26 of his 30 races. He was also the first horse for 31 years to have a walkover (no rivals turning up) in a major race, when he was awarded the Woodward Stakes. Spectacular Bid even managed to win the Santa Anita Handicap, a race famously associated with the endeavours of Sea Biscuit – the people's horse - during the Depression in the 1930's, following the US Stock Market collapse in 1929.

Chris had already witnessed Spectacular Bid at Churchill Downs where he won the Kentucky Derby. This had come about because the Senior Brand Manager, on a Premium (meaning giving a gift away in the box) Detergent, William McGinty, shared Christoph's interest in horseracing and invited him to join him at the races. William McGinty drove from his home in Ohio, the Buckeye State, to Louisville, in the Blue Grass State of Kentucky. They arrived in plenty of time and were able to enjoy a mint julip, the traditional drink for the race, in Centre Field, soaking up the atmosphere on a warm early May afternoon. This was a great bonding exercise between Client and Agency and Chris has to this day the two glasses from the Triple Crown races he attended in 1979, in his study.

In August, due to the intense heat and humidity, in New York City, the whole racing world moves lock stock and barrel from Belmont Park to 'Up State' New York and the wood panelled, terraced, colonial houses that make up the characterful town of Saratoga. For Chris this was a 'must see' and so taking the train beyond the State Capital, Albany, having followed the Hudson River past the military academy of West Point, Chris arrived with many other racing enthusiasts at Saratoga. This is truly a beautiful racecourse with baskets laden with brightly coloured geraniums and petunias contrasting with the dark wooden slatted stands from which they hung. This really fired up Chris's imagination and he would joyously return on a number of occasions in his later life. But back then he had gone to follow a filly Pearl Necklace in the Turf Classic. When the race came around late on the card he plunged big on her and she rewarded his confidence by romping home, more than paying for his day, and making the trip even more memorable. Amusingly, Christoph who was never renowned for his sartorial elegance or good dress sense was approached by a couple of punters separately who wanted to know which horse or stable he was associated with, taking him to be a trainer or trainer's assistant or a racing manager. Needless to say he played this up and led them to believe he had come over from 'Blighty' to 'the former Colonies' to see Pearl Necklace run. At least in his bullshit he had given them a winner!

Chris had realised early on in his Account Management days that the trick was to dress efficiently and effectively. On meeting colleagues from France and Italy who wore grey flannel trousers with a white shirt, tie and blue blazer he embraced this 'habit'. Clearly with his horsey tie and the binoculars with the many badges from a mis-spent youth this made him appear to be a 'sportsman of the turf'. Later in his career, while still at Gris Advertising, he would carry out appraisals on his staff and one of them cheekily remonstrated that he should be permitted to do an appraisal of his 'Boss'. Christoph agreed to this and when his Appraisal was carried out he rather fortuitously received much praise, but one major criticism was expressed which was 'that he looked permanently like a crumpled unmade bed'! It was certainly true that with Christoph's tousled mop of very fine but slightly too long unkempt fair hair that never fell, let alone stayed in a neat parting, he could, not unlike the Prime Minister, Boris Johnson, appear as though he 'had been dragged through a hedge backwards'.

Again, shortly after Christoph had joined his final agency, McKillans, the Director of Human Resources (Personnel!), approached him commenting on his appearance. He suggested that given the importance of his position as Client Services Director and Deputy Managing Director that he should really wear suits. To help him improve his look and image he was going to give him a clothing allowance, as a benefit-in-kind valued at £1,000. Some weeks later this same gentleman caught up with Christoph and observed that he had not noticed any change in his attire. Chris smiled back and said "No you probably wouldn't have but come Royal Ascot you will be able to appreciate my new Morning Suit and at any forthcoming formal evenings you will be able to admire my smart new Evening Suit/Dinner Jacket, both which I am truly most grateful to you for." The grey flannels, white shirt and double breasted blue blazer uniform continued unabated.

When Christoph arrived in New York he quickly perceived there were no betting shops and that the daily newspapers by and large did not cover racing to any great degree. However, undeterred he located a seedy looking place at Grand Central Station with the letters OTB writ big above the shop front. He discovered on entry through the thick smoky bullet proofed glass door that OTB stood for Off Track Betting, and operated for all intents and purposes like the Tote in the UK. He always just went in to this smoke filled bear pit of hardened types, made his selection, placed the bet and removed his personage from the premises with alacrity. What highly amused him was the slogan in the window that more or less summed up his own approach and philosophy on betting, 'Bet with your head not over it'. This line was delivered by the former famous US jockey, Eddie Arcaro. With Chris's fascination for racing stories to enhance his love for the sport he set out to find out about 'Banana Nose' as his colleagues called him (possibly due to his misshapen face, having damaged his nose on a number of occasions from falls off the equine beast) or more flatteringly 'The Master' by the affectionate public and media for his supreme style of riding, judging pace and switching his whip from one hand to the other effortlessly. Eddie Arcaro rode his first winner when he was just 16 and would race ride for 30 years before retiring in 1962, by which time he was already a 'Hall of Famer' (1958). He was a top rider in the USA in the 1940's and was leading money earner in 1942, 1948 and the year of Christoph's birth in 1950. Riding for his stable Calumet Farm, he won the Triple Crown (The Kentucky Derby, The Preakness and The Belmont Stakes), on Whirlaway in 1941 and on Citation in 1948 and is still the only jockey to have achieved this feat twice. 'Big Cy' as Citation was often referred to is along with Man O'War and Secretariat considered by many to have been the best American racehorses of all time. When Arcaro was in doubt as to which horse in the yard he should ride, in the forthcoming Kentucky Derby, and was considering partnering with Coaltown, the trainer of both, Ben Jones told him, "Citation will win, because he can catch any horse he can see – and there is nothing wrong with his eyesight." Arcaro rode him and after the third leg win at Belmont, where he won by some 8 lengths, he stated, to the media, he could beat any horse over any trip, "from ten foot to ten miles." In fact, Citation having won 8 of his 9 races as a 2 year old, won 19 of 20 races as a 3 year old, over distances from 6 furlongs a sprint distance (8 furlongs make a mile) to 16 furlongs a stayer's distance (2 miles). He completed 16 consecutive victories. Eddie Arcaro was special with 2 Triple Crowns given there have only been 13 horses to have achieved this, starting with the first, Sir Barton, in 1919, with the most recent being Justify in 2018. Chris was working in New York, in 1978, when the diminutive chestnut Affirmed won his Triple Crown, defeating the luckless dark bay Alydar by a diminishing distance in each race. Little did Christoph realise that it would be the last time the Triple Crown would be achieved for nearly 40 years when American Pharoah succeeded in 2015. Eddie Arcaro died in Florida in 1997, aged 81.

Christoph had gone to the US a frisky, flashy, headstrong colt but returned, two years later, in 1980, a much more mature, accomplished and finely tuned racing machine (hardly a stallion, however!). His passion for horse racing continued and indeed most Saturdays were spent with his housemate 'Bags' and her family at the racecourses in Southern England. Holidays were taken to coincide with Royal Ascot in mid - June and Glorious Goodwood end July early August. There were the odd occasions when racing crossed over once again with his professional life. One such episode came when one of his favourite and most admired colleagues, Jenny Chase, was leaving Gris Advertising to join her husband whom had been sent out on a long term posting to Spain, in 1983. Jenny's farewell luncheon was hosted by Chris, her immediate boss, who had been instructed by John E Goldman not to exceed a figure of £400. However, due to a large number of attendees, twenty and the high level of consumption of wine when the Italian Trattoria's bill eventually was brought to him it was well over £100 above the budget ceiling. Chris thought for a moment and then asked if everyone could give him £1. He then instructed them all to have another coffee, disappeared and headed up Cleveland Street to the William Hill betting shop. He invested all the money on a 5/1 shot ridden by Willie Carson and trained by John Dunlop, which won comfortably. He then put £85 on a 6/4 favourite in the next race. When this also won he walked out with £212.50 and when he got back to the restaurant he paid each of the invitees their £1 back and promptly paid the bill, much the amusement of everyone present. Jenny Chase never forgot that experience and it continues to be recounted by her with much amusement for both her and also Christoph to this very day.

By 1985, Christoph had moved on from Gris Advertising to Premium White, a fashionable boutique agency run by a group of spirited entrepreneurs. They somewhat surprisingly hired Christoph to bring control and discipline to balance their uncontrolled flamboyancy. Uncharacteristically, this two year chapter saw Christoph mix romance with horses, not just once but twice. The first was out of fascination the second out of financial necessity.

Christoph had encountered an attractive well known Event Horse rider, whom had been side-lined by a serious leg injury. This was a totally new world to Christoph and became much more involving then simply being a spectator or gambling investor. As Juliette Hartnell gradually recovered from her traumatic wound, the fascination gradually turned to romance and an equally short-termed passion with the eventing fraternity. Christoph found himself for a while spending weekends chasing Juliette around the country to events far-a-field, as she rode and competed, though more often she would be training young horses and teenage riders, and increasingly judging the dressage. It was not long before Chris was sitting beside Juliette taking down the dressage scores and then actually buying young horses to be brought on and in most cases developed, turned over and sold. Finally, Christoph persuaded Juliette to write a book about her observations on training horses and riders for Eventing, building off her reputation. This was recognising that after such a serious injury she would never again be able to reach the pinnacle of her sport. Juliette liked this idea providing that Christoph agreed to actually write the book with her - which in the end meant, and became, writing it for her! She had agreed to do the notes building on her knowledge. The only problem being that while Christoph produced a Dictaphone for Juliette to record her thoughts and information, given her hectic schedule, the only time she could record was as she was driving the horsebox from home to one event or another. The net result was that her thoughts and voice were drowned out by the protesting rumbles of the ageing horsebox engine above which, on the dashboard, sat the recording machine! Christoph was left to try to interpret this and then order Juliette's ramblings before he could even start writing the book. It truly was a labour of love. In the end he worked on the disseminated material for 16 days and 16 nights, then did the illustrations, in ink, himself, before organising for a top equestrian photographer to take the real pictures as determined by Juliette. The book was successfully published both in the UK and the USA and was well-received by the media. What they particularly liked about it was its non-lecturing, friendly and accessible tone of voice. However, Juliette and Christoph fell out over the final version that was delivered to the publisher, as he had wanted to have anecdotes, real circumstances and true life experiences to bring some of the points to life. Juliette did not want these. She was also majorly upset when the cover did not feature her but another world leading lady rider, whom had been a rival and competitor of hers. At that juncture the romance cooled and finally ended when Juliette sold their best horse, to America, for a large sum, without any discussion beforehand. This all happened, despite her doing quite nicely out of the royalties and the down payment, on delivery of the book. But as she put it 'That's business and horses are my livelihood.'

However, the book had never been about the money for Christoph. For him it had been a challenge to see if his love for writing could actually be expanded to write a book. As a child he had written poems and then started writing short stories from a young age. He had learnt to read, appropriately enough, from the advertising on the sides of buses in London. The written word had always fascinated him. And though he never fulfilled his dream of becoming a full-time copywriter he had been allowed to write on a number of accounts, so long as

A life above the line – just!

30 second TV was not involved – as this was far too constraining a format for him. The sheer challenge of writing a book was therefore exciting for him. The Equestrian book was the perfect project to test whether he had the discipline and capability to complete such a long work. Christoph was therefore happy to forego on the money, other than seeking a £400 advance, for the poor typist, who had to read his illegible hand. Only time would tell, how far his pursuit for writing would take him, once his advertising days were at an end.

The idea of the Eventing book had started while he was still at Gris Advertising as indeed had his pursuit of Juliette and horse ownership. Their fruition really came about after he had joined Premium White. There had been a somewhat bizarre encounter with the Financial Director when he had been negotiating his deal at this new agency. Christoph had asked for a salary of £35,000, a figure significantly higher than that he had been on at Gris Advertising. When questioned about this discrepancy Christoph explained it this way, "Well firstly your agency is having to pay for the fact that due to my loyalty and longevity, at Gris Advertising, that I have been grossly underpaid. Secondly, you don't know this yet, but you are hiring a workaholic, who will give you all the hours God gave us, so you will certainly get more than your pound of flesh. Thirdly, I have three hungry mouths to feed." At this point the savvy Financial Director looked at Christoph's CV, assimilated the information and then remarked, "But Christoph you aren't even married." Christoph smiled and leaning back with his hands behind his head he responded, "True but I have a trainer and two horses to feed. Additionally, I would like to ask that as I don't drive and therefore don't need a company car whether I could take that multi-horsepower and apply that budget to my powerful horses in training." The Financial Director laughed and to Christoph's amazement his terms were agreed in full, with no further questions asked, though he had to have a real car, which he gave to his mother to drive.

It was fortunate that Christoph had had his financial demands met as his second romance was a highly charged affair - in every sense. 'The Turnip' was a shapely, strawberry blonde, with blue-eyes, snub-nose – hence her nickname – American spitfire. She had arrived on the scene through Christoph's housemate 'Bags' and her family had connections in riding and eventing with 'Bags' parents. Because 'The Turnip' was living over here, 'gaining work experience' in the City of London, it was suggested that she move into the spare room in their house in Fulham. It turned out that she had been an accomplished rider back home in Columbus, Ohio. Not surprisingly 'The Turnip' quickly saw the merit of being with Christoph. She persuaded him to 'borrow' his company car from his mother so that they could drive to the events at the weekend, where she could then ride or at the very least exercise the horses. She also saw the benefit of having a relationship with Christoph as she could share his bedroom and avoid having to pay rent for the spare room upstairs. Christoph was completely bowled over by this pushy fireball with her bouncy flowing locks and vivacious and captivating personality, even though she was really high maintenance. She liked to dine in all the top restaurants, attend the best race meetings and expected this and her excessive and expensive lifestyle to be paid for by Christoph. Fortunately, her time in his life, coincided with an exceptional and unusually good run on the horses. It seemed like 'The Turnip' brought him amazing luck on the wagering front. A number of major coups were had at Ascot, Sandown, Windsor, Epsom and Lingfield and these paid for their lavish lives together. But deep down Christoph knew it couldn't last; neither the relationship nor the run of luck on the betting front. He knew she was not the one for him long term and though he fancied her rotten he was never truly in love with her. This was a good thing as she was flighty and totally unpredictable. There were times when she would leave in high dudgeon for no apparent reason, take the car, and Christoph would have to find and make his own way back to London, usually by public transport. In restaurants she would just take off for no apparent reason and leave him in the middle of the meal. Christoph handled these emotional outbursts with good humour, mild amusement and without rancour or annoyance. He would just smile, shrug his shoulders with surprise, pay the bill and with mild embarrassment depart. Finally, 'The Turnip' decided it was time to leave for good and head back to Columbus Ohio in the United States. He was sorry at the time as it had been a blast,

A life above the line – just!

good fun, an exciting and exacting chapter and she was certainly never dull or boring. However, he was not overly upset – except for the fact that the flow of winners dried up almost immediately - so normal service on that front was resumed!

These two romances more or less covered his time at Premium White and with a new agency came fresh challenges. The Equine book was finally widely released after he had gone on to his 'new shop', McKillans. As fortune would have it McKillans gave Christoph, as part of his management responsibilities, Corporate Entertainment. His job was to determine the financial viability, cost effectiveness and practicalities associated with many long standing events. At the time they had debenture seats at Twickenham, Lords, Wimbledon and Covent Garden as well as two boxes at Ascot Racecourse and 100 tickets every season at Glyndebourne and two seats every Tuesday at The Coliseum. But sadly 'times they were a-changing' and this kind of profligate outgoing, literally and financially, truly could not be justified, even in 1985/6. Clients no longer expected or even desired to be entertained in this manner. Indeed, in some cases they were suddenly concerned that this type of hospitality could be deemed a bribe, or benefit in kind, or some kind of inducement. However, needless to say, Christoph managed to retain the two boxes at Ascot Racecourse and he ensured that they were used extensively and quite often by Christoph himself. He used them to build relationships with clients or to impress the senior managements of clients or prospects and sometimes even his own agency's International Overlords. As a host, Christoph found himself much in demand, as he made a day at the races fun with his knowledge of the history of the course, the jockeys and the horses themselves and also he had a jackpot in every race. With 12 attendees being the norm this meant that there was potentially £72 (six chances of winning £12 per race, thereby having an interest without actually having to bet) on offer throughout the afternoon's card. Additionally, he would take the table through each of the races over lunch and divulge as much information, and side stories, as he could, to aid people's enjoyment and selections. Then he would either put the bets on for them or show them how to do it for themselves. When other directors or Associate Companies in the Group took the boxes Christoph, over his 17 years at McKillans, with his reputation and passion for the sport, would often be asked by them to attend as a compere, or as a quasi-authority, and if he could find the time he would most surely and willingly attend. Christoph's favourite memory of acting in this capacity came on June 22nd 1995 at Royal Ascot.

A few weeks before, Jane Eyrie, who ran the PR Company in the Group, rang and asked Christoph if he would attend as an 'informed' guest in her box. A doyenne of the PR world Jane Eyrie was a woman with an impressive list of influential friends and contacts. Talented, articulate, sharply dressed and with a no-nonsense business approach, the ageless Jane possessed a lovely wicked sense of humour, flirtatious nature and a rich husky voice. Christoph often wondered how many men had fallen under her bewitching spell. The day before the races Christoph called Jane to agree last minute details. He advised her to ensure her entourage left London early to avoid the long tailed back queues and to ensure that they got there in plenty of time. They agreed to meet in the box at 12 noon. Jane Eyrie had arranged a stretch limousine to pick up all the guests so that they could then quaff champagne all the way down from London. By the time they arrived at Ascot and got to the box, at 13.40 (only over 100 minutes late!) they were totally pie-eyed. Among the guests, which included a number of Americans, was a thin, attractive English woman in a bright yellow satin jacket, tight black pencil styled skirt and large black brimmed hat, whom, it became apparent, worked for a prophylactic company and she was involved in their consumer rubber products. Christoph got them all to sit down as soon as they entered and had lunch served promptly, while he proceeded to give them 'the bunny' about the day's racing, rattling through each race, giving them pointers and possible selections for consideration. Once completed he then got them, in mid-mouthful, to go outside at the front of the box so that they could see the Queen drive down the course from the mile start, as she does every day during the Royal meeting – and why not - after all it is her racecourse, having been established by Queen Anne in 1711 (the first race every year on

A life above the line – just!

the first day of the Royal Meeting is called the Queen Anne Stakes, in her memory). Once this piece of pageantry was over they returned to their lunch oblivious that the first race had even taken place, without them having got a single bet on.

It turned out to be a prosperous day's racing for Christoph on what was a very warm June afternoon. A true stayer, Double Trigger, won the Gold Cup for the then up and coming trainer Mark Johnston, who had moved from Scotland where he had graduated as a vet to Yorkshire, where he set up a training yard, which was proving highly successful. Double Trigger was ridden by the heavily under-rated jockey, Jason Weaver, now a popular television pundit, on flat racing, for ITV (who had taken over Horse Race coverage from Channel 4 in 2017). The emerging darling of the flat was Frankie (Lanfranco)Dettori, and he rode three winners that afternoon, for three different trainers. The first was on 'So Factual' in the Cork and Orrery, for his retained yard, the Maktoum's, (Dubai Royal Family) Godolphin operation, with their former public transport driver turned trainer, Saeed bin Suroor. This operation would compete with first Robert Sangster and then the Coolmore Operation (involving a number of characters from Irish racing including John Magnier, Michael Tabor, Denys Smith and even the legendary jumps owner 'JP' McManus) from Ballydoyle primarily, but also Prince Khalid Abdullah from the Kingdom of Saudi Arabia, and in Europe The Aga Khan, and the Niarchos and Wildenstein families. Frankie's second winner was on 'Lucky Lionel', in the Norfolk Stakes, for the likeable and brilliant trainer of 2 year olds, Richard Hannon Senior, who many years later handed the reins over to his son also Richard. Richard senior would end his career deservedly being twice Champion Trainer before retiring in 2013. In The Ribblesdale, Dettori rode a hugely popular winner, 'Phantom Gold' for her Majesty the Queen, trained by Lord Huntingdon. The Chesham was won by 'World Premier', ridden by Brett Doyle, for the ever green Clive Brittain, a canny trainer whom had enjoyed his best days as trainer for Lady Beaverbrook (who had many good horses, perhaps the best being Bustino, trained by Major Dick Hern, who as a 4 year old, went down so bravely to Grundy, the 3 year old Derby winner, in the 'Race of the Century' in the King George and Queen Elizabeth 11 at Ascot in 1975).

All these events had gone by largely unnoticed by the PR contingent who, by now, was completely 'gonzo-ed', though at least in the second race Christoph did urge some of them to part with their cash on 'Lucky Lionel'. This was on the basis of the Americans saying "Here's a tenner - I'll do whatever you're doing Christoph". They were well pleased when Christoph secured them the odds of 8/1 and turned up with £90 for each of them. After that the level of interest diminished noticeably but to be fair regarding Christoph's selections they only missed out on the winning short priced Double Trigger as his other choices were still running, one even finishing plumb last!

However, when it came to the last race of the day Christoph had a strong inkling that this could be the one for a good bet in a big and highly competitive field, for the King George V Stakes. He managed to get the ensemble's attention for just long enough to explain again what he thought might happen in the race. His chief selection, Diaghilef (not to be confused with the brilliant miler Diaghilev) was slightly biased by his love for dance and ballet in particular, but he did believe it was well in on the weights and was likely to run well. Christoph also felt that the favourite 'Bobs Ploy' ridden by Frankie Dettori was a real danger. Christoph's advice was for the team to bet Diaghilef each-way and then to do the two selections in a Dual Forecast (Exacta). The lead American said giving Christoph the money 'Well you've done me alright so far so I'll go along with both bets here's £10 for the each way and £2 for the forecast.' This set the trend for the rest, until it came to the prophylactic lady who looked in her purse and then looked up at Christoph somewhat disconsolately and stated, "I've only got £2". Pausing and searching questioningly at Christoph, she asked "What shall I do?" Christoph smiled and said "Not to worry you can do the Forecast." Once they had given all their money to Christoph, he went and put the bets on while they returned to 'guzzling' yet more champagne. They, subsequently, showed no interest in the race or the contortions of Christoph as it drew to its close.

The race was an extremely untidy affair with the horses at the front closely bunched up and there was significant interference and scrimmaging coming around the bend into the straight and as they made their way up the tough incline to the finishing line. Darryl Holland (known affectionately as 'The Dazzler' in the weighing room) was an excellent jockey who failed to get the quality of rides his talent merited, until he rode abroad, particularly in Asia. Riding Diaghilef, he rode to instruction perfectly keeping his mount up with the pace on the inside with the rail to help him, thereby covering the least distance. As the horses flashed past the post it seemed clear to Christoph that 'Diaghilef' had just held off the late thrust of the favourite, 'Bobs Ploy', priced at 6/1, with the fast-finishing 'Monarch' in 3rd. It went to a photograph and this alone took a lengthy time and then not altogether surprisingly the claxon sounded for a Stewards Enquiry, which was confirmed over the public address system.

Chris's head was spinning. He was exhausted and speechless having watched and run almost every inch of the race himself as 'Diaghilef' was there to be shot at, at the head of affairs throughout. Then there had been the added tension of a print photograph and the time it took to be interpreted and the result confirmed only then for a Steward's Enquiry to be called. In the box no-one really cared although one person did ask what the result was but as Christoph explained it seemed too convoluted for him to comprehend in his inebriated state and he lost interest returning to his drink. After what seemed an eternity, but in reality was around 20 minutes, the result came through and the result stood – Diaghilef had kept the race and Bobs Ploy was second. Diaghilef was 33/1 on the books but paid £100 to £1 on the Tote while the forecast paid £400 for a £1 stake. Needless to say Christoph was one of very few people collecting with these returns from the Tote windows, many of which had closed soon after the race was over. He literally collected thousands of pounds for the box, from an amalgam of different Tote payers. When Christoph returned to the box with their winnings they simply couldn't believe their eyes. The prophylactic lady who had made hundreds on her forecast for her meagre £2 investment decided she was suddenly in love with Christoph and wanted to take him out for dinner and learn more about him. She had already lost her broad-brimmed black hat in her effusive, passionate kisses and embraces, by way of gratitude. As tempted as Christoph was by the kind offer he thought it would probably be wiser and safer to make a discreet withdrawal. And so he quietly left the box now full of very loud elated and considerably richer clients. He nodded knowingly to himself as he too had made a significant return on the day. He smiled as he thought how he could probably have walked away with all their winnings and they would have been none the wiser, but the sheer delight on their faces had made his honesty more than worthwhile. Besides it had been a great day, with an unforgettable occurrence and a memory Christoph would reflect upon many times over the years. Jane Eyrie and he would laugh about it often in the future.

Christoph had much to thank Royal Ascot for in relation to McKillans. Even as he was being interviewed by them for a senior director's position there back in 1985 he had had to have a final interview with their Executive Creative Director, Tony Baker. The only time in this busy man's schedule was on the Tuesday morning of the first day of Royal Ascot. The interview was conducted as Tony Baker, a genial giant, changed into his hired Morning Suit from Moss Bros. Tony was far more interested in Christoph's knowledge of the turf then what he thought was good or bad advertising. He was particularly impressed by Christoph's encyclopaedic knowledge and the fact that he could go through each race, the horses, jockeys and trainers without a newspaper being at hand. Tony and Christoph subsequently were both convinced that Tony had only endorsed Christoph's hiring on the strength of the five winners that he had given him that day (purely for interest they were Rousillon at 11/4 in the Queen Anne; Never so Bold 4/1 in the King Stand; Sure Blade 3/1 in the Coventry; Bairn 6/4 in the St James's Palace and finally Wassl Merbayeh at 6/1 in the Queens Vase). On such fine lines are careers made and certainly the odd – literally - hiring!

Even his earlier foray into Eventing paid dividends many years later. When he had been appointed to work on Neptune he quickly found himself being fronted to the owners of the business and having to

A life above the line – just!

make a major presentation on their confectionery business. Christoph had discovered that one of the owners had a passion for Eventing, having been an accomplished rider and was even then sponsoring and supporting a rider in the USA. Never one to miss an opportunity Christoph, at drinks before lunch presented her with a signed copy of his book. Nancy one of the owners of Neptune was so delighted, surprised and intrigued that she insisted that he sit next to her. Their friendship blossomed and remained solid for the next fourteen years of Christoph's involvement in the business. She liked his difference, his lack of fear and the fact that he had honesty and a good sense of humour, even when under the stiffest of attacks and situations.

Indeed, it was while working on the Neptune business that Chris re-established contact with Mark Jones (formerly at Thomas Healey). Mark came and went twice during his time on Neptune. Christoph organised his two leaving parties the first at The Savoy overlooking the River Thames. This was a sit down dinner with a number of good rude speeches and much ribaldry. When Mark finally left the company Christoph with a friend and colleague at another Agency on Neptune's rostrum, arranged a box at Sandown Park. They designed two large cards the first that portrayed an overweight Mark riding out a finish with much gusto and cheeks blowing out air from a scarlet face. The second depicted Mark as a ruddy faced bookmaker with the names of the runners being the brands he had worked on – the odds reflecting their relative success. The Agencies also presented Mark with a framed racing print from the Marlborough Galleries in Cork Street, off Bond Street, in the West End of London. Mark would go on to have racehorses and take on various prestigious jobs in the sport, including hospitality of dignitaries and winning connections at Grade 1 race courses.

It was Mark who persuaded Christoph, when both were still ageing bachelors, to partake in and have an interest in racehorse ownership. This they did initially through being part of a trainer's syndicate and then later on owning a horse together. The initial sortie did not go well as the syndicate collapsed with the trainer basically being the only one to make money out of the venture. To his credit he used this money to salvage a race course under financial pressure, successfully preserving its future. Chris, in fairness only lost about £2,000. The second adventure was far more costly and risky and made Christoph realise that horse ownership for the small player was an expensive hobby, enjoyable, unpredictable but most definitely not financially rewarding. Very few are lucky enough to make a return on their investment and this is often only through betting on their charges, with the benefit of inside information, at the right time. It is the big operators who can afford to buy well or breed their own stock that dominates the sport.

Mark and Christoph bought a 4 year old chestnut mare called Winderless, despite her coming from a female dealer of questionable repute and linked to a trainer with an even more dubious reputation and unfathomable credentials. Christoph quickly learnt that just like advertising horse ownership was about selling dreams. Each new season dawned with such optimism and promise and the genuine belief that one had a world beater on one's hands. The off-season months had been a time for building up hopes and expectations with every report coming from the yard bringing and building ever more reasons to believe great things lay ahead. Even Christoph's first visit to the yard was reassuring as he was treated with deference and respect while encouraging noises were made about Winderless, having raw natural talent and speed and that she was certain to be a money spinner. Christoph was entertained, in the kitchen, with 'bacon butties' and a steaming hot mug of coffee before being shown diligently and respectfully around the yard and its occupants. Importantly, when Winderless was trotted out she appeared to have 4 legs with one at each corner, a bright eye and a rich chestnut coat. This, however, was to be the high point in the relationship between the trainer, the horse and her two owners. From here it would move slowly at first, then building up speed, before accelerating out of control on its downwards spiral, before smashing into smithereens on the ground with all participants maimed for life! The reality kicked in for Christoph. It all started with 'a minor training set-back', then 'she got a knock' now 'she's got a slight temperature' (nothing compared to that of the owner Christoph could assure you!), followed by 'she's pricked her hoof' and then 'she's

A life above the line – just!

not eaten up' (though on the bills Chris was paying for feed she could have been eating regularly at The Ritz!) before 'she's gone in her coat' (well for Gawd's sake buy her a new one then!) and finally 'she's dull and not quite right' (yes, well we can't all be exciting all of the time but we still have to get on with life and the job in hand!). However, just as Christoph believed Winderless would never be entered at a racecourse, let alone reach one and actually run the trainer rang to say she had been 'entered up' (meaning the trainer enters the horse in various races, each costing a small fortune, as an entry fee, and then the trainer decides which one to go for having lost the money, for the owners, on the ones it doesn't race in!). In fact Winderless was due to race the very next week in an inaccessible part of the country where (as it happened fortuitously) there would be few spectators. Excited and with adrenalin pumping through his body Christoph set off on his expedition despite it being a cold wet day in late March – post The Cheltenham Festival.

He was much relieved to see such few racegoers as from the moment Winderless entered the paddock she behaved appallingly. It started with here whinnying endlessly and nervously, and then she began moving very skittishly 'on her toes', before spinning around so suddenly that she broke free from her handler and then promptly crashed through the rails, which were fortunately made of plastic, so she did not incur an injury. Eventually she was caught and then Christoph watched with some embarrassment as Winderless had to be checked over by the course vet before being allowed to partake in the race. The young jockey, who possibly had only just got out of being ridden around in a pram, he looked so young, small and vulnerable was now not unfairly looking decidedly concerned. He had no sooner jumped up on her back than he was unceremoniously and ungraciously deposited on his posterior on the ground as Winderless reared up with what Christoph could only describe as a malevolent look in her rolling eyes. Now it was not only the jockey's pride that had been hurt, but finally after remounting (read; getting back up on her back into the saddle!) her on the course rather than in the paddock they made their way down to the start, fighting each other every inch of the way. Even down at the start Christoph could see through his binoculars that Winderless was giving her jockey an exacting time tossing her head and pulling hard on the reins. Finally the race got underway and now her jumping would be put on trial and under scrutiny. Over the first two obstacles her jumping was pedestrian and very deliberate but she managed to get to the other side without mishap. Fingers crossed and the exhalation of air came from sheer relief. Too early; as at the very next hurdle she decided she had had enough, ran out, crashed through the plastic wing at the side of the fence and then had to be pulled up – for her the race was over and her day was done. Chris, ever the optimist, thought that this was just a bad start, first night stage fright and that surely things would improve with the benefit of experience and time. No; Winderless was a mad mare.

There were all sorts of excuses proffered, following each of her subsequent runs, 'the ground wasn't right' to 'the field was too small' and 'she needs to be covered up' (too right she needs to be hidden from sight thought Christoph) to 'a stronger jockey would definitely help' (frankly by then any rider would have been entitled to ask for danger money to ride the mare) and then 'she needs a faster pace'. In the end after this barrage of excuses Christoph reached the only viable conclusion and that was that Winderless had about as much chance of winning a race as he himself had and it was time to cut his losses. He gave his share to Mark with good humour taking a thumping loss understandably on his initial outlay, never mind the training and vet fees and bills. Ironically, the luckless Winderless, then no longer weighed down by Christoph's involvement, ownership, cash and expectations, enjoyed a dramatic change in fortune. In her very next race, at Newton Abbott, watched intently by Chris from the comfort of the betting shop he saw her benefit from the runaway leader and hot favourite falling at the very last hurdle when well clear of the field, leaving Winderless to win at the princely sum of 5/1. At least, out of old time's sake, Christoph was able to recoup some of his losses, purely as a punter, by having had a reasonable bet on her.

In hindsight Christoph realised that enthusiasm had got the better of his judgement. He had forgotten the words of Juliette and that was to avoid chestnut mares, because as she put it 'most chestnut mares are

A life above the line – just!

mad, bad and dangerous to know, but if you get a good one she could be very good indeed'. It was the 'but' that had promised so much, for Christoph, but Winderless was not a 'good'un' and even her name suggested she might be 'winless'! However, Chris would watch with admiration as Mark Jones would go on to win many good races with his horses, including once at the Holy Grail of racing, Cheltenham. Their friendship was totally unaffected by the Winderless experience and Mark sold his share after her win at Newton Abbot believing that lightening seldom strikes twice. In fact she never won again and was retired to the paddocks where she became a brood mare – no doubt in more senses than one!

Even at the very end of Chris's advertising career racehorses would play their part. In 2000, when Neptune management changed in Europe, the new broom wanted a different and new carpet to beat! Christoph's team was disbanded and his deputy, Roger, was very sadly made redundant. Roger's farewell took place over Christmastide. As part of his leaving present, Chris presented, Roger, with a £20 win betting slip, on a horse running, that self-same afternoon, at Cheltenham, most appropriately named 'Go Roger Go'. Christoph had taken an early price of 7/1, as it had come over especially, from Ireland, being trained by Eddie O'Grady, and was to be ridden by Norman Williamson, a top flight jockey. Imagine everyone's delight when it won netting Roger £160. Christoph felt it was a fitting end to a great friend's career in advertising.

When Christoph, himself left McKillans, in early September 2001 he went quietly with no fuss, party or even a present. However, on his last visit to Ascot before his departure Christoph put his name and telephone number on stickers, which he then attached, to the five Fores racing prints that adorned the last remaining box in McKillans name. In May 2002, the Ascot Authority contacted Christoph, shortly after the new management at the agency had decided to give up having a box at Ascot entirely. Christoph had predicted this would happen. Having found his details on the back of the prints Ascot had contacted him as he had hoped. And so on the late May Bank Holiday Chris was driven down to Ascot, by Fiona Sole, picked up the pictures and brought them back to London.

Mind you Christoph never felt very happy about the surreptitious way he had acquired these pictures, some might even say purloined, and so much so he never hung them up but kept them under the spare bed. He was right because several months later in early 2003 Chris was contacted by the Agency's Head of Maintenance and asked about the pictures. Ascot had directed him to Chris. Chris did not deny having them nor did he dispute that they were the Agency's property. He was instructed, on the authority of the Financial Director to return the pictures to the Agency. The claim quite rightly was that the pictures belonged to the Agency though Christoph suspected that the real motivation was the desire of the Head of Maintenance to keep them himself as he was another known keen racing man. Christoph chose to ignore the initial demand deciding to wait and see what would transpire as a result of his not complying with this instruction. Some weeks later the same man was on the 'phone this time demanding aggressively to have the pictures back and seeking to arrange transportation to collect them from Christoph's residence. However, Chris was able to resist this arrangement, and redirect this character to the Management of the Agency, as in the interim period he had appealed to the new head of the Agency, Brian Pullet, whom he had known when they had both been working on the Training Committee of the Advertising body, the IPA (Institute of Practitioners in Advertising). Christoph had written in his letter that he had had a long association with these pictures, and had looked after them, at Ascot, through various manifestations of the boxes and their decoration and refurbishment. He also pointed out in the letter how shabbily he had been treated at the end of his time at McKillans, having to slink away one late afternoon, forbidden to even say goodbye to the staff, or to have a farewell drink or a party, never mind a gift from the agency. In July 2003 Christoph received a simple and short reply, by e-mail, from Brian Pullet stating that in light of his sad departure from the agency he had given so much to he should keep the pictures 'in lieu of no announcement, no cards, no present and no party'. He finished up with the simple statement 'You must Chris, keep the pictures as a souvenir and memory of happier times at McKillans.' And to this day they sit on Christoph's study walls.

As Christoph looked back on his working life as an employee in advertising he appreciated the obvious parallels between horses and advertising. He felt he had literally and metaphorically run both in tandem. Christoph would say, using horseracing as his metaphor, that 'it had been a glamourous and colourful life, a truly run race with stiff opposition, and while the conditions were testing, the pace had been an honest and consistent one and he had kept up the relentless gallop right up to the finishing line – even if he was subsequently nobbled by the stewards in their enquiry!' But on review it was judged that he had won and had run the race of his life!

─────────── CHAPTER 3 ───────────

'Never underestimate the power of a woman' Advertising Slogan for 'Ladies Home Journal' 1946 (USA)

If horses and horseracing in particular, had run in parallel with Christoph's life in advertising, women were most certainly interwoven throughout his career. Women always proved something of an unpredictable, surprising and even an incalculable gamble for Christoph. They were however, definitely one of the four cornerstones of his life – horses (and gambling), finances, work and women.

Christoph had always loved women. That said Christoph was no great lover, womaniser and certainly no lothario, but an admirer, a dreamer, a romantic and at times even a fantasist. He loved their manner, behaviour, movement, looks, their shape, their variety, the way their minds worked, their perceptions and above all their company. They definitely appealed to a strong feminine side in his nature and character. He infinitely preferred the association of women to that of men, which was curious given his love of sport, be that team games, such as rugby union, or the more individual pursuits of tennis and athletics, all at which he had proven to be highly proficient. Regrettably his participation in 'rugger' had distinctly not improved his looks having broken his nose three times and every finger on both hands as well as a crucial bone in his right foot. None of these injuries had either enhanced his appearance or indeed his mobility.

A life above the line – just!

Chris truly revered women and held them in the highest regard. His encounters, at least romantically, were often in direct contrast to his business dealings. Whether it was the way their minds were wired, or their sensuality or their aura that took over Christoph never really knew but suddenly he seemed to lack sureness, confidence, immediacy, bravado and boldness. The result was that he could often appear tongue-tied, uneasy, and almost non-communicative, fearing that anything and everything he might utter would be deemed banal – which indeed it often was! Even as a young blade, having successfully and somewhat dishonestly, conned his way onto the social elite lists, he had used flippancy and humour or repartee to overcome his inadequacies when it came to female encounters. In those days Christoph wore velvet suits in bold colours, always donned a red rose in his button hole and a deep red handkerchief in the top pocket of his dinner jacket. Chris more often than not felt he was 'tilting at windmills' and as such was much more of a Don Quixote than a Don Juan. The positive side of this lack of self-belief in his liaisons meant that he was never envious or jealous and never fought for a woman, believing that it was their choice, and if they chose against him, he would try to convince himself that it was their loss.

Yet for all this obvious lack of self-confidence, a series of missed opportunities, some poor judgements, Christoph was 'lucky-in-love' and batted way above his level of entitlement. He had no idea of how or why – perhaps they saw something in him which he most definitely did not. Certainly, women found Chris polite, charming, quick-witted and tolerably amusing, as well as archetypal British. In defiance of the quote 'Charm is a woman's strength, strength is a man's charm' Christoph had bucket-loads of charm. Indeed, it was this charm that got Christoph out of many scrapes and man made holes, often of his own creation, throughout his life.

Even before Chris found his way into advertising and was collecting his dole at Hythe House, in the Shepherds Bush Road, he employed his gift of the gab on the female representative at the Job Centre. This meant he was able to spurn the jobs presented to him instead using the time allocated to him to discuss her ambitions and life while also recounting tales of his tender years to date. Invariably, at the end of each weekly session she would end up reluctantly saying to him, "Well Chris I don't think you really are suited to any of these jobs so I'll see you next week and we'll see if anything more suitable has come on the books"; and so she did, until he finally got his break at Gris Advertising.

In his initial years at Gris Advertising women within the agency played no part in his life, though when an ambitious Personal Assistant, Christine Walcott, was promoted, rightly so, to oversee Chris in the Information Department/Library, he did fantasise about having a relationship with her, as she was an attractive older woman caught up in a problematic marriage. She had a fresh outlook, a wealth of experience of life and had achieved so much against almost impossible odds. Despite some innocent fun mutual flirtation it was a desire and a dream that would never be fulfilled.

In fact it was only when he was championed for a move into Account Management in 1976 that his senses became truly aroused. The cheerleader of his cause to have Christoph promoted, from the Library and his Desk Research job, was a very Senior Personal Assistant, Megan Cutler. Christoph had resisted this proposed move as he still sought to be a copywriter and build a reputation in the creative department. He had had some minor successes with poster, leaflet and press work for a number of clients, but these forays, done in his own time, had not resulted in a job offer from the Creative Director. Megan, on the other hand, had seen Chris's responses to the requests made to the Information Department and had appreciated the analysis he provided and the perspective and viewpoint offered, on each project he tackled. Her perspective and positive views she had expressed strongly to the senior management. She advocated that Christoph was a prodigious talent that should be harnessed to the Account Management Department and that he was being wasted or, at the very least, restricted in his current role. She even went as far as to suggest his presence could actually strengthen the Account Management Department, especially as his career grew and developed. Separately, Megan sought out Christoph and informed him of her thoughts on him and asked for his support over her entreaties. Christoph was completely bowled

A life above the line – just!

over that anyone would go to bat for him in such a fevered manner. He was also totally bewitched and entranced by her confidence, articulate nature, her cheekiness and sense of the future. She was in every way a beautiful woman. Mentally she was a live wire with strong opinions. Physically she was most attractive with her porcelain complexion, her large green-hazel eyes, the full lips, the delicate frame, shapely legs all enhanced by her stylish, expensive, conservative dress sense. Megan was real class. Christoph did everything he could to woo this woman, some 10 years older than him, with writings, poetry, dinners, flowers – red roses- and evening drinks. She truly was his 'Dulcinea', but she was always fully in command and control. Yes, he could wine and dine her, hold her, kiss and caress her, but that was as far as she would ever let him go. Megan was the sensible adult and needed to keep this young spaniel puppy under control and keep him directed and focused on his future career.

Eventually, despite his reservations expressed as, "Account people in his experience and dealings, lacked brain power, showed little initiative or intuition and possessed no selling skills whatsoever", Megan did persuade Christoph to give it a try. She convinced him that this was truly the route to the top of the agency and if he felt so damningly about account managers he should work to change the status quo. Christoph was sold and besides he thought incorrectly that it would provide many more opportunities to see Megan. He made the switch and never looked back. She was right he was a 'suit' through and through. On reflection, Christoph realised that without Megan's belief in him and her intervention he would probably never have made the transition and he always knew he owed her a great debt of gratitude. The fact was that his career success was initiated by her and her foresight meant that he always remained grateful and appreciative of this and her throughout his career. Regrettably, for Christoph, they would lose touch when he went to the United States, some two years later, and whilst he was away she moved to Australia and married a man over there.

As a 'suit' his first client was a leading cosmetics company where he was initially allowed to continue to use his creative copywriting skills to develop 'Beauty Adviser' ads for the local press. This was in addition to his mundane job of proof-reading and ensuring that the mechanicals and artwork were signed off by the senior client, before being released to the publications/magazines. Despite being advised never to have liaisons with clients Christoph became emotionally involved with a similarly aged very bright, talented, flashy, slim, long raven haired, deep red lipped and beautifully made up and turned out beauty assistant in the Public Relations Department, Susannah Crofter. Fortunately, this sortie did not last long as Susannah was in much demand and she was spoilt for choice on the male interest front. Christoph while nice enough was by no means a strong candidate on virtually any criteria. Philosophical about this, once he moved off this account, he moved on with his life too. Interestingly, though Christoph had flirtations with a few clients, over the ensuing years, he had no further relationships and no other associations evolved into passionate affairs from there on in. Christoph did attend Susannah's wedding reception, to a highly successful banker, held at The Ritz Hotel in London, some years later and was most amused when they moved into a house next door to the one he had been brought up in, in Kensington.

However, 'fishing off the company docks' was an altogether different matter. Christoph from even before he had joined the agency business had had a perception that the advertising industry provided rich fishing waters in which to trawl. It was well known in those days that advertising was a magnet for young ladies seeking careers as PA and secretaries. Some even viewed it as a way of meeting potential suitors. It was the time of the raving- raging '60s and '70s – the time of 'free love'. His early years, being largely bereft of funds and time, were remarkably quiet inside the agency. Then he had become completely besotted with Megan Cutler. However, as he grew within the organisation so his confidence levels and his self-esteem rose and at the agency Christmas Party of 1977 Chris found himself much taken with his 'big boss's' newly arrived Personal Assistant /Secretary, Brenda Mere. Brenda, had already had an interesting life, long before Christoph met her when she was just thirty. She had started out as a model and then after an early abusive childless marriage she had turned her very real skills and mental aptitude to teaching most successfully young children. She had proven to have a natural affinity with her young pupils. Over time however Brenda had determined she wanted a more social environment in which to work and also had a desire to explore the world of commerce and business. This had brought Brenda to the advertising industry and Gris Advertising specifically. Chris found this woman alluring with her dark short cropped hair, deep dark green eyes, bold crimson lipstick, slim, tall and classically elegant attire underpinned by her level of maturity and confidence emanating from her life experiences. Brenda had a positive bouncy disposition, a natural vivaciousness and a bright smiling countenance. Her re-found optimism and assuredness manifested itself in in having a great sense of fun, cheekiness and a ready smile and laugh. To Christoph she was both captivating and exhilarating. Brenda was more than prepared to deal with his sometimes unreasonable demands in terms of hours, his workaholic tendencies, his outspokenness, the occasional emotional outbursts and sometimes bad behaviour of a talented, well-meaning but also often insecure, Christoph. That Christmas Party Brenda, who knew exactly what she, wanted, led him back to his back office and then seduced this more than willing partner and they made mad passionate and frenzied love across his desk. This was the start of a heady nine month long romance that was only ended when Christoph was 'banished' to New York.

Christoph truly loved Brenda and he found their relationship novel, exciting, intellectually challenging and sexually exhilarating. In every sense she taught him things he had never known or done before. Shamefully though he never felt ready to give himself entirely to her nor did he perceive her as his long term partner in life. Indeed, their relationship was conducted in private and in an almost clandestine manner. The friendship existed totally apart from his social life and never with the knowledge of the agency. In hindsight Christoph realised he had been selfish and insensitive to a woman that had given herself to him and educated him so much mentally, physically and emotionally. In the Agency they were the sole of discretion, so much so, that his boss, John E Goldman, in a laddish moment would jocularly suggest, "I'll bet you'd like to be giving Brenda one" or "I'm sure Chris, if you could you'd love to have an affair with Brenda". And when Christoph would reply "Yes, well we're actually living together and have been for the past six months", John would laughingly retort "In your dreams mate!" Nobody suspected that this was in fact the truthful account of their situation and relationship. Chris appreciated that Brenda was highly desirable and a very good catch and far more than he ever deserved. He knew that he had been extremely fortunate that they had been an item and a partnership for so long. In retrospect, he always wished he had been less egocentric and career driven, giving her more of his time, sharing more experiences and with greater involvement in his overall life. It was no more than she deserved. When they parted, at the same time as he left for the USA, they were both sad but decided that they would not stay in touch but both should lead their own lives. The inevitable result was that Christoph never saw or heard of, or from, Brenda again after he left England's shores in September 1978.

New York provided very different experiences and Christoph found it a lonely place to be. It took him a while to find his feet and gain confidence, but once he did he realised it truly was in every way 'the land of opportunity'. His initial flurry with an American lady came via a striking mischievous flirtatious Receptionist on the Management Floor at Gris, New York. Nannette was a well-connected privileged JAP (Jewish American Princess) who proved really hard to date. Eventually she agreed to go out with Christoph, mainly out of sympathy, after hearing how he had been ill with 'irritable bowel syndrome' that required a hospital visit in the middle of the night. Nannette totally dictated terms to Christoph. They had two very expensive dinner dates, the first at 'Once upon a Stove' on the Lower East Side and the second at 'One if by Land and Two if by Sea' in Greenwich Village. It had to be said Christoph was completely at sea and drowning way out of his depth with the vivacious Nannette. Imagine therefore his surprise when Nannette stated, as dinner ended, that she would like to spend the night with Christoph. On the strength and success of that she would determine whether they would spend the weekend together. Needless to say, or perhaps under such pressure, Christoph's performance clearly

A life above the line – just!

did not pass muster. The following morning Nannette announced that it had been very nice but that she had decided she did not want to get involved with, as she put it, "a transient Englishman." It had been fun and exhilarating and a solely physical attraction for both but that was it. Christoph would see Nannette often, over the next 2 years, and she would continue to flirt outrageously with him but that one night had been the beginning and the end of any possible relationship. He was history in her eyes.

After this 'rebuffal' it was therefore somewhat surprising that the next female encounter at Gris Advertising would lead to true love. Indeed, it was altogether rather Mills & Boon for Christoph. It owed much to luck, good fortune and even coincidence. The background was that Christoph whilst working on the cosmetic business in the UK had been involved in a number of conversations with a senior Account Director in the New York office, a certain Shelton Blaine. When she discovered that Christoph was being transferred to the New York Office she insisted that he get in touch with her, so that they could meet up in person. To begin with he had not taken up this offer as he sought to find his feet in the Big Apple and besides he felt he needed to prove his worth, to the agency and on the Thomas Healey business before making contact. Initially too he was not even sure how long he was going to be based there in New York. However, one day Chris got into an 'elevator'/lift and there was this stunning looking girl with a mane of glossy black hair, full red lips, pale olive Italian American complexion and deep large dark brown eyes and a shapely full figure. He was totally smitten by her appearance. When she got out of the lift he curiously felt a sense of loss and more frustratingly he had absolutely nothing to go on - no name, no department, no account or client details. A few days later Christoph was fortunate enough to run into this paragon of beauty once again. This time she was carrying artwork and mechanicals. While the lift environment provided no opportunity for an introduction never mind a conversation, as everyone, largely automaton-like men in grey suits, merely looked ahead austerely, waiting for arrival at their floor. As she was getting out a brash unthinking man pushed arrogantly past her and knocked the mechanicals out of her grasp. The man did not even apologise or give her a second glance. Chris, however, deftly stepped out of the lift and came to her assistance. Bending down he helped her pick up the mechanicals which had dropped to the floor outside the lift. As she knelt her hair, which had been held back by a large bulldog clip fell forward. At this the young lady became somewhat flustered and as Chris smiled sympathetically she blushed a deep crimson glow, hurriedly thanked him for his gallantry and kindness and then bustled speedily away seeking desperately to regain her composure, dignity and poise. Christoph watched her walk away with a smile on his face which when she turned around, as though she knew he was looking at her, he laughed and gave her a large wink while nodding his head approvingly. The good piece of fortune that came out of this chance encounter was that he now knew what account she worked on, as the artwork and mechanicals were stamped with the Borcella mark.

It was now clearly the right time to contact Shelton Blaine, as Borcella was her account. He rang her on the internal phone and was duly invited to meet for coffee, up in her office, a few days later. He was desperately trying to think of a way of finding out who her colleague was without seeming like a sexual predator, or stalker, more especially, as he really didn't know Shelton that well. However, he need never have worried as he and Shelton got along famously from the start and indeed they would become good friends right up until Christoph left to go back to England. At the same time Shelton departed Gris Advertising to take up a senior tourist position, promoting trade on and to the West Coast. They kept in touch for many years after, as Shelton, ever business minded, sought to persuade Chris to come out himself and also encourage his friends to visit the American West Coast. As they had been conversing, on this initial encounter, Christoph became aware of the presence of someone lurking in the doorway. Turning around, in his chair, he found himself looking straight into the face of the Italian American bombshell. As before she was carrying artwork and mechanicals, this time for Shelton's signature and approval, and also, as before, some in the middle seemed to slip from her hand falling onto the floor. Promptly, Christoph leapt up from his chair and helped her gather the pieces up. Once again, the young lady got

A life above the line – just!

flustered, blushed and her thick glossy hair came out of its sizeable clip and cascaded down bouncing onto her shoulders. Smilingly, Chris observed to her, "We're beginning to make a habit of meeting like this." Shelton exclaimed excitedly, "Oh I am so glad that you two have met each other already as I was intending to introduce you to one another, as I suspected that Christoph would not know anyone in New York." Standing up Christoph explained that they had never been properly, let alone formally, introduced but had had a couple of chance encounters. Shelton said "Well then let me introduce you, Christoph this is Anita – Account Executive on Borcella; Anita this is Christoph, who has joined us from London, England to work on the Thomas Healey account." In a truly classic British way they shook hands and smiled knowingly at each other.

Now, at least, Christoph had a Christian name to go on with her position and Account details. When he got back to his office he searched through the extensive telephone directory of employees at Gris Advertising, seeking to find any Anita's associated with Borcella. To his relief there was only one Anita and that was Anita Paulina. Summoning up all his courage he 'phoned her. Ridiculously he asked her out for lunch, which was never going to happen, as lunch, at 'the sweat shop' that was Gris Advertising's reputation, was a sandwich or salad and soup taken from the canteen and consumed at the desk, commonly referred to as the 'work station'. Anita was warm and charming, if not somewhat taken aback by Christoph's forwardness and instead of lunch, when, she quite rightly and sensibly, stated there would be insufficient time to talk properly, let alone in a relaxed manner, she instead proposed drinks on the next Thursday after work.

And so it was that following Thursday they met outside the offices of the agency and headed for Crawdaddys situated close to Grand Central Station. Crawdaddys was famous for its cocktails and fried zucchini. Anita despite her initial demureness on their previous 'encounters' turned out to be open, direct and disarmingly honest. She even admitted to having a long-standing boyfriend, Jerry. As such Christoph realised he was being subtly warned off the patch. Given that he was supposedly returning to London, at Christmas, on the completion of three months, he was realistic and willing to accept that they could only really be platonic passing friends. However, they got on so well that it wasn't long before Anita was taking the piss out of Christoph's very English accent and his curious phrases and expressions. Evidently, Shelton had 'bigged' Christoph up as being a potential 'high-flyer' in the Gris organisation, so his PR was well-covered. Indeed, Anita even used the opportunity to seek his advice on what she should do with her career and what suggestions he might have on how she could best progress. Christoph liked the fact that she was so clearly ambitious, extremely bright, very sharp and quick witted as well as out-going, gregarious and conscientious. Borcella had clearly only ever been for her an entry point to get into the advertising industry in New York. Christoph was totally intrigued by her and was captivated by the sincerity of those big open dark pools that stared earnestly at him completely consuming him. By the end of this first date he had persuaded Anita to have dinner with him the following Thursday.

It was on this second occasion that they kissed for the first time, though Anita would only allow him to kiss her gently and tenderly on each cheek. But from then on Thursdays became their regular weekly date, even to the point that Christoph eventually asked Anita, "Why is it that we can only ever meet on a Thursday, as it feels a little like the Carvel Ice-Cream advertising campaign – 'Wednesdays is sundaes at Carvels'?" Anita laughed and confessed that this was because Jerry was a very possessive boyfriend, who worked on a building site, but went scuba diving, with work colleagues every Thursday evening. And so it was that Thursdays became 'sundaes' with Anita!

When shortly before Christoph was due to return to London it was decided that he would be coming back to New York after the Christmas and New Year holidays, and that an experienced American Account Executive would replace him in London, everything in his romantic life had the chance to change. Christoph realised that the relationship with Anita could now potentially blossom and be allowed to develop into far more than just friendship. He knew that he was mad about her, possibly even in love with her. He knew that they had great fun together but also that she was already spoken for and she had, after all, never led him on or given him any hope or encouragement. They had already shared a lot but this had been primarily focused on their ambitions, work, advertising and the agency. All over the festive season, in London, he had time to think about the Anita situation. He found himself missing her desperately and even took the time to call her from London to wish her a Happy Christmas and a Happy New Year, both which took her completely by surprise – but it was really simply to hear her voice.

Once back in New York he knew he had to be honest and tell Anita how he felt about her and that he truly loved her. Anita was a little confused as this was going to change the dynamic of their relationship and besides he was still a foreigner - 'an alien' – as the US Immigration liked to refer to non-US citizens at that time – and he would quite probably still return to his home country. He certainly had never seemed committed to living full-time in America let alone Manhattan. And then there was not the inconsiderable problem of her current relationship and feelings for Jerry, her boyfriend, whom was known and liked by her family. In the end a number of circumstances conspired to work in Chris's favour. The fact that he had come back to New York established some grounds for furthering their relationship. Then Lucy, Anita's sister, working at another agency, BBD&O, really liked Chris and most especially because he was light-hearted and positive. This apparently was in direct contrast to Jerry whom she saw as being overly intense, over powering, controlling and seeking to force and dominate her sister in a way she found both irritating and demeaning. Christoph seemed to bring the fun out of her sister. Finally Anita was offered a position working as a Senior Account Manager in the Medical Division of the Agency. She knew that Chris, with his past experience, would be able to help her put together think pieces, competitive analyses and develop through the line ideas and concepts, in a fun and stimulating manner. Inevitably, this brought the two star struck lovers ever closer and they started to meet far more often after work. They gradually got closer and closer until one evening, after a lengthy work session the barriers came down and they embraced passionately. It was not long before they were tearing each other's clothes off and making mad uncontrolled and fervent love. Their pent up desire for each other was now successfully and beautifully fulfilled. The need and want for each other washed over them and the fervour and excitement was exhilarating and took Christoph to a new emotional place, he had never reached before. It was bliss and they really loved being together though Anita was very reluctant for Christoph to see her naked or to go to sleep fully undressed and insisted on wearing her Notre Dame College American Football shirt.

Anita eventually confronted the luckless Jerry and he was not only abusive to her but became threatening. Chris also knew he had to go and meet Anita's parents and this he eventually did and they were very accepting of him, without in any way taking sides. They were not unnaturally worried that he was an Englishman, not an American and not even a European, even if much to their surprise and relief he had at least been brought up and educated as a Catholic. At this same first encounter Jerry came over and asked to see Christoph outside. Jerry swore at Chris as he stood before him and threatened to punch his lights out there and then, snarling abusive remarks and spitting in his face, even pushing him seeking to provoke him into a physical confrontation. But to no avail. Chris calmly pointed out that Jerry was in danger of making a fool of himself with this public display and that this was neither the time nor the place to show, or even articulate, his fury and hurt. Christoph stated he would be prepared to meet him on a separate occasion for a drink or a coffee. Jerry stormed off warning Christoph that he would have him 'done over'. Anita's parents expressed genuine concern that this might not be an idle threat given his building trade connections and that Christoph should tread very carefully and be ever vigilant. As things transpired, by and large, Jerry only resorted to abusive intimidation with telephone calls in the middle of the night. On one occasion he did turn up at Christoph's apartment on the Upper East Side, late one evening, making a scene outside until neighbours complained and railed him for disturbing their peace and quiet at such an anti-social hour. However, they never squared up to each other again.

Anita and Chris's relationship went from strength to strength and Christoph knew she was the most wonderful girlfriend, bright

A life above the line – just!

and personable, loving, and attentive, companionable, amusing, warm, affectionate and very easy going. For all her beauty she was extraordinarily self-conscious and modest. They shared so much in common and Anita really enjoyed working with Christoph on her projects and using his very different slant to balance her own more disciplined thoughts and opinions. They enjoyed each other's company going to shows and dinners and really exploring New York's cultural offerings together. 1979 was a truly memorable and remarkable year, which he shared blissfully with her.

Just before Christmas, over one year on in their relationship, Christoph had to go to a festive lunch with his team and two mid-weight clients. His boss, not the most sociable of animals, chose to have a few too many Jack Daniels and then feeling decidedly the worst for wear, wisely excused himself. The more senior of the two clients a thickly set man from Idaho, wearing a string tie and a metal tipped collar shirt, and donned in black leather cowboy boots proceeded to get completely wasted on Bloody Marys. He even ordered steak tartare at St John's Restaurant & Bar situated on a mid-town corner of 1st Avenue and then proceeded to send it back because it wasn't cooked. He then made a leering pass at his attractive but quite reserved and slightly prim and prudish Brand Manager, a situation from which Christoph was subtly able to extricate her. He ended up so drunk he had turned his chair around so that he was now conversing with the wall. The Brand Manager, whom Christoph liked and respected as a really bright prospect within the company, through all this harassment, was trying to maintain a sensible conversation with Christoph. Once she had finished her meal Christoph suggested that she should use the afternoon to go shopping while he would take responsibility for getting her boss into a cab and back to his hotel. Once both had left Christoph admittedly now himself feeling somewhat inebriated went to his bank extracted US$4,000 and headed for Tiffany's on 5th Avenue. Once there and seeking to maintain an upright stance without wobbling and a sober appearance he selected and bought an engagement ring, using the total amount and then had it professionally gift-wrapped by them. Fortunately, before Christoph made matters worse he went home and fell asleep on his sofa. Only when he woke up feeling absolutely ghastly with a splitting headache and hangover, did he realise what he had done. Christoph never gave Anita the ring as he knew she would have been truly alarmed had he done so, as there was no way she was ready to get married or settle down, however much she might love Chris. In the end Christoph had to go back to Tiffany's, concede and confess what had happened and sell the ring back to them. They were most understanding, probably believing deep down that his proposal of marriage had been rejected, a somewhat more than common occurrence for them. They offered to give him his money back but only in the form of tokens to be used in their store. That year everyone, especially his mother and sister, got extremely nice Christmas presents as indeed did Anita! It truly was the best of times in every sense.

Things however were sadly to change dramatically for them just a few months later. At the end of March 1980 Christoph, after a series of very difficult meetings and presentations with Thomas Healey, decided it was time to return back to London and pursue his career there. He had learnt many salient lessons, but had realised the politics at Gris Advertising in New York was slowly stifling him, and while he was highly regarded by the team he found he had lost much of his respect and admiration for them. The tough challenges that lay ahead on Thomas Healey in the USA were certainly not going to be solved by him, in either the short or midterm. As he projected himself forward into the future he could not see himself becoming a major player among New York's 'Mad-Men'. He would definitely not miss the cut and thrust of account work fought out in the maelstrom of political ambition, promotion and success. He realised he had grown and gained a lot in a relatively short time and this had brought some real tangible successes but already he missed the regular inter-departmental contact back home. He found the New York Account Group suffocating, rather parochial, overly superior and distinctly paranoid. Besides he knew, as the token Brit, he would always be 'the outsider' in this Group. In truth his view of working in New York had suddenly become somewhat soured, even though in time, on reflection, he would look back on this period as one of the greatest experiences he had had in both his career and overall life.

The really hard part of this realisation and the inevitable decision to conclude his time 'on the other side of the pond' was Anita. He didn't want to be an 'also-ran' as this was not him and in this capacity he would not gain the admiration or earn the respect of Anita. To her eternal credit, while she her family and their friends did, and tried, everything to dissuade him of his negative views over quite a lengthy period, she ultimately accepted that it had to be how he felt that really mattered. Christoph asked Anita if she would come to London and see if she felt she could live there, even though deep down in his heart he knew it would not work for her. You could take the woman out of New York but you couldn't take New York out of the woman especially when it came to the very close ties she had with her family. Anita, to her credit, did come over to London and stayed with Christoph for a fortnight and everyone she met there loved her to bits. Sadly, as he had predicted, whilst she enjoyed her time she truly didn't feel at home there. They had tragically reached an impasse. Anita didn't feel she could live in London; Christoph didn't feel he could live in Manhattan or New York and yet both wanted to be together and still really loved one another. They both realised it would be totally impractical, impossible and even unfair to try to conduct their romance from a distance of over 3,000 miles with just occasional trans-Atlantic visits. So they had reached the end of the road and would have to split and let each other go. Christoph was heartbroken and was not proud that he had been the catalyst for this change and was now the cause of such a level of hurt. Anita had given him so much, mental stimulation, fun, excitement and love and he was now coldly and hard heartedly turning his back on her and their partnership in the pursuit of his career. There were false hopes that he would try to get back to the States at some stage. There were valiant attempts to keep in touch, on both their sides, but these became somewhat acrimonious and ever more painful. In the end this chapter in his life was over and it was time to close the book. He was not proud of himself and a part of him would always love and regret the loss of the talented and vivacious Anita.

For her part she did move on and eventually even got a moment of revenge on Christoph. Over the ensuing years Christoph would make a number of trips to New York, but, however difficult, would always resist contacting Anita, even though her flat was within walking distance of The Berkeley Hotel, where he inevitably stayed, and indeed close to the Gris office. On one occasion someone had forewarned Anita that Christoph would be coming to New York. Imagine his surprise when upon checking into the hotel he found a hand-delivered message from her asking him to call her. His heart missed a beat and he was genuinely excited. Even though by the time he got to his room it was already 9pm, on a hot and humid August evening, he called her excitedly. He had noticed that the security at check-in and in the lobby was more intense than normal and all guests were instructed that they could not open any windows which opened up on the side facing the Waldorf Astoria Hotel. Apparently, the Senator, Edward Kennedy, was coming to town the next day to speak at this hotel and so everything was on high alert and in a locked down state. When he got through to Anita she asked him if he would mind going over to her flat and meeting up with her. When he got there she decided they should stay in and have drinks there rather than go out. Her apartment was hot and stuffy but they chatted amiably and even slightly flirtatiously, the chemistry between them was still quite obviously there.

Eventually, Anita said she would really like to spend the night with him and asked if he would let her stay with him in his hotel room. How could Christoph refuse such a wonderful and exciting offer, truly living up to Oscar Wilde's observation 'that a man can resist everything except temptation'? Anita looked absolutely stunning despite the heat and he truly craved her closeness and touch. Anita packed a few things into her shoulder bag and they made their way back to the hotel. Given, it was now late Anita stated that she was going to get ready for bed, but would change in the bathroom, and was most definite that she would not allow Christoph to undress her. She did, however, deliberately leave the bathroom door ajar so that through the reflection of the mirror he could see her strip down to a tantalisingly sexy matching black crimson laced bra and briefs. When she came to bed she refused to allow

A life above the line – just!

Christoph to remove her smalls, or to caress her body, only allowing him to kiss her gently on the lips and face. Then she simply turned over and went off to sleep. In the morning when she woke up she went straight to the bathroom, showered, made up and dressed. Deeply frustrated Christoph couldn't comprehend her behaviour and had to ask her why she had ever bothered to come and stay the night with him. Mischievously, she smiled and laughed, and replied "Oh thank you Chris. As you will recall our air conditioning was always on the blink and currently is not actually working at all. I just fancied a good night's sleep in a comfortable air-conditioned bedroom." Then kissing him gently and affectionately on both cheeks and brushing her lips against his she bade him farewell and with a flick of her hair departed leaving him a little bemused but also highly amused. Christoph was full of admiration for her brazenness and loved her all the more for it!

Over the next few years back home in England there were a number of meaningless dalliances and even 'one-nighters' but for a long time Christoph's work place romances were curtailed. Christoph had few liaisons at Gris Advertising and at Premium White, his personal life and activities, with the fairer sex, were kept outside the portals of this Agency. It was only when he got to McKillans, his final agency that inter-agency affiliations reoccurred. Christoph was never a man who ever thought about using his status, power or position for sexual gain and never respected other men who did. He was intrigued by women and was always 'shooting at the stars' when it came to his ambitions over them. His initial foray at McKillans was with a highly-esteemed Board Director, Denise Alwyn. Denise was well-regarded as a superb and effective Account Director, with great input, service and strategic nous as well as possessing real people skills. Clients liked and respected her enormously. She was also earnest, sophisticated, well read, a culture vulture of theatre and dance and very feisty. They never worked on any accounts together but Christoph had worked with her and been responsible for staffing on her accounts. He was admiring of her talent, commitment and loyalty to both her clients and the Agency. She was clearly a force to be reckoned with as an operator on demanding and challenging business. Denise was a striking blonde, well-dressed to suit her shapely and diminutive frame, a pointed and determined chin and with sincere questioning blue-grey eyes, that gave little or nothing away. She was seemingly very private, independent and reserved. They got along famously and Christoph was able to get her to relax her demeanour and laugh easily through his easy happy go-lucky nature and approach to life. She liked the fact that even in the darkest days of the agency he didn't take life too seriously and always had a really positive 'can-do/can make it happen' attitude. She also admired his combative, out-spoken approach and the fact that he was apolitical, strong, definite and decisive in his role as Client Services Director and Deputy Managing Director. As a hard worker herself it was easy for her to relate to Christoph's work ethos and his desire to commit totally to his clients with a real sense of purpose. Their relationship developed slowly and positively through a series of drinks after work and then dinners. There was no real romance but a raw sexual tension was emerging and building up. They knew it was probably only a question of time before they succumbed to these urges and when it happened they decided to become 'an item'. Denise was a well-experienced and exciting lover who was experimental and as demanding of her partner as she was of her team at work. Christoph enjoyed her company enormously both in and out of bed. The only downsides were that she lived a long way away, for a non-driver, from the agency, on the west side of London which was hard to get out to late at night. Secondly, she had a jealous male cat that did not admire or accept any intruder into what had been his previously sedate life. When he was ejected from the bed, at night, he decided that was too much and so one night whilst the humans were in the throes of passion he jumped on top of Christoph's back and dug his claws into his back. This was definitely sweet revenge and an immediate coolant of ardent ardour. As time developed, even though they were not in love with each other, Denise wanted to spend more time with Christoph. His workaholic behaviour at that time did not allow for this. Eventually, one evening over dinner at Drones in Pont Street, Knightsbridge, she issued him with an ultimatum, "I need to see much more of you or otherwise our

A life above the line – just!

relationship is not worth continuing," she stated. Christoph in trying to diffuse the situation responded cheekily, "But Denise you have seen all there is to see!" Denise was not amused at this wisecrack and told him he was 'pathetic', and clearly exasperated she threw down her napkin onto the table, slapped him across the face and walked out of the restaurant in high dudgeon. Smarting, embarrassed and a little ashamed at his stupidity and insensitivity he finished his meal, quietly paid the bill and slowly, deliberately and as confidently as he could left the restaurant to a mix of sympathetic and quizzical faces and went home. That was disappointingly the end of their affair. Christoph and Denise remained good friends and highly supportive of each other publicly, as well as being professional work colleagues, but from there on in Denise kept Christoph very much at arms' length.

But Christoph's time in advertising would end with a long-lasting romance and a dream – just as it had begun all those years before. Christoph had been asked to interview a Senior Planner being considered by the Agency for a job in 1994. Her name was Fiona Sole, a short reddish orange haired, long eye lashed, large open blue eyed Scotswoman with a light frame, pale complexion and beautifully sculpted ballerina shaped legs. Clearly Fiona was very bright, astute, sharp as a pin, experienced and extremely competent as well as being supremely confident and forthright. Christoph was much taken by her and made this clear to the Head of Planning, though couldn't resist a totally inappropriate sexist remark, " Great legs – I would hire her for those alone. Seriously though what he had seen was a great character; a woman with great insights; strong creative vision and an outstanding Curriculum Vita with Planning Awards a-plenty. Hers was an amazing track record. She even has a healthy regard for good Account Management and that in itself was something of a rarity!" As it was, Fiona turned down this job offer choosing instead to join another agency, so his charm had clearly failed to impress her. Indeed it is questionable as to whether she had even noticed it! Therefore, imagine Christoph's surprise and astonishment when a year later he was passing down the corridor and saw this same woman sitting at a desk in a large corner office. He went in immediately and reintroduced himself.

Sometime after this Fiona was assigned to work on Neptune UK business where Christoph was the Group European Account Director. Their initial contact was minor and limited to European country meetings and assemblies discussing how creative briefs in individual countries could potentially affect the development of creative work more broadly across Europe. They worked really well together and both embraced the need and desire to change Meteor's brand platform from a somewhat quasi healthy female direction to a broader and more fun positioning based on the product's shape and consistency – after all confectionery was made and meant to be enjoyable! This turned out to be a battle royal both internally, especially with the senior agency management, and externally with the client at both local UK Brand Group and International Franchise level. As the Agency's European head succinctly put it, "I'm not supporting you and if this goes down badly you'll both be going down with it." But the two of them persisted and won, leading to some highly effective creative work, which only got better over time, and not only built the business in the UK but then when a new production line was required to meet the new demand for the product the brand was rolled out into Europe.

During this exciting but tense and stressful selling-in process the two of them had to go to Strasbourg for a major European meeting. Arriving late, the night before, at the Strasbourg Hilton Hotel, there was a very typical, sexist and old-fashioned inappropriate French moment. The Desk Manager noticing Fiona and Christoph checking in together then took it upon himself to ask for Christoph's key. He then changed his room to one that was adjoining Fiona's, which as it turned out even had an internal inter-connecting door. Fiona was not amused, when they both realised what had happened, and as soon as they got outside her room presented Christoph with the papers she needed him to read overnight. She then quickly entered her room slamming the door in his face and very pointedly locking it. Christoph was mildly amused at the Hotel's sexist ploy. However, they were both married to other people and at that time neither was considering any kind of romantic or physical

A life above the line – just!

liaison. When Christoph entered his room he was surprised to discover that it had clearly been set up for a European Minister, attending the forthcoming Council of Europe and the European Parliament. There were background documents, a bottle of fine Alsace wine, a beautiful book of photographs from the Black Forest & Alsace Region and a box of different coloured and flavoured vodka shots. Naturally, Christoph treated himself to these goodies taking the wine; vodka and book back to London with him.

The working relationship between Fiona and Christoph went from strength-to-strength and Chris found himself often brought in by Fiona to advise on UK thinking on the Neptune business. In late 1996 Fiona was asked by McKillans to work on the 'Reigning Cats & Dogs' business. Christoph by now having done over 5 years on the international confectionery business requested a transfer to this pet care account. This was not totally ridiculous, let alone implausible, as by then this account was being handled as an International business. Christoph's request was readily granted by McKillans management as they had been experiencing major problems with staffing on the account, having made a number of poor and ill-judged selections in replacing a well tried and tested team. Only recently they had lost a significant portion of the portfolio, including a key local brand that had been a long standing piece of business for the agency. And so it was that in January 1997 Fiona and Christoph teamed up on the account which he would continue to work on until his departure from this agency and indeed advertising generally in 2001. Fiona for her part would only do two years on the business before moving back on to UK orientated accounts. It was during those two years that their association really blossomed and grew.

Perhaps what was most surprising was that they were so sufficiently discreet that no-one knew about their relationship and few if any ever suspected it. They travelled into work separately as Christoph was a lark, while Fiona would come in later being an owl. They never lunched nor left together and they rarely dined in the Agency's locality, choosing to dine at Christoph's club, the RAC, or in restaurants situated in North London. They invariably travelled abroad together but then they seldom travelled with other team members or even other work colleagues. They attended major meetings with other agencies' representatives on the 'Reigning Cats & Dogs' business, but would just dine together, as rarely did the Senior Clients attend these dinners. This made travelling fun and they ate and drank well and slept even better. The very demanding tough times on the business were more than compensated for by the enjoyment and intrigue of their burgeoning relationship. Fiona became Christoph's great love, true companion in life and his best friend. Fiona was a stalwart, always there for him, through thick and thin and as adviser and supporter through all his personal and occupational hardships and challenges. They proved to be a buoyant, upbeat and strong team. Even when he left McKillans he had no resentment as through them he had found Fiona. They would remain together through all the difficulties life threw at them – a true and loving partnership, sharing their joint passions for the arts, travel and good company.

When it came to working with or for women this had never proven to be a concern or problem for Christoph. He treated both sexes the same feeling that one of the attractions of advertising, as an industry, was that it believed wholeheartedly in equal opportunities and even equal pay. Many women had already excelled in the business long before he had joined Gris Advertising in 1973 and Christoph recognised this as being quite right and normal. Indeed, from fairly on he had in any case to accept this, as when Louis returned to his Professorship in the States after the summer ended, he found himself reporting to a highly competent woman, Christine Walcott. Having had total freedom up until then, as Louis took only a passing interest, and gave only advice when asked for it, now it was to become very different. Christine he found to be strong minded, at times overbearing, controlling and seeking to be involved in everything he was doing, even to a point of irritation and frustration. There was a need for a 'clear the air' discussion and once their roles were properly defined they began to work constructively together and became ever more productive and effective. They were a good combination with very different skill sets.

A life above the line – just!

Christine's strengths lay in being strategically sound and had the natural skills of a disciplined, controlled planner. Christoph's strongest suits lay in being more visionary and creative, backed up by in-depth research and comprehensive background investigations. Their combining meant each could work on separate projects while also divvying up the work to play to each other's perceived strengths. This worked well and productively for both the department and the agency as a whole. When Christoph moved on they parted as the best of friends.

Christoph's first two immediate bosses in Account Management were both women. Louisa Hethersett, on an industrial piece of business, was a delight and really helpful, relaxed and composed who took great pains to get Chris fully up-to-speed. There was some urgency behind this, as she was due fairly shortly, after he came on board, to depart to give birth and take maternity leave, from which she never returned. Louisa was mature, charming, professional and astute and guided Christoph purposefully in those early days. As an Oxford graduate Louisa was bright, articulate and while slightly blue-stockinged, had no care for her appearance. She was tall, thin and pleasant to look at in a natural, unmade, confident and unconcerned way. Louisa was great company, good on detail and very precise in her guidance on the way forward and steering Christoph in the right direction.

However, on the other side of his first portfolio of accounts, things were quite different. Here, he was reporting to Marina Hadlin, a doyenne in the world of fashion and cosmetics. She was truly a 'Queen Bee' in her area of the industry and her status, image and fashionable appearance were all crucially important to her. She was wined and dined by all the leading fashion magazine editors, went to all the major fashion shows and was regularly entertained at the salons of the leading fashion houses. Truly she was something of a minor celebrity and was on the A –list of invitees. She was fascinating to look at being 'plump-ish' with unmarked pale fair complexion with striking deep red hair and daily wore pillar box red coloured lipstick. Her private life was exactly that - private. No one knew whether she had a partner or a lover of either sex. She never walked anywhere but took black cabs, on account, everywhere. She was totally dismissive of Christoph seeing him as a nuisance, an encumbrance and an 'up-start' lacking both style and finesse, who didn't even have beautiful looks. Truly in her eyes he had nothing to commend him. Her approach was simply to instruct and dictate to him on Borcella and neither guided nor explained anything. She grudgingly acknowledged his work on the Beauty Adviser advertising, but this was incidental to her as it was not the core or even really a serious part of the business – at least as far as she was concerned. Christoph respected her position, her stylish front with expensive clothing and beautiful handmade shoes, her crafted make-up and various professionally orchestrated hair styles. He even admired her aloofness, her total self-belief and assuredness and her depth of knowledge of every facet and person related to the fashion industry. There was something distinctly feline about her whole manner that entranced and intrigued him. She had been mildly amused when it was recounted to her that Christoph on going to get some art work and mechanicals approved by the head of the company had left without them being signed off. He had informed the receptionist that having waited some 20 minutes he was now leaving. When the Director was free he would happily come back, as he was only a ten minute fast walk away. This duly happened and when the Director asked Christoph why he had not waited, Christoph had replied, "Well Sir accepting that you were clearly very busy I thought I could be more use to you on your account working back at the office, rather than just sitting in reception looking at all the beautiful women walking in and out." He had smiled and said "I am clearly going to have to watch out for you as you are evidently a smart arse!" When this event had been fed back, by the senior client, to Marina she had 'bollocked' Christoph for not waiting, though then enjoyed retelling the story.

When Christoph got to New York in 1978 his first boss over there was also a woman as indeed was his operating assistant. The boss-lady, Christine Holly, was a feisty, brash, gum-chewing Brooklyn woman, who lacked any subtlety, refinement or decorum. More often than not she would sit at her desk wearing a very short skirt with her feet on the table so that Christoph facing her would not know where to look. Christine was one tough cookie and she took no prisoners believing it was the survival of the fittest in a dog eat dog world. She was, after all, the only woman at her level in the Thomas Healey group and this male chauvinistic dominated world neither liked her nor wanted to tolerate her. Inevitably, and in Christoph's view most unfairly, the Jewish mafia that controlled the group won out in this political war and she was moved onto another account at Gris Advertising. Even her mental toughness, fast mind and good results could not defeat 'these pricks'. Christoph thought this was regrettable as Christine represented to him a breath of fresh air amongst the stuffy white shirted, slick suited men that ran the account. She taught him what was expected and how to develop ideas that could make a difference and how to sell these up the line in a disciplined rational way without emotion. She was good, direct and while as hard as nails, was as honest as the day was long. Christoph knew exactly where he stood with her. He considered himself lucky to have worked with her initially as she gave him the ground rules and the base from which to grow at Gris, New York. Without her stewardship in those early days he might well have floundered.

As Christoph grew and rose through the ranks he found he reported into fewer women directly but he worked with many across the various disciplines be that planning, account management, production, media, creative and ancillary services such as financial, personnel, sales promotion, public relations or sponsorship. Christoph established good and even great working relationships with most of these working women, both domestically and internationally and many of these remained lifelong friends. Fortunately, few expressed negative comments about his occasional outlandish behaviour. Nevertheless, Christoph's non-politically correct nature, telling it as he saw it approach, would he felt have been under severe scrutiny from the earnest snow-flake feminist politically correct world of today. Certainly his touchy feely behaviour, kissing everyone, expressive directness and colourful language would all have necessitated far greater discipline, constraint and self-control. Christoph could be feisty, flirtatious, charmingly complimentary but at times outrageous, though never deliberately offensive or hurtful.

He could be sensitive, offended and even hurt as on one occasion when a woman he had hired in two separate agencies was asked what Christoph, in his capacity as Head of International on the Neptune account, as well as having been steward of the brand domestically, thought of a new campaign being proposed locally, replied, "Oh don't worry about Christoph's views – he's just an old grey beard." This loyal client fed this back to Christoph, as did other attendees at the meeting, as they had been 'gobsmacked' by her response. He said nothing to her at the time but years later he would rag her about this, especially as he admired her Northern grit. He felt fully justified, in his reaction, as when he did ultimately see the route proposed he disapproved of it. He spotted immediately that the campaign idea was too parochial and would have necessitated being shot and produced locally in every country, which was neither practical nor affordable. Worse still there was damage done with the client on this account for her proposing this idea at all. It demonstrated a lack of understanding by this individual of what was needed for the business and undermined the sense of togetherness and union within the agency. It was an error of judgement that had serious consequences long after she had left the agency, when her ambitions for promotion could not be realised. Thankfully, in time, she went on to much bigger and greater things as well as widespread recognition in the field of marketing.

Towards the end of his time in advertising it would be a woman member of McKillans International Management, Zara Benito, who would be one of the determiners of Christoph's ultimate fate. Zara was a sharp, cold, hard, battle scarred adversary. Ageless, stylish, sleek, tall, elegant and sophisticated she was meticulous about her dynamic appearance. She proved to be a challenging and attractive woman to deal with. She was also a survivor, fiercely ambitious, calculating and scheming. She came across as a quiet, bright, decent, concerned and sympathetic individual but this was largely front. Deep, down she was heartless and unemotional and often non-communicative. Christoph referred to her as the 'ice woman' - but he found that unapproachability curious and interesting. He knew what he was dealing with – fire and ice. Zara, for her part, had always liked Christoph's directness, honesty, bravado, professional presentation skills and quick retorts to clients' criticisms or comments, but she was also wary of him, especially when it came to his speed of response and quick tongue. To her he exuded no fear for himself. On one occasion she had been victim to his quick repartee. In seeking to make small talk, before a Senior Management internal review, she had innocently asked him, "Are you into Dogs or Cats, Christoph?" As quick as a flash he replied, "No, I used to be into horses, but now I am only into women." Zara laughed nervously whilst blushing, a bright shade of crimson. She, with her male senior cohort, and equally titled and positioned International President would seek his views, nine months before he left the agency, only to simply ignore them, and did not even bother to get back to him, on his suggestions and laid out plan for moving forward. He was in her mind by that time superfluous to any of her business requirements.

When it came to the client side women played a massively important role throughout Christoph's career. And almost predictably it would be a woman who would bring him down at the very end. Chris worked well with a wide assortment of women in varying capacities and levels of different organisations. Christoph employed his light hearted approach, his cheeky sense of humour, and his directness and sense of theatre to maximum effect, on client business. He was and always had been a strong presenter and persuasive salesman and had a reputation for being dramatic, surprising, histrionic and entertaining once he had the floor. He exuded confidence and never appeared to be cow-tailed. Intriguingly and unsurprisingly to Christoph many of the more formidable and ambitious careerist women that he encountered and worked with went on to have distinguished careers in marketing, politics and business generally.

Most of Christoph's female client relationships were highly productive and positive and these were quite wide ranging. Some became friends, others confidants while others remained simply professional throughout, though nearly all had their humorous moments. In rare cases the relationships even bordered on being innocently flirtatious. Christoph enjoyed all these different engagements and looked back on many of them with humour and some even with hilarity and certainly none with any regrets.

There was for example Sue Tage, a woman who became head of Public Affairs for Thomas Healey. Sue had started out as a lowly brand manager for a small toiletries and medical company, but once acquired by Thomas Healey she truly flourished. Quickly rising to become an Associate on Personal Care products in the main company she was a breath of fresh air in a fairly stuffy, conservative, and process driven organisation. Her ability to deal with people in a calm and friendly manner even to the point that when she wanted a favour she could flirt quite outrageously, but at the same time totally innocently, which served her well in her dealings with the media on crisis management issues. She was an inspired choice to be Thomas Healey's PR media representative. Christoph and Sue had worked very effectively on Personal Care together and in her new elevated position sought his advice and assistance in dealing with some of the 'hot' issues of the day. Together they tackled teenage concerns, oral hygiene education, and the changing role of women in both advertising and the workplace. Schools Programmes were developed one for oral care protection for youngsters and a second on skincare for teenagers, in the process providing much needed materials for strapped cash primary and secondary schools. They also combined to persuade the dental authorities on the validity of their branded products, enabling them to be in receipt of approval from the British Dental Authority. They created helplines for distressed and concerned teenagers, especially those combating skin disorders or early menstrual problems and for related concerns and uncertainties including a lack of confidence and low self-esteem. Christoph really enjoyed the trust that was built up between Sue and him and revelled in working on these high profile issue areas. They provided exacting communication challenges that often needed to be tackled via unpaid for media and he worked diligently to put together papers and presentations that could be made and or submitted to the authorities or the media. It was rewarding and much was achieved in a short time period in what was for both of them relatively new territory.

A life above the line – just!

When Christoph returned form the US, in 1980, in an exalted position, after his two years away, he continued to work on the Thomas Healey account. Despite a few disillusions towards the end of his time in the New York Head Office, he quickly rediscovered his confidence and leadership skills. Within a few months, of his re-joining the London Office of Gris Advertising he had been promoted to the Board – one of the youngest Board members of a major agency in London at the time (though he was slightly miffed with himself that he had just turned 30 when if it had happened one month earlier he could have been claimed to have achieved this milestone while still in his twenties!). He very quickly reshaped his group, brought in exciting new talent and instilled in them a spirit of 'can do' and 'will win'. His popular motivating demand was "We want more, better, faster!" One of his other famous quotes played back to him many times subsequently was when referring to the company brand personnel he called them 'the turkeys' and even to their faces the rallying cry would be "Hey come on guys you bunch of turkeys – gobble, gobble, gobble". While to his own troops to make them feel confident dealing with a demanding and challenging client he would state 'Don't let the turkeys get you down!' During this time Chris was really tough, uncompromising, and required much, not just of himself, and his team but most especially of the clients. Diane Oakland was a Brand Manager at the time of his return and worked very closely with Christoph on the launch of a new product variant. She found his ideas for leaflet drops, sampling through magazines, outrageous PR exercises exciting, innovative, challenging, but also exhausting. After all who else would think of sampling powered detergents through women's magazines or washing an elephant in London Zoo in the same detergent to emphasise the brand's points of difference?

After six months, from the time of Chris's return from America, the Gris Advertising UK Management asked the client, who had been previously highly critical of the agency and their lack of contribution to the business, for an appraisal on how the new team was performing. They wanted to know whether there had been a change in the Agency's response to the Client's needs over this time period. The report from Thomas Healey came back very favourably, especially for being forward thinking, innovative, committed, with real involvement and leadership being demonstrated. Nevertheless, the report expressed the view that specifically Christoph was being too hard and tough on their Brand Management teams. Christoph was called into the office of Jeremy Clyde, the UK Gris Managing Director and Chief Executive to go through this appraisal. He was very complimentary and appreciative and believed there had been a noticeable, even a phenomenal step change in performance and output. However, he finished by saying, "Christoph there was just one small observation stroke complaint – 'you're being too hard on the brand teams' ". Christoph smiled stood up and shook his boss by the hand and replied, "Thank you Jeremy that is the greatest compliment I think I have ever been paid." And with that he walked out leaving Jeremy Clyde completely 'non-plussed' speechless and unable to react. Diane and Christoph worked well together and when she left she went on to become a Top 100 Marketer, helping to build brands and fortunes for a number of businesses, including even at one time indirectly for the Crown!

On Neptune, Chris encountered many capable, strong and extremely competent as well as successful female clients. One, in particular, that Chris worked very effectively with was Jane Boulder; together they launched a nutritious brand in the then emerging popular cereal bar market. Apart from creating a highly successful press campaign they produced an educational dietary programme for broadcast media at next to no cost. They then teamed up again on a major brand that had languished without sufficient news, support or drama built around it. Together they created a new campaign that was youthful, more physical, and more pertinent to the day's extreme sports thereby making it more appealing and attractive to younger people concerned with their fitness. Apart from the new advertising campaign which produced positive gains for the brand for the first time for many years, they produced a TV Broadcast programme concept and a whole sports sponsorship agenda. This expansion into sponsorship was new and they took this through various sports events with billboards at major international football championship venues, ambush marketing at the Olympics, and support for individual athletes and sports personnel. Over time

A life above the line – just!

this support incorporated minor sports where there was limited or in some cases no funding, athletic regional events and even Schools Sports Fitness and equipment programmes – though this last aspect had to be curtailed because it caused consternation and opposition in the press - Confectionery and health not being seen to be compatible. What was exciting was that there was always a battle of wills going on between Jane and Christoph. Both dogged and determined with strong opinions, this made them challenging and adversarial opponents. Fortunately, more often than not, they would find a point of agreement, except when it came to advertising, where they disputed and disagreed over the creative work, the body copy and the interpretation and even the findings after the advertising executions had run. For all their differences they achieved much together and this enabled them to retain a strong bond and friendship long after both had left their respective posts. Indeed, many years later Christoph breakfasted with Jane at a modern styled restaurant in The Aldwych, in London. By that time Jane had become a much respected marketer in the retail world, as well as developing a keen interest and reputation in the educational sector. She stated to him then, in all seriousness, "Christoph, I am so pleased that you are no longer in advertising as we don't have the time to debate with our agencies; we just want them to do what we tell them to do." Christoph was amused, smiled and shrugged his shoulders and then somewhat ironically replied, "Well they have always said that clients get the advertising they deserve!" Deep down though Christoph had this sinking feeling that agencies had sold out and were no longer challenging the briefs, or getting on the front foot by developing and testing new different and alternative positioning's, concepts, ideas and even executions. If this now was truly the way of the world Christoph wondered what 'added value' agencies were providing clients with and would they even be needed in the future, as presumably it could all be brought in-house.

But disappointingly not all Christoph's clients or counterparts were as open and transparent as Jane Boulder. Some could be duplicitous, dishonest, manipulative, destructive, political, self-serving and highly dangerous. These traits Christoph observed were often those of people insecure, worried for their job or simply concerned with self –preservation. Christoph was not a toady and so cow tailing to these insecurities was never going to be part of his make-up. He was never going to be obsequious or turn a blind eye if he thought their approach was fundamentally flawed and could be detrimental to the brand or the company's reputation. He saw himself as being there to help build brands, through a depth of understanding of the brand's properties and its future potential as well as fully comprehending the brand's current and potential consumer base.

'Reigning Cats & Dogs' brought in an Australian heavyweight, Fran Shilling, from outside the company, via the use of her agent, at that time a somewhat unique situation. The company management, before hiring her, had enquired from their agencies whether any of them had had previous working experience with Fran and what her reputation was. As it happened all three agencies had personnel that had worked directly with Fran before and these provided reports that did not make particularly favourable reading. The primary concern that seemed to be fed back consistently was that Fran Shilling was something of a 'star fucker' and social climber easily impressed by celebrities and A-Listers. A taste for this had apparently come from her previous work experience in the fashion industry. Christoph learnt that Fran preferred to work ideally with other women, but otherwise liked stylish, young, good looking men working on her business. Christoph realised that he was clearly not going to fit this bill, as by then he was late 40s and the word style was not one that sprang readily to mind when considering his appearance, nor indeed would he even score highly on the definition or requirement of being 'good looking'. When the reports were considered by the client, who was largely inexperienced in hiring from outside their organisation, they chose to ignore the agencies findings. Previously they had a history of developing their staff internally through training and experience, in all of their disciplines. On this occasion the company even suggested that these three agencies were running scared of the prospect of dealing with such a 'strong minded, successful and characterful' woman. Fran Shilling was subsequently hired and took over from, coincidentally, another Australian, whom had decided to take retirement so that he could return home to Sydney. Christoph had enjoyed a highly productive working relationship with this predecessor so he was particularly sorry to see him go.

Christoph was asked to present McKillans' credentials and the case histories, on the business, as well as taking Fran through the current projects and advertising on each of the brands she would be overseeing. The meeting appeared to go well and Fran Shilling seemed genuinely impressed by the level and quality of the work in market and the results behind it, while acknowledging that the test copy in place and plans for the future on each brand were forward thinking and adventurous. Against this, however, was McKillans current standing with the Management of 'Reigning Cats & Dogs.' Ever since they had lost a core heavily supported brand, in 1998, they had been on the back foot as an Agency. While they had clawed their way back with the brands Christoph was handling the agency no longer had the lion's share of the business and as such were still vulnerable, in early 1999, when Fran took over the reins. Indeed, it had been Christoph's desire to work with Fiona Sole that had led him to volunteer to work on this account exactly a year before. While they had striven to save the business it had always been a hard ask and in the end though he had given everything the politics and history were insurmountable and too much damage had been done in the recent past relationship. Unsurprisingly the remainder part of this core brand in Europe had gone. In its place, however, as recognition of the late efforts made, the Agency had been given three minor brands, by way of compensation. Internally, at the agency, many of his senior colleagues had become disillusioned with this client and had moved onto other business. The Senior Management had even decimated Christoph's group to save staff costs and overheads, leaving him with a skeleton staff, which while enthusiastic and committed were fighting with limited bullets and little support. Christoph felt that the agency management had lost heart and belief in this client and became much more interested in milking it rather than managing or seeking to rebuild trust, faith and most importantly business.

Fran's agenda quickly became clear; she wanted to make her name through famous advertising and turn the brands, where she could, into luxuries. Christoph was her greatest opponent, in Europe at least, as he opposed this view and resisted her plans completely. She pushed on regardless with her strategy producing a range of luxury premium accessories for pets, amorphous foods and recipes and even a range of chocolate treats for cats and dogs (dogs by and large don't eat chocolate!). Fran, with limited if any knowledge of the business, then announced that she believed that cat owners and small dog owners were one and the same. This premise she based solely on the similar physical size of both animals. She approached Christoph's Management and instructed them to write a paper in support of this view. Christoph was to be the author, but despite a strong instruction to do so, he absolutely refused and instead wrote a paper that gave a very detailed and full analysis of the differences between the two species of animals. He produced comprehensive research on the very different relationships that cat owners and dog owners have with their pets, as well as pointing out the very distinct differences in behaviour and character between small dogs and cats. He even went on to tackle their very different attitudes to food and eating. This paper was later to be hailed as a triumph in comprehensive understanding of these pet types but at the time was ignored and disregarded, while Fran simply saw the Agency as being obstructive and belligerent. Instead she demanded that creative work be done that showed cats and dogs in the same execution. Chris refused point blank to do this. This particular brief was therefore given to another agency and the executions were then shot in Paris, by a high profile celebrity stills photographer – giving new meaning to the notion that 'cat walk' models sometimes feel that they are treated as 'just a piece of meat'!

By this time Fran Shilling had decided that Christoph represented a global threat to her ambitions as he clearly knew a great deal about the pet care categories, and certainly considerably more than her scant knowledge, which was being gained on the hoof! Worse still from her perspective Christoph was not afraid to demonstrate this. That made him dangerous. Simply put Christoph had to go. However, this

A life above the line – just!

could not be achieved immediately as his reputation worldwide both within McKillans and at 'Reigning Cats & Dogs' was well established and his results spoke volumes. Both would be most reluctant to see him removed. McKillans acquiesced to her demand that Christoph be removed off any brands associated with her small dog/cat project and agreed to an all-female team being appointed, sympathetic to the emotional associations deemed to be required. Christoph was relieved and philosophical about this even offering the new team advice and assistance both which were firmly resisted and rejected. He had no doubt, as his paper had borne out, that this whole project was flawed, the thinking fundamentally wrong and the strategy and executions that would transpire from this would unquestionably fail in the marketplace. His major concern was that McKillans could become 'the fall-guy' in this, for even contemplating going along with this, once it became public knowledge. Christoph was barred, by his own management, from approaching any senior members of the 'Reigning Cats & Dogs' board and was forbidden to submit his paper to them. Christoph was not seeking to do this for political gain but to avoid unnecessary costs and expenditure. Somewhat surprisingly the European Management at the client end were prepared to let Fran Shilling have her head, even if deep down, Christoph suspected they must have had their own reservations.

The second strand to Fran Shillings master plan to oust Christoph was totally Machiavellian and even compromised her own people. When McKillans year-end agency assessment came up for the Year 2000 the report was manipulated to give a negative impression of McKillans contribution and performance on their business. This report was fabricated and was a tissue of lies, inaccuracies and bore no relationship to what had been accomplished or attained on this client's brands. Christoph would have been accepting of it had it been simply a personal criticism of him by Fran Shilling. But to be written about his industrious team members who had achieved business building results and also high tracking scores for and from the advertising developed was absolutely unacceptable. One Senior Brand Manager had refused to be complicit in this and had refused to take any part in this conniving masquerade, that criticised people he had had a very positive and fruitful relationship with and in particular Christoph. So much so he had contacted Christoph, given him the heads up and told him he had refused to sign off on the paper even though he was obliged to do so. Christoph, as the client's senior agency representative on the business was also expected to sign off on the report but also withheld his signature. Instead, he contacted all the signatories by e-mail confirming what had actually been achieved on each of their brands over the previous year, 2000. Finally, the main author of the assessment and who had signed the Appraisal called Christoph totally ashamed and embarrassed. Christoph confirmed to her that he would not be signing the assessment as it was blatantly wrong, a travesty of justice, and he expressed a huge disappointment in her ever agreeing to produce it. The composer broke down realising that Christoph had produced his own version of the previous year's track record, apologised to him most profusely and confirmed, what he had already suspected, that she had been instructed on what to write, by her boss, Fran Shilling. She decided that the only fair thing she could do now was to withdraw the assessment and it would not be submitted to either Company or Agency Global Managements - and nor indeed was it. Christoph welcomed this outcome and graciously accepted her apology. He was however, rueful that this situation had occurred at all, even if it had backfired. It left a distinctly bitter taste in his mouth. It also showed that Fran Shilling would stop at nothing and stoop as low as it took to achieve her goals.

The final part of the Fran Shilling strategy was to go to the Worldwide Management of McKillans and request the removal of the two senior members of Chris's team. This his gutless management agreed to and by the late Spring of 2001 they had gone. Christoph too by this time had had enough. He never disliked or resented Fran, as he saw her for what she was. In some ways he admired her bright lively mind with its plethora of ideas, some of which he was sure had merit. He respected her, as a highly effective feminist, promoting the rights of women in the workplace. He didn't even mind her transparent and overt ambition and desire to attain public recognition at all costs. What he didn't like or respect were her tactics or her judgement and the way she sought to force her ideas through and dispel anyone who knew more about the business than her, instead of harnessing their know-how and knowledge. Nine months after Christoph had left McKillans the luxury small dog and cat project, came to a shuddering halt, was scrapped having been judged and proven to have been an abject failure. With a wasted cost of some £20million on this activity Fran Shilling was immediately shown the door, by her US management. Years later she would reappear in her homeland, of Australia, as a spokesperson on the music and fashion industries, with a high media profile in broadcasting, supporting feminism and women in the workplace; probably having found her right vocation and place in society.

Christoph had learnt never to underestimate the power of a woman – but then, to be fair to him, he never really had!

CHAPTER 4

'Go West Young Man – To The Land Of Opportunity' (attributed to Horace Greeley (1811-1872) Founder and Editor of the New York Tribune, in an address to the young, at the end of The American Civil War (1861-1865), encouraging westward expansion in the United States).

Christoph had never been much of a traveller; certainly not beyond the 57 race courses in the British Isles. He had not even shown much interest in 'seeing the world'. His views had perhaps been slightly soured by the boat trips he had had to endure between Dover and Ostend, as a boy, to visit his Belgian cousins annually, in their beachside summer place, at Le Zoute. His lack of sea legs meant Christoph spent most of the journey retching over the side of the ferry or curled up close to the luggage hold, on the ship's deck, where at least fresh air was

A life above the line – just!

aplenty. In fact, until the age of 18, Christoph had only ever travelled abroad to Belgium.

On leaving school and in defiance to his recently separated parents he embarked on a hitch-hiking tour of Europe. Dressed in baggy thick cords and brightly coloured kaftans, adorned with beads and long hair, kept back off his face with a bandana, he closely resembled the hippies of Woodstock. Behind this excursion was a deep desire to learn more about the Italian Renaissance that had been a part of his history studies at A-Level. After hitching with a school colleague they had got as far as Milan together when his travelling companion announced his passion for the landlady's daughter in Turin meant he had an unquenchable desire to return to her. And so Christoph progressed on alone, narrowly avoiding becoming a sexual victim to two unsavoury characters, who sought to assault him, whilst on the road from Ferrara to Bologna. His expedition covered Turin, Milan, Verona, Padua, and Sienna and then concentrated on Florence and finally Rome. He wrote up his artistic observations in a book as he went along and it was a record of the wonderful art he saw as well as his amazement at the plethora of pictures, monuments, churches that he viewed and visited. He shamefully never did anything with this work but kept it as a memento of a different, somewhat naïve time in his life. For survival he did odd jobs, such as unloading water melons off trucks and setting up stalls, taking food as compensation. He slept mainly outside under the open sky, on park benches or in the case of Rome on the marble slabs outside the disused and abandoned Gymnasium built for the Olympic Games of 1960. Almost marrying, in a drug induced state, a beautiful German girl travelling around Europe, Christoph realised it was time to move on, pull himself together and get a real life. He took an overnight train to Paris and then found a flight to the Channel Islands and then a local Aurigny flight to Alderney where his father had moved to, with his female partner after leaving his family, his job and his life in London, after a serious accident. These under such duress were Christoph's first air travel experiences.

For the next 7 years his travel would be limited to the occasional Aurigny flights between the mainland and Alderney when he would go and visit his father and newly acquired step-mother. These small twin propeller planes, holding either 12 or 20 people, would fly fairly low and the pilots would encourage the passengers to look for and witness tankers cleaning out their tanks in the English Channel. There were financial rewards, for reporting this polluting and illegal behaviour, from the fines imposed by the maritime authorities.

It was only when Christoph started to work as an Account Man that the prospect of flying and travelling the world appeared to be a realistic possibility, as much of Gris Advertising's business involved International Accounts. But even early on in this time in his new role he had no particular enthusiasm for travelling far and wide. However, all this was soon to change. Once he was assigned to Thomas Healey he found himself frequently flying, on Dan Air (known affectionately as Dan Dare) or BA (British Airways an amalgamation of BEA, British European Airways, and BOAC British Overseas Airways Corporation) to the North of England, be that Teeside, Manchester, or Newcastle from either Gatwick or Heathrow. In those days Newcastle, for example, was little more than a log cabin at the end of the runway. A far cry from the burgeoning International Airport it gradually became.

His first business flying experience came when he was asked by, John E. Goldman, 'the nervy one' (so nick-named because he was so thin that he could actually wrap his arms around his body and they would virtually meet to shake hands with himself, which he tended to do when he was feeling pressurised), to accompany him to meet the senior clients and visit their offices for the first time. Chris, not unnaturally, was quite excited as he felt he was being treated as a responsible grown up. Things however, did not go quite according to plan. When they got onto the plane Christoph asked the stewardess where he should put the large art-bag that he was carrying. She suggested that the best place to put it would be at the back of the plane, behind the final row of seats, as despite its size it was relatively thin and light. This he did and then came back to his seat, situated quite far forward towards the cockpit. Immediately he sat down John enquired in a somewhat concerned voice, "Where is the art-bag, Christoph?" Chris looked at John and reassuringly informed him that it was safely tucked away at the back of the plane. John then remonstrated, "Don't you realise what a security risk that is?" and then continued, "There is the equivalent of over £3million worth of advertising there." Christoph, frankly, was a little bemused by this reaction and in an endeavour to calm his boss he responded by stating, "But John, firstly only you and I know what is in the art bag, secondly I haven't seen anyone on this plane that looks sufficiently interested in it or looks that desperate to want to take our art-bag, especially as given its size it is quite hard to conceal. Thirdly, short of jumping out of the plane with a parachute we have a reasonable chance of seeing anyone leaving with it." John considered this for a moment and then remarked, "Yes, but if, on landing the stewardesses open the doors at the back then someone could get off the plane with our art-bag before we would even know about it." Christoph had no answer to this but just closed his eyes, partly contemplating that this could be as very long flight, never mind day, and also slightly relieved, given the cramped nature of the area in front of his knees, that said art-bag was not squeezed up against them, even if they had been allowed to keep it with them, which seemed extremely unlikely. With these thoughts in mind he then fell asleep, even before the plane had taken off. Christoph was only woken by the bump of the aircraft landing and John jumping up and making to head down the aisle. In this endeavour he was stopped promptly by a stern, hostile looking stewardess, who literally put John firmly in his place, "Will you please sit back down immediately, Sir and remain seated with your seatbelt on, until the plane has come to a complete halt and the fasten seatbelt signs have been switched off." A somewhat red-faced and shamed John retook his seat. By the time John was able to get up again and repeat his manoeuvre to secure the art-bag at the back, he found himself fighting the oncoming tide of a flow of people coming in the opposite direction to get off the plane at the front. Christoph calmly remained in his middle seat, now with no one on either side, and waited for John's return. Imagine his surprise when he suddenly heard shouts of 'Oh, ah, ouch' followed by the expletives 'fuck, bugger, blast'. Christoph immediately recognised those rather less than dulcet tones to be those of John's voice. Speedily, Christoph made his way to the back of the plane where he was confronted by a remarkable scene. Two stewardesses were trying to control themselves from bursting out in laughter. John was dancing about like a stung bear or a maddened dervish as he was assaulted by thick foam coming from a red cylindrical object, pointing up at him from ground level. Christoph immediately perceived that what had happened was that John in seeking to pull out the art-bag from behind the seats had got himself stuck between the aisle and the back of the plane. In his haste he had accidentally set off the fire extinguisher and being unable to move had taken the full force of its emission in a significantly sensitive part of his anatomy. As such was it not only coming at him at a considerable force, being under pressure, but on arrival was forming a sizeable area of white foam. This had, by now, spread from John's knees to just above his belt line. Without actually laughing out loud it was impossible to remove the smile from Christoph's face as he sought to extricate John from his delicate predicament. Once achieved and off the aeroplane Christoph asked John what he would like to do – next. Ever resilient John, realising that there was insufficient time before the scheduled meeting to go into town and get a fresh attire, applied his Boy Scout's mantra 'Be prepared' . Opening his somewhat dilapidated, unsightly, black fibre glass brief case he extracted a carefully folded but well-worn thin grey/navy raincoat. With a flourish of triumph he donned it and sallied forth heading for the taxi rank queue.

However, John's pride was about to be pricked once more. When they arrived at Thomas Healey's offices they were shown into the meeting room and waited for the clients to gather, John sat in his raincoat displaying no evidence of his earlier adventurous mishap. The Senior Advertising Manager entered the room and as Christoph and John both stood up he looked somewhat surprisingly at John and queried, "Not planning on staying long then John?" John was totally flummoxed and became somewhat flustered and never really recovered his composure. By the end of the meeting behind his chair was a small pile of broken pencils which John had nervously intermittently snapped throughout this forum. Christoph sought to make the best of this his introductory meeting and under the circumstances presented the new advertising reasonably well, more especially given his nervousness at this first encounter with these senior 'bods'. It truly had been a memorable 'flying visit' for him.

Even before Christoph ended up working in New York he would make two earlier trips to the 'Big Apple'. The first was when he was asked to accompany Gris's International New Business Director and deliver a case history on Protac Industrial, a client of his in the UK. This was to be made to a worldwide White Goods (washers, dishwashers, driers etc.) manufacturer. Even before they left Christoph had, not unreasonably, questioned the relevance of a presentation of an industrial company's advertising case history to a fridge and washing machine manufacturer. And so it proved to be, as despite running through his case history, to demonstrate that the agency was more than just a packaged goods operator, his was the first part of the presentation to be axed. As the Head of International, Adair, rightly and fairly pointed out "Never mind Christoph, if nothing else it has given you exposure to the Senior Agency Personnel at Head Office. They now know who you are and likewise you can now put a face to their names." Little did he, or Christoph, realise how true and apposite that was, as less than a year later he would be working there, in NYC, full-time. The other excitement and indeed benefit of this trip was that in order to save time they had flown on Concorde, which even then had only been in service for just over a year (the first commercial flight had been in 1976, only 20 of these beautiful but noisy planes were built and they ceased operations some twenty seven years later but still remains the only supersonic commercial airliner). Concorde travelled at Mach 2, faster than the speed of sound and one could hear the sonic boom, as it reached this speed. It landed at John F Kennedy Airport at a time earlier than when it had taken off from Heathrow. Christoph would be fortunate enough to fly on Concorde a number of times and he always thought that it's almost pencil line gave it an eyecatching aerodynamic shape and design. But with its very low cabin height it truly felt a little like travelling by luxury bus or coach, with the seating in pairs on either side of a narrow aisle.

The second occasion Christoph went to New York was equally

unexpected and definitely unplanned and was certainly no less eventful. One Friday summer afternoon in 1977, shortly after lunch, Christoph received a phone call from the Communications Manager, from Protac Industrial asking if he could pop down to their offices in Victoria, bringing with him any stock shots of applications of their products in the USA. Sensing the urgency Christoph took his pad and examples of possible art work and by the end of the afternoon working diligently, in the client's meeting room, to an impromptu brief he had designed a layout, a headline and suitable body copy for a possible advertisement. This was approved there and then not only in London but also over the phone in the United States. There was only one tiny little problem and that was that the client ideally wanted the ad to run in the Wall Street Journal and New York Times, to coincide with a major trade announcement on the very next Monday. Bearing in mind that this was long before the technological age of computers and Smart phones it really seemed impossible to achieve. At a party he attended that same night Christoph was mulling over this problem and finally resolved to do something about it himself. The next morning he borrowed £400 from his mother. He then rang the American Embassy and asked for the Visa Department. He was informed that this particular Department was not open at weekends. Undeterred Christoph, appreciating that the Chairman of Protac Industrial coincidentally had the same surname as himself, Aitkin, decided to take a flyer. As bold as brass he informed the US Embassy representative that his father was Lord Aitkin and that this was an industrial matter of major international significance for both countries. Sufficiently persuaded he gave Christoph a time when he could come down and be issued with a temporary Visa (imagine trying that in this day and age!). This was duly provided and stamped into Christoph's passport. He then made his way to Heathrow and sought out an airline that would get him to New York that same day. Air India had a flight at 4pm and there were seats available. All he had with him was a small bag and the artwork and mechanical for the advertisement, in a smallish studio sized art-bag, which he was able to keep with him on the plane. While he waited to board the flight he exchanged some sterling into US dollars.

A life above the line – just!

By the time he got to JFK it was already early evening. Emerging from the airport, after a lengthy wait in the queue for 'Aliens' (read 'Non-Americans'!), he got into the back of a large black and predominantly yellow chequered cab, with a grill between the driver and the passenger seats. There was just a small slot in this grill for payment. Much to Christoph's amusement there was a large printed sticker, with black lettering on a yellow background, which simply stated 'This cab is driven on Gas, Grass and Arse'. Christoph smiled appreciatively at the humour as he truly knew he had arrived in NY City (or as they popularly state 'A city so great they named it twice' – having formerly been founded by the Dutch who had called the port and place New Amsterdam!).

The chequered cab drove Christoph to the offices of The New York Times - conveniently and appropriately located in Times Square - which of course is how this sector of midtown had 'gotten' its name. Walking into the building with total self-belief Christoph requested to see the Print Manager. When he arrived Christoph asked him if he had had the telex booking space for Monday's edition, which, not surprisingly, he hadn't as it had never been sent. However, Christoph was able to secure a booking with a reasonably impactful space size, as there was space available, with the cost of this being invoiced back to him in London. Christoph then set about preparing and setting the ad. The Print Manager was happy to oblige and told Christoph that if he came back in 3 hours' time it would be done so that he could approve the setting, proof read the ad and agree the whole layout with headline and body copy after which a final block pull could be run off for him. In the interim he suggested that Christoph got a room at The Algonquin Hotel, just down the road on West 44th Street (this hotel and its close neighbour, The Iroquois, are both named after North American Red Indians/Native American tribes. They are also the oldest hotels in Manhattan). The Algonquin as Christoph soon discovered had a characterful small bar in moody dark wood with green velvet seating while beyond this sat the legendary Round Table (not that of King Arthur fame) where famous writers sat lunching in the 1920s. This was attended by the Rothschild related Dorothy Parker and 'The Literary Circle' (often referred to as 'The Vicious Circle' because of their acerbic wit and biting commentaries and observations). It was here that Harold Ross decided to start The New Yorker and for which Dorothy Parker wrote along with her regular contributions to Vanity Fair. The plush red velvet seating and the by then slightly dated setting with its sense of the presence of by-gone literary cognoscenti fired Christoph's imagination from the moment he entered the fairly modest and unassuming portals of this hotel. Even a failed copywriter like Christoph could not be anything other than impressed. He booked his room and then retired to the bar, chatting happily to the amenable barman, to while away the hours.

Returning to the New York Times offices, some three hours later, he made just a few very minor alterations and corrections and was then able to approve the proof of the final advertisement in the proud knowledge that it was now ready to run in the Monday edition. Taking the proof with him he then headed downtown to the offices of The Wall Street Journal and repeated the process though with the proof the time involved was greatly curtailed. He finally was able to return to The Algonquin Hotel totally exhausted but relieved and got some sleep in the knowledge that he had done all that was humanly possible to achieve the goal. He never for one moment considered that this would not be attainable, or that he could have fallen flat on his face, an abject failure.

On the Monday morning, after a restful Sunday spent wandering around Manhattan and New York's Central Park, Christoph picked up copies of both newspapers and was delighted to see both had carried the advertisement. He then rang the US office of Protac Industrial and agreed to meet with their Head of PR. This man was so impressed that he bought Christoph lunch in Smith & Wollensky's, on 3rd Avenue, to celebrate the achievement. After lunch, as the restaurant was situated close to Gris Advertising's Head Office, he decided to pop in and meet with the International Group. Christoph was given a tour of the offices. After they had heard the story behind his 'flying visit', which they were truly amazed by, they booked him business class on a red eye flight back to London that evening and even paid for him to be

A life above the line – just!

chauffeur driven to the airport. They seemed astounded by Christoph's initiative and even more so for pulling it off, with such cheek and bravado. On Tuesday morning Christoph went straight to the Protac Industrial Offices in Victoria and slammed the papers down on the desk of the PR Manager, stating cheekily "Job done". Not surprisingly the client was both astonished and delighted; never in his wildest dreams believing that this would have been possible. It cemented their relationship and their friendship was enhanced by the commitment shown to the business!

Therefore when Christoph was sent to New York 'for training and disciplining' he was to some degree already prepared what to expect. He arrived in September 1978 for what was meant to be just a three month stint. However, this became extended and subsequently lasted for over eighteen months. It only ended when Christoph himself sought to return back to London. Christoph seemed well suited to New York and vice versa. The city of Manhattan was undergoing change but it was still a tough, uncompromising and even dangerous place. This was most especially at night, or when travelling the subway or if one was caught up in the wrong place such as the Meatpacker area – Tribeca, or the Lower East Side or above Columbus Avenue heading towards Harlem. These were places, at that time, where a 'white honky' was well advised to avoid. But to Christoph New York was simply mesmerising. It was a city that for Christoph truly possessed a pulse that throbbed with excitement and intrigue. It truly was a city that never slept! Mind you Christoph had a couple of near misses and one or two tense moments. On one occasion he was caught in a cross-fire between police and a 'hoodlum', across the tracks at Grand Central Station. He had to hit the deck very fast as the police told everyone to get down. As bullets flied around Chris was more worried about being hit by a ricochet, than a direct bullet, but in the end everyone was safe the police made an arrest, as the gunman with no place to go gave himself up. On another occasion Christoph was heading down a side street on the Lower East Side, making his way to the University Hospital, when he caught the glint of something in the shadows. He promptly moved to the centre of the road but became aware that he was being followed by a guy in a hoodie brandishing a knife. Realising that this was not the kind of impromptu incision he was seeking Christoph took flight. Fortunately, despite suffering from a stomach blockage he was able to outrun his would be assailant and get to the hospital in one piece – alarmed certainly, in pain definitely, but at least reassuringly alive. That hospital experience was bizarre too as he was offered a menu of options and various procedures that could be carried out each with a cost figure shown alongside. Christoph chose the low cost item of a simple exploratory procedure and after that the discharge pills, which he had to pay for immediately before being allowed to travel back to mid-town by cab. Fortunately a few days later he was better and the problem had relieved itself and he was not ill again during his time in NYC. He was also able to look back on his night time escapade with good humour and relief.

The true New York spirit came to the fore when travelling with his old Head of Research boss from London, Pedro Vasca and his wife, Lois, on the subway. They were old hands as Pedro and Lois were both originally from New Jersey, but were over visiting friends and family, whilst on summer vacation. The subway was hot and stuffy and the carriage they were in was over-filled with people seeking to make their way home after a long day's work in the extreme heat and humidity. Suddenly Lois fainted and Christoph and Pedro tried to prop her up while giving her water. A tall well-built muscular Afro-American, who had been watching this scene unfold most attentively, came to the rescue and literally hoisted a guy out of his seat telling him "Man; you're now standing." With that he ushered Lois to the seat and she now had space and water a combination that slowly revived her colour and disposition. Pedro and Christoph looked at each other both thinking that when this knight in shining singlet got off they were all done for, more particularly as the previous occupant of the seat looked none too happy about his situation. However, as though reading their minds, the saviour of the moment, had clearly anticipated the potential problem, as he leaned over, and smilingly said, "Don't worry guys I ain't getting off until long after your stop wherever that may be". He was true to his word and all three of them thanked him profusely for his trouble and invaluable assistance when they finally reached their destination. He even refused to accept any payment for his kindness despite persistent attempts by Christoph to recompense him for his valiant service.

The whole New York experience proved to be tough and challenging but in a positive way for Christoph. He found himself with no personal, financial or family responsibilities and was being paid well, with free accommodation. Mind you when Christoph moved into his first flat in Murray Hill on East 38th and Lexington he discovered there were already a number of prior occupants. Hundreds of inch long brown cockroaches with twitching antennae had been attracted by the French Cuisine of the previous tenant, who being a Parisian had a love for cooking. Stamping them out was not an option as they appeared from every nook and cranny, crevice, work surface and floorboard. It took a pest control exterminator to deal with the problem and after that Christoph used gallons of Raid to keep these unwanted guests at bay. It was a gloomy flat, with windows only overlooking the well at the back, which Christoph found deeply oppressive. Accordingly, Christoph was eventually able to persuade the 'powers that be' that while the flat was modern and fully equipped it offered no natural light and was very dark and depressing. Chris was moved, as a result, down to Gramercy Park on East 19th Street, where there was a flat with a short lease but which was currently unoccupied. Close to Washington Square and popular areas such as the lofts of Soho, characterful Little Italy and Chinatown and the low lying buildings that made up Greenwich Village and the centre of the University life down there, Washington Square. This was a much more relaxed setting and had a young positive vibe and feel about the place, in direct contrast to the hustle and bustle of mid-town. For now Christoph was in a trendy relaxed Bohemian artistic environment where the smell of 'weed' (hashish) pervaded the streets and made him smile, as it took him back to his time as a hippy in Italy, less than a decade before.

Unfortunately, as this was only a short let, once it was known that Christoph was going to have his stay extended, by Gris Advertising

HQ, he was moved to a flat owned by another colleague, now based in Europe, on the Upper East Side – situated on East 81st between Lexington and Park Avenue. This was a great area for the traditional American long bars as well as for art with the Guggenheim, Frick, and Metropolitan Museums, all within walking distance of his 'digs'. However, Chris was living illegally there as he was effectively a sub-tenant and once found out he was inevitably going to be moved on. This did eventually happen and then he had to leave. He spent his final few weeks at The United Nations Plaza almost opposite the UN Building itself and, of course, close to the East River. This was a very modern purpose built flat with all the mod-coms and stunning views on all sides but it had none of the character of the old brownstone building on East 81st. Christoph had loved the fact that this ground floor flat had had a double bed high enough in the air to allow for a work station and cupboards and closets underneath. Though this was comfortable Christoph felt slightly claustrophobic with his nose virtually touching the ceiling. Accordingly he chose to spend most nights on a large green velvet sofa in the living room. Certainly by the time Christoph left New York in the late Spring of 1980 he felt he had got a fair idea of the various areas of Manhattan through his numerous residences.

But these residences were really only places to lay his head down as the days were long and exacting and he spent very little time in them. Gris Advertising, 'the sweat shop' was hugely demanding and a tough environment to work in. The hours were excessive and he was usually there before 8am and seldom left before 8pm, at the end of the day, plus at least one day of every weekend would be consumed by work. Worse than the hours was the somewhat stultified work style, which without regular banter, made Christoph at times feel like he was working for an Accountancy firm, or Management Consultancy, rather than for an exciting creative Ad Agency. Any interaction with the creatives and their output was all too rare. Christoph had quickly comprehended that Thomas Healey was the premier account at Gris Advertising and he also had seen that people could be deemed to have failed on this account and survive in the agency, where as to fail elsewhere in the agency was almost certain dismissal. It was a highly stressful account and he was not surprised by the daily ritual, at circa 11am, when doors of the management on the account would close for their regular snort of cocaine. This seemed to be the only way they could get through all the pressures and tensions of working on this highly charged account. For Christoph this was not a major concern as he was not accountable in that way but he was even as a relative junior expected to deliver at an extraordinary rate and to perform at a consistently high level. What Christoph gained, in his time in the US, was an exceptional and highly professional and thorough training. He saw how many of the beneficiaries of this in-depth training, around him, went on to achieve great things in the communications and marketing industries, having departed Gris Advertising to find their fame and glory.

One such character was Dan Felton, a tall thin man impeccably dressed, always in white shirt, made to measure dark pinstripe suits and high quality leather lace up shoes, who sported a receding line of dark black curly hair and wore light tortoise shell horn rimmed spectacles. Dan was a stickler for detail and Christoph learnt that this extended even to the recording of meetings and conversations in the Contact Report. The draft that Christoph would submit would be scrutinised, corrected, and in some cases even had to be rewritten to be precise, accurate and convey exactly the right emphasis. Christoph learnt that Dan and many others around him saw the Contact Report as not just a record but also a selling tool. From Dan he learned that the power of a good and effective presentation lay in the preparation. It was about how to argue the case and how to anticipate ahead of the meeting the likely comments, issues and questions that might be raised by the client(s). These he was encouraged to cover off in the preamble, set-up or strategic piece prior to submission of the work. It was not surprising to Christoph when Dan left to set up a highly successful Marketing Consultancy with an outside partner.

Another character who had a major influence on Christoph during his time in New York was a second generation Irish American, Edward O'Brian, who was a true New Yorker through and through. As he put it succinctly to Christoph, "When you're out of Manhattan you're out of America!" Edward O'Brian was also the quintessential business advertising Account Director, who believed somewhat arrogantly that they were superior to their clients in marketing know-how – and in fact at that time he was probably not wrong! Short in stature but big in personality he had a very short fuse and when he saw red this was matched by his short cropped reddish blonde hair. He habitually wore buttoned down starched white shirts with cufflinks. Wonderfully theatrical he would sit with his hands joined, fingers outstretched as if in prayer or with his arms behind his head leaning back, looking lost and diminutive in his large imposing black leather bound desk chair. When sitting forward he was always careful to hold his arms aloft, leaning against the front of his desk, to ensure that the cuffs did not get dirty or soiled by papers, ink or dirt on the desk surface. When he got angry his face would go a mixture of red and white patches and one hand would incessantly smooth down the hair on one side of his head. Much of Edward O'Brian was about affectation with well-versed clichés abounding from his lips. However, he backed all this up with courage, guts and a quick mind. Christoph came to like Edward and respect him enormously and for his part he more than tolerated Christoph. What he admired about Christoph was his ballsy, seemingly fearless, approach to the business and his unquenchable desire to learn.

Edward O'Brian's ego manifested itself in a myriad of ways. He would come into Christoph's darkened inner office and ask, "Hey Christoph, do you like my latest US$600 Brooks Brother suit?" or "Okay Christoph, let's compare orchid files?" He would then produce a folder full of notes from clients and senior agency bodies' alike complimenting him on a job well done. These he collected and then gave each signatory a points rating dependant on their level of seniority. Another of his games would be to come in and state "Christoph, let's compare the number of letters on our briefcases." Given that Christoph only ever used a canvas Land's End holdall with just CPA initials this was a no-brainer for Edward to win. He had a very expensive briefcase in dark brown padded leather with gold fasteners and five initials. Beyond this superficiality and shallowness when it came to the business Edward lived it and loved it. Like Christoph he saw it as a game to win.

A life above the line – just!

Whilst being the consummate professional he did possess a wicked sense of humour and much to Christoph's surprise he had a number of interests outside work. He had a fascination with 1960s popular music and the Beatles in particular. He also was politically extremely well read beyond simply America. He was also a connoisseur of good whiskies, though after a tough meeting he would only sink Jack Daniels on the return journey to La Guardia (domestic internal airport for Manhattan).

There were many great learnings and words of wisdom that Edward expounded to Christoph. After one particular meeting in which the agency had fought its corner bravely he smiled and peering at Christoph through his large thick horned tortoise shell glasses, stated, " Christoph the enemy is not in Moscow (a time of the 'cold war'); the enemy is not in Hanoi (the Vietnam War having only ended in 1975 after President Nixon had withdrawn the American troops in 1974); the enemy is in New York (Agency's HQ) and Columbus (the base city of Thomas Healey) – beware of friendly fire!" On a separate occasion after Christoph had been at Gris Advertising for a year he was called into Edward's office for a review. "Christoph, its appraisal time and I'm going to bust your chops." Alongside Chris was a second telephone for conference calls and so he picked up the receiver, dialled his PA, Gloria (a characterful, optimistic, cheerful black lady who laughed at just about everything that Christoph said to her). When she answered Christoph said "Gloria could you please book me on the next Laker (discount airline operator) flight, back to London, England". To which her only response was "Oh Gee Christoph you are so funny" and with that she put the phone down! Now both Edward and Christoph looked at each other totally bemused but for completely different reasons. After a very thorough, detailed and almost clinical review, Edward concluded by saying, "But what we really like about you Christoph is that you are both involved and committed and that's not the same thing. It's like bacon and eggs the hen is involved but the pig is committed." To this day Christoph was never able to work out what this meant or what the differences truly were in this irrelevant analogy!

On a trip to Thomas Healey the Creative Group Head had travelled with the Account team, which was unusual as most of the time the

Creatives preferred to stay in New York and let the 'suits' present and sell their work. In what was a tough presentation the Creative had done really well and stood her ground and then made the suggested changes immediately on the spot. The meeting ended with the work getting approval to proceed to production. As Edward and Christoph had other work to go through with the client the Creative left and caught an earlier plane back to NY City. Sometime later when they were on their flight Christoph, reflecting on the success of the meeting, remarked, "We really ought to find some way of thanking the creatives for their efforts". Edward, who was knocking back Jack Daniels, while reading Newsweek looked up momentarily, and stated, "They get paid don't they?" Undeterred, Christoph continued, "Yes, but they really pulled out all the stops today." Absolute silence from Edward and then after some minutes, during which time Christoph felt he had been completely ignored and even felt a tad uncomfortable, Edward stopped reading and turning slowly to stare at Christoph dubiously said, "Maybe your right if you want to eat ham you've got to go down there and feed the pigs."

Edward was undoubtedly most dangerous when he had had a few drinks and on one occasion Christoph and he were at the States Fair Convention in Baton Rouge, where Edward was totally outside his comfort zone. Bored and obnoxious he started to comment on the attire of the assembled delegates. "Oh my Gawd, Christoph have you seen those white plastic shoes - they're gross. Look at those guys with their string ties they suck." – and so on. It finished with the two of them sitting and talking, having had way too much to drink. Then Edward said "I hate these drinking glasses." And proceeded to snap the stems of a number of them, before getting up; and in a defiant gesture wrapping the contents of the table in the white table cloth and hurling it at the plate glass window. The weight was sufficient for it to smash the glass, bringing a number of staff to the scene. Christoph thought that would be the end for him and that he would face deportation from the United States following a night behind a police station's bars, after the 'heat' had been called. However, this was averted by Christoph taking full responsibility and offering immediate compensation, via his

American Express card, to the on-site manager of the establishment. A figure of US$250 was arrived at and agreed. Nevertheless, even getting Edward to his room quietly proved to be a monumental task as he insisted on shouting out expletives at the top of his voice – "Wake up you bunch of fucks." Needless to say the next morning at the Convention, Edward, and to a lesser degree Christoph, appeared totally 'comatosed' and though Edward was breathing shallowly he never moved a muscle and when it came for his contribution to the meeting there was a deafening silence. Christoph stepped up to the plate and stated, "The agency agrees with the direction (whatever that was heaven only knew and certainly not him!) and we'll get back to you with suitable creative directions and materials next week."

Edward was a rule unto himself and on a flight to Columbus they ran into a former agency colleague now working on the same account but for another agency. "Hey Ed, are you looking forward to having a good day?" in a bright friendly tone. Edward just looked at him with total disdain and responded, "My friend, they'll be the judge of that." Leaving this character somewhat bemused Edward got into the cab and immediately discussed how he wanted to conduct the meeting, "I'll do the numbers, and you do the bunny." The meeting was going to be tricky as it was a new direction for the brand that had not been especially well received by the client to date, though had come through research fairly positively though by no means overwhelmingly. Present, for this Mid-Western WASPish (White Anglo Saxon Protestant!)Company, was going to be the highly competent, bright, challenging black Associate, Reg Hayes. It was, as expected, a fiery meeting with a great deal of emotion spent on both sides and at one stage Reg Hayes looked across the table and stated, "Edward, you're misusing the numbers, Christoph you're full of shit!" In the end after a valiant fight by the agency folk the Client finally conceded, "If the Agency feels that strongly then we must, on the evidence provided, reluctantly concur."

Feeling jubilant, as winning was what the game was all about; Christoph excused himself and headed for the bathroom. He was just relieving himself at the urinal when the Advertising Manager came and stood alongside him in the next stall. A likeable man he was extremely astute, shrewd and highly regarded. He was a man that respected honesty, directness and real input from his Agencies, whom he genuinely viewed as partners in their marketing and not merely providers and suppliers of advertising. Roundish in size he more often than not had a pipe in his mouth which did not need to be removed from his lips in order to speak. "So Christoph what brings you to town today?" he asked innocently and light-heartedly. Christoph looking slightly sheepish replied, in a non-committal way "Oh this and that on the copy front." "Well, I hope you're not still trying to sell that copy you presented to me before because, you know, you're never going to fly that one past me," he stated chuckling as he left his urinal berth and made his way to the wash hand basins. "Oh No Sir" Christoph mumbled somewhat unconvincingly, knowing that was exactly the advertising that they had just sold lower down the line that very day. It was difficult for Christoph to maintain some self-control and he ended up pissing all over his shoes. It had suddenly dawned on him that his claim to fame was about to be – 'this was the man that lost an advertising campaign down the toilet!' People would say that he literally and not metaphorically 'had pissed it away'! Not a good position to be in.

Emerging from the gents he re-entered the meeting room and asked if he could have a quick word with Edward outside. Explaining what had happened and the now impossible situation they found themselves in Edward played Pontius Pilate, and rubbing his hands said, "Well Christoph sometimes in life, and indeed in management, there is a need for delegation, and this is one of those God-given moments, so let me hand this one over to you!" Walking back into the room, Christoph said to the assembled clients but looking straight at Reg Hayes, "Edward and I have been discussing the situation we have arrived at today and we feel that in the interests of the good working relationship and partnership we enjoy, that it is beholden on us to take the learning we have and seek to develop an alternative route to test against this route and hopefully this will be one that we can all agree with and would be happy to progress." Reg Hayes looked astonished and was clearly completely taken aback, but could only agree and thank the agency for their responsible attitude and maturity.

This was extremely gracious of him given that this was this same individual who on a previous encounter, when Christoph had presented some work, which had not been well received, called Christoph out, beckoning him with his index finger, at the end of the meeting. On that occasion, he had stated, "Christoph, nothing personal, because I actually quite like you, but you're a god-damn limey and if I was you I would go home and tell my mother to sell the shithouse, because you've just lost your arse." That time Christoph had got back on the plane and had taken Edward's lead example and got bombed out on Jack Daniels – tomorrow, was definitely going to be another day!

Above Edward O'Brian was a very different styled man, Samuel Rosensteen, an amiable man, stout and short, with a very quick New York Jewish sense of humour. Samuel was always 'unfazed' and never let the business get to him as the greatest priority in his life was his wife and children. Regrettably, this was ultimately to prove to be a 'perceived weakness' as far as his senior colleagues were concerned. He would be moved off onto cereal and pharmaceutical business, where he proved a great success and where he was fully appreciated. Indeed, he was happy to escape the intense daily pressures of the Thomas Healey Account Group. Christoph recalled one disastrous Brand Review, with the then Advertising Director, a small, humourless, charmless, uncompromising individual with a short temper and a low tolerance level. He almost seemed to feel he had to behave in this way to be successful; as the sole token Jew in the organisation. He was tough on everyone but most particularly on the agencies as he seemed to especially dislike them and detest their personnel viewing them as arrogant, self-confident chancers - truly 'low life'. Having worked unbelievably hard at preparing for this Brand Review, with an excellent and highly promising female client Brand Manager, Christoph got to the meeting in an exhausted state. Worse than that he had been compromised as he had been forced to go forward with two routes which he felt showed a lack of clear commitment and direction. However, because the Agency

Management had liked one route over another and the Brand Team had the reverse opinion it had been decided both would be presented, with a view that both were good enough to go into test. It was arguably the worst meeting of Christoph's entire career in advertising as it was the only time that he felt he had lost his nerve and 'bottled it' under severe pressure. His preamble was not appreciated by the client and he was castigated for proposing the two routes and not having a definite opinion and point of view.

Eventually, with the Agency on the ropes over no preference Samuel came to the fore. Looking around the table of disgruntled and downhearted individuals Samuel started "Well, you know how it is…" stopping in mid-sentence to knock out the old tobacco from his pipe's bowl before filling it afresh with 'bacci' very deliberately while all watched him intently. He then continued "We didn't all travel in the same cab from the airport, but as the Senior Agency man on the brand, I would like to recommend Route One" To his credit the rest of the discussion was spent defending the merits of this single copy route. At the end of the meeting Samuel came up to Christoph and put a consoling hand on his shoulder and smilingly said to a disconsolate Christoph, "Hey Christoph it's not so bad, nobody died, and sometimes you get Beluga Caviar and sometimes it's just chopped liver. For you today it was the latter." They both laughed, with relief, as put like that it was surely a learning experience and it truly wasn't the end of the world.

When Samuel knew that Christoph's mother was coming to visit him in New York he asked Christoph to ask her to bring him some Havana Cigars, as his Edward VII's were not true Cuban tobacco. The only problem was that he forgot to tell Christoph that Cuban Cigars were banned in the US. So naturally Christoph's mother was almost arrested at JFK Airport on her arrival, but with her charm she expounded her innocence and in the end they let her and the cigars through Custom Control. Samuel truly knew about the good things in life but he also had his priorities absolutely right.

Another likeable rogue in the group was Dick Dereto, a smartly turned out, swarthy, solidly built Italian American, who did the absolute minimum amount of work but his team continually delivered for him. He was bright and pretty astute and a real gambler be that with work, women, cards, or life. Dick and Christoph used to play Poker with the numbers on the dollar bills on the flights to and from Columbus. Calling out the numbers, sometimes on a good flight, half the plane would become involved. It often got to the point where stewardesses would close down the game as it was getting too rowdy, or too many people were walking up and down the aisle. Again Dick was another who did not survive the tough regime at Gris Advertising, on Thomas Healey.

Certainly flights on American Airlines, TWA and Delta were seldom dull quite apart from the occasional dates that Christoph secured with stewardesses. On one flight realising he had lost a button he took the spare from the base of his shirt and then was trying to sew it on himself. Seeing he was clearly struggling the man in the next seat offered his assistance and successfully sewed the button onto the cuff. When it came to introductions Arthur Trujillo only turned out to be the Mayor of Santa Fe, a city in New Mexico.

There were many characters that flew back and forth and one such person was Mary Wells of Wells Rich Green Agency. On one flight Christoph was on she got on in her mink coat and expressed deep indignation that there was no First Class, nor a Company limousine to meet her on arrival at the destination. This dramatic lady was light boned, short in stature, immaculately dressed, if not overly stylish and was one attractive hard-nosed woman. It was alleged that one Christmas she sent all her senior clients a Mont Blanc pen. Unfortunately one of the recipients was the Bic Biro Company whose North American CEO (Bic Societe being a French Company, famed for its Bic Cristal/ 'Bic' ballpoint pen product, with its famed slogan dating back to 1959 'writes first time every time') was less than impressed by her insensitivity in the choice of present for him and fired the agency from their business. Mary Wells realising her error of judgement was mortified. She tried to contact the gentleman in question on numerous occasions but without success, as his staff had been informed not to take her calls and definitely not to put her through to him. Exasperated and in desperation she flew down to their US Head Office, no doubt, in her familiar long real mink coat and requested to see the CEO in person. But still she was refused access to him. Never one to take no for an answer she refused to leave the offices and after three days she finally was granted an appointment to meet with him in person at his office. Apparently, she fell at his feet dramatically and expressed profuse apologies for her lack of judgement. Embarrassed by this behaviour but also impressed by the level of importance she clearly gave to the account, the CEO reappointed her and her agency to the business. Quite a performance from a true legend of the industry!

Gris Advertising, during Christoph's period in New York, was a premier division side, in the 'Mad Man' Agency League Table and working on Thomas Healey was as good as it got from the standpoint of prestige, honour and learning. This was even more so for Account Management as they were cast as the Planners as well as the day–to–day servicing and selling personnel. They were expected to be business thinkers, strategic planners, and creative briefers, based on an in-depth understanding of consumer research and business insights. They also needed to have a thoroughly comprehensive understanding of the competition and sales performances, as well as a deep knowledge of the brand's properties, formulae and manufacturing so as to ascertain genuine point(s) of difference. Christoph loved all these aspects and was a solid performer at all of them but it was really the cut and thrust of selling that became his most conspicuous and defining strength. He loved the gamesmanship that involved tactics and strategy to make a sale. To this he added theatre and performance and this made him a popular frontman as he sought to make his presentations fun, dramatic, effective and memorable. He was viewed by many as a true showman.

When Christoph first arrived at Gris Advertising in New York he was put on a premium detergent that gave purchasers a gift in every box. These premiums varied by cycle and could be a flannel, tea towel, a bar of soap, a plate, a glass or even a Mills & Boon romance styled book. This business was most definitely skewed geographically

A life above the line – just!

to the poorer regions of the States and had a strong business profile in the Deep Southern most States. Cope Detergent had a reputation for giving away quality items and also benefitted from a longstanding female celebrity spokesperson, Molly. She represented and articulated good common-sense ideals and the importance of value "Molly says Cope with it." The task given to Christoph was to come up with a premium to relaunch the brand with, for which might be its last premium, as the company was thinking of rationalising its brands and abandoning premium detergents, as they were deemed by many to be dated. It was agreed this should be a smoky brown goblet styled glass, which the team designed and gave to it the distinguishing name of 'Royal Heritage'. Christoph, using his British background, of course, had no problem coming up with the name for this newly designed glass! He was then requested to develop and produce a Spot TV and Spot Radio campaign and put together an on-the-ground promotional and sponsorship programme through the State Fairs. However, it was during this process he rather let himself down, when he was attending a State Fair Convention in Las Vegas. Even before he had got there he had compromised himself, on the flight there, by chatting up a very attractive woman, with long legs, long blonde hair and blue eyes. She turned out to be a Show Girl in one of the hotels on 'The Strip'. Unfortunately by the time they landed she had drunk so much that she had to be taken off the plane in a wheelchair.

When Christoph checked into the MGM Hotel he discovered that to even get to reception he had to cross a gambling area, full of slot machines, the size of Wembley football pitch. Christoph was sorely tempted by this mecca of gambling and ended up playing the tables for four days and four nights, only just managing to pick up the published literature from the State Fair Convention Office prior to his departure back to the airport. He was absolutely knackered but at least after some initial losses he had finished up making a profit once he realised that on Black Jack (Vingt et Un), the croupier had to draw on 16 or below. The free drinks and food presented to him at the table kept him engaged especially as there were no clocks to check easily on the time, not that this was a concern to him. The lovely, leggy, show girl also made for a delightful distraction from work, while further broadening his level of entertainment. When he got back to New York he was rather less enlightened about State Fair policy but 'Polyester City' had more than lived up to its reputation of being an 'Adult Disney'.

The brand Manager on Cope was the delightful William McGinty and they worked really well as a team. He was straightforward, direct, unassuming and as he lacked real vigour and imagination was only too happy to let Christoph take the lead. For this both were deeply appreciative!

With the successful restage achieved on Cope behind him and it having been a real feather in his cap Christoph was promoted to work on another powdered detergent this time with a fabric conditioner built in, New Wave. Not unsurprisingly as an 'Alien' from that 'piss-pot little island' across the pond he was limited to ancillary tasks on this important main brand! However, this gave Christoph considerable latitude as he had a fairly free rein on how to tackle the Hispanic population on the East Coast of America, deemed to be the 13th largest market in the USA at that time. Christoph surprised a number of his management by putting together a team that included promotions, public relations and media. The lead promotions person was the formidable and diminutive Joanne Berco, a bright well-connected and extremely competent and experienced woman, who wore her hair short cropped that highlighted her flashing deep brown hazel eyes. Joanne exuded charm, elegance and refinement in a wonderfully artistic and stylish manner. Living down in the 'Village' (Greenwich), she became a great friend, to Christoph, as a fellow neighbour, during their time working as a team.

Together they initiated some great fun ideas that gained a lot of free coverage and publicity for the New Wave brand. It was with Joanne that they came up with the idea of washing an elephant, in Chicago Zoo, in the detergent to show how it became cleaner, softer and smelled fresher. The notion of sampling a detergent in a regional paper and eventually in women's magazines was also down to them. This proved to have some teething problems, early on, as the loading up of the papers led to the weight bursting the sachets and on one wet evening there were soap suds everywhere at the printer's depot. By placing the powder in ribs this stopped the powder all collecting at one end of a sachet, but it was still facing the weight from the piling up of papers that proved a secondary problem. The piles had to be kept small and then this explosive problem was finally resolved. The idea of developing information leaflets that could be distributed in magazines or delivered door-to-door was far less problematic and with coupons encouraged trial. Christoph himself came up with the idea of showing a mnemonic of a demonstration of the product formula, a powder detergent and a liquid fabric conditioner combining, in a funnel device, to give a powdered detergent output on the advertising placards/transit cards in public buses that travelled to and through the main Hispanic Communities. Working with the Media department this efficient and low cost medium was employed successfully. They also developed an imaginative and affordable media plan that covered local Hispanic (Spanish speaking) radio stations and even their own spot TV Channels, that brought this mnemonic to life verbally and visually. It was a very simple visual to tell what would otherwise have been a complex story to explain. The 'magic' of science taking place in the funnel, of course, meant there was no clumping!

Disappointingly for Christoph these successes raised his profile in the Group and when one of the senior members of the team was moved off the business he found himself promoted to working on the mainstream advertising for the brand. With this came all the petty politicking that he had spotted from afar and so skilfully averted up until then. There was some relief from the number crunching, competitive reviews and daily analyses, when Christoph was asked to do a circuit of Company internal presentations showing the factory workers and distribution points what had been done in terms of communications. None of his colleagues were at all interested in doing this and so he was able to put together a slide and acetate presentation with fun visuals and video clips to make it involving and interesting for potentially quite demanding audiences. Before leaving on tour he ran it past his masters who enjoyed it but showed little interest in the content. Christoph found himself visiting a number of selected plants and depots of Thomas Healey that took in primarily the Mid-West and North East, including Boston, Pittsburgh, Chicago, Des Moines and Indianapolis. For Christoph the most memorable presentation was to the factory workers in Boston, who were actually making the new Wave product. The part that Christoph always enjoyed the most was the Questions and Answers at the end of each session. On this occasion Christoph was asked about sexy and racy characters he had worked with and any which might have been cast on any of their Company's brands advertising. He had had to think very quickly on his feet but recalled that Linda Lovelace, a movie porn star, had in an earlier part of her career appeared in some domestic product advertising. Being from the United Kingdom he was also able to relate to them how Fiona Wright, a former model, had become renowned for being Burton Retailer's, Chairman and CEO, Ralph Halpern's squeeze and had nicknamed him 'the seven times a night man', while she drove around in an E-Type Jaguar, with the number plate FU2. Another apocryphal story he recounted was associated with a Procter & Gamble dishwashing product in the UK called Fairy that had received the Royal endorsement which entitled it to state on each product the words 'By appointment to Her Majesty the Queen'. On one print run a small piece of fluff had blotted the wording and it read 'By appointment to Her Majesty the Queer'. This brought the house down. Christoph truly saw this as 'show time' and he loved the whole theatre of these occasions. It proved to be great training in how to deal with a demanding and challenging audience and how to adjust the material to suit them. He realised that he had to show he could never be shocked and to give as good as he got! The reports back from these 'whistle-stop' tour presentations, was very positive from these critical audiences. It served to enhance his growing reputation as a presenter of note and also helped further build his stature and worth within the Group.

For Christoph it was important that he did not only work on Thomas Healey during his time at Gris Advertising in New York but had the chance to widen his vision and experience. To that end he was happy to be utilised on new business projects and even on smaller accounts. One of the latter was Chessingdon Fields, a traditional old-fashioned toiletries company that included deodorants, scented and non –fragrant soaps, cleansers and even a shaving foam product called Close. On one occasion the Agency was summoned for a meeting with one of the senior family members, Mr Fields, with the title President. He specifically asked for Rich Harper, the then Creative Director of the Agency to attend. Rich was a very refined gentleman creative with a penchant for well-tailored sports jackets and sharp lace up brogues. He always wore a flower in his buttonhole usually of buttercup, primrose or cornflower blue in colour. He was slightly fey, if not effete, in manner and was extremely self-conscious. One thing such an eminent man was unlikely to take kindly to was being called 'Harpo' as this had all the connotations of his being a member of the Marx Brothers. Of course, Mr Fields called Rich Harper 'Harpo'.

Duly the members amassed and took cabs to Chessingdon Fields offices. On arrival they were ushered into a large impressive oak panelled room with an imposing central rosewood table and matching chairs. All round the walls hung paintings of previous distinguished members of the family. A portrait of the current Chairman was evidently being completed, as a ladder stood by, with painting materials on the sideboard. Around the table sat a number of senior members of the Board and there seemed to be a stilted and uneasy feeling in the room. Among the Agency team there was even a slight concern and underlying fear that perhaps they had been gathered to be told that the Agency was being fired from the business. Suddenly the door opened and Mr Fields was wheeled in by a male nurse/attendant dressed in a white coat. He directed the wheelchair to the head of the table where a space had been left vacant. "Thank you, gentlemen, for coming at such short notice. I truly appreciate it," Mr Fields started in a Marlon Brando gravely type godfather voice. Intermittently, he would strike his trembling left hand at the wrist with his right hand, making a loud smacking sound. "You know my product Close", he continued. At this point the ever keen Christoph interjected and stated, "Oh most certainly Yes, Sir. We are pleased to inform you that the business nationally is up 5% year on year and in the extra spending area of Charlottesville the business is currently indexing at 118." "Thank you young man I know all that stuff," the old man replied, neatly dismissing Christoph's impromptu support, for the Agency's contribution, to the business on Close. Looking directly at Rich Harper, he continued "Harpo I've called you here because I've had this terrific idea and I want to share it with you. Harpo, I want you to talk about my product, Close, as 'the original'." There was a deadly hush in the room as everyone sought to take this in. As no one seemed prepared to comment Christoph felt obliged to raise his head over the parapet, once again, "Sir, it is undoubtedly true that Close was the first shaving foam on the market. However, being the first after so many years does not necessarily make that one the best in today's world. Furthermore, as you know, the market sector for shaving foam has evolved considerably since those pioneer days. Today there is gels, products with lanolin, or moisturiser and others that offer a range of fragrances, while others have variants for differing skin conditions." Totally ignoring this input and interruption from Christoph the old man continued "Harpo, Close was the original shaving foam and this is something that we have never before capitalised upon against our competitors be that Gillette, Wilkinson's, Colgate or Noxzema. Only we, with Close, can own the territory of being 'the original'." This debate or semi-discussion went back and forth for some time between the owner of the business and Richard Harper, until almost in frustration Rich said, "Well. Mr Fields we hear you and understand your idea of our building a campaign around the idea of Close being the original but let me ask you how would you see this being communicated meaningfully in copy terms?" Mr Fields leant forward in his wheelchair with his eyes gleaming with excitement and responded "Listen Harpo" he said, "I give you the idea – how you communicate it to the consumer – that's your fuckin' problem!" And with that he then had himself wheeled out of the Boardroom. For the next 2 years the Agency developed copy to 'The Original' idea and it successfully built the business – so what do us agency smarts know, thought Christoph?

There was a second occasion that Christoph encountered Mr Fields and that was in the Agency. On this occurrence Mr Fields had called the Head of the Agency, Chuck Deal, and asked to have an Agency

Review. This often spelt and smelt of trouble. Accordingly the Account group was gathered and were informed that they had a fortnight to prepare for this meeting and nothing was to get in the way of this work. Christoph spent day and night working over the numbers and putting a full slide and acetate presentation together, as well as compilation tapes of their work and competitors. Everything was included from shipment and share data, to research findings, test learnings and even performance by region and individual store outlet be that groceries or pharmacies. All the stops were pulled out and Christoph was virtually on his knees by the time the big day came around, especially as so many minor changes were made at the run-throughs. Physically and mentally exhausted the team was living simply on adrenaline and the passionate desire to win and impress sufficiently to retain the business.

On the day itself the old man arrived on his own, bar his carer, and Chuck Deal stood up and made his opening remarks. Chuck was by no means the great presenter and had an annoying habit of jangling keys or loose change that he kept in his pockets. But Chuck Deal was a brilliant reader of situations and he had the ability to be so well informed, prior to any encounter, that he could impress all the senior clients with his knowledge of their business. He started his 'spiel' by stating that Gris Advertising's success mirrored and coincided with that of Chessingdon Fields. As they had grown as a business so had Gris Advertising also blossomed. He went on to talk about the length of the relationship, dating back over some twenty years and the pride that he personally had felt in handling their individual brands and on seeing these flourish. This patriotic unification monologue went on for some twenty minutes and was truly a 'tour de force'. At the end Christoph was just getting up to start the review for real, when Mr Fields stepped in verbally and in his husky Brando godfather voice stated, "In my twenty years of working with your agency, Chuck, that's the finest presentation I've ever heard you make. I know my business is in good hands with you. Thank you gentlemen and good day." With that Mr Fields left – leaving behind a stunned room, who didn't know whether to laugh or cry – but in the end simply collapsed with fatigue and relief. Christoph wondered to himself, if maybe just maybe, the old man couldn't face his presentation and simply got out early! These may have been tough times, in the late 1970s, in New York, but they were never without humour.

It was certainly a great time for him to be there at one of the top agencies. Gris Advertising had its critics for its work ethos and some would call 'its lowest common denominator advertising' but it worked and made many brands hugely successful and even famous. They were especially effective and strong on Fast Moving Consumer Goods clients. As these grew and sought global expansion so Gris also expanded internationally. It was inconceivable for Christoph to initially comprehend that brand's such as Procter & Gamble's Tide the leading US detergent was billing over US$20million annually in advertising alone. This brand's expenditure alone exceeded the entire billings of Gris Advertising in the UK at this time. Christoph realised how lucky he had been to have been given this chance. The fact that they thought, with his public school accent, he must be related to royalty meant he gained a little unmerited and deferential respect. The only really successful Englishman in New York, up until then, had been David Ogilvy, who was the founder of Ogilvy and Mather, and whom had already become a legend in the 1950s and 1960s. He had made his mark with his campaign for Hathaway Shirts, that featured a man with a black patch over one eye but dressed in a Hathaway shirt and Rolls-Royce motor cars – 'where the only sound you'll hear is the ticking of the clock on the dashboard'. In the future there would be many more individual British success stories and this move was underlined when there was the reverse takeover of Garland Compton by Saatchi and Saatchi (March 1982). This inevitably led to freer movement of personnel between offices and regular exchanges of staff.

Christoph was smart enough to ensure that not all his time was spent working. Paying no taxes or rent meant he had the money to go to shows, theatre, dance and museums and art galleries. He fell in love with Twiggy (Dame Lesley Lawson), the 1960s waif like model (the face of 1966), all over again, as she moved from fashion to becoming

A life above the line – just!

a Broadway star. Natalia Makarova, the former Kirov dancer having defected from Russia in 1970 had also shown her versatility appearing in 'On Your Toes' with the tall, elegant, charismatic mover, Tommy Tune. There was the sensual, dark haired light blue eyed, sensational long-legged muse of Bob Fosse, Anne Reinking in 'Dancin' and also in the revival of 'Chicago'. (Anne Reinking would in later years take on her mentor's jazz-like, fluid style in many revivals of 'Chicago' initially created by Bob Fosse in 1969 (he had died in 1978 aged just 60).

New York at that time was also the centre of ballet in the world and many of the great companies visited, unquestionably drawn by the brilliance of George Balanchine's New York City Ballet, that had taken up residence along with the American Ballet Theatre and Metropolitan Opera, at the recently completed Lincoln Center, where different facilities opened between 1962 sand 1969. NY City Ballet boasted a galaxy of stars from dancers such as Suzanne Farrell, Gelsey Kirkland, Merrell Ashley and Mikhail Baryshnikov to choreographers such as Jerome Robbins ('West Side Story' fame) and George Martens. The latter choreographed John Curry's ice skating Olympic Gold routine, in 1976, to the music of Minkus's Don Quixote. The great Anthony Dowell, from the Royal Ballet, was dancing for The American Ballet Theatre, where the long legged Cynthia Gregory, standing over 6ft 1ins on pointe, excelled and where another Cynthia, Harvey was just emerging as a prodigious talent, at a time when they also boasted the services of Natalia Makarova. Christoph appreciated he was spoilt as he also saw other great local entities, such as, Martha Graham, The Harlem Dance Company, The Joffrey, Alvin Ailey and Merce Cunningham companies, perform regularly and inexpensively. London at that time had nothing to compare with this variety and contemporary approach to dance. So many other dance companies visited New York – even The Bolshoi. Perhaps the most striking was Alicia Alonso (1920-2019), whose company founded by her in 1948 but renamed in 1955 as The Ballet Nacional de Cuba. Alicia Alonso despite being inflicted by an eye disorder that made her virtually blind continued to dance until she was 90 and who was already nearly 60 when Christoph saw her dance. She truly was a tour de force.

And as if that was not enough the Metropolitan Opera boasted the brilliant Luciano Pavarotti (1935-2007) as their resident Guest Tenor. New York suited this flamboyant character and he was even prepared to spontaneously sing Carols from the steps of St Patrick's Cathedral, on 5th Avenue, in the 1979 Christmas Season, which Christoph was fortunate enough to witness.

Most Sundays however were spent at The Belmont Track where Christoph would take the train across the East River. Even in those days it was a top quality track and Christoph was only sorry to have got to New York after "The Kid" Stevie Cauthen had won the Triple Crown on the diminutive chestnut Affirmed, beating in each leg – by a diminishing margin – the luckless Alydar.

When Christoph had arrived in September 1978 the weather had been quite exceptional and continued to be for some weeks, providing the most picturesque of autumns, as the leaves turned from green to a canvas of yellows, browns and reds set against bedazzling sun-rich, crisp, sparkling blue skies. At the same time New York's Yankees – 'God's own team'- were busily making up the deficit against their arch rivals the Boston Red Sox. In the evenings Christoph had begun to follow 'those Goddam Yankees' whom at one stage in late July had been 14 games behind. On the very last day of the regular season the Yankees lost to, their newly appointed Manager, Bob Lemon's former team, the Cleveland Indians, whereas Boston won. This meant they were tied and a play-off game had to be arranged, at Fenway Park, the home ground of Boston, the location having been determined on the basis of a toss of a coin. In a tight, tense making game the Yankees won 5 to 4, thanks largely to one of only 5 home runs, all season, hit by their short-stop, Bucky Dent, as the team scored 3 runs in the 7th innings. This same player went on to become the MVP (Most Valuable Player) in the World Series against the former Brooklyn Dodgers whom having moved out West had become the Los Angeles Dodgers. Earlier the Yankees had seen off the Kansas City Royals. In the World Series they lost the first two games to the Dodgers. In the second of these losses a rookie pitcher, Bob Welch, had struck out the legendary Reggie Jackson with

A life above the line – just!

two men on base and a full count against him, thereby saving a three run scenario. Back came the Yankees and in Game 3 their star pitcher Ron Guidry ('Louisiana Lightning') did the business and in Game 4 they were saved by their relief pitcher Rick Gossage ('The Goose', as the crowd would sound). With the Series now tied Jim Beattie pitched an entire game for the Yankees (normally a starting pitcher is relieved in the 6th or 7th innings as his arm tires after throwing over 60 to 70 pitches and sometimes even up to 100 pitches). Then the legendary Jim 'Catfish' Hunter won the decisive Game 6 in what was to be his final moment of glory as a major league pitcher.

In support of this pitching was a phenomenal performance from the batters with 7 of their players hitting over 300, including the captain and catcher, Thurman Munson, who tragically would be killed flying his own light aircraft the following year. Another player to achieve this stat was Reggie Jackson (known as 'Mr October' because of his post season form. He scored 18 Post Season home runs and even had a chocolate bar, "Reggie" named after him). In Game 6, Christoph watched on television as, Reggie Jackson exacted his revenge on Bob Welch. With one runner/man on base, Jackson walked towards the mound where the Dodgers pitcher stood and waited and Jackson pointed over his head with his bat to the furthest part of the ground where he intended to hit the ball. Settling down in the batter's crease he awaited the delivery. The very first pitch he received he hit it exactly to the spot he had indicated for a 2 run homer. The Los Angeles crowd who had jeered Jackson in Game 2 were now awe struck and silenced. It truly was a great moment to savour.

Almost equal to the batting had been the quality of the fielding and catching especially around the bases. Craig Nettles, twice a holder of The Golden Glove award for best fielder in a season and possibly one of the greatest third basemen of all time, had been stupendous. Ably supporting him were Brian Doyle at 2nd Base and Bucky Dent at shortstop, both whom had made memorable plays and shared the MVP Award.

Christoph was there on the street for the second tickertape parade in consecutive years. Millions of New Yorkers turned out to acclaim their heroes. They were truly a comeback side who never seemed to know when they were beaten.

Christoph enjoyed going to the games at the Yankee Stadium and despite the level of crime at that time in New York there never seemed to be many incidents on game days not even on the public transport. The whole experience of a game entranced Christoph. The passion the fans had for their heroes, the nick-names, the noise and buzz, the smell of the Yankee Franks (frankfurters), the Crackerjack toffee popcorn salesmen, the plastic containers of light beer available in one's seat, all made for a fun day/evening out. At the '7th Innings Stretch' the game stopped for people to make loo visits or obtain yet more food and drink. The groundsmen, from around 1979, swept the cinder track and bases to the Village People's hit YMCA (1978), the letters which they executed with the arm gestures at the appropriate time in the song. The intensity throughout a game was heightened by the sound of the Wurlitzer Organ that often accompanied the singing of the National Anthem, but which really came into its own, when it geed the crowd up to support a pitcher or batter and again when it played for the crowd to sing-a-long to, 'Take me out to the Ball Game' or 'New York, New York'. The competitions, spotting people in the crowd, and announcements, as well as the 'Let's Go Yankees', all added to the spectacle and theatre. The devoted fans seemed to be on first name terms with their players, their gods and devoted they were, with 3 million turning up, in a single season, to 'the house that Babe built' due to his alluring attraction as a player. Babe Ruth (1895-1948) being the player traded from the Boston Red Sox, in the close season of 1919, the same year he had broken the record of home runs in a single season, at a count of 29. (Boston did not win the World Series for 86 years after that which became known as the "curse of the Bambino". Ruth would go on to surpass his own record for home runs in a season three more times, raising it to a figure of 60. Not bad for a man that started out as a quality pitcher that could bat! He retired in 1935). Today there is a new stadium where the Yankees won the World Season in their first season playing there in 2009.

Christoph because of his heavy work load in New York really

A life above the line – just!

only had Friday nights and part of the weekends to party. Most Friday evenings he would end up in St. John's Bar in the Turtle Bay neighbourhood, closely situated to Katherine Hepburn's house. Many a night Christoph would struggle to get home somewhat the worst for wear and on one Friday night after hitting the Bloody Mary's bigtime Christoph had to make his way from 49th Street to 38th feeling his way round corners and reeling drunkenly across roads. Hardly dignified but he was sufficiently drunk as to pass any interest from assailants or down-and-outs. The worst of his ailments therefore being just a sore head the following morning! The attraction of St. John's was that it was well known to a number of 'Brits' then working in New York, most being English, working in the financial sector. It was a fun loud crowd who knew how to drink and have a good time!

Occasionally the account team would make for PJ Clarks on 3rd Avenue, where Woody Allen, the film director, who as an accomplished clarinettist, could be heard on a Tuesday evening or George Melly playing his kind of 'trad jazz' would do a star turn. Another haunt was the Copter Club at the top of the Pan Am building, which later became The Metropolitan Life. This skyscraper sits above Grand Central Station and looks down 5th Avenue. In those days Pan Am had a helicopter pad at the top of this building. The building itself still serves as a fond memory, for Christoph, of those halcyon days working in New York.

Of course, restaurants come and go and areas change. At the top of the Beckman Towers down by the East River, close to Sutton Place, was a romantic unassuming spot, while 'Tavern on the Green' inside Central Park was another to survive the test of time, for incurable lovers, romantics and tourists alike. As Christoph moved around town so his watering holes changed too. One of his most favourite places was the Valentine Room at the top of the restaurant building, 'Once upon a Stove'. Here all the artefacts on the walls that included pictures, wall brackets, stuffed animals and furniture, including school type chairs, were for sale. Here too the waiters, many of whom were students at The Julliard School of Music, also based at Lincoln Center, did a turn, some singing, others playing piano, violin, viola or cello. This complex of restaurants seemed to regularly fail the Health & Safety inspections and as such was only open intermittently – but well worth it when they were!

As Christoph reflected back on his time in New York he realised he had had the best of times. He had 'worked hard and played hard'. He had been sent out in 1978 as a young, uncontrolled firebrand with lots of opinions and views but little depth or substance. He came back to Gris Advertising in London, in 1980, a man, toughened and experienced with a passion and fire to play a senior role back home. He felt he had the depth of knowledge now to make a difference and to bring fun and challenge to the job. The 'Big Apple' had more than met his expectations and now he needed to go back East.

―――――― CHAPTER 5 ――――――

'International White Trash in New Markets'

<u>('white trash' was a derogatory term for loose women in the 1950s with Beulah Poynter's book, in 1952, entitled this. In 2017, Nancy Isenberg, wrote a similarly titled book, referring to the 400 year old untold history of class in America)</u>

If Christoph thought that the New York experience would be his only taste of being an International operator, he was quite mistaken. Barely had his feet touched the ground, back in the UK, when the US Management at Gris Advertising sought to send him out to Tokyo in Japan, as the Senior Account Director, on the Thomas Healey business. Christoph, more out of politeness and courtesy, than desire, went to New York to be briefed and then flew direct from there to Tokyo. However, what his three days 'recci' told him was that he was not ready to take on another international assignment so soon after his US experience. Christoph did not like the place, nor as he discovered did the client, another Englishman. This man hardly inspired him with either enthusiasm – seemingly being there only under sufferance – or confidence. The cultural differences were extreme whether it was in terms of the purchase of soap which appeared to be a gift rather than something one bought for oneself or the usage of disposable diapers, where tradition had it that the grandmother passed down cotton nappies. While finding the people gracious and almost reverential in their respect there was little humour or joy about them and to Christoph, perhaps naively, he found the women all looked the same - short, raven haired with dark eyes and a pale complexion – 'not a genuine blonde amongst them' as he cheekily wrote in his refusal report.

Despite this rebuttal, 7 years later, he would find himself on the International treadmill and this would pretty well continue unabated, right up until his retirement in 2001. Christoph discovered as the world got ever smaller and new countries opened up and emerged these needed servicing, educating, management input and the need to learn the tools of the trade to perform well on difficult and demanding clients seeking consistency in performance, unilaterally. Many clients simply expected the same level of professionalism, expertise and contribution they got in the traditional developed markets they operated in. In addition to this geographical expansion clients themselves were increasingly moving to more centrally controlled operations with what were termed 'centres of excellence' – something of a misnomer in Christoph's view! These were often referred to as 'Hubs', where communication ideas and even executions needed to be able to cross borders and boundaries. In time Christoph would discover that many major multinational clients treated whole countries simply as being test markets or to be perceived as being 'abnormal' to the rest of a region. He watched this gradual evolution with foreboding and initial disappointment. In time this would become a fascination and even curious interest before finally he became a somewhat reluctant but active participant and even convert. Christoph came to realise that over time as technological advancements extended the reach across geographies this would inevitably lead to immediate access to more relevant targeted communications. This need to think more widely would in itself bring far greater efficiencies in resource, manpower, time and costs. Regrettably and sadly this would not necessarily bring better, more relevant or clearer communication and seldom a higher level of creativity.

A life above the line – just!

For Christoph his entry point at 'Going International' would start with the Middle East. How, by 1988, he had become jokingly known as 'Christoph of Arabia' he never really comprehended. Certainly the Middle East proved to be one of the more enlightening periods in his entire life. It was never dull and the characters involved made this time both challenging and adventurous. By the time he finally handed over the reins for this region in 1993, after some 6 years in charge, he felt it had been like a lifetime. Indeed the region had changed dramatically, almost beyond recognition, in just that short period of time, due to internal and external factors alike. To McKillans, when Christoph came on board in 1987, the Middle East was of very little interest and even less significance. This whole geographical area was simply perceived by them to be a hot, arid, dry desert where people travelled by camel, beheaded people for theft or adultery. They saw these people as strangely different as they wore long white robes (thawb) and red and white tea towels (keffiyeh/ghutrah) on their heads and women were subordinate and covered their heads (hijab) and in many cases their faces too. To the rest of the world this region was simply important because of their vast oil reserves. The only reason for the Agency to have a presence at all in this part of the world was to service the needs of Neptune, who had pioneered their business interests there – though the demand for chocolate, to Christoph, seemed somewhat limited given the extreme heat. Thomas Healey was also showing some interest in developing their global brands in these markets.

At that time, a world long before the internet, it was impossible to run advertising without actually having a presence in Kuwait or Saudi Arabia and the notion of pan-regional advertising was simply alien to them and a faraway dream. To develop advertising in these markets necessitated having a licence and until then most of the work was done through a network of affiliates and these were almost exclusively run by Lebanese operators. As it was put to Christoph advertisers had found that it was impossible to control whether the right messages were being broadcast, let alone when, and whether in fact they were actually appearing as they were being told. What seemingly was needed was a trusted representation on the ground that was operating legally and working in the interest of the advertiser. In McKillans case some ground work had been started with another agency group's affiliate, which was run by a highly capricious and calculating Lebanese businessman, whom had divulged Mckillans plans unscrupulously to their parent company. Not surprisingly trust had broken down and McKillans had been forced to send an operator, unfortunately a person whose career was going no place fast, to service the small budgets involved and whom would be prepared to live locally in Jeddah, on the Red Sea, in Saudi Arabia. George Plaster, a low calibre operator back home was quickly found to be completely out of his depths and not surprisingly things were rapidly spiralling out of control. In fact the situation was becoming even worse than before his arrival. This was definitely not helped by his association with a minor prince, of the ruling family Al Saud, whom he had met through one of his aides. This had proven to be a dubious relationship all round. The minor prince had no advertising or communication knowledge and no licence to operate in these fields. The only way that the agency could operate and buy media let alone run advertising was by bringing in bucket loads of dollars into the country and paying for everything in cash. Not totally unexpectedly this had been open to misuse and possibly even corruption especially as there were no accounts, no receipts and no paper trail. The chaos was inconceivably compounded yet further when McKillans decided to appoint a Regional Head, William Swallow, early in 1987, on the simple basis and premise that he had lived in Beirut and claimed to know the Arab mentality. However, as it transpired, this had been acquired only as a military man and not as a marketer. It was shortly after this hiring and following fairly vigorous complaints from the local clients that McKillans US and UK managements began to have their suspicion that things were about to blow up in their faces. They had now seemingly hired an uncontrollable Exocet missile, with his own agenda, which seemed to be to spend as much time in Beirut in the arms of a long established love tryst, seemingly paid for by the agency. This red wire haired, scrawny, blue eyed Scotsman had a strong penchant for whisky and beautiful Lebanese women. When sober he was characterful, great company and had a quick mind and a library full of stories. He had

A life above the line – just!

already failed, in his first instruction, to remove George Plaster. His mission had been to fire George on grounds of incompetence and for operating without a legally acceptable licence. When questioned on why this direct instruction had not been carried out William Swallow simply stated that he had chosen not to do so – demonstrating that he was clearly a rule unto himself.

The realisation to the McKillans Management was that they needed 'one of their own' whom they knew they could trust 100%. The person selected, at that time, had to be male and be a strong operator with a respected reputation on their core businesses. The decision to turn to Christoph was not a major leap as he was already working on Neptune in the UK, and had been assisting them to develop work on their brands being sold in the Middle East, in an advisory capacity. Christoph also had a wealth of experience on Thomas Healey the next major client likely to require and even demand local assistance in the region. Their only reservation was that Christoph was a man who did things very much his way, but they felt at least he was Company loyal and well-regarded by the clients. They judged this risk to be a fair trade-off.

As a foretaste, before his appointment, Christoph was asked to attend a review meeting with William Swallow and the Worldwide CEO, Group Financial Director and his own UK Management. Christoph's first encounter with the gentleman in question was his turning up in full Scottish regimental uniform, including tunic, kilt, sporran and even a skie-an-dhu (a Scottish clansman's dirk or jewelled dagger) and holding a battered water bottle. The meeting got underway with William Swallow being asked for his current perspective on the region. He started off by stating, "Ah so Gentlemen you want to know about the Middle East. Well if you had fought as a soldier, in the Kings Own Border regiment, in the Arab conflicts (for him circa 1965-1974) you would have had to put yourself at risk and your very body on the line against the might of Islam. Now you see this water canteen; well these dents were made by shrapnel. The man next to me 'wasnna so lucky', his head was blown apart like a watermelon." The US Management paled visibly and Christoph could see they were wondering what the hell this inebriated character was doing giving them his version of history rather than a business review. Why indeed did he smell of whisky at eleven in the morning? Christoph, using all his guile, suggested they have a break, for coffee, even though the meeting had only been going a short time, stating he needed to make a vital telephone call. In this agreed interlude he found a way of extracting William Swallow from the meeting by assuring him that he would find the next part thoroughly boring as it was to review finances and likely investment in the region from the Group Financial Director. When the meeting reconvened Christoph explained that William had been taken ill and had gone home, but that as he, Christoph, was present, as an observer, he would ensure any important decisions taken would be relayed to William. The UK Management smiled, behind their hands, knowing Christoph well. This was truly a baptism of fire!

As, the now, newly appointed Head of Middle East Operations and International Board Account Director on Neptune it was clear this was going to be a difficult task. It was even more difficult, for him, as he was only able to do this from Friday until Monday as he had his own local clients to deal with in the UK. Fortunately, the weekend over here did not coincide with the Middle East where their weekend was Thursday and Friday. It did mean though that he was working 7 days a week. His first job was to take control of the situation and bring William Swallow to heel, in particular, as he was clearly running amok. While Christoph's major goal and priority was to develop a base in Saudi Arabia and then find an affordable way to work in Kuwait and The Emirates, William's sole agenda seemed to be to develop the business in the Lebanon. William had even based himself in Beirut and was actually operating under the protection of General Michel Aoun and from here he was able to travel freely to and from Cyprus by military/'presidential' helicopter. It got to the point where in May 1989 William actually came to Christoph with a proposal to develop an image and tourism campaign for the Lebanon. Christoph by this time had become a far more experienced operator in the region and saw the perils and ridiculousness of this notion at that time. General Aoun (born 1935), a Maronite Christian who had been Head of the Lebanese Army was the Christian Leader in a fundamentally Islamic Region.

A life above the line – just!

While he was Acting Head of State and Prime Minister, in 1988-1990, he initiated the "War of the Liberation" against their neighbour, Syria (this war ended badly for General Aoun who became an exile in France, for some 15 years (1990-2005), before returning to the Lebanon, and becoming the country's President in 2016). It was not difficult for Christoph, even with the offer, from the State, of around £10k a month, for the first year of creative development, for him to reject any notion of a tourism campaign. The former 'Garden of the Middle East' Beirut and the beautiful wine region of the Beqaa Valley lay situated in a war torn country with threats both internally and externally. Interestingly, news of this possible activity, no doubt broadcast afield by William, had led to Syrian interested parties warning Christoph and the Agency in London of potential repercussions if they pursued this course of activity. Christoph was very quick to make it public knowledge that any rumours of marketing of this nature were completely unfounded and would not be being considered let alone pursued. The dangers could not be exaggerated and indeed in 1988, William himself had had a lucky escape in West Beirut when badly injured in a car chase in which a journalist was killed.

Even despite all this William returned to London to take umbrage with Christoph for his lack of support in his tourism idea. However, he was very sick; suffering from alcoholism and Christoph along with the Director of Human Resources had to have him attended to by the Company doctor. The doctor sent William straight to hospital where he was effectively 'sectioned'. Christoph went to visit him and William, looking furtively around, and then seeing no-one of authority, proceeded to take out of his cabinet a bottle of Scotch. "Very good to see you Christoph so you'll join me in a wee dram. Pull up a chair and tell me all the news". Christoph called a nurse over, removed the bottle from William's hand and then sat down and told him in no uncertain terms, "William if you are caught with a drink in your hand whilst you are in hospital, or if you leave before you have medical clearance, or if you fail to complete the medical programme prescribed, I will fire you instantaneously on the spot. Do I make myself clear and do you understand me?" William looked shell-shocked and then mumbled,

Oh, yes, Christoph – that's perfectly clear." To his credit William did pretty well over his period of convalescence and got better and then went back to Beirut. But sadly by June 1989 William had become too much of a liability and a real risk trading off the Agency's name. Christoph decided it was time to 'part company'. Christoph ensured he got a good severance package, including a sizeable payoff, to be paid in two tranches, six months apart, and conditional upon him neither 'compromising' nor 'embarrassing' the Agency over this period. Christoph was relieved as it had taken two years out of his life to try to control unsuccessfully this likeable, talented self-destructive character. However, the 'Ghost of William Swallow' came back to haunt him when in September 1990 an unpaid American Express bill for just under £30,000 arrived on his desk. This was for travel, subsistence, meals, entertainment and 'purchases' incurred by Mr Swallow in the Middle East. This was in addition to the Company Diners Club which he had also maxed out on. Christoph had to find a way of settling these enormous overages, which he managed to do in the next year, through stringent financial control.

It seemed a long journey from his first visit to the region, when William Swallow had prevaricated over getting him an invite, to the Kingdom of Saudi Arabia, in order for Christoph to secure the appropriate visa. When Christoph got off the plane the temperature in Jeddah was over 40degrees Celsius and yet it was very early in the morning. To his amazement he was met by George Plaster whom had supposedly been fired. After freshening up at the hotel and insisting that George got hold of William and instructing him to meet him for breakfast, they sat down and talked. Christoph was furious, when after a relatively short time, and a very sketchy discussion William informed him that he had to go as he was in danger of missing his flight to Beirut. William would realise in time that he had clearly misread Christoph both as a man and as a scrupulous operator. Christoph was now in the hands of George whom he neither knew nor respected. He was slightly nervous when George said he would drive him around and show him the surroundings and the city and then proceeded to drive him out on the desert road, towards Mecca (the holy city where the prophet

Muhammad (570-632 AD/CE) had his first revelations that became the Quaran/Koran and is situated 340kms south of Medina, where the prophet completed his revelations and died) and Taif (the location of the King's Summer Palace, Shubra, situated in the mountains). So there they were on the desert road when George pulls over in the blazing heat and says, "I thought you would like to see where we shot the last spot for Neptune, featuring quad bikes racing "over sand dunes". Christoph already concerned about being in unfamiliar territory was cautious enough to ensure that he was always between George and the car betting on his speed to out run his companion, even in the sand. He was mightily relieved when they got back in the car and headed back to Jeddah.

Sorting out George Plaster and the problems he had caused was no easy matter. As Christoph quickly discovered scandal abounded in Jeddah and George was unpopular and had put the fledgling agency operation into jeopardy. Christoph finally paid off George at the end of 1987 thereby ensuring that he could do no more harm to the Agency's already damaged reputation. He also negotiated a settlement with the minor prince, in order that he did not lose face – even though he had never held the appropriate and necessary advertising licence – and would not stand in the Agency's way as it sort to expand and develop its business interests. This was a tough negotiation as it started with a demand for US$100,000, but through face-to-face discussions with the prince in Jeddah Christoph was able to negotiate a deal. He was totally transparent over what the business was currently worth and the suspicions that had reached him about his aide's behaviour, involving George. They finally arrived at an agreed figure of US$30,000. It was decided this would be paid in cash to this young refined and sartorially elegant prince in person by Christoph in London at The Carlton Tower Hotel off Sloane Street. Over a drink this was accomplished to everyone's satisfaction in a cordial professional manner and both shook hands with a smile each knowing what it had cost!

The plans Christoph had put in hand by then could now be accelerated. By moving as quickly as he did he squashed the threats and attempts by the 'Lebanese mafia' to stitch him up and force him, through blackmail - about outing the agency for operating illegally - into working with them for survival. The first thing Christoph did was to appoint 'a grown-up' whom he could trust to secure the business base. Roger Tetley had worked for Christoph before and so he knew his strengths and weaknesses and whilst a poor politician was a strong and reliable account man whom the clients could count on. He also knew he could rely on Roger to be his eyes and ears when he was not in the region. Simultaneously, Christoph identified a sponsor who not only had an advertising Licence but who would want to build a partnership out of the relationship and not merely be in receipt of a fee. Chris was adamant that he did not want anyone just being a distanced uninvolved name on a piece of paper. He discovered as he met all the clients that a small local client of the Agency involved in heavy transport vehicles had an English Finance Director, James Rennie. Seeking his advice and gradually getting his confidence and friendship Christoph discovered that a number of his bosses were involved in other major businesses. Indeed, the President of his Company was a close cousin of the then king, King Fahd (the ruling Al Saud family), while his Executive Vice–President, whom had been a soldier and an overseas diplomat, was a respected Sheikh. James arranged for Christoph to meet these two esteemed gentlemen. It became clear to Christoph that the aloof President was not really interested in being involved in such a fledgling operation and was already a sponsor of their major client, Neptune, which could pose, for him, a conflict of interests. The Vice President, even though he also had a relationship, though more detached, with Neptune, was stimulated by Christoph's vision and sense of adventure and was entertained by the idea of working with him. When Christoph offered him a management role, with a monthly retainer income and a share of profits plus the position of chairman of the Local Board, which Chris had there and then decided to create, he was totally sold. Significantly, he held the all-important Advertising Licence.

The plan had to be sold to Neptune and Christoph was able to sell the arrangement to them as a positive, as the people involved were clearly highly regarded and there would be no-one involved with the agency that was actually working with Neptune. The Senior Client

A life above the line – just!

who knew Christoph from the UK would however only condone the arrangement if he had a written guarantee that Christoph himself would be the working Senior Board Member and the signatory on the contract. Additionally, he insisted that Christoph should be totally involved in the development of the advertising on their business, approve all work and attend all reviews. And so it was before any dirt could stick or mud fly Christoph had set up a legal entity and the past was the past. Christoph's speed and dexterity had been masterful and he had outplayed his potential enemies, whom he then turned into friends, by wining and dining them, and thanking them for their understanding and patience. This transparency and sudden air of respectability unnerved them and he had no problems from the Lebanese run operations from there on in.

Those early pioneering days for Christoph proved quite a challenge. Prior to the two Gulf Wars the mood in Saudi Arabia was distinctly pro-American, with their co-development of the oil fields in Saudi Arabia, under the Aramco name. In direct contrast they were decidedly anti –British whom they viewed as arrogant, quaint, out-dated, old fashioned colonialists. Christoph had to overcome this and also learn the Arab, and especially the Saudi, customs in order to get the most positive results. Simple things like never showing the soles of his feet, especially when crossing his legs, and accepting two cups of sweetened tea, but equally always refusing the third and to bear with long silent pauses in meetings were all quickly learnt. When Christoph would get on the plane to the Middle East region he would put the freneticism of his London job and life behind him and slow everything down. This prepared him for the unwelcome reception he all too often got when he landed at the other end. Being British he could expect to be sent to the back of the queue, at Passport Control, rather like a naughty school-boy. Unlike many of his countrymen who got riled and frustrated he would smile ruefully, shrug his shoulders and carry out the instruction. His tactic was then to stand cross-armed with his eyes firmly fixed on the Officer's glass room and watch him studiously as the occupant did nothing other than have the occasional cigarette or have a conversation with a colleague. This trick would invariably work, as the Officer, conscious of being stared at, and evidently feeling uneasy, would bring Christoph forward to the front of the queue so that his papers and passport could be speedily processed. But this was only the first hurdle to overcome, the second was Customs and here often he would be asked to open his bags and then his clothes and papers would be strewn all over the place. He would then be told to repack them. Sometimes the advertising materials would be confiscated or reviewed. Throughout this ordeal Christoph would remain passive, always being courteous and polite allowing nothing to surprise or faze him.

While the seven days a week working schedule inevitably took their toll he found the fascination of his weekend job more than compensated for the physical demands. It became even more extreme during Ramadan as he could be awakened from his sleep in the hotel to attend a meeting at 2am to avoid the locals having to attend meetings during the day when they could neither eat nor drink and could be hungry, distracted or simply irritable. The locals also enjoyed putting Christoph to the test. He felt at times like he was a contestant in a 'Japanese Game Show'. Guest of honour at one banquet led to his being presented with the local delicacy of a sheep's eye. With everyone watching attentively there was no way of quietly discarding it in his pocket or coughing it into a handkerchief. It had to be done. Imagining it was simply a liquid surrounded gobstopper Christoph swallowed it in one and then took a long draft of water. At another feast, where again he was deemed to be an important guest, he was confronted with the delicacy from the other extremity of the sheep - his testicles. These were presented cooked and each resembled a small ball of calamari. Christoph convinced himself that that was what was on his plate and he proceeded to cut through them and seemingly unabashed so as not to lose face, chewed them thoroughly, drinking deep, on water. On completion of eating them he made appreciative remarks regarding their taste and expressed his sincere and deepest gratitude.

Christoph enjoyed the freedom of his job in Saudi Arabia, where, of course, he was able to call the shots. He admired their different culture, respected their religious fervour and the Shariah law based on the Koran. He acknowledged the importance of earning trust and through this friendships were established. He was fortunate enough to make many good friends across the Middle East over his time in charge of the region. In Saudi Arabia he built up a strong working relationship with his appointed Chairman and enjoyed their time working together building up a prosperous business. The Sheikh was a good friend and confidant and full of surprises and insights. At the very start he came to London to see McKillans first hand and he arrived not in his robes but in a very expensive looking, almost certainly Saville Row, handmade suit. When they went to The RAC where Christoph was a member - despite never having driven in his life - the Sheikh, normally fairly sombre, sober and quite serious, chuckled and requested a double Black Label Jonny Walker on the rocks and asked if he could see the wine list from which he then chose an excellent Chateau Beaumont. So much for the abstemious tea drinking Sheikh in his local garb! Then at the very end of Christoph's time in the region he was asked by the Sheikh to attend a dinner in his honour at his home, a real privilege in itself. On this occasion he presented Christoph with an Ebel watch, but as this was the third watch he had presented him with Christoph thought nothing of it. Imagine his shock when he got back to London and discovered the same watch in the window of Mappin & Webb, in Regent Street, priced at over £2,500.

A major problem Christoph encountered was finding good enough people to work in the region as local Saudis were impossible to hire as they didn't at that time need or want to work. They were maintained by the ruling family through grants. Women at that time were not permitted to work in the same offices as men. Good Internationals were very costly and so it was a case of relying on Egyptians, Lebanese or Asians, whom he could train to be reasonable operatives. As the business grew Christoph embarked on broadening out of Saudi Arabia and opened up negotiations with Agencies in Kuwait City, Dubai (UAE) and Cairo (Egypt) and established a registered office in Cyprus and an association with an agency in Tel Aviv (Israel). The last appointment necessitated having to have a separate passport so as not to offend his Arab hosts. Christoph loved the whole sphere of negotiation, wheeling and dealing, and he proved to be a natural at it being a tough and skilful negotiator. He secured different deals in each country always, protecting McKillans and ensuring minimum risk and exposure for them, whilst ensuring good returns and profit capabilities for the core agency. In Saudi the deal had been profit related with the costs being met by the turnover of the entity; in Kuwait it was also profit based with the local entity meeting all costs. Egypt was seen as being an 'investment for the future' and becoming the central point from which to service the whole of North Africa. In Dubai the deal was based on turnover as the local entity was receiving the business through referral from Christoph. These all worked in their own way. Cairo, however, was a drain on the resources as the press and poster media was at such a low cost and there was no television advertising at that time. It was almost impossible to make sufficient money to fund an operation of skilled personnel and meet the overheads of a local office. Yet this was what the local Thomas Healey account expected their agency to fund on their behalf, insisting on there being a local agency presence. The temporary solution Christoph came up with was to do all the work himself in London and then fly out and present the work as though it had been done locally. Even Christoph realised that this 'smoking mirrors' way of operating could only last so long, in fact only until the long arm of Internationalism stretched from Head Office in New York. Fortunately this took time and Christoph had a good run until then! Indeed, in the early stages of Dubai's development Christoph was able to convince his overlords that life was really tough there and he had to travel by camel and sleep in tents in the desert. The truth was that he was living in luxury at the Hotel Intercontinental with stunning views of the Creek, where he could watch the dhows dock and off-load their goods from Pakistan and Bangladesh on the walled shore, overlooked by emerging high rise buildings. Later when his team developed a highly successful campaign for promoting business and tourism in Dubai he had to come clean. They could see the pictorial and video evidence of the modernity of the place. But even he could not have foreseen how Dubai and Abu Dhabi would expand to become the very 'heartbeat of the Middle East' and the former the playground for celebrities – even becoming the venue, at Meydan Racecourse (opened in 2010) for the World's Richest Horse Race (until Riyadh, in KSA, somewhat surprisingly took that mantle in 2020 offering a purse of US$20million for a single race, the Saudi Cup, at King Abdulaziz Racetrack with US$10m going to the winner – the US trained and owned Maximum Security). So, so, different from his early days when the first golf course had not even been built and the Creek was just seeing the first high rise buildings being constructed and where all the concentration was around Deira and Jumeirah Beach. Racing was limited to Arab horses and Camel racing at Nad al Sheba both hugely respected and important sports, in their own right, and continues to be so. A top Australian Camel could fetch US$3Million, even at that time.

For the locals Christoph's perceived strengths were evidently his total integrity and honesty. He was offered many private side deals and refused them all. On one occasion when the business had proven both effective and profitable to everyone in Dubai he was informed that a separate private bank account could be set up in his name and money siphoned off into it. This could have been to the tune of well over £100,000. Christoph laughed and said, "What and give you a powerful card in your pack on me? – I don't think so." Continuing in this similar light hearted manner he went on "You see this ugly face of mine? Well every morning, when I get up and shave, I have to look at it and I don't ever want to say I did anything dishonest or that anyone had anything on me. I like to know I played it straight and beside I'm well paid for what I do!"

On another occasion the local management, in Dubai, came to see Christoph prior to a major new business presentation and asked him how much they should put in a brown envelope for the prospect's key decision maker. Christoph was indignant and stated sharply, "Absolutely nothing at all. If we can't win this account with the quality of our thinking and the creativity of the work we have produced then so be it." His colleagues persisted and said "Well then we won't win the business." Christoph was adamant and replied "If we can't win this business fair and square and the decision is made on the biggest bribe then these are not people we should be doing business with and I would rather not win." Christoph's colleagues were dumbfounded and highly dubious and very worried as this was potential new business they had been nurturing for some time. They knew if they could win this account it would make a huge difference to their fortunes and the reputation and image of their agency. However they also admired Christoph's confidence and belief as well as his resistance to backhanders. They went into the presentation, which Christoph led, with complete assurance and he gave them an exhibition of salesmanship and conviction, backed up by some really strong research, and attention getting creative print, poster, brochure and video work that won the day. A process that had started in November 1989 with 12 agencies briefed, had come down to just 3 agencies for this final presentation in June 1990. McKillans scored 9 out of 10, while the other two agencies both received scores of 7 – perhaps Christoph cheekily remarked afterwards they would have given 10 out of 10 with a sweetener!

When Christoph retired from the Middle East position in late 1993, the Head of the Agency in Dubai presented him with a Montblanc set of a burgundy coloured fountain pen and ballpoint and separately a gold Cross propelling pencil all which he uses to this day. They had come a long way together in just 4 years and there was much to reflect on proudly and with real satisfaction.

Certainly much changed over his term, some due to geographical conflicts, some due to technological advancements, some to a more open policy and some down to his own efforts and desire to see change happen. He had been determined in Saudi Arabia to do advertising differently and not merely to meekly accept the status quo. He accepted that advertising was viewed by the authorities as being 'educational'. What he didn't accept was that this should mean that all television advertising should be contained in a thirty minute or one hour programme of commercials with sometimes as many as 55 spots in a single half-hour. Even the greatest lover of advertising could be forgiven for being bored to distraction. Besides as an advertiser was it best to be first in break, half way through, or at the end? The number of competitive ads in a single break also further exacerbated the problem. This all seemed to Christoph to be totally ill-conceived and he embarked on a two prong attack to alter this. To achieve a

A life above the line – just!

point of difference and capitalising on the opportunity to provide better television he conceived of the notion of producing sponsored programming with strong branding throughout. In order to get the authorities on side he decided these would have to be game shows so that they could be viewed as being educational. He was able through his team to produce a number of these for different advertisers, be they in healthcare, food, confectionery or soft drinks. The questions were devised to centre on Health or Sport or General Knowledge. The result was phenomenal as the authorities appreciated better made programming that still was seen by them to be educational. The viewers particularly liked the game show format where they could win prizes such as holidays, cars and other luxuries. The advertisers benefited from the impact of the unsubtle branding and also from consumer good will towards their brands. These programmes became so popular that they were soon broadcast across the whole Middle East region.

The second arm to Christoph's strategy involved having to take on the Heads of Media and Communications, in Riyadh, the capital of Saudi Arabia. He had to persuade them that what his agency McKillans was already doing was producing material that would better educate, inform and entertain the people. He urged them that they could go further to produce and make short public information films that could be sponsored by respected organisations and tackle issues such as anti-smoking, anti-drugs, safe sex, oral hygiene etc. This was being championed by the Ministry of Youth Welfare. From this Christoph was then able to build the argument that commercial breaks could and should be looked at differently. To win this argument he was able to show them potential short sponsored spots from major advertisers in support of their national football team. It required all of Christoph's persuasive skills and tactical nous to get the authorities to agree with him. They needed to see the benefits in terms of quality of the messages, the professionalism of these ideas and the involvement of advertisers in financing and promoting good and necessary causes. The line between the view of the religious leaders and the communicators was a very fine one that had to be trod most carefully. Bear in mind that this was a religion that believed in a car crash involving a Westerner and a local Arab the Westerner would always be to blame as if he had not been there the accident would not have happened. An indisputable fact! Additionally, the normal tools of research and consumer feedback were useless and suspect. In research consumers always seemed to utter what they thought the moderator wanted them to say and hear. But, Christoph never gave up and his persistence finally paid off when he was granted access to the actual Minister for Communications, Information and Media. A series of hardnosed discussions took place and his fervent belief in what he was doing and the Department's view that things had clearly improved dramatically, meant he was listened to. They liked the fact that he asked nothing from them except concessions and was prepared to offer workable solutions and innovations at his own Agency's cost. The fact that these proposed solutions made sense, in the end, led to the structure changing, from one programme of consecutive ads to commercial breaks, as were familiar in the Western world. There were unsurprisingly conditions such as the role of women – they had to be covered and could only be featured in advertising that was relevant specifically to and for them.

With this significant win under his belt Christoph then started to produce commercials locally featuring Saudis. This too was acknowledged by the Authorities, as it showed to them a commitment in doing things specifically tailored for them and by them and were not just re-edited foreign imports. Christoph was clever enough to give the credit for this to the Authorities in the entire PR that ran fairly extensively. It was also an accolade for the advertisers' who were seen to be building bonds and relationships locally and not just seeking to sell their products. These seemed like major wins at the time, and indeed they were, but by the time he left the region pan regional campaigns were running, local offices were no longer essential and with the internet everything became global.

Indeed, in 1990, the first Gulf War took place and for the first time a war could be watched live as it unfurled before one's very eyes. Christoph had good reason to remember 'Desert Storm' as he made a massive miscalculation in a major meeting in London that took place on August 1st, 1990. The meeting had been convened to

A life above the line – just!

discuss the progress that had been made in the Middle East and what the programme was for the future year and what the financials were looking like. The International Management were in attendance including the Worldwide Financial Director. At that same time, it was common knowledge that Saddam Hussein had been building up a significant body of troops and firepower, including tanks, on the Kuwait border with Iraq. The Financial Director asked Christoph what he thought the prospects for war were in the region. Chris genuinely believed that Saddam Hussein would not invade as he would face the might of the Americans, British, French and Saudis to mention just a few opponents and responded that he thought it was just, as he put it, "sabre rattling on the part of Hussein". He went on to express the view that this was largely media-hype fuelled literally and metaphorically by the oil traders and producers. Talk about getting it majorly wrong! The very next day, the 2nd August, Saddam Hussein took over Kuwait in a 45 minute invasion in which nearly 600 people lost their lives in the face of 25,000 well-armed and fully trained and equipped troops. Rightly, and not surprisingly, Christoph was teased mercilessly by this gentleman over the next 10 years working together – "any predictions for tomorrow Christoph? Or are you just sabre rattling?" he would jest chortling loudly. They would both laugh!

The immediate concern for Christoph when the invasion took place was for the welfare of his staff, especially in Saudi Arabia where Saddam Hussein had directed and fired his SCUD missiles, and Kuwait City which he had captured with relatively little resistance, but where Christoph's people had had to go into hiding. As soon as it was permissible Christoph took a flight out to Kuwait and then from there went on to Saudi Arabia to ensure everyone was alright and that they had what they needed. A black pall of thick smoke with flying debris greeted him in Kuwait City as Christoph realised that Saddam Hussein on his retreat had dynamited and detonated all the wells in the Burgan Oil Field (second largest in the world) and also the Wafra Oil Field. Many of these were still burning freely as they had not yet been capped by Red Adair and his team. Along the roadway from the badly burnt airport were the shells of Iraqi tanks, armoured vehicles and trucks, which had been damaged or destroyed by the allies, in their counter attacks. Many of these had been brought together around the perimeter of the airfield. Christoph also saw a compound where more transporters and vehicles were bombed out in their failure to get back to Iraq. Kuwait City itself had been badly damaged and many former Hotels, Government buildings and Palaces all bore the scars of invasion, offensive action and occupation. Fortunately, his team were all safe and were delighted to see Christoph and receive his assurances that as a matter of priority the funds would be put in place to reconstruct the agency and make it properly equipped and fully functional. He also guaranteed the staff their salaries to tide them over the period of recovery and the absence of income from advertisers, whom he knew would be slow to come back and invest.

As for Saudi Arabia fortunately everyone had got back safely to Jeddah and as such had been out of range of the SCUD missiles. Unsurprisingly, as in Kuwait, advertisers had lost confidence and belief in the region and were slow to come back into these markets. It did happen and by 1999, less than 10 years later, there was an annual growth rate of 10-15% and the regional spend by advertisers was in excess of US$600m, with the Kingdom of Saudi Arabia making up some US$245m of this total. Even just 3 years after Saddam Hussein's invasion the growth had come back and the expansion plans were in place. It was at this juncture that Christoph felt he had got the agencies in shape with talent and good people and he was leaving McKillans with a strong base in the region from which to grow.

The Middle East had suited Christoph's cavalier 'can do' attitude. His entrepreneurial skills and the absence of a controlling management gave him the ideal platform to get things done. He knew he had wanted to do things differently, break the mould and make things better. It had been exciting, challenging and hugely rewarding. Things had not always gone according to plan and some events had been way beyond his control. Christoph would look back on those pioneer days with pride. He had achieved much, developed a region, built teams, grown in knowledge, established long-lasting friendships and built trust. Above all they'd had a hell of a lot of fun doing it!

A life above the line – just!

However, his expanded international assignment into Central Africa was a different story altogether. The Senior McKillans Management had seen this as a logical extension to Christoph's Middle Eastern brief and remit. They had no clear or apparent reason for doing this – other than the fact that no-one else wanted to do it or was deemed suitable. It was arguable that North Africa was Arabic in influence, religion and in some cases culturally. Indeed, Maghreb ('place of setting' relates to the countries north of the Sahara desert, west of the Nile and in line with The Atlas mountains) and Mashriq ('East rising' - as in the sun – relates to those countries East of Egypt and North of the Arabian Peninsula) are by origin Arabic words.

Christoph loved Cairo. It was totally mad and frenetic. Back in the early 1990s every car seemed to be a beaten up Fiat 500. On three separate visits he encountered what can only be described as 'unforeseen circumstances' in these cars driven in a manner akin to dodgem cars at a fair. On the first trip, to Egypt, Christoph was coming in from Cairo's airport when the car started to overheat and steam and smoke were arising in growing amounts accompanied by ever louder hissing sounds of complaint from under the bonnet. Eventually the driver, who by now could no longer see out of the windscreen, informed Chris, not totally unexpectedly, that he would need to stop to let the engine cool down. Chris watched as endless supplies of dirty water seemed to be being poured into the radiator, from a vast container extracted from the boot of his car. On closer inspection the radiator seemed to have become riddled with holes and now closely resembled a well-used kitchen colander. After some twenty minutes the temperature seemed to have cooled sufficiently to allow progress and the hotel was reached without further mishap. The second time driving across town the fan belt suddenly broke bringing the vehicle to a complete and shuddering standstill. The driver seemed neither concerned nor surprised but rootling around in the glove compartment he eventually extricated an item of lady's hosiery – later identified through a toothless smile to have been his wife's contribution to this ready-made mechanical solution. He proceeded to wind this thick stocking, which appeared to be at least 100 denier, around the mechanism under the bonnet. Tying a knot in the underwear provided a short term solution and substitution for a rubber fan belt. It thankfully lasted long enough to get Christoph to his destination without further stoppages. The third Fiat experience was again on a ride into town from the airport and perhaps unwisely he had got into a particularly bruised and battered version of the Fiat 500. It looked like it had done a number of rounds with the stock car fraternity and taken quite a hammering. Even the door when he got in did not close properly and Christoph was advised by the driver to hold onto the handle pulling it into him. This was easier said than done as the pilot clearly had been watching far too much Grand Prix Formula One Motor Racing as he seemed to take great pride in throwing his car around at breakneck speed down the rough and poorly maintained highway. Christoph found himself tossed from side to side sprawling across the seat and struggling to hold his footing whilst all the time purposefully trying to hold onto the handle of the door to avoid an expedient exit. The added complexity to Christoph's plight was that he had ascertained that the floor beneath his feet was a rust bucket and he alarmingly could see the road rushing past just inches away from his foothold. Pressing down hard did not seem to Christoph to be a particularly good option. The relief at arriving at the hotel was not inconsiderable. As he slowly unwound his hand from the door handle which gently creaked opened on its own, he felt, rather like the car itself, he had been a punch bag for a heavyweight boxer. It had been one of the more exacting journeys in Christoph's life with not much of a safety net let alone a safety belt!

But there was something truly magical about Cairo with its sprawling untidiness and dishevelled buildings and narrow unkempt roads, its beautiful palaces, (the Abdeen and Manial to mention just two) the magnificence of the Nile, the Giza pyramids on the outskirt of the desert and the wondrous museums (Museum of Egyptian Antiquities; Gayer-Anderson Museum, Egyptian Museum, The Coptic Museum, The Museum of Islamic Art, to select just a few!).The spectacle of over 12 million people gathering in this hectic place with their differing religious views in markets and rough brickwork housed streets was truly astounding. One of Christoph's most memorable trips was taking a camel round the pyramids from the suburb of El Giza and seeing the Sphinx for the very first time. Christoph felt himself transported to a different time and age as he beheld these awesome structures that held so much history of a great former dynasty (the tombs of three pharaohs of 4th Dynasty circa 2515-2465 BCE). As uncomfortable as the camel was as a means of transport he weighed up its advantages over the local Fiat 500s and realised there really wasn't much to choose between them!

Cairo was also the first time and place that he had ever been arrested by the police. Amusingly Christoph was not even visiting Egypt on this occasion but merely changing planes at Cairo International Airport having flown Egyptian Airways from Jeddah on his way back to London. He was scheduled to transfer there on to a British Airways flight. However, when they touched down at Cairo he found himself along with six other passengers taken off the plane by a military police escort, arrested and put into custody at the airport. The cells were wired cages, with visibility on all sides, giving a total lack of privacy. Outside stood or sat a number of rifle carrying guards or members of the military police. Some of Christoph's companions became quite distraught and concerned about this situation. Christoph was not fazed at all and spent most of the time reassuring the more emotionally upset that they had nothing to worry about and they would be totally safe. The fact that he knew the country and had been there many times gave them some comfort, hope and optimism. He tried to convince them that they were highly unlikely to be hostage victims to be ransomed or negotiated over in an exchange deal between the respective countries. Over time each of the 'captives' were questioned in turn and then returned to their cage. When it came to Christoph's examination the military officer in charge, in a small bureau, wanted to know why he was travelling via Cairo and not direct from Jeddah to London. Christoph explained that he wanted to be back in London, for business meetings, the next day and there were no direct flights flying from Jeddah to London that particular afternoon or evening. The Officer in charge had his passport and tickets so he knew this was the case, or at least could easily ratify this explanation. Nevertheless he continued to probe Christoph seeking to uncover some plot or great plan, where none obviously existed. Christoph was used to this style of persistent questioning from his Saudi experiences. He just sat back relaxed and quietly answered the barrage of questions. Finally, he was asked why he showed no fear worry or concern about his predicament. Christoph smiled nonchalantly and replied telling him that he knew he had done nothing wrong or untoward, his office could vouch for his story and they knew his movements. He also pointed out that he was a regular visitor to Cairo on business and that he had established an operating office there. Christoph did however point out that this might not be the best form of PR, especially for his co-prisoners, who were frightened out of their wits, for a country that was so dependent on tourism for their economic well-being. None of them were criminals and none were planning on extending their visit, or indeed were even scheduled to stay in Cairo, but were simply using Cairo as a place to change planes. No answer was forthcoming to this but the officer simply smiled at Christoph, shrugged his shoulders and then had him returned to his cage.

By the time he got back his 'co-passengers' were expressing concern as to the whereabouts of their luggage and personal effects. Christoph was able to placate them and assure them that their belongings would be fine as the Egyptians would not want to create an International incident with so many people involved. It was getting very hot, stuffy and claustrophobic, which added to the discomfort of being cooped up like chickens. In time water was brought in a jug, which Christoph refused, as he had a policy of only ever drinking bottled water with sealed caps when outside Europe. He just sat on the floor closed his eyes and thought about the scrapes he seemed to get into and smiled ruefully to himself. He even nodded off for a while and was brought round with a start when he was told to get up by a guard. He and his co-conspirators were shepherded out of their confinement given their papers and passports and then were led under heavy guard supervision across the now dark and barely lit deserted airport to a massive hanger. Here they were told, without any guidance or assistance, to find their luggage and then reconvene at the entrance. Given that the hanger was

A life above the line – just!

packed with apparently errant suitcases it could have been a case of finding a needle in a haystack. Some of the passengers looked dismayed. Christoph suggested they split up and as soon as anyone had located relevant tags or better still their own luggage to call out as the others would almost certainly be in the same place. This plan galvanised the team and the task was then implemented with enthusiasm as each wanted to be the discoverer. After a relatively short time one of the group called out having found his suitcase and sure enough all the luggage was situated close by. Once everyone had retrieved their bags they marched as a solid unit to the front entrance, where the guards awaited them. Surprisingly, the soldiers did not even bother to check whether the right people had the right luggage. They led them straight to the Departure Terminal, where once they were inside the soldiers then departed. Greatly relieved the group shook hands as though they had bonded over this experience. Some even thanked Christoph for keeping their spirits up and remaining so calm in the face of adversity. Christoph nodded, bid them farewell and set off to find a flight to London. As luck would have it the BA flight had been delayed overnight and so he was able to check in and board at 8am. Christoph felt a little bemused, exhausted but satisfied that he had got through this episode and kept everything intact – not least of all his marbles and his luggage!

This was only the first of his arrests in Africa. The others took place in Lagos Nigeria. Christoph's first encounter with the Nigerian Police came when he was travelling with James Mutella, the CEO of McKillans' affiliate, Moonshift. A blockade had been erected in the street and James Mutella's car was pulled over. There was evident dislike on the faces of the police. This may have been envy for the smart modern white Mercedes Benz, which clearly suggested affluence, that James drove, or it could have been a tribal difference that they distinguished. It could even be that what they saw was a local black man whom had seemingly befriended a white colonialist. It may well have been all three as both James and Christoph were roughed up by the police, seeking to goad them into a reaction. Both remained calm and detached and took the pulling, pushing and body punching without retaliation. There was much anger being displayed, a lot of gesticulations and considerable shouting, especially directed at James. Christoph was smart enough to realise that he could contribute nothing to this discourse being carried out in front of him, in 'Pigeon-English' where only some words were discernible to a pure English speaker. He remained silent. He tried to remain dignified and positive throughout this affray, which given the heavily armed nature of his assailants was probably a sensible course of inaction! In time after all the papers had been thoroughly, one might even say microscopically, checked and considerable DASH, bribe money, had been handed over they were permitted to carry on their journey – bruised, angry and licking their wounds but at least alive.

The next occurrence with the police was altogether more alarming. This came at the end of a very long and deeply frustrating day. Christoph had been seeking to find a reputable research company that could provide reliable data of different sectors in the market. This had proven to be well-nigh impossible and the information was apparently not available. Christoph had also been looking for competent moderators that he judged to be trustworthy and personable and who could undertake consumer groups among women. This too had proved to be a fruitless venture. So by the time he and his colleague, Bob, had decided to call it a day they were both tired and irritable. The last thing therefore that Christoph needed was to be pulled over in their chauffeur driven car. Chris apart from the courteous salutary greeting with the driver in the morning had exchanged no words with him all day. The car ground to a halt and curiously Christoph was the only person instructed to get out of the car. As he climbed out Bob who knew how angry and tired Chris was said to him, "Christoph just give them the money and whatever you do don't be a smart arse." Chris smiled at him wickedly and responded, "No way!" He was confronted and surrounded by six young policemen armed with rifles one of which, an old bolt rifle, was pointed at his head. He was spun round roughly and made to lean against the car with his legs spread and his arms on the roof. He was body searched for a possible concealed weapon all the time being harshly manhandled, jostled back and forth, as his assailants

A life above the line – just!

laughed. After this somewhat denigrating and unedifying examination he was allowed to turn around and face them. Most of the police felt they had had their kicks and were lees interested in Christoph but the one with the rifle at Christoph's head pressed it even harder against his temple. He was a very jumpy, menacing and angry looking individual with an obvious hatred of white and possibly more specifically British people. Almost spitting out the question he demanded, "What have you got for me?" Clearly he was looking for Dash (bribe money) but Christoph totally deflected this intention and replied, "Well here is my passport" presenting it to him. The police officer thinking the money might be contained in this flicked through the pages, before realising there was no money concealed with in the sheets. One of his colleagues looked at the photograph and compared its likeness to that of the man before him and once satisfied handed it back to Chris. The angry young man pressed on excitedly, "Yes, but what have you got for me?" Again Christoph chose to ignore the monetary demand behind the question even despite catching Bob's ashen face in the car mouthing 'just give him the god-damn money'. Instead he took out the official paper that legitimised his doing business in Nigeria as an associate of Moonshift. This paper was unfolded and held up for the young officer to read by another colleague which from a cursory glance once again revealed that it too contained no money. This paper too was then handed back to Christoph. Now the young officer was getting even more irate and asked even more brusquely, "What have you got for me?" with real emphasis on 'me'. Christoph by now was feeling in control and completely relaxed even though he knew that the bolt could jump out of its holding and release a bullet straight into his head. He took out one of his business cards and handed it politely to the police officer stating simply, "Well, this is who I am." The man looked at the card with total disdain and his colleagues laughed at the stupidity of the white man and the failure of their colleague to get his message across. They started to walk away leaving Christoph with just one furious policeman, who clearly felt he had lost face with his colleagues. Christoph folded his arms and stated "Now let me tell you why I'm here." And with that he proceeded to give the man a lengthy monologue about why he was in

C. P. (Charles Pierre) Altmann

Nigeria and Lagos in particular and what he hoped would be achievable between the various people he was working with. Eventually even this officer had to concede he had lost this battle and was now tiring of the boring, tedious monologue. So he ended up hitting Christoph across the head with the rifle barrel and then angrily instructed Christoph to get back into the car. He then walked away to join his colleagues down the road. The driver who had said virtually nothing all day turned right round in his seat and looked Christoph in the face, then smiled and nodded before stating, "Man – you're one cool fuckin' dude." Before Christoph had time to answer Bob replied "No, one fucking idiot." At this point they all laughed and headed back to The Sheraton Hotel in Ikeja in much better spirits – many more of which were consumed at the bar as they relived this bizarre episode and how Christoph's boring presentation had won the day!

Encounters, with the police, were one thing, but being kidnapped in Nigeria was quite another. Christoph had already heard of kidnaps in the highly corrupt and extremely dangerous Lagos Delta area. He knew this was not an uncommon event back in the 1990s. Companies such as Shell, Unilever and Procter & Gamble could all testify and vouch for this. The key for Christoph was not to become just another statistic with a small column mention in The Times of another Englishman, or white man, found naked without any possessions or worse still discovered dead in the scrubland. He later acknowledged that no-one knows how they will react in a crisis or a war situation or when kidnapped. Some people are naturally brave and courageous, some foolhardy, some find an inner strength they never knew they had and some have an inherent survival instinct. There are others who find anger a motivator while others simply find the resolve to survive and get out alive and ideally in one piece. But there are also those who bottle it or break down crying and become quivering wrecks, even pissing or crapping themselves. None of these very different reactions should be judged as everyone Christoph knew were different and only when one is in the situation does one find out how one will react under this kind of pressure. In Christoph's case he was fortunate to keep his wits about him, ride his luck and escape the worst with a modicum of bravado and a considerable amount of bull shit/hutzpah.

His story started on August 19th 1992. Christoph had flown into Lagos on a delayed British Airways flight. This meant that by the time the plane landed and the passengers had disembarked it was well after 10pm locally. There had been the usual, and now to Christoph the familiar, bad body smells and bedlam at the luggage carousel. This combined with the acrid smell that always seemed to hang in the Lagos air. All the jostling and banging sounds only contributed to Christoph's feeling of exasperation and fatigue. In those days the local currency, the Naira, could only be obtained on arrival at the airport and then had to be exchanged before departing the country. When changing money at the monetary exchange everyone received a docket showing how much had been changed and at what rate. This docket had to be resubmitted with any remaining Naira, which would be exchanged, at the airport prior to leaving the country. The hope always was that in the interim period the currency had not been devalued dramatically. This had happened to Christoph, on a prior visit, when the Naira had lost 50% of its value in a single day. On this occasion however Christoph was not thinking straight being so tired plus he was anxious to meet up with James Mutella and get to the hotel for a good night sleep. In his befuddled state he forgot to collect the docket of exchange.

Finding James outside with a welcoming smile was a relief. After checking in to the hotel they went to the bar and had a drink to catch up on news and the major presentation that Christoph was scheduled to make the following day to all of Thomas Healey's local management. Spotting how tired Christoph looked James suggested they call it a day and that Chris get to bed. At the entrance to the Hotel they bid each other goodnight and James confirmed he would pick him up at 9am. Christoph went up to his room slept soundly and undisturbed.

The next morning Christoph was down in the foyer shortly before 9am. At 9.05am one of the lobby attendants, a bell-boy, approached him accompanied by another man, who asked for Christoph by name, addressing him as Mr Aitkins. This man then informed him that the 'Director' was tied up in a meeting and he had been sent to collect him and bring him to the office. Given the time, the fact that the man had addressed him in person by name and the plausibility of the excuse, Christoph had no reason to be suspicious. Once they got outside the hotel entrance another man came over and offered somewhat insistently that he take Christoph's work bag which he then put in the boot of the car. Christoph assumed he was the driver which indeed he was. Christoph sat in the back while the two men sat in the front of a small Fiat car. To begin with nothing seemed untoward. It was only when Christoph became aware that they were not heading in the direction of the office that he became concerned. His worries and suspicions were then confirmed when one of the men asked to see the money docket he should have received at the airport. Instantly Christoph appreciated he was in a spot of bother. He calculated that his three main priorities were firstly to stay alive, secondly to retain his passport and papers and thirdly to get back to the hotel. Christoph explained what had happened the night before but without informing them how much money he had changed into Naira as he realised he might need these at some juncture. He was informed that what he had done was a very serious matter and as he did not have the transaction slip they would have to take him to their Head Office where their Director would need to speak with him, and to determine the appropriate fine and penalty to impose upon him. Christoph was not unduly worried about this as he could see this was just a ruse and he was part of a scam. The non-driver then asked Christoph what monies he was carrying on him as they would need to make a note of all the cash he had and ensure via their serial numbers whether they were legal tender or not. Here they got very lucky as Christoph was carrying much more money than normal as he was due to go on holiday the day after he returned to the UK. As such he had French francs 2,810 (circa £310) and United States Dollars 420 (circa £225) and £65 in Sterling. The passenger in front pretended to make a note of all these currencies while his driving companion spent the entire journey complaining that this was an encumbrance, as though it was on Christoph's volition, meaning that he could not be with his sick sister at the hospital. He clearly viewed Christoph as a 'nuisance factor' and was evidently not a happy or contented employee. In a further

A life above the line – just!

attempt to worry Christoph the passenger informed Chris that having failed to obtain the correct papers this could have meant that he might have been arrested overnight in the hotel, had a room-by-room check been carried out. This was he stated a regular occurrence normally executed by internal hotel Security, Land Security or by the police. All these fear tactics and threats had no effect on Christoph, who knew they were complete bullshit, but he nodded along apologetically but saying little or nothing.

Of course by now Christoph was fully aware of his predicament and that he had been abducted. He subtly concentrated on identifying landmarks and roundabouts on their journey. He also watched the height and flight path of the airplanes flying in and out of Lagos Airport to determine where they were in relation to the airport. Additionally, he resolved to play along with their game and made them think he thought they were plain clothes security people working for Inland Security.

Eventually they arrived in a wide but quiet residential street where at the end in front of them sat a large high walled building with an array of satellite dishes on the roof. The car was parked up close to the gates of this building and Christoph was instructed to get out. However, he refused to move forward to the the building until he had his Land's End bag returned to him from out of the boot. After a somewhat heated exchange they conceded and his bag was returned to him. They clearly wanted to avoid a fracas that might attract notice in the street. It was probably at this juncture that Christoph should simply have attempted to make a run for it. However he had to consider that there were two of them and whilst he knew that one was carrying a knife in his belt he was uncertain as to what arms the driver had, if any. Anyway the opportunity was missed and Christoph allowed himself to be guided through the gate where he was confronted by a compound courtyard with about 10 rifle armed militia. He noticed there was even a guard house. Christoph was ushered up a flight of steps on the outside of the main building and into a small dark room where the curtains had been drawn across and where he was sat down surrounded by 4 guards. He was close to a television where CNN news appeared to be blaring forth. The sound was presumably turned up to drown any conversation or cries for help. After what seemed like an interminable amount of time but was probably only a few minutes his two original escorts entered the room accompanied by a large imposing man dressed in fine blue and white patterned cotton robes. This was clearly 'Mr Big' (alias 'The Director'). Christoph surprised everyone by standing up, turning down the television volume and moving forward with his hand outstretched to greet 'Mr Big'. The armed 'goons' were completely taken aback and nonplussed and looked furtively at each other wondering what to do and whether this was a possible assault on their boss. As a purely natural gesture the top man held out his hand which Christoph shook vigorously. Good humouredly Christoph said, "Good morning Sir, thank you so much for giving up your time to see me and I apologise most profusely for any inconvenience I may have caused you and your security!" Mr Big seemed totally befuddled and even more so when Christoph went on "May I say how enormously impressed I am in your homeland security and vigilance in Nigeria generally and in Lagos in particular." Mr Big was looking quizzically at Christoph not sure as to whether this man before him was totally all there, barking mad or was for real and being serious. He cautiously responded to Chris by saying that it was a matter that could take some time to resolve satisfactorily and to create the appropriate paperwork and that he would have to wait for this to be undertaken. Christoph seizing the initiative stated, "Sir, I don't think that will be necessary as since you have my currency already if I leave these with you, your people can complete the documentation and then at your convenience one of your able bodied men can drop it off at my hotel." Once again Mr Big was perplexed and now he was uncertain as to whether Christoph was playing a game or was a totally naïve idiot or if he genuinely really did think that he was Head of Inland Security. But before he could make up his mind which of these options was most likely Christoph went on to say, "Oh and I shall be meeting with Mr Nezeribe this afternoon and I will be sure to tell him of your efficiency and concern for foreigners visiting Nigeria and would be delighted to put in a good word for you personally if you would think that could be of any benefit?" The name Mr Nezeribe seemed momentarily to flummox Mr Big who stutteringly asked,

"You know Mr Nezeribe? ……And you say you have a meeting with him this afternoon?" "Oh, most certainly, Yes" responded Christoph going on to state, "We have a session to discuss the marketing and communication of his campaign to become Governor of this region and because of this time for me now is of the essence." What neither Mr Big nor his henchmen knew was that Christoph had simply got the name of Nezeribe from posters and pictures of this man that were plastered all over telephone kiosks, market stalls and bus shelters along the roadside.

'Mr Big' then politely asked Christoph to sit down and then with a further glance at Christoph he left the room with the original two abductors. Christoph could hear them talking but could only discern the odd word such as Sheraton from the Pigeon English dialect being used. When Mr Big came back into the room and Chris once again stood up he came over to him and informed him that one of his men would accompany him back to his hotel and as he had suggested the appropriate paperwork would be delivered to his hotel later that day. His tone was almost deferential as he clearly now suspected that Christoph was seemingly well-connected, carried influence and clout and was not just another eccentric English businessman. Christoph thought to himself 'so far so good'.

However, when Christoph saw that his companion was to be the mean looking henchman dressed in a vivid green close fitting t-shirt and bearing a large knife who had initially duped him in the hotel foyer he realised his troubles might not yet be over. This man had a hard mean face, with tribal incisions on both cheeks, and showed an abject dislike for this white man and quite probably any international travellers. Nevertheless once they were outside the compound Christoph felt he had evened the odds and he just needed to keep a wary eye on this malevolent character, especially if he drew his knife. He had no doubt in his mind that his companion would have no hesitation in using it. When they got to the main road which was a fairly busy highway with three lanes in each direction, split by a central reservation, this character, rather than stopping a cab, simply stepped into the busy thoroughfare and stopped a clapped out dark brown Ford. He then offered the driver 40 Naira but the driver wanted 50, to take them to Ikeja. The driver agreed to do this and Christoph was pushed into the back. Christoph was aware of the very circuitous route that his captor was instructing the driver to take. Initially Christoph thought this route was planned to confuse Christoph ensuring he would not be able to ever find his way back to the compound where he had been but when the driver was asked to stop the car on a long narrow road where both sides were surrounded by high growing sugar cane he became rather more suspicious and fearful. Christoph was aggressively instructed to get out of the car but this time he refused. He had had enough. Despite verbal abuse and strong language with threats about how he had to meet another Government official there Christoph remained static. He was not moving. Steadily the henchman became more menacing and annoyed and by now was pulling and even punching at Christoph but his blows were only falling on Christoph's Land's End bag. Then, much to the worry and concern of both the driver and Christoph he drew his knife, but his thrusts with this weapon came to nothing in such a confined area and Christoph was easily able to parry these. This whole commotion and the sound of the aggressive assailant's voice had drawn a crowd of people who suddenly emerged from the plantation and surrounded the car, watching with obvious interest, intrigue and bewildered fascination. This seemed to panic the would-be assailant and he decided he would have to leave empty handed and certainly with neither Christoph nor Christoph's possessions. He went round to the driver's side and made him promise, under a penalty of reprisals, to say nothing about what had occurred. The driver quite sensibly stated he had seen nothing and therefore there was nothing to report. With that the man ran into the crowd and disappeared.

A somewhat bewildered and terrified driver turned round and faced Christoph and asked tentatively, in a somewhat shaky voice "What was all that about?" Christoph asked him how good his English was and once he had it confirmed that the driver had formerly been an English teacher Christoph asked him to drive him back to the Sheraton in Ikeja. He promised to tell him the story in full on the way there, with the added incentive of a good payment on arrival. The crowd outside the car, realising the show was over had started to disperse and the driver was able to make his way easily down the road. Christoph gave him the bare bones of the story which did not seem to surprise his companion. In fact he spent most of the journey bemoaning his own bad luck and the failure of having had any real opportunities in life and how he was now a poor struggling individual. Christoph felt the demon drink must have been the route of his problems as he was clearly an educated man with exceptionally good English. For him this was going to be a good day as he was going to receive double payment for a journey he had admittedly undertaken without much say so. When they got back to the Sheraton Christoph gave him the equivalent of US$40 in Naira that leaving him with just $10 worth. The driver was overjoyed and became completely animated getting got out of the car laughing, thanking and hugging a slightly embarrassed Christoph. He finally got back into his beaten up Ford and Christoph watched him drive all the way down the approach road with a rueful smile. He had, after all, got him back to civilisation and safety.

There were a number of ramifications and consequences that arose from this episode. Christoph was livid as he had deduced that the bell-boy or porter at the hotel had been in cahoots with the people from both the airport exchange and with the gang that had abducted him. He took the matter up with the Manager of the hotel who was deeply shocked and apologetic offering him the world by way of compensation and assuring him the perpetrators would be singled out and dismissed. Christoph agreed with this course of action but he also wanted assurances that the security would be beefed up at the hotel. He proposed that all number plates should be recorded and logged while all guests and visitors should be asked to show valid ID and that there should be CCTV installed in the foyer and car park. With the assurances given that these steps would be taken he then asked for the Manager to contact Moonshift. When he got through Christoph spoke to James and asked if he could come and pick him up so that this time he could ensure he arrived safely at the agency!

When James arrived he immediately asked why he hadn't been there when he came to pick up Christoph earlier that day. Christoph gave

James a brief synopsis of what had befallen and assured him he was fine. They both agreed that in future all employees including Christoph and himself would have Moonshift ID cards, which would have to be presented on any occasion they were picking up or collecting personnel. James did not feel Christoph should make the presentation after such an experience but Christoph insisted. He did ask that absolutely nothing was said about his adventure until after all the Thomas Healey clients had left. By now the adrenalin was pumping in his veins and the challenge of a presentation was just what Chris felt he needed. And so it was the local clients and his agency's colleagues knew absolutely nothing of what had befallen Christoph. At the end of the meeting the clients expressed appreciation of his time, input and creativity and were highly complementary of the style, delivery and content. Christoph himself felt he had pulled it off especially as nobody present had an inkling of the preparation he had had! When the story of his kidnapping had got around the agency people were just amazed that he had been so relaxed in the meeting. They treated him like a hero and with a new found respect and a bunch of people he already regarded well truly bonded in friendship.

Once the presentation was over James Mutella called Christoph into his office and over a drink asked him for a fuller version of the events. They discussed the option of reporting this incident to the police but both felt that the level of corruption in the police force, at that time, made this an unwise route to pursue. Indeed, there was even a fear that the police might actually tip-off the gang. James did however insist that Christoph report the events to a good friend of his who was Air Provost Marshall for the Nigerian Air Force and based in Lagos. This gentleman insisted that Christoph come down to his base and meet with him and his security team. When Christoph arrived he was shown into a room and was confronted by three officers in full military dress with medals and stripes while at either end a plain clothes man sat at a long trestle table. The Air Provost ushered Chris to a chair in the middle of the room facing them and asked him to recount his story in as much detail as possible. This he duly did but he could see little surprise and even less interest in his tale. There was almost a look of 'well it was your own bloody fault' about their demeanour. However, things changed dramatically when Christoph played two trump cards. Looking straight at the Air Provost Marshall Christoph asked, "Would I be correct in my assumption that you were trained in Kaduna?" This took the man completely by surprise and when he confirmed to the affirmative, Christoph went on "And would I be correct in my assessment that you were trained by Wing Commander Martin Malbeck?" The Air Provost was amazed and stated that he had indeed been taught flying under the tutelage of this man, Malbeck. "Well gentlemen Wing Commander Martin Malbeck is my cousin, through marriage to his wife Pamela, whom you probably also know or can at least recall." The Air Provost responded by saying he remembered both with great affection and held them in the upmost regard.

This alone had been quite a flyer but now it was time to play his second trump card. "Gentlemen, if you are interested I can take you back to where I was held." Now there was heightened intrigue in the room and a complete change in attitude as well as total disbelief. One of the plain clothes men said, "How can you do that? You don't know Lagos? You only come here infrequently, it's simply not possible." Christoph smiled and asked him to check whether the aeroplanes were still flying in the same direction as they had that morning. He went out of the room and shortly after returned to confirm that they were. "Right," exclaimed Christoph "Then you have nothing to lose. If I fail to find the place in three attempts then we give up." The two plain clothes men were detailed to get a car and follow Christoph's instructions and directions. Following the flight paths and remembering the landmarks and roundabouts that he had mentally noted they made the journey north of the airport. Time was important as dusk was beginning to close in. Christoph knew he would only be able to identify the location in daylight. On the first sweep he made a mistake and failed but on the second run he found the street and the building with its satellite dishes and compound, where earlier that day he had been hostage. The NAF security men were astounded and one of them agreed to maintain a watch and got out of the car, while the other drove Christoph back to his hotel. The surveillance continued for the next 24 hours by which time the NAF felt that they had enough proof and evidence that this whole operation was illegal and potentially criminally dangerous. They had followed up the leads at the airport and at the hotel and taken people into custody and were now ready to burst into the compound. Christoph was asked if he would like to join in their raid and serve as a witness as he had been so instrumental in bringing this armed militia gang down, but he declined. Christoph felt he had played his part and did not want to be in fear of his life not knowing how deep the tentacles of this organised crime operation might be.

Christoph did notice, on his next visit, that the road blocks were being carried out by the military and not the police. This was for a myriad of reasons but became operational when a senior military man in plain clothes had had his head blown off when he objected to the police treatment of him. Christoph returned a number of times in both 1992 and 1993 and still continued to stay at The Sheraton Hotel in Ikeja. On his first time back, a month after the incident, the hotel gave him their Presidential Suite with a fully stocked bar for his use. The security at the entrance to their grounds had been stepped up and cameras had been installed. Moonshift presented Christoph with his own ID card. But not everything had changed for the better. It still took him 10 payments, tips ('Dash') from the hotel to actually get on the plane returning home!

Christoph did not recount his kidnap experience to his family till some years later when he was no longer involved with travel to Africa – and by then it was just a good story. He did, however, have to produce a full report for the Agency Management, which he wrote longhand, on his way back to England and then left on his secretary's desk to type and send out, as he went off on his scheduled holiday. She was boggle-eyed as she read and typed this account and the management were aghast, reimbursed his taken money, agreed that no women should travel there alone and that kidnap insurance coverage should be put in place. In fact from October 1992 Kidnap/Ransom and Extortion Coverage, up to US$3million, was initiated for all travelling employees. A witty senior American also working on the Thomas Healey account wrote to Christoph saying, "Let this forever be known as the Christoph Aitkin amendment!"

Christoph never suffered a sleepless night over his escapade. He did write at the end of his report 'I thank God it was me and no one with a different disposition, who might have panicked, argued, resisted or simply broken down physically or emotionally with the potential to have been mentally scarred for life.' For him it had merely been a further adventure in his rich tapestry of life!

Christoph's time developing operations in Central Africa was largely exploratory. In Kenya he found a country in turmoil under the powerful and repressive military that supported the dictatorship of Daniel Moi 1924-2020, President, after Jomo Kenyatta, from 1978-2002. This had bubbled over into tribal led protestations, demands for fair elections and depressing levels of devaluation in their currency, the Kenyan Shilling. Nairobi, the Capital, and Mombasa had become increasingly unsettled and dangerous places, which always intensified in election years, such as 1992, which Christoph witnessed first-hand. What Christoph admired and liked about Kenyans was their warmth and sociability, which was in stark contrast to the bulk of Nigerians he encountered. Despite their official language being Kiswahili he found everyone spoke excellent English. Their friendliness seemed even more extraordinary to Christoph when he considered the atrocities of the past committed by the British around the Mau Mau, led by Dedan Kimathi in the 1950s (1952-1960). These events led to the country's Independence in 1963 under Jomo Kenyatta. The countryside was beautiful and productive, with tea plantations, flower growths and many fruits and vegetables. It also possessed stunning and extraordinary wildlife visible in its large protected parks and game reserves.

Christoph discovered that most of the media world and communications was controlled by the Asian Kenyans who for the most part had emanated from India. They were well informed and astute business people. The problem as he sought to find the right partner(s) to work with was the conflict of business interests, between the clients they held and the client prospects Christoph was seeking to introduce. Christoph would far rather have worked with dynamic Asian

Kenyans but in the end had to do a deal with a small Kenyan British run operation – safe and sound but not really go-ahead. Christoph was able to provide them with clients with real billings and therefore revenue for which he received media planning and buying and local creative adaptation services.

Life in Kenya, in comparison to Nigeria, was positively tranquil for Christoph and he avoided getting too close to the protests on common land, preferring to watch these unfurl from a safe distance. He did, however, have one potentially life-threatening experience. After a particularly positive meeting with the local senior client at Thomas Healey this English gentleman asked if, prior to catching his plane back to London, whether Christoph would like to visit the Kenya National Park. He leapt at the opportunity. The roadways were particularly bad made more so by heavy rains that had fallen recently and these masked the potholes that lay lurking under the puddles. With the inadequate fencing around the Park's perimeter it had meant that both lions and crocodiles had been found roaming around housing estates closely situated to the Park and not far outside of Nairobi itself. Notices warned people to stay in their cars and not to venture outside except with extreme caution. Imagine then Christoph's concern when their car came across one of these hidden potholes that broke the camshaft on their return journey. This left them immobilised and basically stuck as the persistent rain raised the water level around them. Fortunately thanks to modern communications they were able to get an emergency service to send out a four-by-four, attach a strong rope, to the fender, and tow their Volvo back to town. Both were greatly relieved and Christoph had just enough time to bid his client farewell before heading to the airport. Apart from the drama of the car he had lasting memories of having seen a black rhino and giraffes at close quarters in their natural habitat in the wild.

But Nigeria was oh so different. This vast country gained its independence from the British Empire in 1960, when the First Nigerian Speaker of the House, Jaja Wachuku took the Independence papers on October 1st. The first Prime Minister was surprisingly a Hausa tribe leader Sir Abubakar Tafawa Balewo, but his tenure was short-lived. Since 1966 until 1999, with the exception of the short period from 1979-1983, when there was a civilian leader, Nigeria has been under military control. Even today the military has considerable influence on events that take place in this country. At the time Christoph was working there Major General Ibrahim Babangida (1985-1993) was in control until he was ousted in a coup in 1993 by General Sani Abacha (1993-1999) – the latter who promptly dissolved all political parties. Christoph had discovered that Pigeon English was the most commonly spoken language, though the Hausa, Ibo and Yoruba tribes all had their own dialects. Curiously English was still the official language. Christoph came to like many of the indigenous people he met and did business with. Outside of this circle he always sensed a dislike and even hatred for the white man and there was clearly no love for the British. Christoph always felt it was a country with so much potential that had been wasted in the quest and greed for oil revenues. There was so much sadness, dirt and poverty in Lagos, where at that time, 40% of the people were living on scrubland and in abject conditions. The roads were lined with beggars, many whom had been crippled in tribal conflicts and feuds and others who had been victims of self-mutilation.

Christoph was delighted with the arrangement he had drawn up with James Mutella and his agency, Moonshift. They were a creative agency with strong personalities and serviced the needs of Thomas Healey, a particularly demanding client, effectively and professionally. They liked Christoph as they enjoyed his energy level, light touch, his sense of humour, apparent lack of fear, his braveness and his desire to teach them new skills. They recognised he wanted to train them and would only lead when they needed him to. Having won over their trust he was able to strengthen their credentials presentation, improve their selling tools and challenge their strategic thinking making this more robust and informed. He was always willing and proud proud to lead from the front for them when requested to do so.

When Christoph finally handed over the reins at the end of 1993 he felt he had done a lot to open up new regions, new markets and specific new countries for McKillans and their key international/multinational clients. He felt he had been a pioneer and had witnessed first-hand some remarkable historical landmarks which in time would lead to a rapid expansion and opening up of these markets in both the Middle East and Africa. Christoph was truly honoured to have played a small part, on the ground, to effect change; though he knew that the new technology of the World Wide Web and the Search Engines and Social Media would make this uncontrollable and unrestrictive in terms of communication. This would change the map for ever. In his pioneering role Christoph had discovered that the price of life in many parts of the world was cheap. He had wryly seen himself as 'International White Trash', to the locals, in these markets, and to his own management alike. He enjoyed the moniker, using this unflattering label and expression about himself – and he would continue to refer to himself in this way until he retired in 2001.

CHAPTER 6

Internationalism – 'The way of the world'

William Congrieve Restoration Comedy 1700 (Society's acceptance of abuse and inequality)

Nicholas Bouvier's 1953 book on a car journey, of two men in their 20s, from Serbia to Afghanistan – a voyage of self-discovery

Cambridge University definition – 'Types of behaviour and ways of doing things that would typically or generally happen to and between people'

When Christoph had joined the advertising industry in 1973 'international' was something of a dirty word. Certainly the people in the International Department or doing international jobs were looked on with disdain, by their local counterparts. It appeared to Christoph, who was not in a position to comment or criticise, that these 'internationals' were either elder statesmen, whom had done their time in the cut and thrust of the front line, or people whom had failed to impress and had been effectively side-lined or in a few cases had been moved there to avert political dissent. Often Christoph perceived they were personnel that had political nous, were not ready to be put out to grass, fired or retired, but who instead could play a role in the geographical expansion of clients' business and ensure consistency in service across markets. Thus it was these people travelled extensively and became a financial drain on the embittered local office, through their travel costs and subsistence expenses, high salaries and overheads. These local offices more often than not failed to see their true value or even their purpose and benefit to them or the organisation as a whole. What Christoph perceived was that these men, and they nearly always were men, were often bright and competent savvy politicians but were 'Yes Men' without real drive, genuine authority, much personality and little real initiative. They seemed to take other country's past or current creative work and simply adopt, or at best adapt, it for use in other markets. They were seldom able to have blame attributed to them or be held responsible. There was the seagull association about them as they would fly in, squawk a great deal, crap all over the place and then fly away before they could be held to account. Regrettably, Christoph noticed they seemed to be distanced from the regular advertising folk and were not welcomed or accepted by them. They could criticise from afar – literally – but were not contributors or initiators. At McKillans, even in the mid- 1980s, they sat on a different floor in their own area. In some ways and in many instances they saw themselves as superior simply because of the strong contacts and bonds they had at the senior level of Clients, usually at their Headquarters, which more often than not were based, in those days, in the United States. At Gris Advertising, in Christoph's earliest years, they were based at the Agency Headquarters in New York and took their instructions and orders from the Board or perhaps more likely the CEO, Chuck Deal. Some of these characters would have the responsibility to set up operations abroad and find agencies that could be acquired or become suitable partners or affiliates. Sometimes too they would train people locally and very occasionally they would be in charge of a start-up. They had graduated to be business men but were not the 'classic day-to-day suit' and were seldom creatively inclined or minded.

A life above the line – just!

In the space of just 30 years, Christoph witnessed a sea change that was truly dramatic. Early on US Businesses, in particular, were still seeking to get geographical expansion for their products and brands, following the Second World War. Then products from Japan began to make massive inroads. Finally it would be the Chinese that would rule supreme. However, as was pointed out earlier, it was technology that became the major driver ultimately in this turnaround. The world through its accessibility became an ever smaller place and this technology suddenly was in everyone's grasp. The message could now be delivered immediately and in a more and precisely targeted manner via a far more direct medium. Clients too, Christoph observed, had changed as they appreciated the cost-efficiencies of having International Hubs and Centres ('Centres of Excellence' as they somewhat inappropriately called them!). From these marketing and advertising could be controlled across a whole region, sometimes irrespective of language or culture. At times it truly was lowest common denominator work. These clients, as mentioned before, could see the cost savings both at their end and also with their suppliers, but they wanted to have the best expertise working on their behalf. Christoph saw that this regional perspective meant that individual countries could be viewed and used as test markets or as a way of adapting messages or trying out different communication to determine what might be better than their current mainstream advertising. In the former days the mantra had seemingly been 'Be focal, think global, act local'. Now Christoph perceived it had been amended to 'Be local, think focal, act global'. The worry in Christoph's mind was that this could often lead to simplistic communication, or advertising based merely on executional gizmos, devoid of a consumer insight or a strategic idea emanating from the product or the brand behind it. In effect Christoph noticed that the production techniques and their originality became the vehicle – even literally in the case of car advertising – substituting for product facts, details, and performance credentials and in many cases without any brand values or communication of their assets.

Of course too, Christoph realised the people in international had changed demonstrably. The internationals were now often the smartest people in the agencies, their strongest salesmen and often too their best financial administrators and presenters. The skill set had changed and the old politicians simply acting on the will of the senior clients and sweet talking them had gone. Christoph liked the new face of internationalism as he felt this gave a far greater canvas upon which to ply his trade. It also gave him a much larger audience to address. For him though maintaining integrity and producing ever better creative work that was effective would remain of paramount importance to him, even in this 'new world'.

Initially Christoph watched this transformation and transition from the side-lines. It was only in 1992 that he first put his toe in the water. But it would not be long before he would become totally immersed. The catalyst was when after being part of the rebuilding and restructuring management at McKillans from 1985, he felt that, 7 years on, they had lost that drive and ambition, which had been such a hallmark of their success. In its place he felt there was now complacency and arrogance. Big name hiring's became part of this which they had never needed, or sought, before. Saving accounts and the will to win at any cost had changed and now what was being seen were accounts being resigned on matters of principle and style. Christoph felt the agency's hunger was no longer there and that after so many years the same management had been in place too long. For him it was time to move on and explore new avenues. So in the spring of 1992 Christoph took the unprecedented step of resigning from the UK Management Board, where at that time he was Joint Deputy Managing Director and Joint Client Services Director.

Christoph also acknowledged that he had become restless, back home, after his experience of running the Middle East and Central Africa. There he had few if any constraints and greater freedom to determine policy and direction. Strangely he felt that the UK Agency was too parochial and myopic in its thinking and this meant that if he was to stay with McKillans he would need to expand his 'International' credentials. Perhaps he could work on the major international accounts which had the big budgets but it seemed like there were no openings for him at that time? But then timing as he well knew was everything.

A life above the line – just!

Neptune had recently moved to a centralised European Operation with regional control from a single location and though this was heavily resisted by the major local markets it was being mandated from Head Office. The brands would be split between the Company's most experienced marketers whom were expected to embrace a cross Western European approach. Not surprisingly Neptune expected its agencies to mirror this way of thinking and operating. In response McKillans set up a new centre in Brussels, Belgium, headed up by a senior US operative. Naturally, this appointee knew nothing of Europe, the region he was now in command of, and immediately sought to build a team reporting directly and exclusively to him, who could come from any of the Western European countries. The McKillans UK Management fearful of losing Christoph altogether from the organisation put his name forward to be the Number 2 in Europe. Christoph's initial impression of the US appointee was that Dick Shiltz was a man mountain, tall, with a thickly set frame, topped with thinning deep red hair and a ginger walrus moustache and piercing blue eyes behind clear plastic framed glasses. He was clearly bright, direct, business focused and well regarded by the Neptune Senior Management, from his time working on their business in the States. Dick was also a gruff, no nonsense, and inelegant person with little subtlety and even less small talk. He came across as something of an intolerant mid-western American red neck. This was so different to the refined, cultured thespian, Christoph, with his mischievous lack of respect for authority, seeking to always break the rules and always challenging in nature. Christoph and Dick were no-one's idea of an immediate fit and many thought that they would never be able to work productively together. It could be a case of oil being poured on troubled waters! But what Christoph liked about Dick was his directness, his clear ability to take on the top men and the fact that like him he was prepared to have the fight with both his own management and, as importantly, with the Clients. After a fairly short initial meeting they agreed to give it a go, besides neither had great alternatives or options at that time!

However, things did not start off too well. Dick asked Christoph what his terms for the job would be and then baulked at Christoph's demand for a £100k a year salary. Christoph also wanted to appoint an Account Director, Jimmy Firefoot on £50k. Dick requested a full justification for both and asked if there was any room to manoeuvre. Christoph was clear in his response, "No it is non-negotiable. We will be working all hours God gives us, travelling extensively and excessively meaning Jimmy and I will be away from home a great deal. No doubt too I will be writing and preparing multi-media presentations and speeches for large numbers of attendees. On the positive side I will never come to you asking for a salary increase as that is simply not my style." Dick stated that he needed time to think about this and mull it over. By the time he came back the job had already started. Dick informed Christoph that the deal with Jimmy Firefoot was fine but that he could only go to £92k on Christoph's salary. Christoph looked at him directly and said, "That's a real shame and a big mistake." Accordingly the next few weeks were strained between the two men. Christoph and Jimmy got to grips with this new way of working and meeting the key clients and determining how best to keep all the agency offices in Europe motivated and informed. When it came to reporting up the line to Dick it was kept formal, distanced, largely through printed status reports issued weekly while any actual encounters were decidedly stiff and non-cordial. Eventually Dick called a meeting for just the two of them to review progress. Dick started out by being highly complimentary in how things had been set up to show great transparency while keeping everyone informed and in the loop. He only had two negative points and the first was that he felt Christoph was 'desk managing' rather than getting out into the markets and making himself better known as a person and building familiarity with the local personnel. Christoph accepted this criticism and observation and agreed to travel to the markets more. Dick then tackled the more sensitive issue and that was that he didn't feel that their relationship was built on total trust and friendship. Christoph's response to this was direct and from the shoulder, "Dick you chose not to listen to me when I laid out my terms to you, that I stated at the time was non-negotiable. You chose to short change me and that pisses me off. As such I only have to respect your authority and report in to you but I sure as hell

A life above the line – just!

don't have to like you." The very next month, July 1992, Christoph's salary went up to £100k. He never asked for a rise and they never discussed money again though he did get an increase and bonuses. So began a partnership that would last 7 years and a friendship that would be life-long. They fought many great battles together often playing the tactics of 'good cop, bad cop'. Dick preferred the direct approach and being a straight shooter. What he liked about Christoph and his team were their presentation skills, tactics, strategic thinking, the creative output and their commitment and belief in team motivation.

As early as 1993 the newly formed team found themselves competing to save their lead Neptune brand for McKillans against one of the most popular agency's in London at that time. This agency had taken the initiative, gone to the senior clients, in both the US and Europe, speculatively pitching ideas on brands that they were not assigned to. Christoph admitted that his predecessors at McKillans had been complicit, having taken on board some woolly thinking and a strategic directive from the Head European Client, which had blown the lead brand off course and led to some very ordinary ho-hum advertising. Christoph took charge of this challenge to retain the brand. He started by debunking the client strategy as being soft and generic 'Everyday should be this good'. Christoph then worked with a top planner in the UK, whom he had had the experience of working with on Neptune before. Working through possible avenues one late night they arrived at a positioning that could be articulated and understood in just three words, 'Energy for Accomplishment'. They also went on to define the attitude of the person 'You've got what it takes inside' – be that mental, physical or even emotional. Shortly after this working with two of Christoph's favourite creatives two storyboards were developed. These he then had put into research against the current work running and when they had confirmed that this new direction appeared to be spot on and the executions had been acclaimed they were ready to present to the European Client Management. This might have been difficult but Christoph played the card of how this had been a valuable learning exercise on how to build on current thinking and move it forward. The day was won with seemingly no one losing face.

C. P. (Charles Pierre) Altmann

The threat of the other agency was seen off and they were snuffed out, though would remain a consistent and constant enemy, from there on in, keeping Christoph always on his toes, never allowing him to get complacent. The advertising when made was well–received by the markets and grew the business even in the most developed market. On this particular experience Christoph had learnt that it was possible even on a lead brand to build new meaning and interpretation out of a brand's heritage. It was also feasible to communicate this in a modern, relevant style. Encouragingly the payoff came when this brand was evolved into different market sectors, with a range of variants, giving it even more life and greater contemporaneity.

From his time in the Middle East Christoph had appreciated that major brands could be marketed cost-effectively in external activities, be that education, culture or sports. His Middle Eastern experience with programming and sponsorship he now brought to his new geographical area. This soon led to the lead brand getting involved in Sports Sponsorship with Football Championships and major Athletic Events, including, even ambush marketing, at the pinnacle of sport, the Olympic Games in 1992, 1996, and the year 2000. Christoph, being sports mad, loved this part of his job and finding teams or individuals who needed sponsorship was an added joy. He also knew it was a powerful tool for the brand. This activity was not just about the supreme athletes but working to support the sports at the grass roots level. Through 'Schools Programmes' materials and equipment could be provided that would increase learning, understanding and ultimately encourage greater participation in sport generally.

On another brand that offered a bite size offering Christoph and his team decided to move from the physical lightness of the product to the emotional light-heartedness of the product. This still used the dynamics and attributes of the physical product to achieve this but translated this into the fun that people could have with this product. Christoph knew this was a major call especially as he had opponents in the Neptune Company who had the view that this brand should be more worthy and justifiable in the granola/natural bar era. Indeed,

A life above the line – just!

the very brand's existence longer term could rest on this decision. Christoph's team under the guidance of the planner guru, Fiona Sole, fought this through both a nervous Agency Management and the Client alike. Fortunately, the European Senior Clients could see this was the way to contemporise this longstanding brand, in their portfolio. They backed the thinking wholeheartedly and despite the initial creative executions being a little wooden and a bit of a 'walking strategy' in time the advertising would evolve to be truly fun and memorable. The Neptune Company built a whole new manufacturing line on the success of this repositioning. The brand was expanded rewardingly into new markets. Christoph and his team with Fiona's strategic thinking had taken a calculated risk and it had paid off big time!

By the spring of 1995, just 3 years on from inception, McKillans had proven that their creative approach to 'Internationalism' could really work. The team led by the tough and uncompromising Dick Schiltz, ably supported by the theatrical Christoph Aitkins and the suave, debonair linguist, Jimmy Firefoot, were building a formidable reputation, not just across Europe, but worldwide. Jimmy who had, in his own backyard, been described as 'being too senior to be a junior and too junior to be a senior' proved to be the perfect foil and companion to Christoph. He had the ability to bring people along that might have found Christoph's approach too aggressive, hard-nosed or ballsy. Christoph attributed the success of his team to their ability to work closely with each of the markets. Christoph would happily give creative briefs for alternative routes and strategies to other individual markets which could then be tested out via research and where successful be run locally or regionally. This showed respect and not enforcement. He knew how to build close and valued relationships with the key decision makers in each country at both the client and agency. He never simply paid lip-service to these people but got and kept them all fully involved through regular meetings and the weekly status reports.

In the newer markets of Central and Eastern Europe, including Russia, Christoph also changed the way they were operating. Up until the new team's intervention these countries were just running old commercials from other markets or off the historical reel. Christoph insisted they back tracked and ascertained there was a need for an educational step to be undertaken and which had been missed out. As such he developed advertising that focused on the ingredients and gave people a real justification to buy these premium priced products. The results were staggering as the business quadrupled after the first two executions they made ran locally.

Showing flexibility, adaptability and the importance he gave to understanding consumer research, Christoph found that in the earlier developed markets in Central and Eastern Europe there was a transitional need between the 'Ingredients' story and the advertising that was running in the rest of Europe. The positioning for this middle ground he came up with was 'natural energy' that started out with whimsical advertising with soft messages based on the ingredients, done locally. However when the local team changed Christoph briefed the creatives for much harder hitting spots that featured real people doing real jobs and shot them in their working environment. This proved to be highly effective advertising as people could truly relate to these people doing mundane but important jobs such as bus drivers and road cleaners.

What made Christoph's team different was their commitment, honesty and the trust that they built up with local offices. This, for them, had to work both with the local agency and their local client. They never went behind the local agency's back. But also they never forgot that part of the expectation from the Central Team showing up in an individual country or at a forum, or meeting was the theatre of their presentation. This came naturally for Christoph as he was a born showman, wanted to make the job fun, exude enjoyment and make presentations that would be memorable. Interestingly, before this job, Christoph had not been called upon to do major presentations to large forums or to make speeches, but he seemed to take this expansion of his role completely in his stride – rather like the proverbial duck to water! These occasions gave him an adrenalin rush and he loved the sense of power he had with his knowing what he was presenting while the audience did not. The preparation for these major choreographic events was incredibly hard work. The character and style of the charts, visual aids, be it graphs, diagrams, graphics or accompanying slides and acetates and videos was all crucially important to Christoph. He knew if he got this right it allowed him to be outspoken, sometimes outrageous and nearly always humorous. He knew the limitations of the multi-media equipment and when things went wrong he was ready to carry on relying on his quick-wit, and ad-libs to overcome the glitches. It was reported back to him that one of his team when asked "What is Christoph going to say?" replied, "I have absolutely no idea and knowing Christoph I seriously doubt, at this moment, if even he knows what he is going to say!" It was certainly true that Christoph never made the same presentation twice as he just felt that he couldn't do justice to the content if he did.

Mind you things didn't always go according to plan. In 1994 Christoph had to stand in for Dick Shlitz and it was his first experience of making a speech to a large assembly of unknowns. This was at the National Confectionery Association of America (NCAA) with the topic having been given to him being 'International Confectionery Advertising'. This, for Christoph, necessitated flying to Orlando in Florida and staying at The Disneyland Hotel. His presentation was scheduled for Friday afternoon on the last day of the Conference. By the time he stood up most of the delegates had had enough, surrendered their pass keys and made for the hills and home. Of course Christoph surmised they may also simply have been disinterested in the specific topic, written on the agenda as 'Cross border advertising for confectionery and snack food brands.' Whatever the reasons there were only a handful of attendees and delegates in the vast auditorium which was hardly inspiring and made the whole thing what Christoph recalled as 'being a bit of a damp squib'. The only comfort was the courteous, polite and complimentary comments passed on to him at the end - possibly more out of embarrassment for the poor attendance rather than based on the merits of his speech. Certainly this was not the great start that Christoph had been hoping and looking for as he embarked on this new part of his career; that of being a public speaker.

One thing was for sure Christoph never minded being controversial and raising his head over the parapet. He firmly believed that confectionery and snacks were not bad foods in themselves but they could if eaten in excess be part of a bad diet. He strongly argued against lobbyists, medics, dentists, often two faced politicians happy to take the taxes from the companies involved but wanting to be seen on the 'good side' of the consumer as well as some 'do-gooder' elements within the media who sought to ban advertising of these products. His view was simply that if it was legal to sell the product then it had to be right and permissible for it to be marketed and communicated and, of course, advertised. Despite being opposed to smoking he applied this same argument in that category, of tobacco, as well as alcohol, soft drinks and confectionery. In the case of snack foods and confectionery he firmly believed that it was up to the Government and authorities to better educate people, in personal hygiene, about moderation and the need for a balanced diet and the importance of daily exercise. This Christoph felt was far more preferable than the knee jerk reactions, higher taxes and 'nanny state' approach that was proposed and even taken against advertisers and manufacturers of soft drinks and snack foods. He always advocated that people should be allowed to make informed choices. The increasing sedentary lifestyle, which came with computers and the games they supplied had unquestionably resulted in a lower level of exercise. This Christoph observed also coincided with successive Governments reducing the time and facilities for children to exercise within the school curriculum. Schools were not providing sufficient time for exercise of its pupils daily. Worse still local authorities and successive Governments were turning playing fields and green spaces into housing developments.

It was on the strength of Christoph's defence of advertisers and the promotion of manufacturers with sugar in their products and even defending the continued use of longstanding slogans by said advertisers that Christoph was asked to make a speech at the Food Forum in 1995. Christoph's speech was always going to be provocative and even the title caused eyebrows to be raised, 'World Trends and Consumer Behaviour in Food and the Real Killers'. The speech caused quite a stir especially as he chose to depict those foods that taken in excess can threaten our lives - as coffins. It was a punchy, upbeat, positive presentation which so delighted the sugar industry and specifically British Sugar (formerly Tate & Lyle) that they asked if they could use the content and graphics for their own use and in subsequent presentations. Christoph was only too happy to oblige.

Many senior players at Neptune were present at The Food Forum and requested Christoph to develop presentations for them to present higher up the line or at major gatherings of their teams. They also asked him to become one of the key contributors to a paper produced by the Advertising Industry defending confectionery and snack foods advertising which he did with relish.

On the subject of confectionery, at one time, each of Neptune's agencies were given a key competitor in the category and asked to produce a review of their business and advertising. McKillans was given Antonini, famed for its quality moulded products. Christoph was specifically asked to undertake the work and prepare a presentation for a meeting of all the individual country Heads of Neptune's European markets, in Brussels. Dick Schlitz, Christoph's boss, was in attendance along with all the other agency gurus in Europe. Poor Dick nearly had a heart attack going absolutely puce when Christoph compared Antonini's perfectly moulded, aesthetically pleasing products with Neptune's value for money shaped products which in the case of the latter he likened to 'turds and rabbit droppings'. If Dick had not had a recent bad skiing accident necessitating his leg being in plaster and stretched out on a stool he probably would have chased Christoph around the room and killed him there and then. The audience, however, had responded to this analogy with howls of laughter, but Dick remonstrated, "God damn it Christoph you can't go around calling your client's products 'turds and rabbit droppings' comparing them with faeces. Why have you always got to be so God damn controversial?"

In fact this presentation became so talked about that Christoph was asked to present it to the Neptune Board at the Annual Review in New York. This turned out to be one of those occasions when it was harder to present to his agency management than to the client company. Three times McKillans CEO, Ray Teflon, interjected anticipating a point that Christoph was about to elaborate or make and proffered 'his assessment' or 'considered view' and three times he got it completely wrong! On each occasion what he said was directly contrary to what Christoph was going to say and in a couple of cases actually show on his next chart. Each time, Christoph had to find a way of salvaging the situation and avoid making his own CEO look a complete arse. 'I think Ray makes an interesting point here but, of course, there is another way one could look at this…' and 'There are differing viewpoints on this aspect and it could equally be argued that…' and finally 'This is a really complex and challenging area and indeed initially many thought exactly as Ray has expressed, but subsequent analysis has shown that possibly it could be…' Christoph came out of this review meeting absolutely exhausted but also elated and contented by the complementary and positive way his presentation had been received by the Neptune Management. A senior agency colleague, also working on Neptune, from the US Office came up to him and jocularly said, "Christoph that was a masterful exhibition on how to extract your own management from their own self-made bear traps! You did that with style, panache and good grace – a lesson for us all!" He then asked him to join him for dinner and a few beers in Gallagher's' famous steak house off Broadway and another lifelong friendship was established.

Neptune's European Management increasingly turned to Christoph for lively presentations on subjects that could be potentially fairly dull. One such case was 'What makes a Brand?' This had started out as a low key presentation for the Scandinavian markets, which had requested an overview on the subject of branding. However, on the strength of its reception by the Scandinavian Management it was developed into 'a Magnus Opus' and into a full speech. It was also adapted to be a training tool for Neptune internally and indeed for McKillans. It explained the importance of brands and branding as opposed to simply being a product. It also provided a number of cases where product names simply did not travel, be that Colon Detergent, Skum Fluffy Mallows, Mukk Yoghurt, Plopps and Ploppsie Chocolates, Pschitt Lemonade or Bonka Express Coffee. During 1995 and 1996 Christoph

A life above the line – just!

and his European Client counterpart gave numerous versions of this presentation right across Europe from Russia and Poland in the North down to Spain, Portugal, Greece and Italy in the South, as well as many countries in-between. In the ensuing years it would be plagiarised by academics and other marketers – possibly the best form of flattery? It became a reference for examples and arguments and it was still being adapted, and in some countries adopted, for understanding the importance of brands and how to maintain them, in a product life cycle. Christoph knew from travelling the world that Heinz Tomato Ketchup had built up an emotional association which was far stronger than just the taste and enjoyment of a sauce.

In 1996 Christoph made two other major speeches on behalf of, and sponsored by, his client Neptune. The first was titled 'A thought provoking look at the future of Advertising' for the Biscuit and Confectionery Alliance whose forum was held in Dresden. Christoph used this opportunity to look ahead and speculate on the evolution and to some degree the revolution that would take place over the next 5, 10 and 15 year periods. He was delighted that most of what he predicted then was more than fulfilled and that the technical age and technological widespread advancements did, as he forecasted, change the industry, agencies and messages completely and forever. At this forum there had been simultaneous translations that proved a complete nightmare for the translators as Christoph, as per usual, failed to stick to the script! At the end of this presentation and speech a senior member of the Cadbury family came up to him and as good as offered Christoph a job presenting him with his card and asking him to contact him directly! He had found it as he eloquently put it 'a stimulating presentation that had provided much 'food' for thought.'

The second presentation was for 'The Marketing Week Conference'. Christoph was able to use some of the work he had done earlier, but expanded it more widely, to cover a broader remit within marketing communications. He titled this 'Alternative Marketing techniques and communication Vehicles in the Confectionery World'; not exactly snappy or catchy but explicit! He covered the wider use of the Internet, Instant Win Promotions, Product Placement in films and on television,

Sponsorship of relevant programmes and subjects, including sport, music and culture, as well as ' idents', before and during programmes; Interactive Websites and the use of Experiential media and events. Christoph's views stimulated much discussion and concern, especially when it came to control, ownership and responsibility. Christoph expressed worry that brands could be associated with concerning and less desirable material on sites and that the obvious absence of control by the providers was a genuine long term problem that the industry faced. Christoph had seen how control of the message by so many of these on line providers has proven well-nigh impossible and the damage was often done before the offensive material could be 'taken down'. Agencies, from his viewpoint, had been too slow to embrace the new technology or to obtain the expertise in-house. This would, he felt, inevitably lead to greater fragmentation of the agencies with more specialist shops and boutiques emerging, capitalising on these new and distinct media opportunities.

The difficulty for Christoph was that his reputation as a speech writer and presenter was leading to his being increasingly used for training people both at Neptune and at McKillans, which was not what he was about. He was not a professor nor an academic, or even an expert, and his content was simply there for interest, stimulation, consideration, discussion and reaction. He did not want to become removed or distanced from his real day time job - the implications of his thinking on the development of ever more relevant advertising. He did, however, accept he had a responsibility to train people and he was persuaded by Neptune to produce challenging presentations for their new marketers and junior personnel to better understand advertising, how to asses it and therefore how to produce better briefs to and for their agencies. Because Christoph was an 'outsider' he could make the training fun and interactive and involving as well as be a little irreverent. There was only one condition he insisted upon and that was that he would not give feedback or make a judgement on any individuals. That way the attendees would know they were not being assessed or reported back on and so could voice their opinions and views freely. Christoph's training programme was extended from the

UK to cover the Central European markets, the Nordics, Southern Europe and even some of the more traditional markets, like Holland, Germany and France. In 1997 he was asked if he would work jointly with an outside consultancy that Neptune was using for their Training Programmes. Christoph had huge reservations about doing this, which he articulated, as he really didn't want to be sucked into consultancy or training any more than he already had. However, in the end, he produced a presentation, entitled 'Good and Bad Advertising' with a show reel of specific cases of each, which could be continually updated, as better and more contemporary examples presented themselves, in any given market. Christoph provided mini case histories on each, also offering strategic and executional opinions behind each advertising example. The format gave the attendees the chance to question the strategy, determine the brief, evaluate the creative idea and debate and assess the merits of the actual advertising produced. This was well-received and Christoph was forced to deliver this on numerous occasions though finally refused to do it any more when he came to loathe even the best commercials on the reel! There was one radio spot that Christoph always loved and that was because in his definition of advertising he had always said 'Advertising is pictures that sell' and used the Heineken Apollo 11 Moon Landing, (July 20th 1969) radio commercial to demonstrate this point. The pictures he felt were conjured up in one's mind as Neil Armstrong fluffs the words but after having had a Heineken he gets it right –'That's one small step for (a) man, one giant leap for mankind' and ends on the brand's famous end line 'Heineken reaches the parts other beers cannot reach'.

Internally, at McKillans, he became one of the go-to annual presenters on the Agency's UK Graduate Training Programme. His session was called 'An audience with Christoph Aitkins'. Christoph liked this as he had a totally free rein and could be highly controversial as he was when he nominated Princess Diana and Saddam Hussein as examples of specific brands in successive years. This made for interest, debate and conjecture - not altogether surprisingly. Needless to say these did not travel internationally!

Towards the end of his time on Neptune, Christoph was asked

by the Company if he would work with the Head of Planning, a well-esteemed woman, at McKillans, in the UK, on a presentation about the changing face and role of women and how they were being depicted in advertising. The balance of her disciplined, simple, clear graphics and thinking, with the theatre of Christoph, was always going to be an interesting combination and balancing act. Despite their contrasting styles they put together a stimulating presentation, 'The Changing Face of Women'. Christoph edited a short film with cuts of women from advertising, featuring different depictions of women in various guises, be that working, playing, fashion, alluring, practical, right through to organoleptic. These he had cut to the track of Manfred Mann's version of the Bob Dylan song 'Just like a Woman' – both which were recorded in 1966. From the time they presented this to Neptune in the autumn of 1997 right up until Christoph's departure four years later it became a much used presentation internally and externally by both McKillans and Neptune.

Unquestionably, with the highly effective creative work, their involving process and the quality of their presentations, Dick and Christoph had become a formidable duo. They exuded total trust, belief and confidence in each other. The amount of their output was phenomenal and the work they were producing strategically and creatively was both admired and more relevantly proving to be business building in the various markets. The presentations they compiled were judged to be challenging, thought provoking and were delivered in a captivating and entertaining style and manner. People actually looked forward to their attendance and contributions at forums. The positive feedback and reports Dick received led him to create a moniker about Christoph 'TGFC' which when spelt out read 'Thank God for Christoph!' This he posted on Christoph's office wall and door. There was never any envy, jealousy or status issue throughout their time working together. They were just colleagues who got on with the job in hand. It really was for both of them a halcyon period – challenging, demanding, spirited, motivating and rewarding.

Inevitably, they had their enemies both on the client side, among

A life above the line – just!

people they did not work with and brand people not associated with them, but also amongst the other roster agencies, which saw them as constantly out performing them. There was envy, dislike and negativity towards them. Some found the fact that they were always challenging the norm and contesting what was deemed to be 'perceived and accepted wisdom' tiring, threatening and sometimes difficult to handle. Their clear absence of fear and lack of deference believing their end result would win out in the end made Dick and Christoph be viewed by some as being high-handed and arrogant. Christoph had clearly come a long way from his initial scepticism about 'internationalism' and 'globalisation'. From being seen as a 'Little Englander' and rather parochial he had become a champion and instigator and developer of work across a diverse range of markets, though only if it was creatively relevant to that market or set of markets. Like so often in his career, Christoph never believed he was wrong or faltered in his desire to win even against seemingly impossible odds. He never stopped to consider the down side or adverse risk involved. The 'Not Invented Here' syndrome which he had encountered in the early days and was such an impediment to progress had been overcome. Only those that understood this and embraced it fully would survive in this growing International World. Change was and had taken place rapidly but Dick Shlitz and Christoph both knew that good thinking and brave executions could and would travel widely. They appreciated that the world of communication was evolving and that the old world of 30 second commercials on a couple of TV stations was all but dead. In January 1997 Christoph and Dick reached the same conclusion simultaneously that the job had been done and it was time to move on. Heavyweight strategic thinking politicians (a dangerous combination!) with their sophisticated modelling techniques had moved in to senior positions on the client side. Many of these had been hired from agencies and consultancies and were now interfering with brands positioning's' on a global perspective and platform. Dick and Christoph could now see the good and bad of 'Internationalism' and it was the right time to stand back. This would inevitably mean that they would probably have to part company, at least, eventually.

However, before the split came and they would go on to pursue their own goals there was just one more major challenge they chose to face together. They were teamed together to try to save the 'Reigning Cats and Dogs' account for McKillans. This account was in a serious state of jeopardy across the whole of Europe, after serious chunks of business had been lost in the lead UK market and many within the Company had washed their hands of McKillans. Indeed, many at the senior level of the agency had already for some time written off the business. This was just the challenge that attracted Christoph. The stakes were high and everything was stacked up against him – bring it on! Even before he started one of the European Heads at the company, whom he had never met before, specifically came to see him. He advised Christoph strongly against taking on this job, as he had heard good things about him, and this assignment would do his reputation no good as it truly was a lost cause. Indeed, he went on to say they wanted Christoph's predecessor's 'head on a plate'. The dye had been cast and the decision was that the account would ultimately leave McKillans, and that would be sooner rather than later. Christoph nodded sagely and then responded by stating "As for my reputation that counts for nothing. One is only as good as the next job one does, not the last job one did! The past is exactly that the past. I like, and even need, a good scrap and from what you have just said, which I truly appreciate and thank you for advising me over, makes this challenge even more exciting and worthwhile. This agency will not go down without a fight." With Dick heading up the team and Fiona Sole as his planner as far as he was concerned it was 'Game On'.

Christoph could see that this would need a very different way of working to the current process, where everything seemed so set in its ways, with too many long established personnel on both sides of the fence. At the very first meeting Christoph attended, in France, where a new product format in a pouch style packaging with a talking animal on the pack, where this last element was presented as the big idea, brought the reality home to him. This presentation was embellished by a heavily intellectualised justification of this stance by a very short, dapper, verbose, intellectual arrogant Frenchman. Christoph's response was to tear into the thinking stating that it was neither particularly original nor unique as a concept and was not strategically sound but all it had going for it was a questionable executional device. Furthermore, he pointed out, it would be difficult to transpose this advertising to other markets as each language would have to be recorded separately at the outset, or lip synched afterwards, which would be an expensive and difficult job. Much heated discussion ensued with little progress where Christoph repeatedly asked the French team what the advertising idea was as distinct from the executional device. In the end, in sheer frustration, he got up and with a large blue felt tip pen he went over to the diminutive French planner and towering over him said, "Okay write on the board what you think the consumer insight is and what the advertising idea is. I will give you that the executional idea is 'a talking animal on pack' ". This was too much for this self-important Frenchman. He was visibly annoyed and his chagrin shaken and he felt his cerebral thinking was being challenged publicly by a brash Englishman, new to the business. His arrogance pricked he appealed to Dick Shlitz and sought from him control of and an apology for Christoph's behaviour. Dick shook his head and replied, "We are at war and things are going to get shaken up majorly if we are to win. This is just an example as to how things will change and how we must challenge ourselves daily to do better. The thinking needs to be robust and based on consumer understanding and not on anything else. Christoph is right though I accept his style and approach may not be to everyone's taste." There was a long and embarrassing silence until one of the other French team members got up and wrote on the board that the idea was 'for people who have an involving relationship with their pet'. She went on to say that this was paid off in their end-line/slogan 'It is more than pleasure'. Christoph remonstrated and reminded this brave woman, nicely and politely, that her so-called advertising idea was in fact a generic claim for the whole category. The end-line, he felt, was only a half-thought, as this claim lacked any support, reason why or pay off.

When later on some general advertising routes for the lead brand were presented Christoph took further exception at these ideas proposed. Dick Shlitz had seen and heard enough and brought the meeting to a close and while not disagreeing with Christoph's comments said to him "Christoph I have already thrown myself over one of your grenades but my body can't cover a second so I think we will have to leave it there." The French being so advanced in their thinking and work and having already involved their local client were allowed to pursue their talking animal on pack idea. The product behind this route had very limited success despite heavy levels of media support while the advertising directions outlined, as a result of this meeting, were never pursued.

Following this meeting the Frenchman whom had been so offended wrote to Dick Shlitz demanding a written apology from Christoph for his outrageous and outspoken behaviour. Christoph, ever practical, in the interests of peace and harmony, duly obliged and did apologise not for what he had said but how he had said it. In the future there would never be much love between the two of them. But Christoph knew he was not there to be liked, never mind loved, but solely to try to make the difference and the impossible possible on a very short timescale. If that meant treading on peoples sensitive toes with niceties being thrown out of the window then so be it. So long as everyone was totally honest that was all he asked. On the pouch he took this product format to the German agency, gave them a completely different brief and with the advertising that was developed, tested this against the French route and another Agency's 'challenger' work. The German agency storyboard developed won through in the independent research showing that it was still possible for McKillans to do good work for this client.

The second formal meeting Dick and Christoph had to attend was a general presentation of the work orchestrated by the German Agency to the McKillans Senior Management tasked with saving the 'Reigning Cats and Dogs' account. The Global Head of the Agency, Ray Teflon, had come believing that it was his relationship with senior management at the client end that was all-important. Eight campaigns had been produced, which seemed to Christoph to be a scatter gun, rather than a focused, approach to the problem. There was evidently no clear and coherent strategy, a lack of consumer insight and no solid platform for this work to be evaluated against. Christoph felt sorry for this lead agency as it seemed like a case of throwing everything and anything against the wall and hoping that something stuck. The Global Head was putting his weight behind an executional idea that saw the pet pushing his or her bowl, across a smooth surfaced kitchen floor, with their nose. Christoph responded by saying that this was a nice simple visual mnemonic but that it did not currently emanate from the product or the brand and was therefore just generic. The range of routes presented included 'Pets through the Ages' from the pharaohs to today; 'Pets in Literature' including even T S Eliot's Old Possum's book of Practical Cats' the source for Andrew Lloyd Webber's musical 'Cats' and even a route looking at 'The astrology of pets' (thankfully the horse was not included as they all have their birthdays on January 1st!). It was quite clear to Christoph that if he was not going to have to drink the poison in the chalice that had been handed to him that clear uncluttered leadership was required. Little did he realise, at that time that he would literally on this task get poisoned!

Following this meeting Christoph took Dick aside and issued him an ultimatum. He told Dick he didn't feel he could do the job with the current regime and structure and would therefore have to step down. However, he said he would stay on but only if he reported into Dick and Dick alone and the McKillans US Management had to then 'butt out' and let him get on with the job. If these terms were agreed he would take full responsibility and lead the charge. He would want to work with various resources and would then submit the work for final scrutiny, before being presented to the Client on the 'day of judgement'. Much to his surprise this was agreed possibly because the Management now had one target to shoot at if things went badly wrong, which was already the expectation of many! As it transpired the current line-up in the agency had been panned by the client and really they had run out of options so Christoph putting himself forward fitted the need and bill perfectly. Christoph was in effect not just their best hope but possibly their last and only hope!

With this clear mandate Christoph set about learning all he could about pets, their owners their behaviour. From this he whittled down his thinking and understanding so that, for example, he appreciated that with cats they have individual and most importantly independent personalities. Also that with cats the feeding moment is the time when there is a coming together of the two parties and when and where the owner is vital (often the only time the cat allows the owner to have or be in control!). After an intensive four month period he felt sufficiently confident in his knowledge of pet care. On this basis he organised a week away with a number of creative teams in a Chateaux near Orleans in France, so that he could outline his thinking, present his brief and discuss the various consumer insights he had reached. This allowed the teams the chance to question him and to probe for better understanding. After that the creative teams that came from Canada, US, Germany, Central and Eastern Europe, as well as the UK were set to work. On the Friday morning all the work was presented, reviewed and discussed and then after lunch everyone went home for the weekend. Christoph was delighted with the outcome as there were a number of routes that were viable and had genuine potential. The best of these he took and developed with his team secretly so that when it came to the major client presentation on August 13th 1997(of all dates, but at least it wasn't a Friday but a Wednesday) it would all be a total surprise.

The three routes he majored on were 'Chefs knowledge' using popular chefs, with European wide reputations to create recipes that would be healthy, nutritious and appetising; 'Moments' that captured the enhanced and enjoyable relationship that came from feeding the best possible food at different times and circumstances in an animal's life and finally 'First Encounters' that capitalised on the first time the owner met their pet be that, for example, as a stray, rescue, when purchased, or at birth. Here the owner was displayed as the concerned, caring, loving person who wants to do right by their pet. These owners naturally chose 'Reigning Cats and Dogs' brands because of their dominant and renowned position in the market, which gave them all the confidence they needed.

The day before the big presentation there was the customary run-throughs that as the presentation was to be in Germany were held in Hamburg. It was decided that Christoph would lead the presentation supported by Dick and led off by the Global Chief, Ray Teflon. This

A life above the line – just!

was to some degree surprising as the presentation was taking place in the backyard of the German Agency and yet they were not being chosen to present even though they had been the lead agency on the business. The head of the local agency was totally relaxed with this decision and did not ask for a role or even to be present at the meeting. He had worked closely with Christoph in the build-up and prior to that with him on Neptune and he knew and liked Christoph's combative approach and his 'entertaining' presentation style.

There was a nice moment after the run-throughs were completed and they had returned to their hotel, across the road from the agency. Ray, Dick and Christoph were cooped up together in a particularly small lift. Ray was only 5ft 10ins, but squarely set, while Christoph stood 6ft 1.5ins and Dick was a solidly built 6ft 4ins. As the doors of the elevator closed Christoph looked down at Ray and slowly with just sufficient menace in his voice said, "Right Ray, now that we have got you here." At this point Dick was going absolutely scarlet and Christoph could read his thoughts 'Oh my God what is Christoph going to say or do now?' This look only became more concerned when Christoph went on "….There is only one thing Dick and I have got to say to you." Ray understandably was looking decidedly uncomfortable, certainly concerned, a little perplexed and had paled visibly. Christoph carried on, "Win, lose or draw, Ray, we both want off this God damned business!" Dick immediately relaxed and breathed out laughing nervously as he stated, "Ha, ha, ha very funny Christoph – well Ray you know what a joker and maverick Christoph can be – even in moments of adversity he can seemingly find humour!" Ray, too, look relieved that nothing more serious had been threatened or actually occurred.

The next day the meeting went about as well as Christoph could have hoped or expected. McKillans had clearly found its stride, confidence and had come out with all guns blazing and delivered at all levels with aplomb. Christoph was in sparkling form and was really up for the fight despite the pressure the Agency had been under and how the odds had been stacked against it. When he had finished his preamble, laid out the strategic thinking and direction, exposed the consumer insights they had worked to and how the agency viewed the long term future for the core brand, the European Head of the Company stopped the presentation. He then went on to say, "Christoph before you go on I wonder if I could have a copy of your charts and presentation as that was genuinely the most succinct explanation I have heard of where we are and where we need to go." Christoph smiled with a degree of pride and rubbing his chin with his hand cheekily replied, "Well I don't know (pause) as I'm not sure that you've actually paid for this one yet!"

This totally broke the ice and everyone relaxed and laughed, including the US Senior Board Members in attendance from Company Head Office.

The work that Dick and Christoph went on to present was very well received as it clearly was in line with the thinking that had been outlined. It was surprising and different – even for the German Lead Client team whom Christoph knew had spies in the Hamburg agency camp. This was fresh thinking and unseen creative executions even for them. In the question and answer session that followed the Agency, through Dick and Christoph fielded and shared the responses, with supreme confidence and obvious enjoyment. This was an agency back on top of its game answering with knowledge and competence. Truly nothing more could have been done. Whatever the misdemeanours of the past may have been, be that in personnel, attitude or work these had been blown away by an unapologetic, self-assured, sparky, open Agency performance. It had been challenging, forward looking and crystal clear in both its content and direction.

The McKillans team left that meeting, which had been billed as 'the last chance saloon' feeling strangely elated but also totally fatigued. They had given it everything and even Christoph, for once, was silent for quite a while afterwards. He reflected privately wondering and ruminating whether it had been a case of too little too late or was it enough or had indeed 'the dye already been cast'? They went and had an exceptionally good lunch in a village nearby and after Ray had left to catch his plane from Bremen having expressed his huge appreciation of the efforts of Dick and Christoph they stayed on and chatted before eventually making their way to Hanover Airport. There they had a couple more beers before Dick went to catch his flight to Brussels.

A life above the line – just!

Christoph had time to kill so made his way to the small British Airways lounge, which was effectively a long single room with a mirrored bar at one end and limited seating in the central area. Having just sat down the door opened and much to Christoph's horror he was confronted by the Senior Management from 'Reigning Cats and Dogs' walking in. There was nowhere for him to hide, but the Chief Executive, to his credit, came straight over to Christoph. As he stood up this gentleman put a hand on Chris's shoulder and with his other hand shook Christoph's hand and in his heavy cultured Mid - Western American voice said "My friend, that was a damn fine presentation you made today and I want to thank you for that. But.." he went on to say "..some times in life you don't get the result you deserve." And so it was at that moment he knew he had failed in his mission to salvage the brand – close but no cigar! Sadly the decision had gone against him and McKillans.

However, that did not turn out to be the end of the matter. It transpired that the CEO had been both sufficiently impressed by the presentation made by McKillans and equally critical of the decision making process at the Company end that he insisted that if they were going to take away the lead brand that McKillans had to be compensated in some way. Accordingly they received a brand from each of the other agencies on the client's roster. Christoph was pleased for McKillans, as it kept people's jobs, but he felt he had failed and appropriately took full responsibility for the negative outcome, and as such immediately tendered his resignation. He also knew that if he did the honourable thing it would prevent there being a witch hunt, scapegoating or the unproductive and interminable 'blame game' that had become commonplace in these situations. His resignation was not accepted as the McKillans Management never held him responsible for the loss, which they attributed to previous shortcomings, before his appointment to the business. In fact they praised him for his efforts that had led to the agency gaining compensation in the form of three other brands. Christoph would carry on working on the 'Reigning Cats and Dogs' business including running these new brands.

Sadly, though at the end of this exhausting process, Dick and Christoph knew their time working together was now finally at an end. Dick would be appointed Regional Account Director in the Far East, while Christoph would remain based in London ending up as Global Account Director and Worldwide Category Director, before departing in the autumn of 2001. There was still just time for two further instances before this happened that both would remember with amusement. Just two months later in October 1997, the Head of McKillans International called a 2 Day Conference in London on Neptune. This brought together all the operators on the business from across Europe and the US, as well as the Senior Management of the Agency from New York. With them came a two point agenda:-

- To foster superior teamwork and collaboration in pursuing the goals of being the leader in building global brand business.
- To update everyone on new developments with Neptune and to discuss together how to apply 'The McKillan Way' (whatever that was!?) to service this client.

Christoph was invited as he had only fairly recently departed from the account and had built up so many good contacts throughout Europe on this business. Dick had insisted that he was present.

The forum was split up into tables of eight, with assigned seating. This was deliberately done so that people who had never encountered some of the other personnel present would have the chance to meet and get to know each other. It also had the potential to have people with different experiences, influences and thinking to work together and feel part of a single entity. The people on Christoph's table asked him to be their spokesperson when the first challenge of the day was issued. The task was to come up, in the 10 minute time allotted, with a list of either major concerns and or a menu of breakthrough ideas that could, in the course of the following two days, be considered and discussed or reviewed by the forum. Much disquiet, regarding the current modus operandi, was expressed by the people at Christoph's table. They were especially vexed and concerned at how 'Internationalism' seemed to be increasingly and frustratingly governed by what Head Office in New York wanted. It seemed that the American Management believed

A life above the line – just!

that only they had the answers and therefore that it should be them that dictated to all the other countries from afar. This was now being defined as being 'Americanism' rather than 'Internationalism'.

Christoph captured this sense and feeling in a SWOT Analysis Chart, which broke down as follows:-

<u>Strengths</u>	<u>Weaknesses</u>
Few Americans	Too many Americans
<u>Opportunities</u>	<u>Threats</u>
No Americans	More Americans

Dick made sure that Christoph's table presented very early on in the proceedings as he hoped for a bit of levity once he knew Christoph had been nominated as spokesperson. Christoph took them through this chart with a gradual reveal of each element. This brought the house down and there was much laughter and delight. Even his American 'over-lords' took it in good heart and it certainly broke the ice and showed that openness was going to be accepted and indeed even called for. Not surprisingly when Dick finally left Europe he gave Christoph a blow up copy of this chart citing it as one of his favourite and most memorable moments from his time in Europe. At the same farewell party held in Dick's honour he presented Christoph with a card. Dick had always been fascinated by European History and the two of them had shared many discussions about the battlefields in the various countries they visited. The card was headed with the title 'Great British Generals'. Underneath he wrote, 'To a great general – numerous skirmishes, many battles, a few wars and some enduring campaigns. Without you they would have been far less engaging, entertaining or enjoyable. Thank you for allowing me to be one of your subalterns!' With that one of the first truly International partnerships was over. Together they had embraced Internationalism without ever compromising the quality of the creative work. Their partnership at McKillans truly was a reflection on how the way of the world in business, marketing and communications had changed.

CHAPTER 7

A Game of Chance

<u>(where just sometimes winning is losing and where even occasionally losing can be winning)</u>

<u>US Legal definition:-</u>

<u>'..a game whose outcome depends upon an element of chance, even though the skill of the contestant(s) may also be an influencing factor.'</u>

Christoph had always felt that his career in advertising was a game of chance. He played the percentages and he reckoned so long as he won more times than he lost he would be end up ahead. As with his gambling on the horses, he took his losses with a mere shrug of the shoulders, a degree of public grace and dignity and even on occasion some remorse; but most importantly he simply vowed to win next time. All through his career he viewed every day as being a calculated gamble and would reflect on each, at night time, as either having been a winning day, one of survival, or, in the worst case scenario, a day to forget. Sometimes the winning just didn't seem right, justifiable or that worthwhile and he would ruefully reflect on some outcomes, even when technically and publicly he might have been seen to have won.

A life above the line – just!

For Christoph it was never about winning at all costs, or being myopic, selfish or ruthless to achieve the ends. It was playing the game, as that was what advertising was to him, and playing it well and doing it with élan and panache that really mattered.

The 'Reigning Cats and Dogs' decision, not to retain their key brand with McKillans, despite Dick and Christoph's valiant attempts, hurt him deeply. Even the compensation of three new brands could not fully compensate the failure he felt. By his terms he had 'lost' and losing was not an option for Christoph and certainly not one he liked. The only way he could get over the hurt was by working hard to make these three new brands high profile with business building copy behind them. The one thing that had amused him was shortly after the result was known one of his predecessors, whom had returned to his home country, the USA, a defeated and brow-beaten individual, wrote to him stating, 'You've done a bang up job with the shit I left you. You managed to secure a victory from the grips of defeat. No one else at McKillans could have done that, I'm sure.' Maybe he was right but certainly Christoph would never see it that way. He had gambled when the stakes were high and the odds were stacked against him but he had lost.

Earlier, prior to coming off Neptune and having helped, on this client to secure three major brand wins for McKillans, in competitive pitches, against the other agencies, he asked to be in the line up to pitch for an existing granola bar. This product and brand was floundering in Western Europe where it had been launched some years before. The Company was not keen to have McKillans present as they felt they had a considerable amount of their business already. Nevertheless, Christoph insisted that on the strength of the work they were doing they should be given the same chance as the other agencies. He knew that the senior client involved with this brand didn't particularly like McKillans. He was a status man and didn't feel that the agency gave him sufficient respect or regard. However, his reason for not including McKillans initially was actually fair in that he felt they already held two other brands in the same sector and that were close in nature to the product formula in his brand. Christoph's persistent requests in the end paid off and McKillans were granted a late–entry pass, based on his persuasive argument that the client had nothing to lose. They might, he suggested, if little else, get some solid thinking and even some reasonable creative ideas out of the process.

On this occasion Christoph simply got the tactics horribly wrong from the very outset. Initially he had had to contend with just a written brief and no face-to-face meeting for questions to be answered. In hindsight Christoph should have insisted that they had at least a discussion meeting to question and better understand the brief. Christoph felt that the brief was far too narrow. Though instead of answering this brief and then developing an alternative strategy and work done to that, as a follow-up part of the presentation he arrogantly chose to ignore the client's brief. Despite this, on the day, he did, in the initial part of the presentation, seriously question the validity of the original brief. Having done that he then showed the evidence behind his proposed strategy, which he articulated, as 'naturalness fed by natural ingredients' which he had had tackled creatively, by the biggest selling market of that particular brand, Germany. To establish the mood that he was seeking to communicate he developed a film with cuts of the ingredients and scenes of naturalness done to the background track of Louis Armstrong's 1967 No.1 smash hit, 'What a wonderful world'. Unsurprisingly, this all played to the strengths of the natural ingredients of the product be those bran, yoghurt, raisins and cereals.

The presentation itself went well and Christoph fought a vehement defence for his strategy versus the positioning articulated in the client brief. Indeed, it was a battle royal, that had taken the fight head-on to the client and then the new positioning had been defended articulately with work that clearly demonstrated its potential. Christoph's, more or less, solo performance so impressed the CEO of the German agency that he insisted on taking Christoph to lunch at a top Hamburg restaurant. However, even he had perceived that Christoph's presentation had made as he remarked, 'one man very unhappy' and that was the instigator and initiator of the original brief. It was never wise to challenge a brief so vociferously in such a public forum as it either showed extreme arrogance or insensitivity – or possibly in this case both. This observation was correct and a strong client ally of Christoph's whom had also attended the meeting said that that had been the undoing of McKillans pitch. He thought that it was a good presentation with some stimulating thinking but the damage had been done. Needless to say they did not get the business. Occasionally not listening properly, being an arrogant prick, or even on the odd rare instance, complacent, could militate and work against Christoph. No one likes a smart arse/ass or a 'clever dick'. Christoph, to his credit, was the first person to put up his hand appreciating he had got it totally wrong and apologised to all his colleagues who had done such good work but where his tactics had failed them miserably. He was humbled and annoyed with himself for losing a potentially winning position through a lack of consideration and forethought.

The great thing with Christoph was that set-backs and failures were for him a learning exercise and never dragged him down for long. Tomorrow was always another day and he would wake up the next day ready for the challenge. Sometimes the failure would be one he could smile about afterwards and handle equally with humour and humility. He certainly never ducked responsibility, or from being held to account, even when circumstances were major contributors. Such a case was when he was asked by the CEO of McKillans in London if he could put together a team and a presentation to South Eastern Gas. It was at the height of the summer and people were scarce due to it being the holiday season and many being away from the agency as School Holidays had just begun. Finding available people was therefore a problem and it was largely for this reason that Christoph had been commandeered in the first place. In fact he was exceptionally busy himself, as he pointed out, but was informed 'needs must' and 'desperate times require desperate actions'. Time drifted by and on the Thursday before the presentation on the following Monday the CEO returned to Christoph's office to enquire how he was getting on and what progress had been made. Christoph having been so consumed by work on his own accounts had completely forgotten about this assignment. He dropped everything there and then and set about briefing a creative team and a media representative while he worked up a presentation over the entire weekend. This was a massive undertaking as this was not a category that Christoph had ever worked on before. This meant finding research on consumer understanding of Gas supply and suppliers and their attitudes to respective offers from these producers and companies. He also did a full critique on the recent campaigns for the various Gas Boards around the country. He even undertook a comprehensive assessment of the individual Gas Board companies and their various business models and where potential might lie for building business in the future. From all this analysis and comprehensive review Christoph was able to find a distinctive and different positioning, that he felt able to justify, from the evidence he had unearthed. Christoph even went as far as creating a slogan that would be unique to South East Gas (SEGAS). He was able with these snippets and discoveries to keep his creative team updated as to where he was going and they could build this into their work, including the suggested slogan. He managed to find a willing Personal Assistant to type up his charts, produce acetates and even the 'leave behind' presentation document. Taking the budget provided by the prospect the media lady he seconded was able to produce a media plan for their expenditure. By Sunday night everything was ready, even the blown up charts and printed T-Shirts, for the CEO and Christoph to wear under their shirts and suits. The great day dawned, coinciding with the first day of the All England Lawn Tennis Championships, at Wimbledon, in 1987. It was a truly hot, humid and muggy late June day, with showers and a continual threat of rain. There were two important and significant discoveries that came to light immediately. The first was that only the CEO and Christoph were available to present as the media and creatives were already committed elsewhere. The second was that the slogan on the T-shirts could be seen through the white shirts that Christoph had purchased for the CEO and himself to wear. This would necessitate wearing their jackets done up, throughout the meeting, despite the temperature. Worse still Christoph had discovered that in his tiredness he had failed to realise that he had a mismatching suit on with the jacket being dark grey and the trousers navy – so much for suave and sartorial elegance!

When they arrived at The South East Gas offices the previous agency pitching for the business was just leaving, with an army of personnel. Additionally, they appeared to be laden with equipment and materials, including video cassettes and radio cassette tapes, charts, screens, sound equipment and large boards. McKillans somewhat sparse numbers, notably two people, and a simple art bag rather paled into insignificance next to this heavily armed legion. When the senior 'potential' client came out to greet McKillans, he looked around and seeing just the two of them asked quite reasonably and innocuously, "Are we waiting on some others to arrive?" Quick to recover the CEO stated confidently "No we believe in quality not quantity. We also like our representatives to be hands-on and so we have elected to field only those members of senior management who would actually be working on your business should we be fortunate enough to be appointed." Looking a little surprised, if not even slightly perplexed, the prospect replied, "Well you had better come along to my office as you clearly won't be requiring the Board Room."

The background, the overview of the market, the competitive environment and the identified opportunities for South East Gas were received with nods of approval and tacit agreement, as well as general acceptance. Nothing mind blowing or hugely revealing but equally not much to really criticise or have conjecture over. Only when the CEO (a natural falsetto) and Christoph (bordering on a bass but just about bass-baritone) started to sing the Julie Andrews song 'My favourite things' (1959 Sound of Music), with the lyrics changed to sell the benefits of South East Gas, did a wry smile cross the face of the prospect, who at the end applauded the rendition in good faith.

However, when questioned over the validity of the claim and positioning and what research had been undertaken to determine the relevance and appropriateness as well as acceptance of the proposition, the CEO responded – probably breaking the hearts of numerous researchers and planners, in his agency, if not across the country, in the process – by stating, "We don't believe in presenting ideas backed up by the views and reactions of a limited number of consumers, as we would rather sell the idea first. Besides what agency is ever going to field an idea that has research tested badly?" A fair comment if not quite an honest reflection of the fact that there had simply not been the time to do any research!

The final 'coup de grace' was yet to come. Earlier they had been asked if they would like to remove their jackets but both the CEO and Christoph had declined, despite both sweating profusely in the conditions of a non-air conditioned office in the height of the heat of the afternoon's overcast muggy conditions. Now was the moment to reveal the slogan. Unfortunately, Christoph in pulling his shirt open had forgotten to undo his jacket and as such found unwanted resistance and had to pull even harder. The next thing he noticed was the Marketing Director taking cover under his desk as he was attacked by a barrage of M&S white buttons and a large grey suit button, spinning towards him, which narrowly missed his right ear. And the slogan read 'You've got to SE(e) Gas to believe it!' At this juncture both the CEO and Christoph dissolved in laughter amidst profuse apologies for the missile attack on this senior prospect! The outcome was reasonably predictable – McKillans did not get appointed to the business! They had made the cheapest of presentations (possibly in more ways than one), had had an absolute 'gas' – literally and metaphorically and provided a fun after dinner story for the Marketing Director. In fact a few months later he caught up with McKillans CEO at a Gas Conference and he was still talking about this 'infamous presentation'. It had been unforgettable for all the wrong reasons for all concerned. Christoph penned a note to those who had not been present but had assisted in the background, which he titled *'Stormy Monday'*:-

'There are some times in our lives when things do not go according to plan. Flaming June turns into a deluge. Church Shoes ruined by the mud tide at Royal Ascot. Fancied horses losing bogged down in the mud and then on to the next week......

Monday started with the sun breaking over Turnham Green at 6.00am, only to turn to drizzle by 10.30am. Not a ball was served on Wimbledon's hallowed turf,

A life above the line – just!

not a ball was bowled at Lords. It was a hot, humid, muggy day. Dressing as normal, though seeking sartorial elegance Christoph elected to don his only fitting suit. However, on arrival at the office it was pointed out that while he had the suit jacket on the trousers were completely unrelated and even a different colour.

The significance of the team presenting to South Eastern Gas was that due to unforeseen circumstances it had been whittled down to just the CEO and myself. This became even more apparent when it was discovered that the previous agency McCaufield had fielded a team of eight, each carrying large amounts of visual aids, special presentation screens; audio and visual tapes, plus research boards. In stark contrast there were just the two of us and some cardboard, some acetates and a T-shirt.

The presentation was an unmitigated disaster for which I can only apologise to you most contritely. However it was not without its memorable moments:-

1. *The explanation at the outset by our illustrious CEO as to our somewhat beleaguered team went something like this. "We believe in a hands-on approach to business and like our management to be totally involved and committed in the business. We have elected to field only our assigned management team."*
2. *The singing impression of Julie Andrews and her famous song 'My favourite things' by a combination of falsetto and double bass, encouraged, rather than perfected, by the practice on the way down past Croydon. This nearly resulted in a crash by the chauffeur's uncontrollable laughter and mad hysteria. The practice paid dividends as the delivery when it mattered most was met with applause and a cracking of the prospect's stony face.*
3. *The final coup de grace came when re-iterating our 'hands on' approach and 'shirt sleeves' philosophy, the redoubtable duo ripped off their designer label St Michael shirts to reveal the slogan, 'You've got to SEGAS to believe it!' Unfortunately one of the team had forgotten to undo his jacket with the net result being that an almighty rip to the only wearable suit in his wardrobe occurred, with the large button flying off at great speed, along with numerous white shirt buttons narrowly missing the right ear of the Marketing Director, who had to take evasive action and duck down*

beneath his desk. *The Agency team dissolved into laughter and after that had to make a fairly speedy exit.*

I suppose it will be small comfort to say thank you for your efforts and I am only sorry we didn't do better – but it was the cheapest presentation to date – (on so many levels!) – and we had had - yes you've got it - 'A Gas'!
Christoph'

It may not have come good but it had been a fun experience and sometimes, as Christoph knew, making the impossible possible – is actually impossible!

It was not unknown for Christoph to go against the grain in order to achieve the end result he sought or to show a level of commitment. He knew that this could necessitate taking a punt, which if it went wrong could have dire consequences for him and even his agency. Working with Jenny Chase had always been for Christoph a pleasure and a delight. They worked in two agencies together and she was unquestionably, the quickest mind and the most considered person he knew. Jenny had a great wit and a healthy positive attitude on life. They had many a good laugh together. This great working relationship had led to the development of some highly effective advertising. One of these beneficiaries was a pharmaceutical, toiletries and drugs company, Pharmacia. Part of their portfolio was dental and denture products. One of these was a denture fixative product that appealed to the then 20% of the population that was edentulous (without teeth - in some cases where ill-fitting dentures had even been passed down the generations in a family!). Two new advertising routes had been produced and put into research. Both routes had come through strongly but Gris Advertising had a definite preference for one of the directions as they felt it would make for better and more memorable advertising. The final decision would be made by the client, and more specifically by a complex, suave individual whom, as Marketing Director, always liked to be seen to have the upper hand, and especially over the agency. Christoph informed Jenny that he intended to recommend the other route – Route B. Jenny was aghast and deeply concerned and certainly dubious about this strategy. They got to the meeting and went through the research in painstaking detail. When it came to the Agency's recommendation Christoph conceded that it was a very close call, especially as both routes had done so well. Nevertheless, the Agency marginally opted for and preferred Route B. The client thought deeply during which the tension was unbearable but then he complimented the Agency for having developed two highly effective routes, and confirmed that he was in total acceptance of the research findings, which were evidently very positive. He then paused again and looked steely eyed at Christoph to try to read his set, sober, unmoving game face and then he spoke. He said he disagreed with the Agency's recommendation and that on judgement he viewed Route A as being the stronger piece of advertising. Christoph made a half-hearted attempt to justify his recommendation, for Route B, keeping a straight poker face throughout. He then relented and accepted the client's view and assured him it would make a fine piece of advertising. And so that was how the right decision was taken and everyone was happy; the client felt he had got one over the agency and made the ultimate decision; while the agency got to produce the better piece of advertising and the one they truly wanted to make! As Jenny surmised, afterwards, when she was finally able to explode with laughter, in the cab back to the railway station, it had been a demonstration of how knowing one's client could be crucial. Understanding the psychology of the client in any given situation, especially where there was space for them to manoeuvre was paramount. It had been basically a game of poker and playing the hand with a straight face giving absolutely nothing away. Christoph had bluffed his hand and the client thought he had called him out. If he had bet his hand the other way the Client would still have wanted to impose his will and so Route B would have been selected rather than Route A. A less good piece of advertising would have been the end result.

When Christoph had gone to Premium White the first account he had been asked to work on was a biscuit manufacturer. On one particular brand the agency had had great difficulty selling a new advertising campaign, even though they had a highly creative route which had proven itself in research. Even against the longstanding campaign it had done exceptionally well but the client seemed reluctant to move the brand on and so they had reached an impasse. The Marketing Director was a very able and affable man, highly regarded in the industry, holding a senior position within the Marketing Society. From the start Christoph and he had got along famously and they worked closely on a number of projects including support for two old favourites and the launch of a new biscuit brand in the highly cluttered 'bran wagon' arena. Through the use of good PR and selective Trade Advertising they had achieved excellent distribution. Based on a strong store presence it had been viable to do consumer advertising. On another brand, targeted at kids, Christoph had surprised this client by suggesting they run advertising developed by a previous agency as it still had legs and would save on production costs. But, for all this, the 'problem brand' still had not been resolved and resistance still lay here. Premium White, Christoph knew, was counting on him finding a way to sell the new creative direction. Christoph felt that this might have to come down to tactics and backing his track record on the three other brands by this stage where success could be pointed to. He appreciated that overwhelming this client with numbers and research findings was not going to persuade him. He determined to go down on his own and tackle the case face-to-face. Christoph laid out the background, why there had been a need to move on with the communication, the thinking behind the new work, the research findings in comparison with the previous work running and what the costs were for making the new advertising. The client was appreciative that Christoph had come down on his own and had not tried to pressurise him by bringing the legions or other members of management with him. However, he was still uncertain and prevaricating, seeking, yet again, to defer making the big decision. Christoph chose to go for the shock tactic and left the client in no doubt how strongly the Agency felt when he said, "I am leaving now to catch my train back to town. If I don't have a telex or fax from you by the time I get back to my desk at the agency, you leave me no alternative, but for me to recommend to the Agency Management that we resign the business." The client gasped at this affront but even he realised it was crunch time. In truth all the way back to London Christoph was sweating bullets wondering if maybe he had gone too far, overstepped the mark and whether this punt would pay off. It was high stakes poker! Much to his relief, on his return, there was a fax on his desk which simply stated *'If the Agency feels this strongly and clearly is so committed to the direction then we should go ahead and make the film. Good luck'*. When Christoph told the Agency they were delighted. However they were less enamoured by the tactics he had employed to sell the work. Indeed, it could be said that they were horrified and he was severely reprimanded for the threat he had made. But even they accepted that he had won and were delighted and praised him for finally getting the outcome they had been seeking for so long unsuccessfully to achieve. As a footnote, the commercial when made won a Silver Lion at Cannes and Campaign's Ad of The Week. In the marketplace the results were more circumspect and less conclusive, as it received very limited levels of support, so its true worth could neither be fully evaluated nor proven.

Working at Premium White certainly brought its own challenges for Christoph. The Management were creative led and no one was supposed to take, let alone present, or sell work, without strong creative representation being in attendance. This could prove to be more problematic than beneficial on occasions. The difficulty for Christoph was that he firmly believed that it was a case of 'horses for courses' and in his experience the people who had developed the ideas were not always the best at selling their work. He felt that Account Management more often than not had the better salesmen as they were less emotionally attached or directly connected to the work. He recalled shortly before leaving advertising that the UK Creative Director, at McKillans, came to see him and thank him for making a very difficult sale of some creative work and where ther creatives had wanted to make all three executions and not just the two the budget could afford. The Creative Director said to him, "Christoph, can I ask you why do you care so much about this creative campaign? What is it that made you fight so hard to get the extra money to make all three executions?" Christoph smiled and replied, "I don't care especially about this work though I think it is pretty good. I see my job as being a salesman. I am paid to find the very best way of selling the work once I have been convinced it is on brief and on strategy. My opinion of the work itself is irrelevant. Before that work ever runs I will probably have had to sell no less than four other campaigns and possibly more. My opinion therefore really counts for little and my emotional attachment even less. My task is simply to sell and the pride for me comes in making the sale and winning. For me advertising is a business. The work is not a piece of art hanging forever in an art gallery. In time people won't even recall this advertising!" The Creative Director nodded his head a little perplexed but then before leaving philosophically conceded, "Well, you seem to be pretty good at your job. It is much appreciated in my department. Thank you."

A further consideration had to be the tactics and the ability to read the client, both which could be crucially important. Such was the case on one account he worked on where the Premium White Agency had taken on the assignment because it provided the opportunity to do high profile show case advertising, even though the budget was small, and the ability to make money from this business was infinitesimal and inconsequential. The media budget for this Engineering representative body was £140k with £35k allowed for production, which even in 2020 would have been a total spend under half-a-million. Christoph worked on this account very closely with one of the most senior creatives in the agency and a man who had rightly earned a great reputation from writing issue, political and crisis advertising. He was tough, uncompromising, and thoroughly professional but could be intolerant, impatient and testy. He had found it deeply frustrating that this client seemed always to be operating through Committees and that their PR man was not the sole decision maker. Christoph acknowledged that this could be time consuming and at times exasperating, an emotion this particular creative could not hide and which the client contact was well aware of. Because of this, Christoph took the brave decision to front the client himself through the final stages of the process, right up to the development of the full black and white pages in the newspaper campaign. The series of ads were built around the insight that 'Engineers did not get the recognition or acclaim that they deserved'. Premium White devised a series of brilliant ads; one that featured an interior view of Westminster Abbey and commented on the fact that while there was a 'Poets Corner' there was no representation of 'Engineers' – *'Why isn't there an Engineers Corner in Westminster Abbey?'*. This execution represented the past glories but there was another that represented the present. This showed a series of nine cricketers in different batting poses, under the headline *'Once more the world is beating us at our own game. And it's not cricket.'* Under each was a nugget, a fact, that Christoph's investigations had gleaned through discussions with various engineers e.g. *'After the war Britain was the third largest steel producer. Now we are tenth'* and *'In 1900 Britain made 60% of the world's shipping. Today we make 3%'* and another fact was *'Britain once exported motor bikes to over one hundred countries. Now we import nearly every machine we buy.'* With very minor tweaks Christoph went to the Council Executive and sold the campaign, on his own, as he judged that he related better to their members than the creative guru, a view shared by the day to day contact client. However, when he got back to the Agency he was severely berated and 'bollocked' for not having creative representation present - a sine qua non – for the agency. Christoph was relaxed about this as he felt he had made the right call and had done what he thought was best to get the desired result at the time. He never once thought what would have been said, or indeed happened to him, if the campaign had not been sold lock, stock and barrel!

Perhaps the greatest testimony to this campaign came in the Thatcher Government's March 1985 Budget (The Chancellor of the Exchequer, was Nigel Lawson) when it provided an extra £42million for Sciences in Universities and places of Higher Education. The campaign itself entitled *'Fighting to help Britain make it,'* received significant press coverage including a sizeable article, featuring part of the Cricketers ad in the Financial Times on January 10th 1985. It borrowed its headline from the third ad in the campaign that talked to the future, *'Make engineering a dream'* and featured a boy lying on a hillside dreaming of what he was going to be when he grew up. At the end it simply stated *'He wouldn't dream of being an engineer, of course'*. The Director General of the Council claimed he had been inundated with telephone calls and letters of support – in excess of 275. Even the Minister of Education, Sir Keith Joseph lauded the campaign publicly. Schools, and industry alike, requested block pulls of the ads, to use as posters for display or for career information packs. The post awareness campaign research, in the papers, in which the ads ran, notably The Times, Telegraph and Observer showed an awareness level of 37% among its readers and 28% amongst the general public. The Public Affairs Department at the client stated *"....the size and quality of the public reaction to the campaign was so remarkable to be beyond the previous experience of the Public Affairs Directorate, who have seen many similar campaigns..."* From the creative standpoint it won the much heralded D&AD Award for Copy, which was quite an achievement for such a low level campaign, but thoroughly merited.

What Christoph learnt while at Premium White was that their need was for a well-trained and disciplined Account Management department to work alongside their creative emphasised platform. The art of selling that Christoph saw as such a major part of the job was absent. The Account Management were simply client contact people, bag carriers and there to follow up on decisions reached in the meetings. Christoph felt that as the agency grew it would have to change. He valiantly tried to put into place initiatives to encourage 'self-starters' and to help get work out of the agency spontaneously rather than solely responding to clients' briefs. However, this never got off the ground as the creatives would only deal with what was briefed to them by a client. Christoph then decided to take a real punt and that for and in an agency that did not believe in having a powerful and influential Account Management! He decided to challenge this and take their creative led philosophy head on. To that end Christoph determined he had to raise the standards of Account Management and to open their eyes to the potential within the job. They needed the tools of the trade and so he produced a

A life above the line – just!

Training Manual. Christoph conceived of this in a ring binder format so that it could be continually updated and added to. Better thinking, wiser contributors, new technologies and new media opportunities would all be candidates for inclusion in the future. It was however, in the first instance, his best thinking, views, experience, knowledge and information. Some of this he gleaned, begged, adapted, stole and garnered from other agencies, which already had training programmes in place.

There was a very basic structure and layout to what Christoph titled 'The Account Management Procedures Manual'. It started with a section on Definitions and this outlined the roles and job performance at each level, of Account Management. This also looked at People Skills expectations, Financial responsibilities and Evaluation measures. The second section was 'Disciplines and Reports' which included tips on how to compile a Facts Book; the headings for a Work List; how to lay out a Status Report; how to write a Business Plan; how to conduct a Brand Review Meeting; how to format a Marketing Plan and what is essential to include in a Creative Strategy as well as the structure and key elements for a Creative and Media Brief. The third section was 'Helpful Hints for Account Management' covering how best to run a meeting; how to sell work; how to deal with issues pertaining to the ownership of work and copyright; how to manage new business and the costs involved in a pitch; as well as how to best use an Information Department or in-house Library – if one existed! Additionally, it covered how to write a brief Client Case History with examples provided and also dealt with Client budgeting explaining different ways clients arrived at advertising budgets. Finally this section covered how to conduct an Interview with people new to the industry such as Graduates but also for the more experienced people applying for a job. A sub-section Christoph developed was 'How to be more effective'. Another whole area included in this manual was 'Production' that covered systems that would help to get better work from initiation to final production and how this differed for print and broadcast. The penultimate section was 'Financial Services' that sought to make people realise that they were in a business and not Walt Disney cartoons. This looked at how to try to get increases in budgets, assess the effectiveness of the advertising on the client's business and how to increase profitability for the agency. Given a responsibility to stakeholders and shareholders as well as potential interest from investors and the City generally Christoph saw it of paramount importance to make sure that his teams gave accurate Projections and Forecasts for billings and revenue on a month by month basis. Finally, the last section covered 'An Account Trainee Programme'. This started in April and went through until September and culminated in each graduate internee giving a presentation to the Board, which was then followed by a dinner. There was also a list of external courses available for these trainees to potentially sign up for and participate in.

Once Christoph had completed his work and agreed the forms with the respective and relevant departments he printed off the binders and the content and then presented it to the Premium White Management. He took them through it and they were clearly impressed by the level of input, the commitment behind it, the range of topics covered, and delivered in a non-preaching guiding helpful, constructive and user-friendly manner. They much to his amazement embraced it wholeheartedly seeing it as a way to instil more discipline into the Agency's modus operandi, while raising the expectations from their Account Management. Even the Creative leaders who ran the agency realised that they needed a better way of getting the work through the department. They embraced the way Christoph had come up with timetables and steps to ensure that the work was done in a controlled manner. They were complimentary and liked the way he presented it with a degree of humility, recognising that it could be updated and changed as time passed. The gamble had paid off and it was now up to the players to rise to the challenge.

But what really shocked the Board was that at the end of this presentation Christoph announced his intention to leave the Agency and presented them with his letter of resignation. The Management were completely taken aback, surprised, disappointed and were deeply shocked. Christoph did it with a smile and no bad feeling at all. They did everything to try to change his mind but in the end unsuccessfully. Christoph felt he had done his best, built a fully functioning Account Management Department, created a Graduate Training Programme and left them with a Manual that gave them the tools of the trade. He truly had decided he had no more to give to Premium White. He resigned with no job to go to and due to his workload had not yet even put his Curriculum Vitae into the marketplace. As luck would have it Christoph received a number of overtures, approaches and job offers. Christoph opted for an agency that was International but was facing some major problems – just the challenge he felt he was now ready to embrace. That gamble also paid off, as for his last 16 years, in advertising, he would work for McKillans.

Throughout his career Christoph encountered many situations that were not clear cut or simply black and white. In a self-regulated industry, such as advertising, it was critical that sensible, sensitive and responsible decisions were arrived at so that it did not become legally controlled. It was for this reason that the area of Copy Clearance was established to ensure that advertising was 'legal, decent, honest and truthful'. It was imperative to have bodies of experts who were in charge of controlling the copy messages delivered to the consumers. Within this were many grey areas. Christoph a thwarted thespian and part frustrated barrister revelled in these murky grey waters. From very early on in his time at Gris Advertising he had been involved in seeking to get these bodies to approve and accept cleaning performance claims and demo sequences for cleaning products. Some of these demo-sequences looked more like a Japanese Flag then an authentic stain prior to washing but then would come out stain free. The degree and quality of whiteness would have to be checked and Christoph could relate having to go down by train, to Oxted, to visit a Copy Clearance Consultant and Expert to prove the washing credentials. This would entail standing in a field as the sunlight went down and the Northern light could be seen through the flapping pillow case that Christoph would have to hold up. Even to Christoph this seemed a rather bizarre behaviour and carry–on.

Sometimes too, in those early days, the claims would require qualitative and even quantitative research findings demonstrating consumers understanding of the claims being made and ensuring that they were in no way being duped or hoodwinked by the advertisers.

But winning was not always the outcome that Christoph felt particularly proud of. One such result that really rankled with him was when Thomas Healey had a teenage skin care product that they wanted to advertise on television, using an American execution that had run in the US reportedly with some success. The advertisement highlighted the teenage problem, by drawing a comparison with this concern and a pepperoni pizza, supported by, in Christoph's view, some cruel and unsavoury language, 'Remind you of anybody's face?' When this route was presented to him by a middle level client Christoph was adamant that this should not run in the UK, on the grounds that it was distasteful and insensitive to a real problem that many teenagers suffered from. Despite expressing his views strongly the Client still insisted that it was presented to the Copy Clearance people who upheld Christoph's views and rejected the advertising. Christoph thought that would be the end of the matter. Not so, the US Company Management then applied pressure on their UK counterparts and they insisted Christoph, whom they knew had a formidable record on copy issues, went to bat on their behalf. Christoph was reluctant but the challenge of finding a way to win soon overcame this hesitancy! Accordingly, he put together a powerful defence of the advertising at a meeting of the BACC (an organisation with many names/titles/ manifestations/reinventions over the years from ITCA/ ITVA/BACC/Clearcast). The argument that Christoph made to this 'independent body' was that this was the way teenagers spoke to and about each other. As such the route had 'yoof' 'street cred'(ibility). After a protracted discussion Christoph won the day and the copy was permitted to go on air, much to the delight of the client. For Christoph it was a victory he took little pleasure in. He had simply done his job and got the result they wanted. He was secretly relieved when this advertising was pulled after its planned first burst on air following a large number of complaints to both the

ITC (Independent Television Commission) and the ASA (Advertising Standards Authority). Of course, in today's 'snowflake' world, with political correctness and teenage anxiety and mental and social issues Christoph acknowledged this advertising would never have been a candidate or seen the light of day.

Christoph had over time built up a reputation of being a real street fighter when it came to these bodies in charge of copy clearance. The tougher the challenge, the greater the odds against him, the more he liked it. He would fight tooth and nail to keep ideas from being turned down and to win in these 'grey areas'. He had built strong relationships with many members at the Copy Clearance bodies, gaining their friendships, trust and respect. Unlike most of his colleagues Christoph saw selling to them as every bit as important as selling the idea to a prospect or client. There was no point, in his opinion, being able to sell the moon to the client if it then couldn't be aired. In some instances where there were potentially thorny problems on a direction being considered he would seek the experts' clearance or views before ever presenting let alone selling the idea to the client. A tactic he employed was not to tackle any issue over the telephone but preferred to go down to their offices with any, or all, supporting evidence and combat their worries, concerns or complaints face-to-face. Often a word substitution or a change in emphasis would resolve the problem. Where Christoph scored over his peer group was that he never delegated this area to a junior even when he was at the top of the tree in an agency. This was his responsibility, and he firmly believed in the saying, 'never send a boy on a man's errand'. If you've got a hard-nosed combative character you might as well use him! He also acknowledged the psychology of this job. On any given day an individual employed by the copy clearance team would have to deal with 8 to 10 scripts and also have to review 20 to 30 items on the viewing reel – so his particular script might not get the proper undivided attention unless he tackled it personally.

Quite early on as an Account Director at Gris Advertising Christoph discovered that his key contact person at the ITCA (Independent

Television Copy Authority) a delightful innocently flirtatious woman, Jane Elstone, had a penchant for gambling. Once he had picked up on this, Christoph invited Jane to dinner at The White City for an evening of Greyhound Racing. Jane was delighted to accept this invitation but asked if it could be extended to include her husband as well. Christoph was delighted to oblige her request until he arrived as it only turned out that Jane's husband was the Deputy Head of Copy Clearance with whom he had been doing fierce battle just that very afternoon! Chris had also previously bleated to Jane about what a stick in the mud this character was and she had merely smiled gracefully and never let on. It appeared they both loved horse racing and gambling and had landed many a good touch both in England and in France, where they had a bolt hole, and to which they finally retired. The evening was a great success and gave everyone a good laugh mainly at Christoph's expense.

Christoph was convinced that his investment in time and effort in this area had proven to be a major benefit to him and his agencies and clients throughout his career. More often than not workable resolutions could be found through good honest debate and discussion. When and where reversals occurred after transmission he was usually able to negotiate a stay of execution, giving sufficient time to keep the advertising on air, while a replacement copy route was developed and produced.

Occasionally matters could or would be elevated at both the client end and or with the broadcast authorities respectively. In many of these situations Christoph would be the 'go to' man in the Agency, especially during his time at McKillans. Two major wins came for Christoph on Neptune when two of their confectionery brands were under attack from both the HEA (Health Education Authority) and AIS (Action Information on Sugars). The battle had been taken to the ITC (Independent Television Commission) and specifically their Director of Advertising and Sponsorship. By the time Christoph was brought in, on the first case, the bad feelings, stresses and strains, as well as the politics, had become pretty unsavoury, between the various bodies.

A life above the line – just!

There were also enough 'so-called' experts and egos to fill The Albert Hall. Christoph's initial move was to step back, accept that the scientific evidence might be compelling one way or the other but perhaps what might be more persuasive would be the reactions of the consumers themselves. Despite these being identified as the people that needed protecting they had seemingly been largely ignored, by these boffins, and their input missed and unconsidered. To Christoph this part of the argument seemed to be particularly relevant given that the product under review was of a small portion size, a low density and containing considerably fewer calories than other snack foods. The science itself demonstrated that the product when consumed by children provided less than 7% of daily energy requirements and would take just 90 minutes to burn off. In the subsequent consumer research, Christoph initiated, mothers supported the responsible approach being taken in the advertising, showing moderation over indiscriminate eating. A carefully scripted letter was written by Christoph to the respective bodies. This was sufficient to win the argument and the slogan and the advertising were allowed to continue to be used and aired.

The second case was altogether more important as it was on a lead brand for the Neptune Company and the stakes were very high indeed. The arguments were more complex and convoluted and the attack was on a brand logo and advertising slogan that had been in existence since the 1950s. The accusation was that the advertiser, notably Neptune, had contravened the ITC Code, these being stated as:-

-*'generalised claims for properties such as 'goodness' or 'wholesomeness' may imply that a food product or an ingredient has a greater nutritional or health benefit, than is actually the case….'*

-*'no advertisement may misleadingly claim or imply that the product advertised or any ingredient has some special property or quality, which is incapable of being established.'*

Christoph watched as legions of great brains and acclaimed experts were brought into this fray from the worlds of nutrition, food science, health, diet, behavioural habits and attitudes as well as from crisis Public Relations. Christoph, after his relatively simple success earlier, was invited to many of these forums and meetings. What he encountered was a great deal of pontificating and posturing with a fair degree of cerebral pomposity. There seemed to him to be a lot of point scoring without any significant progress. All the while the brand's advertising had been pulled off air. Christoph's viewpoint was crystal clear. Categorising food as being good or bad was misleading and that the key was diet and here there were genuine concerns, exacerbated by an increased sedentary lifestyle and a lack of exercise. Christoph continued to believe that snack foods and specifically confectionery, in this instance, as part of a balanced and controlled diet was totally acceptable especially when consumed in moderation. He would even go so far as to say that it was an enjoyable and acceptable way of providing many of the nutrients that are essential as part of the Recommended Daily Allowance (RDA). On this specific brand Christoph argued that it had always been associated with people actively involved in leisure pursuits, which was and should be encouraged by everyone – including the Government, scientists and nutritionists. The ingredients this product offered and provided contributed to people's ability to perform their everyday activities. The long established slogan reinforced this and in no way implied that anything was peculiar to or exclusive to this particular brand. Christoph, however, was not involved or even allowed to partake in the defence for the Medical Advisory Panel.

As such he decided to concentrate his efforts on keeping the people at the Broadcast Copy Clearance body fully apprised of developments and informed about the discussions going on, way above their pay level and indeed his! This way he retained their support for the brand's right to advertise. Additionally, working with the in-house Company Public Relations Manager at Neptune they devised a programme of market research initially and then consumer research with regard to consumer take out from the advertising and its slogan. This focus on the understanding from the advertising and the slogan was a different tact and this was Christoph taking a big punt to provide a different angle to the argument. The first step was an analysis of the quantitative research where 68% of people felt that the end line was just an advertising slogan and not something that was or should be analysed. The second stage was the qualitative research and here Christoph was gambling on his belief that the slogan was simply advertising 'puffery' and only inextricably linked to the brand because of its longevity. This gamble paid off big time as it became the deal-breaker in the stand-off dispute between the warring parties. The Independent Television Commission even conceded, in writing, with these words, '....*not conclusive but did lend some support to the advertiser's argument.*' They also acknowledged that based on the scientific evidence provided that, '*the product was indisputably entitled to claim to be a convenient and agreeable source of food energy.*'

The time Christoph had invested with the Copy Clearance body also paid off as their Chairman wrote to the ITC forcibly complaining over '*the length of time that was taken to resolve the matter*' and going on to state that this brand /advertiser '*was unable to use a slogan of long standing for the best part of the year. Quite apart from the obvious commercial implications......there is a basic injustice in dealing with a complaint of this nature in such a harsh manner.*' They then went on to state that in their view, '*in such circumstances.....the advertiser should be given the benefit of the doubt during the investigative process*'. It was a comprehensive win and did Christoph's reputation no harm at all as the canny, tactical, games player when it came to Copy Clearance issues.

The only time it could be a complete lottery was when the film had already been made and then rejected. It was then desperation stakes and Christoph would be brought in to try to salvage the film and get it broadcasted. Clearly, given the cost of production the idea of the advertising agency having to write off a film and having nothing to support a brand was tantamount to losing the client's total trust and ultimately the business. As such in these situations the stakes were very high. Quite often these were films that had been made, without any prior discussion, with the copy clearance authorities. There would have been no clearance or approval of the script. This was not something that Christoph would ever recommend doing, and certainly never did.

One such case, amongst many he tackled, did amuse Christoph as it was a commercial for cinema where because of the medium no-one in the agency had thought approval at script stage was necessary. The script for Quartet Toilet Tissue was entitled Yuppie 11. Christoph knew he had a tough battle on his hand when he was brought in after the Cinema Advertising Association UK had rejected the film. The idea revolved around a man sitting on the loo with two telephones and read as follows:-

"It's simple, simple, simple. Have you forgotten my three point plan Giles? You buy, you sack, you sell. Can you understand that? Here let me demonstrate Point 2 'you're fired'" (First phone)

(Second phone rings) "Jane, darling; I'm home tonight so I'd like some dinner. You're cooking?? (Amazed) Then you'd better buy some toilet paper. I want this soft stuff…Quartet. Ciao".

(First phone) "Sarah, send Giles his P45. Oh and if you haven't finished that report pick up yours too. I am going to Jane's tonight so call the wife. Tell her I'm in Zurich.'"

Male Voice Over:- *'Quartet. So soft, it's recommended by arse holes!'*

The issue, of course, revolved around the use of the word or expression 'arsehole' and on grounds of offensiveness and lack of decency the film had been rejected. The CAA quoted Code Clause 5.1 which stated, '…*Compliance with the Codes will be judged on the context, medium, audience, product and prevailing standards of decency and judged offensive on the grounds of race, religion, sex, sexual orientation or disability.'* This was familiar territory to Christoph and once he was brought in he determined to fight the case on the spelling and pronouncement of 'arse' which he claimed would be 'ass'. He also pointed out that in the dictionary one of the meanings given for 'ass' did in fact equate to 'arse'. Furthermore, an examination of other advertisers had revealed that both Nike and Holsten Pils had used the word "shit" as a reaction expression. Christoph also argued that 'asshole' was a colloquial expression for a stupid and self-important person – as per the character depicted in this advertising. Indeed, he went on to state that the dictionary definition for 'arsehole/asshole' was that of 'being a stupid, irritable or despicable/contemptible person.' His final 'piece de resistance' was that while it might be perceived as being a double-entendre it was being used in a wholly appropriate context and for a totally relevant product.

The argument was won by changing the word from 'arsehole'

to 'asshole' in both the voice over and the printed strapline with the condition that the advertising could only appear with Aged 15 and 18 Certified Films. The CAA's ruling and judgement read as follows:- '... *To this end the more commonly acceptable phrase "ass hole" should be used, thereby tilting the meaning towards slightly more sophisticated social readings. The fifteen plus audience includes many who would be likely to take offence at being expected to react to such blunt scatology (obsession with excrement and excretion)."* As such it went on air and Christoph had probably saved the account and a certain team member's career within the agency! It is never great for one's Curriculum Vitae to have to admit to having had to write off a film or to have lost one's job because of a client moving their business because of such an oversight!

Christoph truly enjoyed the sparring, and debates, that took place in those 'grey areas'. This was the area that lay between those scripts that were crystal clear and did not challenge the norm and those that simply hadn't a hope in hell of ever getting made, let alone, broadcasted! Often it was a case of doing the prep work properly and thoroughly, coming up with a positioning, developing the arguments and discussion points. For Christoph it was also about establishing mentally and practically beforehand where the compromises could be made, and where it was subject to interpretation, or where serious debate would be called for. Sometimes he would use pure theatre with amateur dramatics and other times it would be more reasoned with a calm assurance and a skilful and carefully laid out defence. Either way, it nearly always ended up with a 'liquid lunch' with the Copy Clearance team ensuring there were never hard feelings on either side. It seemed to Christoph a small price to pay for a good battle and for maintaining his high winning record! He knew he never expected to lose but he was also aware that it was impossible to win all the time. The fun and thrill lay in finding different ways of playing the game that gave him the very best chance of winning.

CHAPTER 8

'The Risk Taker'

'A person willing to do things that involve danger or risk in order to achieve a goal' – adapted from Merriam-Webster's Dictionary

'I am a risk taker. Fear does not control my decisions' (Rachel Wolchin)

'Risk is the down-payment of success' (Monica Kurhade)

Christoph always played the percentages. This was irrespective of whether it was gambling on horses or dogs, or facing up to the challenges in his working life. Having a good basic knowledge and form to go on was fundamental upon which to assess the odds. Form helped to frame his judgement. But the real high came from betting against the odds and taking on the higher risks, which he seemingly embraced with little or no hesitation at all. He always backed his judgement and seldom thought of the downside risks or the consequences of failure and certainly not to himself. If he thought that something could be done than for him it was worth trying. He took failure badly, at the time, but recognised it was a consequence of taking risks and chances. He learnt much from his failures and mistakes more so than his successes. What Christoph endeavoured to do was never to make the same mistake twice. When something went wrong he would analyse why and how it had gone wrong and what could and should have been done differently. He acknowledged his faults and took full blame, accountability and responsibility and never let his players or team members be culpable. He felt he had broad enough shoulders to take the knocks. He also had no care for his own preservation, as security and an easy life was never something he actively sought. For Christoph it was the sheer thrill of the risk. That was where the humour, fun, satisfaction and adrenalin rush in life came from. Without risks life was merely, boring, dull and predictable. When he was bored or not kept fully motivated and busy he became dangerous – highly critical, dulled, pessimistic and even self-destructive. That would be when he would often resign and hence his moniker of being 'the serial resigner'.

Throughout Christoph's working career there was never naked selfish ambition. He had a sense of his worth and value and that was enough for him. He was not interested in self-promotion, self-seeking glory or working for rewards. He expected to be remunerated fairly for what he was expected to do but looked to others to evaluate what that might actually mean. Even before he asked for £100,000 to work on International business with Dick Shlitz he had deliberated over the opportunity with the Head of Human Resources and conferred about what he felt a fair price for the job was. He then mulled it over before arriving at this figure and how he would justify it. He never in his whole career sought comparisons with other staff members but saw himself as an individual. He believed in meritocracy. Equal pay was an anathema to him, nobody did the same job as him, irrespective of whether their titles were the same or not. He was an individual who ploughed his own furrow, made his own rules, and expected his performance, success or achievements for his agencies to be recognised and rewarded appropriately. Loyalty was something he truly believed in, but he also knew it was more often than not abused and longevity was frequently penalised rather than rewarded. Long term players usually earned significantly less than 'unknown' newer recruits or people 'bought in' at similar levels. The mentality seemed to be 'he's never going to leave, so we don't need to pay him so much'. He had discovered this when leaving Gris Advertising and going to Premium White. Hence he made heavier demands from his new agency than he might have done otherwise. The fact that longstanding servants and operators were seemingly less valued and all too often taken for granted was something Christoph never understood. This was more especially the case when these people suddenly decided it was time to leave, to either earn more, or for new challenges, and then all of a sudden, there were vast sums available in the coffers, of the incumbent agency, to try to retain these people's services. If they had paid them the going rate they might never have looked around, and made them feel unloved or insecure, in the first place.

Overall though, Christoph felt he had been fortunate throughout his working life. The circumstances, the opportunities that had presented themselves, or that had been created (sometimes even by him!), were timely and advantageous. Christoph would fairly regularly be asked if he considered himself to be lucky, being in the right place at the right time, in getting the outcomes he achieved. He would usually ponder and reflect on this for a moment before replying, 'No, not especially. I worked really hard at being lucky and I truly made my own luck.' Deep down though, he knew that in every aspect of life there had to be a modicum of luck, be that with health, finance, birth right, schooling, recognition, success, love, children, and just as relevantly, in gambling and judgement calls. But to these he could add his natural business acumen, a certain flair, a lack of fear, never standing on ceremony, avoidance of political forums, a total disregard for political correctness and taking the risks and chances, many would not even have considered never mind taken. These aspects, plus his phenomenal work ethic and immense output, Christoph reckoned, brought the odds down in his favour. He knew he rode his luck – sometimes even literally! Right from the very start of his career he would often get away with it by the 'seat of his pants'. Certainly, Christoph knew that he relied on charm, and an almost perpetual smile, in the galvanising company of others, to smooth the path. He was always ready with a quip, a laugh, a joke or a piece of theatre to change and lighten the mood and tone. The simple fact was that, throughout his 30 years, he could never take advertising too seriously, and that was quite probably what kept him sane. It was a game.

In Christoph's early days on the Thomas Healey business at Gris Advertising he had to partake in their annual jamboree - 'The Budget Meeting Season'. These were high risk meetings where it was possible to be shot down in flames, lose one's nerve or say the wrong thing with dire consequences. These outcomes often took effect immediately though sometimes could affect a person's career in the long term. The budget meeting was done for each brand singularly and not by category. They were basically a ball-breaking, painstaking exercise, reviewing the business in microscopic detail. The Agency curiously was expected to answer all the questions posed sitting alongside the Brand Manager and his or her team. These poor unfortunate acolytes were expected to have prepared all the answers to a number (even on occasions a raft) of questions, in myopic detail. The questions had been sent down in advance of the meeting by the company management. They had arisen from a one pager Brand Budget Preface that had been submitted by the Brand Manager, with accord from the Agency, a few days in advance of the actual meeting. This sheet highlighted the current status, the progress on the brand in that fiscal year and previous calendar year, and an outline of the proposed plans going forward. There was, of course, no guarantee that the questions would be exactly those posed initially and indeed they seldom were. What was essential was that the answer given to any question asked was short, precise and succinct so that it satisfied the questioner and avoided further exploratory questions, if at all possible! Brevity, accuracy and neat completeness were the order of the day. Christoph had learnt that many a good operator had come unstuck by answering a question too fully and then having to defend the additional information they had inauspiciously provided. Inevitably embellishing a response would only open up a can of worms and the subsequent questions would almost certainly not have been planned or prepared for and would in any case be far more demanding and complex. Less was definitely more. Getting out in the allotted time of three hours was very much part of the game plan. The prospect of coming back after lunch, or worse still on another day was not a situation one wanted to even begin to contemplate, and certainly not be responsible for.

Christoph could see that in many ways these annual forums had real tangible benefits. All the key members in the Company were present and there was this dedicated time set aside to examine in detail each and every brand. Every aspect was scrutinised from business performance (yes even by pack size, by outlet type, by region!), problems being faced, successes achieved by sales, retailers, and consumers alike. There was Christoph always thought a major shortcoming and that was that it was conducted without any competitive analysis or a review of the category as a whole. Another real concern with these forums were that they were truly a lot like 'Mastermind' and as Christoph discovered a huge amount of pressure was exerted on the poor individual in the 'black chair'. The pressure and tension was electric and could almost reach breaking point. Christoph knew of instances when the Agency representative resigned, off the business, rather than face this torture chamber. Others had refused to travel to the meeting, or even leave their house, feigning illness out of sheer terror and dread. In one particular case an individual Christoph knew actually took an overdose and so instead of travelling to the meeting, at Thomas Healey, he found himself being conveyed to the local hospital by ambulance. Christoph had mixed feelings about these interrogations and had a variety of results, fortunately mainly positive, over his years working on Thomas Healey. He fronted for the Agency at over 15 of these brand budget sessions, though his last four or five were considerably less tortuous. By then the format had changed and it had evolved to be more of a discussion between Brand Team supported by their Agency and the Company Management. In a rather perverse way Christoph rather enjoyed them and had only one really bad experience when in the USA where 'he had bottled it' and blotted his copybook. That was when he had been persuaded to put forward two copy routes on a brand when instinctively he felt it would have been best to have a firm recommendation on a single route. On that occasion he took the flak, the venom and was ultimately chewed out by a really

A life above the line – just!

tough uncompromising Advertising Director, whom had displayed a strong dislike for advertising people, even before this encounter! Rightly though, he couldn't comprehend why the combined Brand and Agency team didn't have strong point of view and a commitment behind one route rather than being so undecided and wishy washy. Christoph learnt from this and never made that mistake again!

These were definitely not forums or occasions to show-off in and Christoph realised survival and a good end result with praise for the work, contribution and presentation was about as good as it could get!

Christoph witnessed many strange events at these forums. On one occasion the Brand Manager was so stressed that he went into a fit of flatulence and couldn't stop farting and in the end had to leave in a state of great embarrassment. Another time the Brand Assistant experienced a really bad nose bleed and the Advertising Manager rather than excusing the individual had him lie flat across the table and continue to answer the questions from this supine position. Another occurrence involved a brand manager who despite possessing the same Christian name as the, then recently appointed, Advertising Manager simply couldn't remember his first name. In the end the Advertising Manager wrote on a large card 'My name is Malcolm – the same as yours!' It was quite extraordinary how nerves manifested themselves in some people. It truly was a case of survival – and not necessarily of the fittest!

Advertising was a major part of a brand's support and so not surprisingly came under considerable scrutiny at each and every one of these forums. This could be the actual content of the copy, which was normal, but it could also be the employment of the media – how much and where. It seemed bizarre to Christoph that the most inexperienced and junior agency person would be pushed forward to front at these meetings. As he became more senior he chose to take the lead as he felt it took the pressure off the junior staff and he believed that he could offer a broader perspective. Very early on, however, when he was the new boy on the block and a complete novice Christoph learnt that 'honesty pays' and truly was 'the best policy'. If he didn't know the answer himself then call in the expert most likely to provide the information rather than bluff it, especially as at his junior level he would have scant knowledge. This also had the added benefit of giving the principal answerer time to recover their composure, giving them a short respite and a moment to relax while the focus was not on them. It was Christoph knew only a short moment as he would still be under the hammer, being scrutinised and sensing he was like the Christians being fed to the hungry lions, in The Coliseum, in Rome. One wag Christoph knew phrased it similarly and stated it felt like 'Caligula and the Muppets where one was most definitely the Muppet and one was quite likely to have one's head torn off one's shoulders!' Indeed, in his first ever Budget Meeting, this very first outing became somewhat traumatic and definitely memorable.

Christoph had got through a barrage of questions on brand share, distribution by pack size and brand performance by retailer by region. This had gone reasonably smoothly and even surprisingly well and Christoph was warming to the task at hand. His performance was greatly enhanced by the efficiency of the Brand Team, who produced the relevant information, on acetate, at the right time, from a vast deck of these plastic sheets; which they had printed out in advance, in preparation for the likely myriad of questions that could be fired at the greenhorn, Christoph.

But then suddenly the focus of attack shifted to the advertising where the proposal put forward had advocated for an increase in expenditure. This was behind a long-established testimonial route that was fairly pedestrian and was not exactly leading to 'housewives' frantically pulling the product off the shelves. Three times the Advertising Manager asked Christoph how he felt the extra expenditure proposed could be justified. Christoph felt totally exposed, and distinctly naked, and most definitely challenged! The first time he responded by suggesting that the campaign needed more time and increased support to establish its effectiveness in the marketplace. On the second response he dug deep with a more subjective and judgemental response, claiming that the quality of the new testimonies was of a decidedly superior calibre, which had come about through better casting of women, of a more diverse and characterful nature. On the third time of asking Christoph

A life above the line – just!

appreciated he was going to a well that had gone dry and that the only water for the dried out shrubs was going to be his own spittle. In response, he stated that the intention was to support the brand more aggressively, in the more expensive Southern TV areas, in which the brand leader was more prevalent, in order to be combative and more competitive, and thereby build business and market share there.

Completely underwhelmed by the arguments and responses provided by Christoph the Advertising Manager was about to repeat his question for the fourth time. Christoph was right out of defence be that based on ideas, facts and even bullshit. Now he was looking into the eyes of a major crash, head on. Then salvation arrived from a most surprising direction. The Chairman of the Agency, William Keyes, in his full, deep, sonorous voice, interjected with total understanding of the intent behind the Advertising Manager's persistent questioning and stated, "I give you my assurance that you shall have new advertising to test against the current copy campaign, by June 1st". This was indeed a bold promise given that it was already the middle of March and nothing had been briefed in to the Creatives, to that effect. Nevertheless, on the day, this interjection worked, as the Advertising Manager relented and let a squirming Christoph off the hook, as he stated, "William, I am truly very relieved to hear this. I'll call you on May 31st to find out the progress you have made." The then Creative Director, in what was meant to be an inaudible whisper, but which came out far louder then was intended, said, "I wonder what he'll call you, William?!" Assessing the situation brilliantly William Keyes retorted, "My dear boy that will depend entirely on you!" This caused much hilarity and some tittering around the vast table. And so Christoph had survived his first Budget meeting –just - and in the process earned many accolades for having held his own and stood his ground – even though he felt it was a distinctly shaky terrain, if not actually quicksand!

Over time Christoph realised that these were sessions where it was possible to perform well and also take a lot of the pressure off the less experienced staff and thereby hopefully make the contributions more constructive. He also recognised that from the Agency standpoint, the best thing would be to get ahead of the game in terms of advertising development. To that end he sought to ensure that on all the Thomas Healey brands, held by the agency, that each had a copy platform. This entailed having the mainstream campaign currently on air, an alternative mainstream copy route in test; be that ideally made and actually in a market region, but at the very least in research, an alternative strategic direction and a 'flyer' that could be using other media or an off the wall advertising copy approach to the brand. Christoph's thinking behind this was that it was difficult to criticise the agency, for lacking initiative, or failing to perform, or providing insufficient output if it was being so pro-active. He even modified and introduced this model for International assignments, as the business moved in that direction, from the early 1980s. Here he had to be sensitive as to whether the copy running in one country could actually 'travel' and be relevant in other countries, especially where English might not be the first language and where irony and humour simply might not work. He strongly resisted the American Management view that if certain advertising had run in the USA successfully it could run everywhere and anywhere. This became an on-going battle as Internationalism/Globalisation expanded and ever more Americans appeared in senior roles at both client and agency alike. With them came their US approach to advertising that all too often was inappropriate and proved ineffectual in the European Markets.

Early on, after his return from the States, Christoph experienced first-hand the complexities of dealing with this emerging American threat. A highly politicised and political person, Tom Boxer, was appointed as the Gris Advertising's Franchise Director on Thomas Healey business throughout Europe. This was a character who believed in operating via paper rather than face-to-face. Not only did Christoph find his own terrain being narrowed by this gentleman but he had to contend with being inundated with telexes, faxes and telephone messages. This for Tom seemed to negate the need for any meetings. In the end Christoph's in-tray from these memos became so laden and voluminous that he chose simply to ignore them totally. Besides, he fortuitously discovered that, if he waited long enough one would be contradicted by another, or in some cases merely become redundant.

Finally, Christoph did catch-up with Tom and he asked him why he thought that this was an efficient use of his time to simply fire in one paper after another rather than meet. Tom's answer was that he was always travelling, having ideas which he wanted to share. Christoph suggested that when he was in his hotel room or waiting to board a plane he would help his cause and himself far better by reading a good book, or even a dirty magazine, and abandon 'sharing' his multitude of disconnected and often irrelevant or inappropriate thoughts. This was clearly never going to be a marriage made in heaven as Tom was a snippy Jewish New Yorker – a dilettante and not a worker and he relied on his contacts rather than any genuine interest in the business or the development of good let alone great advertising. Christoph was a direct Catholic Londoner who believed passionately in what he was doing and resented interference that was counterproductive to his process and progress. On one occasion Tom actually said to Christoph, "I'd really like to have a meeting with you but you're so full of vitriol"! (Though there was no evidence that he really wanted to have a meeting in the first place!).

When Tom insisted on foisting himself onto the Budget Meetings, in the UK, with Thomas Healey, by getting himself invited by the client Christoph went ballistic. He was so put out that he stated he would not attend himself. Given that he was the lead person for the agency his UK Management was rightly somewhat concerned. A compromise was reached in that Tom would only attend as an observer and only utter anything at all if and when a question was specifically directed to him. As Chris put it rather eloquently to his management, "If Tom so much as opens his mouth I will get up and ram my fist down his 'effing' throat." Enough people believed he would too so Tom was quietly warned in advance. As it transpired Tom said nothing, the meetings went well and they were a personal triumph for Christoph who was singled out for praise from the Company Management. Afterwards, as was the norm, there was an evening of revelry and much jollity was had, by triumphant and greatly relieved teams, that had bonded so well over this process, on two separate brands. Christoph was having such a good time that he barely made the night sleeper back to London.

Inebriated, exhilarated and exhausted he collapsed on his bunk bed. Disembarking on a crisp early spring morning he felt decidedly the worst for wear and chose to walk from Kings Cross to the agency's West End office. When he arrived there it was still early and relatively few people had arrived. However, when he opened his office door he was greeted by Tom Boxer, sitting at his desk, apparently awaiting his appearance. This was not something Christoph was expecting, nor desiring, least of all, in his current dishevelled worn-out state. Tom started by rather condescendingly and patronisingly praising and congratulating Christoph on his tour de force performance the day before. He then went on to ask Christoph what his problem was with him personally. Chris was in no mood for a soul searching session and he was slightly irked by the intrusion of Tom in his office and for him having taken the liberty to sit at his desk, uninvited. He looked blankly and unemotionally at Tom and then said, 'Tom you are a politician who schmoozes clients. I am an adman who seeks to find effective communication for their brands. That makes you dangerous as you are looking to ingratiate yourself and seeking short term gratification, which is more than likely going to get in the way of longer term solutions to the complex problems I am challenged to resolve. In truth, I think that you are one of the biggest turkeys I have ever encountered and how you got past Christmas without being gobbled up beggars belief!" Certainly not one of Christoph's finest moments, let alone a mature, astute or politically correct response - but at the time deeply satisfying!

Unbeknown to Christoph then was that these would turn out to be his last budget meetings held in this 'Mastermind' gladiatorial style. He would however get a smile and chuckle on enquiring how one of his close colleagues (interestingly another Jewish New Yorker) had got on. Seymour had replied, "Well Christoph you know how these things can go-Sometimes well, sometimes badly. In this instance it was a case of "Lions 6, Christians 2 Jews Nil." But Christoph's end to these came not from the change of format, as this would only occur in later years, but by Tom Boxer exacting his revenge.

Christoph was asked by Tom to attend a major brand strategic review in Brussels involving senior bodies from the agencies in Europe and their client counterparts. Christoph had agreed to attend and he prepared a paper that outlined his thoughts and ideas for this household brand. He had explored a range of different consumer insights and to these he had developed a number of concepts which could be tested out. This forward looking input, at the meeting, was very positively received and led to a very constructive open discussion. The client was especially pleased at the range and depth of thinking which they found to be stimulating, exciting and challenging. Christoph left the meeting feeling that he had made a significant contribution. However, when he rang into the agency from Heathrow on his return he was informed by his PA that the UK Agency Managing Director needed to see him urgently as he was after his blood! Christoph was totally bemused and couldn't begin to think what had gone so wrong in his absence. When he got back to the office he promptly went to see the MD and was informed that this time he had gone too far and that Tom Boxer had rung him, complaining that he had been openly contradicted in front of the clients by Christoph. In so doing Tom felt he had been undermined and this had resulted in a fractious, indecisive, contrary meeting which had shown the agency in a bad light. Christoph was absolutely stunned as this was wholly unexpected. He defended himself by pointing out that this was intended to be an ideas forum on the brand, where openness and exploratory thinking were meant to be discussed, considered and reviewed. He had done preparatory work for this meeting and, in his humble opinion; his input had been well received. But Christoph's defence fell upon deaf ears and he was suspended from doing any work on the whole account with immediate effect. Christoph was shell shocked. He took this instruction very badly, as unfairness was something he had never been able to abide. But at the same time it gave him 'time to consider and review his position'.

As soon as the next day the Managing Director came to see Christoph in his office. Rather sheepishly he apologised and then laughingly stated that perhaps he had been a little hasty in arriving at his decision the day before. He had had the time subsequently to reconsider, especially given a telephone conversation, he had held, with the Senior UK Client whom had rung to thank his agency for having taken such a leading role in this International Forum, and specifically citing Christoph's contribution. On refection, therefore, Christoph was to be reinstated. However, overnight, Christoph had come to the conclusion that he was fed up working with someone whose own ego was evidently more important then what was being done on and for the business. He'd had enough of the 'politicking'. He also felt that the working relationship between Tom Boxer and himself was counterproductive for both the Agency and Client alike. So, smiling ruefully, he looked the Managing Director in the eye and said, "No – last time it was your decision and you chose not to believe me, or check with others first, but accepted the wrong and unjust accusations of a politically motivated individual in Europe. You chose to publicly suspend me and I respected that decision. But now this time it is my decision and I refuse your retracted suspension and instead I tender my resignation off the account. It is time for a change and this should make it easier in the future for both you and the International Management." The MD was astonished and realised he had read and done Christoph wrong. All sorts of incentives in terms of financial remuneration, staffing levels and status were offered to keep him on the business. But the only concession and compromise Christoph made was that he agreed, in the interests of both parties – client and agency – to work on the account until the end of the year so that his replacement could be identified and brought up to speed. This he did honourably and without client knowledge until very close to his departure date. After seven years that had taken him to both sides of the Atlantic, with Thomas Healey, it really was time to move on and face fresh challenges. Most graciously the Company hosted a farewell dinner in his honour and presented him with an inscribed silver tankard expressing their appreciation. It is never used but it holds pride of place in Christoph's study.

Some years later, at McKillans, Christoph would work for Thomas Healey again and would reacquaint himself with some of his earlier client personnel as well as many new faces. Amongst the latter was a General Manager who was a much travelled and wildly enthusiastic

A life above the line – just!

Singaporean. His infectious personality and dramatic restless traits made him quite a character. His standard expression to the Agency was "I want a campaign as famous as the Marlboro Cowboy." At a private session sometime later he informed Christoph how he felt about his family life and travelling with them, "You know Christoph having had our children in Singapore and then having them educated over here in the UK makes me feel like I'm bringing up a bunch of bananas; yellow on the outside white on the inside." They got on well and together did change and free up the advertising over time - but there was no Marlboro Cowboy.

But the person who eventually took over from the Singaporean General Manager, when he left to go to Canada, was another old sparring partner from Christoph's earlier days on the account. Now, in this elevated position, he reminded Christoph on how when the clients would get into a group to discuss the Agency's creative copy recommendations – termed as 'a huddle' he would be heard to say "Come on you bunch of turkeys can't any of you make a decision?" They both laughed it off and enjoyed a new spirited relationship from there on in. In fact it was to him that Christoph made his final three Budget Meetings. These were on Healthcare and Teen Care brands in 1992. It was a very different atmosphere to the past and there was none of the confrontation but they were highly constructive work sessions. Christoph always recalled his last ever review as he had been suffering from a very heavy bout of 'man flu' that had left him temporarily deaf, with a heavy cold and a rasping sore throat that made it hard for him to talk and swallow. Despite his condition and a strong desire to cry off, his team insisted he carry on and lead the agency, at this forum, which he dutifully did. The Client was mildly amused by Christoph's apparent weakened condition and out of sympathy asked whether the agency would like to make some opening remarks. Christoph used this opportunity to anticipate some of the questions that might be raised by answering these succinctly and adroitly in his preamble. Not hearing properly he had come across as making an impassioned speech but done so very loudly. This was so much so that it apparently came over more like a demonic sermon from the pulpit rather then a marketing presentation. Unsurprisingly, at the end of the meeting, the Advertising Manager came over to thank Christoph and shaking him warmly by the hand congratulated him on the plans, the work, and the part he had played in the meeting, but wanted to know if it was really necessary to have shouted throughout. When Christoph explained his medical problem this gentleman smiled and patting him on the arm said, "From henceforth you shall be known as 'The Reverend Aitkin' by me!" And so he was, even if it was an insult to the cloth!

Christoph loved the potential risk of uncertainty, and indeed nothing in advertising was ever certain. Sometimes, however, it was clear that the odds were not in his favour and this inspired and excited him. He would calculate his chances and then take the risk, either because he felt he had no viable alternative, or because at the time it seemed, to him, the right thing to do or even just for the hell of it. This would even extend to situations which were not directly connected with his agency or his clients. One such case involved a friend and colleague of his, who had gone on to start his own agency, working primarily with new companies and conglomerates in the newly emerging technological and communication fields. He truly was an ideas generator and his concepts were often highly visible and subject to strong PR mileage over and above the paid for communication. The problem that he suffered from was that being a small operation it was easy for big organisations to delay payment, adversely affecting his cash flow, or worse still avoid payment altogether, on totally spurious grounds. The nature of his clients also meant that there were takeovers, mergers and affiliations taking place all the time so that his actual client was often a moving target and subject to change, in both name and personnel. With these developments also came unsavoury politics and business greed where properties, entities and messages he had developed were simply transferred in ownership terms to whomsoever these big entities decided. This raised an important legal issue and that was over ownership and copyright of properties developed by a supplier. Additionally, it raised another question and that was whether if a company is acquired the new company automatically assumes they have the right to use the logo, name and slogan developed for the previous company and are there cost implications or usage restrictions and limitations. Christoph was asked by this friend for his point of view and advice alongside many legal minds and boffins he was consulting with. He had become a victim of these complexities, in the telecommunications field. Over time this became a major legal wrangle and a number of court proceedings were put in place over a lengthy period of time.

Christoph felt strongly that this was strong arm tactics seeking to declare this friend bankrupt, through non-payment of his bills and seeking to discredit him and claiming their ownership of the work and right to use it without further payment. Accordingly, Christoph felt a gross injustice was taking place and a need given his 'respected' position to support him, in whatever way he could. This meant he had to defy his own management who neither wanted Christoph to take on anything outside their jurisdiction, especially given his heavy work load, and certainly did not want Christoph to get embroiled in industry issues that could adversely affect him and even possibly their own agency. Christoph in response told them that he was prepared to resign from the agency to support his friend and his fledgling agency that at that time was breaking up and in total disarray and on the verge of going under. However, Christoph conceded that he would support his friend under his own name and that his agency would never be mentioned by name. He also assured them that this extra curriculum activity would be carried out mainly in his own time, except for any lawyer or barrister meetings or any court appearances. McKillans, realising that they would lose Christoph, as they appreciated he would not give this up, backed down and agreed to the placatory suggestions he proposed.

As time elapsed the conglomerate involved determined to discredit this small agency and the individual over an issue pertaining to Trade Description. If they won this case it would weaken Christoph's friend's position in the light of the Court at the subsequent property ownership case. It was at this juncture that Christoph was called as 'an expert witness' on behalf of the defence. What was particularly concerning about this was that he found himself in opposition with his own industry's advisory body whom had been called as experts for the prosecution. The specific issue in debate was that his friend's agency had seemingly borrowed a standard contract from another reputable 'shop' to model their contract on, with and for their clients. In so doing they had failed to delete the claim that pertained to being a member of the IPA (Institute of Practitioners in Advertising), which they were not. The debate raged over how important and relevant this was and by its inclusion of the IPA were they, in fact, guilty of misrepresentation?

Christoph was able to reassure the Court that this was merely an oversight, a genuine mistake, and was a clause that appeared as standard in most established agency contracts. Furthermore, Christoph expressed surprise that the IPA was appearing for the Prosecution as in his view the IPA stood as a representative body for the agencies and was in no way representative of clients, who had their own body, ISBA (Incorporated Society of British Advertisers). Christoph also reinforced his credentials; with regard the IPA, by stating that he had until recently been a core member of their Training Committee involved in developing training programmes for personnel, at different levels, within the IPA registered agencies. Christoph also went on to express his astonishment that this issue had only been picked up now after such a long time in their relationship, and, that perhaps, this was because it bore no relevance to their appointment of this agency at any time. Christoph pointed out that the IPA, while highly regarded as a representative body and resource, actually carried no legal power within the agencies nor was it a governing body. It was reassuring to clients to know that their agency was part of a respected representative body but carried no weight or would it normally, if ever, be a determining factor in the choice of agency. In his own particular case as a senior agency person he had over his career often gone to their library for desk research information, had occasionally sought their advice on particular advertising related matters, had called on them for arbitration between agencies and used some of their historical research. However, all his dealings had been concerned with agencies and never with or about clients.

It was a tense time but in the end it took the jury just 10 minutes to reach the unanimous verdict that neither the individual nor the agency was guilty of infringing the Trade Description Act. So in the end Christoph's friend was not discredited, he had not committed a misrepresentation and therefore no criminal action could be pursued or brought against him, while the contract remained valid and could not be deemed to be void. Christoph's friend would live to fight another day!

Christoph had always felt very strongly that the whole area of copyright ownership needed to be strengthened in law. He was particularly keen that this legal entity should favour the originators and creators. This had partly been his motivation to support his friend to ensure that big business did not ride roughshod over people whose creative product and originality could result in increased business results, but with no profit or gain for them, however long it was used. This concern he articulated in a film shown at the later High Court trial. He went on to expound his belief that copyright should always remain the ownership of the originator, though it could be arguably bought out, for an agreed sum, for a given period of time, mutually acceptable to both parties - the originator and the user. The fact that a message, a slogan, or a film, or a photograph had appeared in the media did not mean copyright and ownership was automatically transferred to the user.

At the High Court trial it was firmly established, and the judgement was made, that the advertising agency owned the copyright of the ideas it develops, and this even extended to pitches, made to prospective clients, where materials had frequently, in the past, been 'stolen' from non-appointed agencies. The conglomerate involved agreed to settle for an undisclosed significant sum with Christoph's friend and justice was ultimately seen to have been done. Christoph was delighted and in fact McKillans were full of admiration and immensely proud of Christoph for having stood up for the underdog taking a clear and strong position and emerging on the winning side, without in any way impairing their or indeed his relationship with the IPA.

Throughout his career Christoph would be called upon to make some risky big calls, genuine gambles and a few good punts. Early on during his time at McKillans when leading the team on Neptune in the UK, he had received a dictate from the client's International Management stating that they were putting an embargo on advertising. This was because they felt that there might be more prudent and cost-efficient ways of building their business and they wanted to identify these and then test these out without the waters being muddied by an advertising presence. These so-called different and distinct ways of reaching their consumers ranged from trade deals, gondola ends instore, better store presence generally, even special displays in store, through to sales promotions and other forms of communication under the nebulous and undefined umbrella of 'presence marketing'. Naturally, the Agency Managements were greatly alarmed as they could see their revenue plummeting.

Christoph on the other hand saw this as an amazing challenge and became excited by the idea of getting household brand names associated with sports and sponsorship in particular. The problem Christoph had was that he didn't have the contacts in the sporting world and therefore advised the Agency Management to invest in building a Sponsorship Unit within the agency itself. He agreed to lead it and appoint a small team of three people to work under him, with skills in sports sponsorship, event marketing and branded programming, for not just the UK, but also across other markets, both traditional and undeveloped, including the Middle East. It proved to be highly effective and it made McKillans the first major agency in the UK to pioneer and incorporate this facility within its main agency alongside its advertising offering.

So now Christoph had the tools of the trade to approach Neptune during this phase of abandoning advertising in the traditional media. He knew that the UK Country Manager, a gruff, middle aged, shrewd, small, dour Northerner with suspicions about everyone and a total distrust of agency folk, would be a tough nut to crack. The start of Christoph's pitch was not exactly promising as at his very first encounter with this particular client, immediately after the introductions, the Client decided 'to have a go' stating, "I think I should bloody well fire you – as you're never honest you flash agency types." Then when

A life above the line – just!

the actual meeting got underway Christoph began by showing a compilation film he had put together to show the potential power of sport sponsorship. This had been edited to the sung musical track, 'Football crazy – football mad' – written by James Curran in the 1880s. As it was playing the Client leant over to Christoph and muttered, "I bloody hate football, now if it was Crown Bowls then that would be a different matter altogether." Despite this rather inauspicious start Christoph battled on with his presentation undeterred which he had titled 'TV- Your flexible friend'. In the course of the presentation Christoph showed the wide use of sports sponsorship and how it was, and could be, captured on television be that via signage, billboards, intros, clothing and/or equipment. He also expounded on how teams and individuals could be sponsored and how this could be achieved, even at the most controlled environments, such as The Olympics, or, expensive events, such as The World Cup for Football, by the use of ambush marketing techniques. Christoph was able to weigh heavily on his work and experiences in the Middle East, as well as his genuine love for sport and interest in seeing Neptune enter this arena.

At the end of the presentation the normally cantankerous General Manager actually smiled and nodded approvingly while offering his hand and looking at Christoph, with a degree of surprise, and even grudging admiration. He said, "Well I'll be damned. I think you might just have gone and done it. It works, it excites, it's different and it could just be the way forward in our current climate. Well done." With that he took the presentation in its entirety. He presented it at a number of Management Meetings both domestically and internationally. He even played the film 'Football crazy' at each of these sessions! To his credit he always gave full acknowledgement to McKillans. It worked as it led to Neptune getting heavily involved in sports sponsorship with football, athletics and yachting, even including 'The Whitbread Round the World Yacht Race', which they fully capitalised on by having a mainstream commercial on a transatlantic yachting crew at sea, coinciding with the event itself. A by-product of this venture was that with the Middle East programming and sponsorship activity it made the Sponsorship Unit a viable entity, for McKillans. It also laid the pipe for the Neptune Company to eventually come back into mainstream advertising, thereby protecting the Agency's revenue. A risky strategy had truly delivered at and on many levels.

No gamble was too big or too small for Christoph. For him it was all about knowing the client, working out the details and then determining the chances of success. When Christoph had been working on Pharmacia, back in 1982, the challenge, as he saw it, was to take a fairly dull and mundane category, such as denture fixatives, and inject new life into it. Teaming up with a tall, powerfully built, fiery, red wiry headed Welshman they were determined to change the status quo. In a broad Welsh accent Gavin presented his work, starting almost in a whisper, "We don't want to hide this edentulous problem with mutterings in the corridors". Then raising his voice to its lyrical full force he boomed, "No – we want to sing it from the rooftops man; with pride, honesty and confidence." And so it was that this product featured normal, youthful looking people biting confidently into hard foods and especially a firm apple with its resounding 'crunch'. Indeed, this became the mnemonic for the brand. To justify it clinical trials and scientific evidence had to be produced, which was accepted by the ITCA (Copy Clearance body). The commercial was made and aired and the lighter tone and natural confidence was well received by users of fixatives and edentulous people alike. It made them feel normal, confident, aspiring people and not dowdy, old and dated. In a single stroke a recessive sector had become mainstream and normalised. Needless to say the leading brand and other competitors were envious of this bold step and sought through counter data to have the commercial taken off air. In the end the controversy led to the commercial being withdrawn, by the client, but they retained the mnemonic and the job had been successfully done for them. Business growth and a change in image had been positively achieved.

There were some occasions when the risks were truly formidable and when Christoph really had to dig deep into his reserves. During the early 1980s Gris Advertising had experienced some notable problems with their Scandinavian operation. Christoph was asked if he would help to reshape the agencies in the region and train individuals in the Stockholm office. The real area of concern was that they lacked sufficient numbers of people who had and could work consistently with other offices in the agency group on major International Clients. They were also lacking the presentation skills to attract and convert local prospects and possible long term leads for expanding clients emanating from Scandinavia and Sweden in particular. Christoph agreed to front at a number of these credential presentations and even a number of client forums. It was a happy and particularly rewarding and enjoyable period in Christoph's life. He found that the chemistry was ideal between him and the Scandinavian operation centred out of Stockholm. They wanted to work hard and play hard. The hours were long and draining and the play was equally demanding involving heavy drinking and extensive late night gambling, at the Casino. It was a fruitful experience as a lot was achieved and good friendships were established. At the end of his time there they presented him with a beautiful cut glass Orefors bowl.

However, it was not all plain sailing for Christoph. He was sent a telex from Norway asking if he could prepare a presentation on the UK Shoe Market as a particular company they were close to and had been courting for some time, was interested in bringing a line of their shoes into the UK. They were especially interested in having a segmentation of the market by shoe type and outlets by regions and an idea on styles and the price strategies being applied. Diligently Christoph put together a major review examining the different manufacturers, brands, imports, and retailers, fashion trends, marketing levels of support and price point analysis. Imagine then Christoph's shock when his key contact in the 'Nordics' arrived and stated how much he was looking forward to Christoph's market overview of the 'Shoe Trees' market. Not, after all, the shoe market but the niche sector of simply and solely shoe trees. Worse still he was expected to fill out such a presentation for circa 3 hours as this was the time the prospect had allocated prior to them leaving at lunchtime. Christoph blanched and getting out the telex he had received he was able to demonstrate that the request had clearly been for an analysis on 'shoes' and that the word 'trees' had been totally omitted. His colleague was mortified and began to panic as he could see his days had just become numbered, once this disaster became public knowledge. "In that case we have no option but to remain silent about the whole matter and I will simply have to 'wing-it'" Christoph remarked.

And so it was and so he did! During the introductions Christoph quickly assessed that among the team of four prospects there was in fact only one marketer, a woman whom it transpired was ex-Unilever. All four members though seemed bright, alert and interested and committed members of the shoe tree brigade! He appreciated he was facing a real task and challenge. Given this appraisal and assessment of his audience he started by seeking to capitalise on the likely fervour for their own shoe trees. He asked them if they would like to show him their products and the likely candidates for the UK market. This they did, at some length, and during this discussion Christoph was able to arrive at a segmentation of the market reflective of the product line up presented to him. He saw that some had a screw mechanism, some had a coiled spring, some had pliable bodies, some were made of plastic, chrome or stainless steel and some of wood and some had side alternators/expanders to accommodate different widths of feet as well as length shapers. From this Christoph then talked about how each model could best fit into each shoe outlet to which he now spontaneously added shoe repairers. He then discussed how some of the models should be affiliated with major shoe makers and manufacturers. It might even be a consideration for certain models to be sold as part of a package in the higher end market sector, be that Church's, Wildsmith, Locke's or Lobb and even Pinet or Russell & Bromley. Beyond this there were obvious tie-ins with the retail sector especially at the top end such as Austin Reed and Simpsons, Harvey Nicholls and Harrods/House of Fraser. At a different level were specialist shoe shops such as Clarkes Shoes where the emphasis was on comfort and suitability where a range of their shoe trees could retain the shape of the shoe here. An analysis of price points was important as each sector selected would merit a different and distinct product and a different price point. Clearly in the shoe repair sector the products needed to be cheap and cheerful, practical and affordable. He started to physically show how each of their products could effectively be segmented by outlet type, price point and style.

By now Christoph felt he was 'on a roll' but time was still his enemy as the minutes seemed to be elapsing ever so slowly and he was reaching the end of his length of rope. He used as much of the Shoe presentation, as he could recall from memory, in seeking to make it relevant to shoe trees, but even that had now been exhausted. It was then that he took the wooden products and smelt each. He perceived the distinctive scent of cedar and pine and this provided him with his next angle. He outlined the significance of the opportunity of linking the freshness of shoes through the essence of their shoe trees. The potential importance of fragrance in this sector had been totally overlooked. Shoe freshness and foot odour were areas of concern that had not seemingly been effectively tackled, only through foot or shoe sprays, from Dr School or Boots the Chemist that could be potentially damaging to shoes and tended to be fairly costly. However, a natural product with a natural fragrance was something completely different and distinct. It might even be possible to sell sachets separately to enhance the original fragrance over time as the initial smell wore off. Perhaps even a spray variant could be considered or an oil that could be applied to the original product thereby enhancing and protecting the wood. Without drawing breath, Christoph then launched into a fragrance defence, demonstrating his knowledge and experience of how important this factor was against different target audiences, be that in perfumes, after shaves, body mists, deodorants and finally bath oils and essences. Here the woodland smells were highly relevant and desired. This included Bergamot, Cardoman, Cinnamon, Citronella, Jasmine, Lavender and most relevantly to them Cedarwood, Fir and Pine. Here he focused then on Pine as this was so prevalent. The value of pine was that it had all the connotations of naturalness, 'outdoors's', escape and freedom into a coniferous world of freshness. What at the end was left was an after smell that lingered in a vibrant, vigorous, heady, non-stale way on both the body and in the bathroom. Hence the importance of Badedas – a luxury, premium product, that led the market in pine essences and was an acceptable gift on any occasion. All through his exploration of other market sectors Christoph was watching the reaction of the ex-Unilever member of the prospect team and she was nodding affirmatively and seemed to be both intrigued and involved in Christoph's presentation. He surmised that she must have simply thought he was a well-trained Thomas Healey account man!

Christoph then brought his presentation back to their shoe trees and stated that the pine essence could be a viable platform for the top end wood products, which could be sold through the premium shoe retailers. Christoph suddenly found that astonishingly he had filled more than the three hour slot allocated and had done so without a single chart. The presentation had given areas for discussion and consideration as well as having opened up a potential avenue to explore, around 'natural aroma' that they may not have even considered before; and a business opportunity through tie-ins with leading manufacturers/retailers. The prospects, as they left, expressed gratitude feeling it had been a stimulating morning and were deeply appreciative of Christoph's input, thoughts and time. As Christoph collapsed into a chair after their departure he laughed aloud, as did his Nordic colleague, who gave him a 'High 5'. Christoph simply put it this way, "Manfred, Bullshit usually smells and this time it was of pine!"

Much later in his career when he was at McKillans he would have a similar experience, that took place in Russia, though this time the stakes were considerably higher, as it was on a well-established client. After the collapse of the Berlin Wall in 1989 and the subsequent break-up of the USSR (Russian Soviet Empire) in 1991, Russia, under first Mikhail Gorbachev and then Boris Yeltsin, became a free open market. Christoph was involved with Russia from those earliest days right up until the end of 1999. That coincided with the end of Yeltsin's term and since January 1st 2000, either in title or actuality Vladimir Putin has been President of the Russian Federation. Christoph was always inspired by the Russian people's 'fatalistically optimistic' outlook, where they accepted their lot, the high level of blatant corruption around them and a sequence of self-politically motivated leaders. And yet for all this

A life above the line – just!

they still believed that 'perhaps tomorrow would be better'. Christoph had many interesting experiences in Russia but the one in the bitterly cold late November 1998 possibly topped the lot.

The newly appointed Account Director, in Moscow, on 'Reigning Cats & Dogs' called Christoph up in London and informed him that a tough, humourless, industrious Australian had just arrived, from the Antipodes, to be the Marketing Director on the business. This was a man clearly seeking to make his mark and establish his credentials, by changing things, as well as, putting real pressure on the agencies. As part of his programme he had demanded a thorough analysis of the dog pet care market not just in Russia or Central Eastern Europe but across the whole of Europe. He specifically was interested to know how the agency viewed the dog portfolio market segmentation and how over time it might be applied in Russia, as brands were introduced and then grew and evolved. The new Account Director, George, panicked as he had no idea how to proceed to answer such a demand. The Head of the Agency, an ex-KGB man, Sergey, advised him to get hold of Christoph immediately and notify him of this request. George was only too keen to off-load this task onto Christoph and the latter then spent a month preparing a comprehensive analysis of the dog food category across the whole of Europe showing how the portfolio of brands had evolved in each domain, giving the competitive context, and importance of pets, by market. He then highlighted how the portfolio could be amended to be suitable to the CEE and Russian markets, given the current competitive presence. In so doing he made particular reference as to how this might be distinctly different for these markets, given where they were then with the sale of the company brands. When he had completed this onerous task he contacted George, whom he 'didn't know from Adam', knew absolutely nothing about, and whom he had never met in person, that he was now ready to present and would come and make the presentation himself. He had heard from a friend in the Company, another Australian, that this client was a 'hard man' and a 'tough as teak Aussie'. His overall impression of agency people was that they were usually lightweights when it came to marketing issues and communication strategies. He apparently 'ate nails for breakfast and I don't mean finger nails' was how his friend had graphically put it!

The Account Director arranged the meeting for a few days later and agreed to meet Christoph at The Sobieski Hotel in Moscow on his arrival. Christoph eventually got to the hotel late in the evening and was greeted by his new agency operative, who had been sitting and drinking in the lounge. George was a tall, thickly-set, high foreheaded, black haired, pale almost translucent white skinned individual, with a forthright confident demeanour. They sat down and ordered drinks which on arrival Christoph toasted 'to a good meeting on Dog tomorrow'. George suddenly started to fidget nervously and looked downcast and concerned, before summoning up the courage to tentatively ask, "Yes, but Christoph, what have you got on Cat?" Christoph laughed and replied, "Highly amusing George. Sorry, my friend, I have nothing on Cat - that would most definitely have to wait for another day!" George was now seemingly trembling with discontent and clearly something was troubling him. Eventually he came out with it, hesitantly, "The client has changed the brief and wants the agency now to present on Cat tomorrow." Christoph was completely shell-shocked and responded saying, "You've got to be joking. What the hell do you mean the client has changed the brief? In this bag (looking down at his Lands' End canvas bag) I've got presentation materials on Dog, dog and f…ng dog, but nothing on bloody cats." Close to explosion Christoph then looked at the squirming George and icily asked, "Well, when did he change the brief and why on earth didn't you think to tell me before I caught the plane here?" George uneasily responded, "I am very sorry but I have been so busy I forgot to tell you" and then in a more optimistic tone added, "But I'm sure you'll manage!" Christoph stood up and looking down at this simpering pathetic man simply said, "You're sorry. You may very well be tomorrow. I'm off to bed and I'll expect to see you in your office at 7.30am to see what we can cobble together before the meeting starts at 9am. Good night." He then strode off in high dudgeon, to the bank of lifts.

Christoph experienced a sleepless night, wondering what the best thing was to do in this situation. He had started by considering going ahead with what he had on dog food and letting George take the rap from the client, afterwards. Then he had thought of simply making this a discussion meeting on cat food. In the end he had arrived at the unwelcome conclusion that he was going to have to do and say something about cat food, as this was what the client had specifically asked for, and was giving up his and his team's time to listen to. Arriving at the offices early Christoph found the Account Director's den. As he would not arrive for at least another 30 minutes or so Christoph had the time to rifle and rummage through the papers lying on his desk. He suddenly came across a single sheet which was a market segmentation of Cat food in Russia. When the Account Director appeared he asked him to make an acetate copy of this sheet. At 9am the 'ball-breaking', suave, well-dressed suited, tied and crisp white shirted Australian arrived with his cohorts and acolytes, many whom Christoph had encountered before. Christoph used the pleasantries to make it known to the new client that he was friendly with his previous boss in Australia, on the basis that anything or any connection might help. Then Christoph embarked on his presentation. With the benefit of his experiences on Cat Food in Europe over the previous year and prompted by the names of the brands on the acetate he was able to recall the general development of each brand and the competitive scenarios in most of the key markets. He trawled through his memory bank on how regions differed between dry, moist, semi-moist, as well as by delivery system, be that can, pouch, tin and boxed. He even remembered which recipes had been most successful in each market and how the specific markets differed in attitude and varied dramatically on price point. Quite remarkably Christoph spoke off this single chart for 4 hours. Along the way there were questions asked and at the end there were more speculative queries raised as to the effect on their own specific market and what hypotheses he would make there. Chris was able to field all the questions posed to him, and to debate and discuss the marketing and historical advertising of the key brands in the category across Europe. He even had a stab at predicting trends for the future with possible regard to technology and packaging and how these might apply to the region and Russia in particular.

At the end of the meeting the gritty Australian smiled warmly thanked Christoph for his enlightening presentation and asked him to stay close to their business. He even asked if he could have a copy of his presentation, which was ironic as there was only the one acetate which his Company had provided in the first place. He felt that the thoroughness and in-depth knowledge of the category had given him every confidence that the agency was on top of the business, which was most encouraging. Christoph stated he would produce a synopsis of his presentation in an easily digestible form with accompanying tapes of commercials he had referenced, and he would promise to be available to the local client on an as needed basis. Reassured by this positive response, as clearly, at that time, they only had their own copious notes, the client withdrew with his team, being ushered off the premises by George. When they left the room Christoph sunk deep into a chair, leant back and looking up to the ceiling he closed his eyes. He was mentally and physically exhausted. Having used up all his reserves and survived on adrenalin alone he had nothing left. He was a spent force. George, the Account Director came back into the room and cheerily said, "Well that went rather well. They seemed chuffed, happy and delighted. I told you, it would be alright Christoph. I must say, though, that talking from just a single acetate for over four hours, even somewhat surprised me and certainly exceeded my wildest expectations!" Christoph was too tired and exhausted to tell George to 'fuck off' or even to have a fight with him. He just laughed and they reflected together how they had truly pulled it off! Interestingly, at no time, did Christoph feel the pressure of the situation or what failure could have meant to the business locally. He had risked it for the sake of the agency and got away with it with sheer bravado, chutzpah and bluff. He chalked that one up to experience and a pretty good memory!

What Christoph had learnt was that George was a dangerous man and he would need to be very wary of him in the future, as he clearly was not into detail or a person and character to rely on. Imagine then his horror when the very next year this same individual was foisted upon him and his team in London, despite his vehement protestations. Indeed, when the prospect of George coming to the UK was mentioned

Chris contacted the Head of Europe, for McKillans, direct[ly] and complained to him strongly. As he pointed out, "Do you not rea[lise] that wherever this man has worked the country and in some cases [the] whole region's economy has collapsed?! When he worked in Brazil the economy nose-dived and he had to move on. He then went to the Far East, based in Malaysia, and here the entire region's economy faced a down-turn. Then he was taken on in Russia and here not only has the economy collapsed but so also has the entire political infrastructure and system (it was this that brought Vladimir Putin to the fore). And now you want me to take him on in the UK – where thankfully the economy and political structures are currently fairly robust and stable. So no thank you we don't need George." But for all Christoph's resistance it was to no avail. The gamble Christoph made to bail this guy out of the hole in Moscow had now back-fired big-time! He had seemingly beaten the odds and still lost!

Taking risks was part of the game for Christoph and he had enough chances to demonstrate that luck played its part, but good basic knowledge and know-how, coupled with experience, were the tools that gave him the edge. The attitude of never thinking it couldn't be done, and never worrying about the ramifications for his career, also definitely helped taking risks naturally and as a matter of course. There was always a goal and there was never any fear.

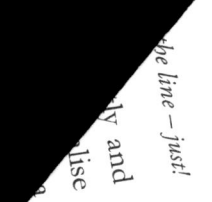

CHAPTER 9

Be the difference & do it differently

'Don't be afraid of being different, be afraid of being the same as everyone else' (Anon)

'The things that make me different are the things that make me' Winnie the Pooh (A.A. Milne 1882-1956)

'Two roads diverged in a wood, and I took the one less travelled by, and that has made all the difference' (Robert Frost 1874-1963)

Christoph always believed that if a job was worth doing it was worth doing differently! He had even made it a policy of his never making the same presentation twice. When it came to developing advertising he was always looking for the next big idea or finding a different positioning on a brand, or finding a new technique, or new media to exploit a brand's potential. On the creative copy front Chris believed passionately in the development and evolution of long term campaigns. His copy platform meant he was always being pro-active, with the next two executions in the existing campaign already in at least storyboard form. He also looked to find a different way of approaching the mainstream strategy on a brand. Separately he would seek to find a varied positioning for a product to see if there was a different way to sell the brand and it or these would then be put into research. He also looked to see if the brand could be communicated in different media to stretch its footprint, in a less expensive vehicle than television, be that in broadcast via cinema, radio, online or via static media such as posters, billboards or press, or use of new media or experiential (based on experience or observation) media or even in product placement and sponsorship. Curiously for someone so inept at using technology Christoph was fanatical about its potential for things to go viral and to use the new media to reach different targets with tailor made messages. This mentality seemed to be reflective of his overall desire to always keep pioneering and looking forward, as if one was always moving, and hopefully with positive momentum, one was a hard target to shoot down. He was totally convinced that if his programme and approach was pursued complacency would never set in and clients would be enamoured by the continuous excitement and development on their brands. As Christoph liked to put it, "It was always about keeping one step ahead of the banana skin!" He did accept, however, that there was always the danger of clients getting bored of their mainstream advertising long before the consumer had and seeking to change it for changes sake. This was simply because they saw something new or felt an advertising spot had been over exposed, forgetting that the number of exposures to the public was far more limited, usually dictated by the high cost of traditional broadcast media.

Christoph's disciplined training from working on the Thomas Healey account and his observations from reading and studying the legends of the past had instilled in him the need and desire to be positively forward thinking and to offer a real point of difference. Resilience and flexibility were also part of this. Chris was always amused by the initiatives shown by a colleague of his back in the 1970s, a time long before mobile telephones and electronic media. The Agency was working on the Co-op (Cooperative Wholesale Society (CWS) – effectively a 'membership' owned business seeking to be of service and benefit to their community), which apart from its renowned and affordable funeral service, ran a national chain of 'smallish' local grocery shops, selling items at very competitive prices, appealing to lower earners, especially in the north of the country. The Co-op featured their best weekly offers in the national press that would normally run on Thursdays and Fridays prior to the then weekly/weekend shop on Saturday.

The Agency was scheduled to present a new campaign look to the Senior Management up in Manchester. The night before the Account Director and Creative Team involved reviewed the work, for a final time, and had a run-through of their presentation. On completion it was agreed that they would meet on the train leaving from Euston Station the following morning. This they duly did and then shortly after the train pulled out the Account Director asked to have another look at the work. It was then that there was the awful realisation and discovery that neither party had brought the work, each thinking the other was bringing the 'schlep' bag containing the creative boards. Ever resourceful the Account Director spun into action, stating, "Right, well we need to get someone to contact the agency and get the portfolio bag sent up by plane." He then had all the members of the team rolling up notes into balls and then they used this ammunition to bombard passengers on the platforms of train stations they flew through. Each note asked the person should they open it to contact the Station Master and ask him or her to call the Agency and request them to send up the Co-op work, in a bag in the creative director's office, by plane to Manchester Airport. Fortunately, fairly early into the journey, a passenger picked up one of these missiles opened it, read it, and acted upon it. They must have thought that they were part of an Agatha Christie 'who dun it' mystery involving a 'run-away' train. The instructions were carried out to the letter and by the time the team had disembarked at Manchester Piccadilly they discovered that the work was already on its way up to Manchester. Taking a taxi to the airport they then patiently awaited the bag's arrival. It eventually emerged and gathering it up, checking that it was indeed the right one, they then proceeded to the Co-op offices. Apologising most profusely for their tardiness they then started their presentation. The work was approved

A life above the line – just!

and everyone was able to celebrate over a job well done. A situation that could have been a complete disaster was averted by a combination of quick thinking, decisive action from many contact points, a sizeable chunk of luck and a totally off the wall solution. This more or less proved the point 'that where there's a will there's a way!' This had truly been brinkmanship at its best and really appealed to Christoph.

Right from the start of Christoph's advertising career he had sought to do things differently and to make a difference. Even as he made the transition mentally from wanting to be a creative copywriter to accepting he was destined to be an Account Manager he still wanted to have input, flair and style in the creative solutions. On one of his earliest assignments for a construction kit manufacturer, in the toy sector, he saw the opportunity to produce a format that would give the company an immediately stylish and instantly recognisable look, that was unique to them and which they could truly own. It was to have five key ingredients, firstly a main picture depicting the kit in action (either a photograph or stylised picture), secondly scaled down plan drawings of the kit (these would have the dimensions of the kit in the real world), thirdly an arresting headline, fourthly body copy that started with a paragraph containing interesting historical fact(s) or background information pertaining to the item depicted, followed by details of the actual kit and finally each would have a border and a serial number, rather as with a blue print, which kit makers could collect. This campaign received much coverage and many favourable comments from the media as it stood apart from the competition. Collectors and constructors of kits were even contacting the agency for block pulls of the ads so that they could build up their historical records and files of the kits, with quality thicker glossy paper versions.

As Christoph's career progressed he realised there was a need to get maximum impact in the media for clients and especially those with small budgets. They needed to have standout in a clutter of messages. When Rolls-Royce was split up after virtually going bust over the development of the RB211 engine, it had to be saved by the Government of the day in 1971. Rolls-Royce Cars was separated from the gas turbine business. Christoph was one of the earliest team members that was actively involved in bringing Rolls-Royce (1971) Limited back into advertising. Needless to say budgets were very tight and the only affordable advertising at that stage, for their gas turbines, were black and white spaces. Initially, Christoph sought to employ a dramatic effect he had learnt when being trained in production and that was to consider the use of woodcuts. This provided a much deeper saturation of ink creating a darker and more dynamic appearance. Based on this understanding he sat down with the art director and head of production and they evolved this thinking to arrive at the notion of using mezzo-tints done to illustrators' eye catching employment of these gas turbines. Their application provided much scope for dramatic pictures as they were the power behind oil rigs or the Siberian Pipeline or in battleships or in power stations and even for helicopters in addition to fighter planes, such as the Harrier Jump jet in addition to being the engines carried in many commercial airlines and freight fleets. These illustrations and the printing technique of mezzo-tints added real stand out and a depth to the subject matter being portrayed and conveyed.

To celebrate the first commercial flight of Concorde on 21st January 1976 the team had chosen to yet again be different using a drawing that focused solely on the back end of this streamlined aircraft. This was at variance to all the other advertisers, in the national press that day, where everyone else featured the distinctive pencil shaped nose and cone. But for Rolls-Royce it was about the engines that powered the aircraft, the Olympus 593 turbo-jet engines, which had been made in collaboration with the French company SNECMA (Societe Nationale d'Etudes et de Construction de Moteurs d'Aviation). The front of the plane had flown out of the page while the headline read 'Rolls-Royce/ SNECMA bring you the three second mile'. It had been a long process as the inaugural flight from Toulouse was, of Concorde 001, on 2nd March 1969, with its first supersonic flight being on 1st October that same year. The commercial flights would continue until the plane was retired on 24th October 2003. It travelled at Mach 2.04 twice the speed of sound and carried between 92 and 128 passengers. Jim, the creative,

A life above the line – just!

and Christoph were proud to have been a small part in the history of this noisy, yet beautiful, streamlined, supersonic airliner.

Never satisfied and looking for yet more drama Christoph and his art director wanted to find an even stronger branding device for the following year's campaign. Late in 1976, Jim and Chris were discussing the work for 1977, which they were relatively happy with, but which for them lacked the real power they believed was possible. The presentation was the next day and yet they were still looking for more and had gone to a Wimpy Bar – the forerunner to Burger King and McDonalds – in the West End, to reflect on the forthcoming meeting. As they were talking over things, as good friends, they discussed what had been done and that was to reflect the various applications through the branded cowling of their engines, which worked strongly to register the Rolls-Royce logo. Christoph felt that it was still a little flat and so he and Jim started to draw a range of different layouts on the napkins. Suddenly Chris exclaimed excitedly "I've got it! Let's take the 'RR' out of the middle of the logo and feature the application there so that it becomes a window to their world, whilst the name of the company will sit at the top and bottom of the picture with the key line of the logo holding in these visual elements." They rushed back to the office and Jim drew various layouts to provide the maximum balance. Together they then developed a number of strong, bold and arresting headlines to suit each application and combat the now large logo that dominated the layout. Down the side of the logo was the body copy. The headlines provided the opportunity to tell a number of attention grabbing, and, to some, surprising, facts e.g. 'RB211. The World weightlifting champion' (on November 1st 1976 a British Airways 747 carried 420 tons beating the previous record by some 20,000lbs); 'Rolls-Royce. One of the world's great air forces.' (Rolls-Royce turbines in 1977 were in service with 94 armed services around the world); 'Rolls-Royce saves another man from drink' (in and around Great Britain Rolls-Royce powered helicopters carried out an average of 200 rescues every year); 'We're the pumping powered behind 800 miles of Alaskan oilway.' (Crude oil from Prudhoe Bay travelled 800 miles across inhospitable terrain and in the toughest of climatic conditions, at a rate of 1.2 million barrels a day); 'We'll keep the AV-8B one jump ahead.' (The AV-8B Advanced Harrier jump jet was ordered for the US Marine Corps as a high performance light attack V/STOL (vertical/short take-off and landing) aircraft); 'We're a fighting force at sea.' (Rolls-Royce in June 1977, at the time of the Silver Jubilee Review, supplied over 40% of all gas turbine warships in 22 of the world's navies, including the Admiralty Board's ship, HMS Birmingham, one of the world's most advanced destroyers); 'Last night in the North Sea we drilled through 50ft. of rock, lit the rig and cooked dinner' and also 'When you're powering a North Sea platform 22 degrees of frost and a force 11 storm is the easy bit.' (When production stops it can cost upwards of £1m a day. Rolls–Royce gas turbines were operating continuously for 16,000 hours in the most hostile and heavily salt-laden marine conditions; Brent, Viking, Leman, Claymore, Cormorant, Dunlin and Murchison all chose Rolls-Royce electrical, pumping and compression energy).

Additionally, the two decided that there should be an even more confident sign-off. Prior to the work being presented the next day the end line had been a simple statement 'Pumping Power'. The campaign evolution approved for presentation had evolved this to read 'Progress is our tradition'. This they liked but wanting to be more than just forward looking and exuding supreme confidence they came up with the line 'World leaders in gas turbine technology'.

By the morning the two of them were completely exhausted but also exhilarated. Ahead of them lay the difficult job of un-selling the work their management had agreed to put forward at the meeting and suggesting the new work they had developed almost literally 'on the back of a fag packet!' Most management do not like the 11th hour surprise or shock but Christoph's enthusiasm was infectious. John E Goldman, an astute former Cambridge University scholar (as he liked to remind Christoph and many others on numerous occasions!) could see the merit in the work being presented to him even though it had not been passed through the correct channels internally. He determined that the original campaign should be pitched first, and strongly supported, as the logical progression from where they had been. On the assumption that this went well the new campaign in its rough form could be presented at the tail end of the meeting as a 'flier'. John had expressed concerns about tampering with the company logo, as more often than not, it was ill-advised to do this as it gave free rein to opportunists to use their logo at will and without control. Company legal eagles and corporate lawyers were particularly protective of their company properties and would stamp on any misuse of these. John genuinely loved the work as he felt it was bold and confident and could only be done by Rolls-Royce but that it was potentially a high risk strategic approach to put forward, as the agency's only recommendation.

This was acceptable to Christoph and Jim as they had, at least, got permission to front their new thinking. From there, it would be a case of how the client responded and would they be brave enough to defend the proposed alteration of their logo. They need never have worried. The Client was very happy with the way the agency had evolved the current campaign. But then the client was completely bowled over by the sheer boldness of the new idea and could see its potential for having a truly dramatic impact even from the simple roughs presented. They could visualise how it could translate to having a very positive effect and influence on their business and image and would exude confidence in every corner of the world in which it ran. In the most extraordinary situation they approved the layouts, the end line, a number of the headlines and the visual treatments suggested, there and then. The agency was encouraged to get on with it. Christoph always applauded and acknowledged the senior client for his conviction and determination to run with this campaign more especially as it was he who took on the lawyers internally.

The campaign, when it ran, was amazingly well-received in the media and won 13 awards in the specialist media it appeared in. It also won both Advertisement of the Year and Campaign of the Year from no less a publication than Business Week in 1977/78. More importantly it did, what Jim and Christoph had truly hoped would be the case, it took Rolls-Royce's Impact and Awareness scores through the roof. It was famous advertising for a famous name.

Christoph stayed with Gris Advertising for eleven years and he truly felt this was the one agency he had been truly wedded to. After that, at his other two agencies, he felt more like 'a hired gun', brought in to sort out problems. But then as he would often argue 'that's businesses for you'. As he was approaching his 10th Anniversary at Gris he decided to host a 'Party' by way of celebration, thanks, and acknowledgement and to mark this landmark memorably. It was as much a way of his expressing gratitude to all those people whom had put up with him, as well as recognition of his endurance and perseverance. He sent out invitations to a 'Tea Party' printed in dark blue on a pink card. Inside, it read, 'Now I am 10' in a child's style and font. At the event itself there were egg mayonnaise and cucumber sandwiches, Victoria Sponge cake, jelly and ice-cream, fairy cakes, biscuits and, of course, a Birthday Cake with 10 candles. The only concession was that in addition to tea and fruit juice he supplied champagne. It was a great event and not without surprises especially when one of the creative teams decided to organise a strip-o-gram, who when failing to arrive, led to him persuading his girlfriend, a most attractive receptionist, to strip down to her black and white polka dot bra and briefs and then sit on Christoph's lap. Christoph was completely taken aback and was absolutely speechless - for once. It was a really different way to signify his first decade in the business all of which had been spent at Gris. It was memorable, great fun and gave a lot of people a lot of laughs, many at Christoph's expense. It truly was a great event though sadly only one year later Christoph would leave Gris Advertising for good.

Christoph was forever seeking to find a point of difference that would give his clients and their brands an edge and standout over their competition. This was not limited to simply advertising and the normal paid for media channels of communication. His belief was that getting brand awareness and registration as well as placement wherever possible – providing the association was in no way demeaning or negative – was all part of his mandate. It was this that had led him down the paths of Product Placement in TV soaps, Sponsored and paid for branded programming and exploitation of sports sponsorship via associations with individual athletes and teams as well as gaining signage and billboard presence. Christoph never felt there were any boundaries, limitations or restrictions that could not be surmounted or overcome. Everything was fair game to him providing that it was positive, legal and decent. These challenges he felt were well worth pursuing. For him what really mattered were brands being out front, ahead of their competition, and above all being talked about. It was different and in some cases new and this occasionally brought its own problems. There were times when the association with a particular personality, or sportsperson, could be risky or even unfortunate, as they could be involved in a scandal, become injured, dropped or simply not selected. Christoph recognised the potential pitfalls but overall felt that even in the most adverse conditions good publicity and news could be attained for the brand. This positive outlook and thinking dominated his working life.

Indeed, even in the twilight of his career, Chris was embracing new methods of doing business and seeking to find ways of stretching the budget. In 2001, on a cat litter product, that could not afford to be aired on television, he worked with his team to produce a viral execution and a 'micro-site' featuring a 'Tiger Wood' styled rat with a set of golf clubs hitting clumps of 'litter' out of a cat's excrement box, as a way of showing how robust the product was and how well the cat litter product worked. This proved to be highly popular in this new medium and got much coverage for its innovativeness as well as receiving a large number of 'hits' (read viewings!) and favourable free public relations.

But simply being different and a pioneer were never goals in themselves for Christoph. It was only justifiable if it had a positive impact on the brand involved. On a tea company brand, 'Brew Morning', that was struggling to find sufficient funds to support the brand in the expensive South Eastern half of the country, where television airtime costs were at a premium, Christoph had to think differently. Despite the brand never having been communicated in a static medium he persuaded the management to use Posters/Adshels, Four Sheets and Bus Sides in London and the rest of the South East. Additionally, when Christoph was made aware of the potential of Product Placement he latched on to this for them. Working with an expert in the field who knew the scene dressers and props department heads of 'the soaps' and popular TV shows they achieved the equivalent of £750k media exposure for a speculative outlay of just £40k. 'Brew Morning' became featured on posters in Coronation Street and even appeared as a box for collecting money for a charity in East Enders. The packs of 'Brew Morning' appeared on the shelves of grocery outlets and newsagents depicted in these popular programmes. To Christoph what made this area even more exciting was that it was deemed to be highly controversial. The broadcast authorities neither liked nor condoned this type of appearance of well-known brands as they felt it was biased and not necessarily representative of a brand's strength in a given area. They had trouble controlling it and the battle raged in the media and in PR giving yet more coverage for the brand. Then it was new and different but today it is truly big business and it can cost millions for brands and products to be featured in films. Watches, cameras, telephones, computers and cars genuinely pay huge sums to be featured in for example a James Bond movie – just think Aston Martin, Rolex, I-Phone and Nokkia!

Another sphere that was equally contentious, but opportunistic, which Christoph was quick to capitalise upon was that of Schools Programmes. Working on a dentifrice product against the might of the brand leader Colgate was always going to be a tough ask. School Programmes was a way of seeking to persuade parents, through their children, of the need to brush their teeth and ideally use the brand that was promoting this activity. Christoph and his team came up with a beaver character called 'The Eager Beaver McIver'. Instructions were provided for optimum brushing and a chart for children to fill in when they brushed. There were also diagrams on the elements of a tooth and how and where bacteria acted in the mouth. There was also information about why brushing teeth and gums were so important and the need to remove bad bacteria that cause bleeding and gum disease. The programme even extended to include leaflets explaining about food stuffs and their effect on teeth enamel and gums through tartar and plaque build up and sugar and acids in the mouth. There was a leaflet on how dentifrice combated problems and what the particular ingredients in toothpaste and dentifrice products were and how they worked individually and in combination. It very much complied with the National Schools Curriculum at that time. Getting ex-teachers to work with the agency meant that the materials met their target accurately and precisely. This programme was much welcomed by the cash strapped schools, which were not only short of money but also learning aids and equipment. Parents also were appreciative, as they received free samples and coupons, plus a willingness on the part of their off-spring to brush their teeth. Christoph felt it was a clever way of building support for the brand without being solely reliant on a television message. Critics, at OFSTED (Office for Standards in Education, Children's Services & Skills – a non-ministerial department of the UK Government reporting into the Ministry for Education), the wider media and even competitors condemned this activity as they saw it as commercial exploitation by companies to sell their products to and through vulnerable people, in this instance, children. Christoph saw it as providing valuable materials, albeit branded, for the schools and letting the brand glow in the positive reaction from schools and parents alike, who viewed this programme as being 'educational' rather than 'hard sell'. The parents and children particularly liked the interactive elements built around the Beaver character, with charts and stickers and a programme that even included a record of their visits to the dentist. In the end many of these Schools Programmes were closed down after severe scrutiny and criticism, not aided by attacks in the media. Product sectors such as soft drinks, snack foods and confectionery quickly became off-limits! Ironically, Christoph had worked on both confectionery and dentifrice categories, with schools, from very early on and was therefore cast as hero and villain alike!

For some time this same dentifrice brand had been seeking, unsuccessfully, to gain endorsement from the British Dental Association. Christoph working with the Company's Public Relations department, their specialist sales force and dental hygiene experts embarked on a programme of making strong overtures to the BDA. There had already been a comprehensive sampling programme through dentists. Finally, after the provision and submission of numerous clinical studies and a number of representations the BDA finally gave their endorsement, which was then used on pack and in the advertising. This was a major victory and Christoph was proud of the small part he had played in this.

Christoph had always been passionate about the whole theatre of presentation and as he freely admitted he was both a frustrated thespian and barrister. He wanted his presentations to be dramatic, memorable, distinctive, effective, hopefully entertaining and enjoyable and definitely different. For him the presentation was a big part of any sale. He loved all the different steps and stages, the set-up, the pre-sale, the content – visuals and language – the concluding remarks and then at the end the Question & Answer session. He truly enjoyed being challenged and he viewed this as being an essential part of the selling job. He knew he all too often would have to rely on his speed of response, his humour, his quick wittedness and his ability to shock or surprise, visually or verbally. In his twenty eight years on the front line he never lost the drive or the desire to present. This was always a challenge he could never refuse. Almost the very last major creative presentation he made was to a European gathering on a new semi-moist dog food product being planned for market expansion. The agency had developed a new advertising campaign that was being presented to the European managers from 'Reigning Cats and Dogs' for the first time. The meeting had started with a lengthy review of the individual countries' business results. It was tedious. It was down beat. There were few highs and many lows. The business picture was not good and indeed the figures were soft. And it was in this cauldron of gloom and doom that Christoph was expected to expose the new creative work for an exciting new product/brand, about to be marketed in a relatively new premium segment of the market. Christoph realised that to present in this negatively charged forum with its depressed atmosphere would be well-nigh impossible.

So when it came to his time to present Christoph smiled stood up and flicked both his open hands, up and down, as though they had been

A life above the line – just!

scalded, and exhaled a deep breath with a loud, "Wow" sound. Then he asked everyone present to take a natural break, to get up and walk around the room three times and finally to remove items of clothing. Christoph set the example by removing his shoes, his jacket, his tie and undoing a number of buttons on his shirt, which he then took out of his trousers. The rest of the attendees quickly and obediently complied and to his surprise followed suit. It also prompted one of the clients to pass a note around the table to Christoph's Account Director, George, which simply read 'Okay, what drugs is Christoph on today?' The reply that came back was 'Oh none – it's just Christoph being Christoph – you know what he's like. Believe me this is quite normal behaviour from him!' Christoph, having got everyone distracted, mildly amused and spell bound, then proceeded to give a fun, up-beat, over the top presentation reflective of the personality of the brand. As he opened up he stated 'Your brand 'Romp' has a happy, positive, fun name and that is the mood you should be in when you receive its creative work.' The meeting attendees really liked the insight, 'Romp adds colour to you and your dog's life.' The executions were loved and were eventually made and went on air in April 2002, some 8 months after Christoph had left advertising. In this instance Christoph had chosen not to use charts or even notes at all but had prepared everything beforehand and learnt the flow and rehearsed what he was going to say back home. There was genuine theatre as he acted out the roles of various dogs on the floor with accompanying sound effects and what the effect of the product was on the dog and the relationship with its owner. It caused much revelry. At the end followed a boisterous lunch with a happy European team in buoyant mood. The French Senior Franchise client turned to Christoph and asked, "Next time, you are coming to present, would you mind if I brought my children as that was funnier and more entertaining than the clowns at the circus!" Christoph though not totally sure took that to be a compliment!

Christoph always displayed great self-confidence even though deep down he would be nervous beforehand and right up until he stood up to present, when the nerves would seem to suddenly disappear. He did have self-belief though was seldom complacent or arrogant and he took absolutely nothing for granted. Chris never minded taking responsibility or being held accountable when things went wrong. He would be the first man to put up his hand, and take it on the chin, when things did not work out the way they were meant to. He was even happy for people to have a joke at his expense. Few people would have allowed themselves to be publicly vilified in the industry's trade press; but then if Christoph could see the benefit of doing this for the good of his relatively new agency then why not? This happened in late October 1986 a year after he left Premium White to help rebuild, a newly merged agency, as part of a ten man management team at McKillans.

The background was that Christoph had worked on a small piece of telecoms business which was shared with another big agency that held the bulk of their business. Splitting the budget between the two agencies that had similar technologically advanced products seemed to make little or no business or commercial sense. Interestingly, both products were fore runners to the light, flexible, and easy to hold mobile telephone. They had the ability to transmit messages, or possessed an alarm system, or locator. There are today new generation versions of these used in prisons, hospitals, residential care homes and even by individuals who feel potentially exposed and/or are isolated or on their own. Christoph pointed out the similarity of the two products and that the duplication of effort would be far better channelled into a single communication campaign featuring both products and offering a choice dependant on need, desire and requirement. Christoph knew that the likelihood would be that his honesty would lead to the Client's bigger agency becoming the agency of record and McKillans would lose out. The senior client was impressed by Christoph's frankness and perspective on how the business could benefit and agreed totally with him. Regrettably, without a pitch, he then chose to go with the agency that held the lion's share of his business much to Christoph's disappointment and chagrin!

As it transpired, this turned out to be the only piece of business that the newly formed agency lost in their first year in business. One of the senior creative teams came to see Christoph and asked if he would be game enough to appear in a very ballsy and confident double-page spread advertisement they had prepared for the trade media. The ad had a lot of white space around a character standing underneath a bold headline that read, 'McKillans. One year old. Fifteen wins. One loss – This is the man who lost it – he came from Premium White'. At the base of the advertisement were listed all the new business wins and new brand assignments from existing clients. The man featured was, of course, Christoph.

Most people were highly amused by the ad and enjoyed the fact that someone was confident enough to feature themselves in it as having been a loser! Few felt that they would have done this but Christoph enjoyed the attention it gave him. The only people who seemed really upset were the management at Premium White. The Managing Director called Christoph stating that they couldn't believe that he would be that brave, or was it foolish, to be portrayed in such a negative context. They also expressed disappointment that their agency had been mentioned by name. Christoph responded by saying that he was sufficiently content in all he had achieved over the previous twelve months, including salvaging two clients about to walk out of the agency. He had gained their confidence sufficiently to have actually been appointed to handle extra business and new product launches from both over that same time period. He went on to say that he hoped that it showed that McKillans management were prepared to have a bit of fun and make a joke at their own expense. As for the mention of Premium White they should be proud rather than critical as it underlined their standing and reputation, as well as showing the esteem in which they were held in the industry. He also added cheekily that they should also be pleased and relieved that they had got rid of a person liable to lose business! Unfortunately, they didn't see the funny side of that argument still feeling it was a slight on them.

When it came to dealing with his staff Christoph always sought to hire people that he felt could potentially be better than him. He believed that if he achieved this they would make him look good and they would add value. He never felt that would be too difficult - but it sometimes was! He always held his team members in the highest regard and tried to give them total respect. He saw it as a third of his job to train them so that they would grow, develop and fulfil their potential. He was immensely proud of a number of the people he had trained as they went on and did great things with their careers. When, in his capacity, as Client Services Director, in all three agencies Christoph had the difficult job of having to let people go he took it hard and very personally. The worst of these occasions was at McKillans shortly after his arrival. A merger took place and suddenly he found himself having to play a major part in reducing the combined headcount from some six hundred to three hundred and sixty. Quite a number of these casualties inevitably had to come out of Account Management. Chris spent sleepless nights determining who could take early retirement, who could and would be alright if released and made redundant and those that would need help finding new positions elsewhere. At the same time Christoph's strategy was to cut slightly deeper than he needed to so as to ensure that there were the funds to keep the people he needed to retain, motivated and incentivised. Few people would have opted to do this but he always felt that, as painful as it was, it paid dividends in the longer term. On the side of caring for those being made redundant he spent a considerable amount of time with the individuals and then with the various head hunters to get them placed in other agencies, or other ancillary services, and some even on to the client side, or into charitable organisations. For all his external mental toughness he truly cared about these people and their well-being and futures. He never ever saw any of these people as simply a number or as a statistic but always as an individual and a real person with emotions. He faced up to his responsibility and never hid behind Human Resources/Personnel. In his particular domain he met with each person individually. It was a really tough period in his life and it left him exhausted, at the end, but he looked back on it with some pride and with gratitude to the friends he made through it and the assistance he had from the head hunters and also from many of his own colleagues, in the industry.

In his dealings with staff Christoph was tough but fair. He refused

A life above the line – just!

to give guaranteed bonuses, golden handshakes or golden goodbyes or parachutes. He believed that only front line staff should be entitled to spot bonuses, and only in exceptional circumstances. He believed everyone worked for a salary, that should be transparent, and that was what should be their payment with no special privileges least of all regarding extra amounts paid into pension pots or future share deals or financial promises. Shares and share options he believed could be given instead of a salary increase or an earned and therefore entitled bonus. Most importantly he believed that every one of his team should be apprised at least once a year. He did not believe that an appraisal was the time for any salary increase but stood alone. Salary rises and increases should be reflective of a combination of performance and the agency's ability to be able to afford to pay it and should be reviewed, for every individual, at least once a year. No appraisal was ever completed or signed off until a dialogue had been had with the individual. This provided the person being appraised to have input and respond to what Christoph had scripted. He firmly believed that the 'appraisee' had the right to comment, criticise and seek redress and changes where it was felt, in discussion, that the evaluation was not deemed accurate or totally fair or representative of that person's contribution. Christoph saw the appraisal certainly as a tool to reflect an individual's current and recent performance and achievements. Perhaps more importantly he saw it as a guide to engineer change, direct ways of getting an improved performance and to be an aid to assist the individual to progress and set new goals for the next period in their career. Chris was always delighted when the individual concerned pulled him up on something he might have said or written. He recalled on one occasion he had described a young woman's success with a particular client as being partially due to her alluring effect on him. She accused him of being sexist and that if she had been a man he would never have written that. She was absolutely right as her looks had nothing to do with her competence or ability to do the job. Indeed it was her feisty nature and ballsy approach to the business combined with her self-belief and confidence in the quality of her work that yielded results. He would also, on occasions, offer to allow individuals to do appraisals on him so that they could feel free to comment and criticise him in a structured manner. This could also be insightful and constructive for both parties!

Letting people go was the hardest part of the job and he never found it got any easier over time. In August 2000 he was instructed by McKillans Worldwide Head on 'Reigning Cats and Dogs' to release his two account directors because the Client's newly appointed European Marketing Franchise Director didn't rate them. In the case of Roger he had no real concerns as he knew he was a survivor and that the redundancy pay-off would see him alright and he would bounce back quickly. However, in the case of George, he was going to struggle and it would be a shattering blow to his fragile ego and self-confidence. Having spent so little of his career and time in the UK he knew George would have trouble finding another job, with so little experience here and therefore no positive reputation behind him. The additional problem facing Christoph was that these redundancies had to be made immediately and George was away in Portugal at the time. Christoph was certainly not going to disturb or destroy George's holiday with such devastating news. He would in any case have wanted to tell him face-to-face. However, in the interim period, he decided to put certain wheels in motion. Contacting George's secretary he asked her if she had a copy of his Curriculum Vitae on her computer or on file. As luck would have it she did and was only too happy to provide him with a copy. Christoph then set about modifying and changing this document even adding an objective at the top linking this to wanting to work in a senior capacity as an International Account Director on major FMCG (Fast Moving Consumer Goods) business, utilising fully his language skills and geographical experiences. At the bottom of the CV Christoph added his own name as a referee and the contact person for any references. Once he was satisfied that it read well, as a selling tool, he sent it off to major International people he knew in other agencies including his old firm Gris Advertising. The Management Supervisor there rang Christoph and asked for more information pertaining to George and she then agreed that, subject to meeting him, she would more than likely offer him a job. Christoph even discussed George's remuneration terms with her. She had wanted to put George on three months trial and on a lowly salary. Christoph recommended that a man of his calibre and international background and experience should be earning £65,000 and that it would be insulting and demeaning to a man of his time in the business to be put on three month's trial. When this had been agreed, in principle, Christoph then set about negotiating the most favourable redundancy terms for George from McKillans International Management, given that he might find it difficult, at his time of life, to find another job, and that he had done nothing wrong in his current position. This was a difficult negotiation but given he was losing his two Account Directors and they desperately needed to keep Christoph motivated, at that time, he was able to win a strong settlement for George. This, of course, was all going on while George was still away and totally oblivious to what was happening back home.

Imagine therefore George's surprise when Christoph met up with him on the morning of his return to the agency, from holiday. After all the niceties and pleasantries had been exchanged Christoph informed George that he had a job interview at Gris Advertising that evening at 5pm. George retorted "No I don't. I've only just got back and in any case I can assure you that no interviews with other agencies have ever been considered, planned or arranged." Christoph then had to explain what had happened whilst he had been away and how his CV had been updated (read 'doctored'!) and how the interview, scheduled for 5pm, that very evening had come about. George's immediate reaction was one of anger, consternation and protestation at what had clearly been a most irregular process. However, when his options were spelt out to him, and a little persuasion had been applied by Christoph, George eventually agreed to attend the arranged interview. He subsequently secured the job, got the full redundancy from McKillans and just six months later received another redundancy cheque from Gris Advertising, when they discovered he was not the person they needed and that, by their definition, they had been sold a pup, by Christoph. Christoph never did find out what George thought of his new CV but then again George never knew the role Christoph had played in securing the deal at Gris Advertising, with the job effectively secured before the interview ever happened! They did however remain lifelong friends and racing buddies.

Perhaps the situation that was both most daring and different, if not somewhat controversial, came again towards the end of his time in advertising. It was on 'Reigning Cats and Dogs'. It was a situation that gave the mischievous Christoph the greatest pleasure. It had all started innocently enough. Christoph was asked to attend a major European meeting on dog food in Europe late in 1998. The thinking behind this forum was to arrive with fresh ideas and brain storm the category to seek an edge for their brands in the marketplace. This so called 'brain storming' session quickly deteriorated into a 'barnstorming' assembly, between an accusatory senior client and the agencies. Christoph had arrived with a number of potential areas for consideration and had even developed concepts to demonstrate how they might be exploited to the consumer and communicated effectively. He had uncovered a number of possible and feasible insights on each brand his agency was responsible for and had delivered some interesting product areas and recipes that could be developed by the client. This thinking had been reinforced by some scientific studies that he had obtained that supported the thinking and gave substance to the notions he was presenting. Regrettably, he might just as well not have bothered as the Senior Client launched into a tirade of abuse directed at all three of his agencies. His biases, prejudices, and abject dislike for agency people quickly surfaced in what was not so much a discussion but more a war of attrition, with one man literally firing all the shots and discharging his big guns! He accused the agencies of shirking and ducking away from the key issues - as ever. Christoph was not fazed by this attack as he had known this character over many years and had many a good run-in with him. He was a tough, uncompromising, bullish (and something of a bully to boot!) emotional individual with an exceptionally honed political skill for survival and a talented but unrestrained mind. Christoph had enjoyed his encounters, with this powerful adversary, as there was always some genuine concern or potential opportunity lurking behind this filibustering, which somehow would need to be eked out and then responded to sanely and in a measured manner. Today's outburst was no exception. The area his advisers and scientific colleagues had proposed was a dog's 'well-being'. This at the time seemed like a fairly undefined and nebulous area, however Christoph was always up for a challenge and he agreed to head up the project himself on behalf of his agency, McKillans. This surprised and appeased the client who was both surprised and taken aback that Christoph would pick up this gauntlet, but in no small part delighted.

Linking 'well-being' to a dog food manufacturer seemed to be quite thought provoking but potentially rather limiting, without getting into extremely scientific and technical areas. This would then be restrictive as it would only really apply to a specialist product or brand in the veterinary or premium dietary sector. This was not the broad positioning that 'Reigning Cats and Dogs' was looking for. The meaning of 'well-being' could of course apply to the training, discipline and physical condition of the dog through control, exercise and activity. However, this was not necessarily relevant to a dog food except if it provided the dog with the right nutrients and diet. Other definitions of 'well-being', beyond the dog's physical appearance overall, could be broken down into specific indicators. These might include anything from the quality of its coat, the brightness of its eyes, the oiliness of the coat, the muscle development, its movement, its weight and of course its fitness. Clearly these could all be end-end benefits coming from the product fed and general maintenance of the dog's diet and the exercise regime. The real proof of the dog's well-being lay in its stools and level of flatulence. Christoph knew right from the start that he really didn't have a 'cat in hells chance' (excusing the pun!) of succeeding with this route with the copy authorities. <u>Shit</u> was not something that had ever been allowed to be visualised on air. He was well aware from all his dealings with legal personnel and copy clearance bodies and committees around the world that it was highly improbable that the area of faeces quality or the topic of flatulence would or should be 'airable'. Broadcasters' natural tendency is to shy away from what could be seen as being unattractive, unpalatable and even arguably distasteful communication. However, it was a potentially interesting route, as far as the client was concerned. This was an area that had raised its head periodically before and Christoph reckoned the only way to kill it stone dead was through a thorough investigation. He knew too that the dogs output, its excrement, did provide the dog owner with a visible demonstration of the nutritious benefit of the product. However, this was an area that could and should best be handled through Public Relations and Information Leaflets. Advertising 'per se' was unlikely to be deemed the appropriate vehicle or medium for such messages.

Nevertheless, in being seen to be totally committed to the project and indeed to the challenge issued by the client and accepted by Christoph he knew he would have to embark on a comprehensive review of the whole subject. To that end he spent lengthy sessions with the Company's nutritionists. Before going down this step he had arrived at a number of questions that would need to be resolved and fully answered. Then when he felt he had enough to go on from his research, analysis and exhaustive study of the subject he established a meeting with a senior scientific animal nutritionist and then worked with this individual through the whole process. It was lengthy and time consuming as it started with Christoph posing a series of questions, concerns and observations, that all needed to be debated, discussed and assessed. As the knowledge built up and became clearer it was then a case of probing possible areas for potential marketing and communication routes. This also entailed trying to associate the optimum brands in the company's portfolio with potential relevant avenues. Christoph came to realise that certain ingredients and combination of elements would lead to distinctive diets with differing outcomes and indeed outputs for the dog. In terms of faeces and excrement, as well as wind and air (flatulence), it became clear for example that a high protein diet would have a very different effect to a high fibre diet. The key question for Christoph was would he be able to communicate in layman's terms what consumers could and should look for. Additionally would there be a way that they, as a dog owner, could better understand that the output could be adjusted and affected by a better understanding of the nutritional facts.

He discovered that there were thirteen different grades of stools that were all resultant on and dependant from what the dog actually ate, and in what quantity. A further complexity was that this could differ depending on the age and health of the animal. The experts graded dog's excrement from dry and crumbly to loose and runny and all stations in between.

This learning led Christoph to the title for the whole project, which had the umbrella title, of 'Backend Performance' and from this the more dramatic and immediate graphic presentation title emerged of, 'From hoseable to kickable'

Eventually after all the background studying and research analysis plus the work done with the expert nutritionist Christoph finally developed eight distinctly different concepts. Each of these concepts put a positive spin on how owners could now confidently judge their dog's well-being, based on being aware of the amount of flatulence and the solidity of their pet's stools. Christoph then picked a particular brand where there was known to be a relatively high (circa 25%) of 'unacceptability' on faeces against the normal and indeed widely accepted standard (circa 7-8%). In fact most companies, at that time, were seeking to bring the figure for complaints down to a level of 5% or less. Christoph developed concepts that built on new product formulas, with different product ingredients, and distinctive mixes of ingredients, to that which was currently available and being sold in the current line-up and range in stores. This involved adding ingredients that included both oils and vitamins.

The three core areas that Christoph finally settled on were Health, Environment and Flatulence. A flavour – excusing the pun - of the type of concepts Chris worked on in these areas were 'See for yourself – you'll see the change at ground level'; 'If your dog is feeling good your dog's tail will wag even more contentedly'; 'Your dog could be suffering – check your feeding your dog correctly'; 'Poor relations with your neighbours – no more slip ups with this new formulation'.

Christoph then set about working up a comprehensive presentation and then somewhat tongue in cheek took it to the European Management and presented to their full team. They were totally amazed and applauded Christoph on his analysis and the work he had done on arriving at both recipes and concepts. Much to Christoph's surprise it truly fired up their imagination. The Senior Client, whom, had in some way, initiated the project, praised McKillans and Christoph in particular, for as he so eloquently expressed it "…..outstanding input to understanding the problem to arrive at the right output".

The follow-up and outcome from this meeting and the body of work Christoph had produced was extensive and considerable. Christoph was sent around the world to make his presentation, 'From hoseable to kickable,' in 1999 and 2000, in all the key markets. It also unquestionably, as a real tangible benefit, forced many people within the company to think much more about the whole area of diet, product formulations and the resultant effect on the dog's 'well-being' as evidenced by its flatulence and excrement. Additionally, with little input from Christoph, the company management, somewhat arbitrarily, divided up the concepts between their brands. Basically, those with a stronger scientific emphasis were tested out for the company's lead brand. Other concepts that were more down-to-earth, and simply more consumer helpful, were left for the cheaper brands to exploit. So enamoured was the Company with McKillans work that they gave the directive that the concepts in their current form should be tested out in the marketplace. Furthermore, they instructed the agency to involve the copy clearance bodies, in different regions, to establish how far it would be possible to go down this route in individual countries.

A rather unflattering result from this work was that Christoph was now seen to be something of an expert in the area of pet excrement. This was so much so that on the strength of this highly dubious and questionable reputation he was able to persuade the company to promote a dormant premium cat litter product. This was targeted to challenge the dominance of the generics and store own label brands in this market sector. Initial success meant that the fortunes of this brand were rolled out cost-effectively across many regions in Europe. Christoph found a way of cutting down existing film material and re-editing the work that had been done some years earlier and which contained a strong and plausible demonstration sequence. Additionally, Christoph and his team produced arresting posters that were featured

A life above the line – just!

on sites close to major supermarket outlets where the product was being stocked. They strengthened this store presence yet further by buying trolley sides in these stores and advertising, where available, actually in the store itself. They finally produced the on-line spot for just £4,000 to create yet further noise around the brand.

Perhaps for Christoph, while it gave him great kudos, far more importantly every time he made the presentation of 'Back end Performance' he always had a twinkle in his eye. To this day, over twenty years later, even those close to Christoph have never known whether he had really taken this project on in all seriousness or had actually really been taking the piss – literally and metaphorically. Perhaps there was a small clue to this answer in the title 'Back End Performance – From Hoseable to Kickable' – no shit Sherlock!

What this whole exercise and presentation had shown was that Christoph was fully prepared to do something different and do his job differently. In his own way it had given him an immense amount of interest and fun. It had resulted in a presentation and direction that was much talked about, discussed and debated, often in and with good humour.

Christoph had always loved advertising as a vehicle to communicate a message for a brand. He saw his job as being to find something different to say about that brand or to express it in a different way, so that consumers could and would reassess the brand. They should be reassured and the advertising should provide a new or renewed desire for that brand. At the very least it should strengthen consumers' belief in and commitment to that brand. Christoph truly believed in brand choice and that how it was communicated could genuinely be the point of difference. Values could be built over time that gave the brand an emotional association with its consumer, far beyond and exceeding its purely functional use. Christoph would always say, "That is why people buy Heinz Tomato Ketchup in preference to anyone else's tomato sauce." Christoph believed his role was also to be different, to stand apart from the crowd and to find ways of doing the job differently, which he could then fully exploit.

But Christoph also knew the risks with his strategy. Some would criticise him for not being a team player, especially when he fundamentally disagreed with a direction being taken. Some would also accuse him of arrogance and even complacency. Some opposed his maverick tendencies, his outspokenness, and at times his flamboyant and even outrageous style and behaviour. He accepted that some of these accusations levelled at him existed at various times in his career. Nevertheless, he found most people regarded him for always being prepared to lead from the front, and to take the top man on. Many liked the fact that he seemingly exhibited no fear even in the most difficult of situations. He was also admired for always taking responsibility for his actions and also those of his team. He would always hold himself to account. Christoph could never have been a politician and he certainly never was politically savvy. What no-one could dispute whom had worked with Christoph was that without even trying he was different and as a result he did the job in a different way. By doing things differently he often made the job more challenging, exciting and a heck of a lot more fun. Christoph truly represented the old idea that 'Advertising was selling dreams, hopes and desires'. Perhaps too, he believed, it was able to offer a little escapism. Even if they couldn't afford the lifestyle depicted in the 'After Eight' or 'Ferrero Rocher' advertising, they could at least afford and enjoy the product.

CHAPTER 10

Beyond Control

'Forces beyond your control can take away everything you possess except one thing, your freedom to choose how you will respond to the situation.' Viktor E. Frankl (1905-1997 Austrian neurologist)

In the four decades that spanned Christoph's career in advertising there were many instances where and when he was in control of his own destiny, for better or worse. There were, however, also times when things happened that were out of, and way beyond, his control. Chris was always fairly philosophical about these situations and seldom, if ever, bemoaned his lot and never blamed it on 'bad luck'. How could he really? After all, he believed that he made his own luck and usually there were reasons, behind, or for, the outcome – be that favourable or unfavourable. Obviously changes in personnel, be that on the client side, or in agency managements, could never be predicted, planned for, or necessarily managed. However, equally expecting, or hoping, that the status quo would be maintained was in his opinion foolhardy, risky and most unlikely if not implausible. What was critical to him was how was he going to respond? Likewise, how he was going to react to unfortunate circumstances, and unpredicted changes, was absolutely vital. Christoph knew, better than anyone, that he was on a rollercoaster, and as long as he was enjoying the ride, he would accept and live with the ups and downs, always in the knowledge that one day the ride would surely have to stop.

Very early on in his Account Management role he learnt some salient lessons. The meeting summary paper, known as the Contact Report, was proven not to be a document, to which clients could be held to legally. This became an issue twice for Christoph. The first time was when he was working on a toy account. Having got established on the business through their kits he was then involved in the making of a commercial for a doll that shed tears, and was targeted at parents of pre-school children. The commercial had been made and had been approved by the client in time for the Toy Fairs that in those days ran early in the year (these events were timed so that they could feature new product offerings for the following Christmas, even though the gift season was 10-11 months away). Many weeks after the commercial had been completed the Marketing Manager decided to dispute the production costs involved in making this commercial. Christoph was looking down the barrel of a £40,000 hit, which if not paid would result in a massive loss for Gris Advertising. Back in 1976, £40,000 was a sizeable sum of money to write off for a fledgling agency. Christoph had been well trained, when under the tutelage of the Head of Production, whom had truly been his mentor. His advice to Chris had been 'always get it in writing from the client before you do anything and if not put it in writing yourself'. He had lived by this principle though it was more often the agency account person who had to put things in writing. In this particular case Christoph produced all the written evidence, with the agreements reached at the meetings. This included the Contact Report where the specifics of the budget for making the commercial had been outlined, discussed and approved. However, much to the agency's surprise the client decided to pursue this matter through their company lawyers. They refuted the meeting report's authenticity, alleging that even though the date of the meeting was accurately reported, in the Contact Report, there was no proof of what was discussed and agreed at this particular forum. Furthermore, there was no evidence what the contents were of that meeting, or that the so-called 'report', had not been trumped up after the event and without the client's knowledge. Finally, as the client had not signed off on the Contact Report there was absolutely no indication that they had either seen or agreed the content. Nor indeed, was there certainty that it had in fact been issued within 48 hours, as was normal practice, so that any issues emanating from the report could be raised promptly and dealt with, and if necessary changed or altered.

Christoph was shell shocked as he had never before encountered a situation where his good intentions and integrity were being brought into question in a manner that he judged to be most unfair. Fortunately the contents of the Contact Report were detailed enough to list the attendees, on that given day, identifying also what the purpose of the meeting was, which included the agreeing to the budget for the doll's commercial production. The Gris Agency lawyers felt they had the information and tools available to go to battle with, even though they were countered by the company lawyers stating that the Contact Report was not a legally binding document, as it had not been signed off or was there proof it had ever been received. The people present at that meeting were brought forward as witnesses and they verified the content. In the end it was 'amicably' resolved, largely in the Agency's favour, and the major part of the outstanding monies was settled. For Christoph the trust in this client and the particular individual involved was destroyed forever and coming off the account could now not be soon enough for him.

The second occasion was in 1983 on the Venice Simplon Orient Express account. After the first experience Christoph had realised that the Contact Report was only really useful as a record of events. It could only be deemed legally binding if it was issued and countersigned and dated by the client within 48 hours of the meeting. The problem was that most clients refused, or more likely could not be bothered to sign, let alone return, this paper, despite its potential importance and significance. But, to be fair, few ever used it as a defence for not agreeing to something and most accepted it as a useful report of a meeting. There were, however, occasions when agency people used the

Contact Report as a selling tool and not simply a containment of plain facts and action steps agreed. On the other side of the fence there were clients who deliberately refused to sign off on the Contact Report as it might be seen to be a commitment on their part if things went wrong. This was basically what happened in this case. The Venice Simplon Orient Express was a train journey that started from Victoria, London and ended in Venice, Italy. It was the brainchild and passion of the American anglophile, businessman, tycoon, James (Jim) B. Sherwood (who died in 2020 aged 86). Sherwood had made his money as the founder and owner of Sea Containers Limited, with its involvement in Ferry Boats, Ship Containers, the Great North Eastern Railways and their hotels. The last named was the catalyst to becoming a major business interest that expanded into restaurants and bars, which included Harry's Bar and The Cipriani in Venice. James Sherwood was a tough, uncompromising, strongly opinionated, bullish businessman who put the fear of God into pretty well everyone who had to do business with him, including Christoph. When it came to the VSOE he had obtained, bought and lovingly restored the beautiful original carriages from the then defunct Orient Express, as cited and featured in Agatha Christie's mystery 'Murder on the Orient Express'. Many of these carriages had been renovated in Carnforth, where the agency had been commissioned to shoot the interiors for a press campaign and brochures.

The creatives had decided on a moody approach and the shots that came back had real depth but not much sparkle and brightness, being overall moody shots of the Lalique and Tiffany glass and the deep rich grain of the range of wood employed. Mr Sherwood's lieutenants had approved the direction and the work. However, when Mr Sherwood himself saw the photography and the layouts he totally rejected them, expressing massive dissatisfaction with the finished retouched artwork and the layout of the mechanicals. This was an even more complex situation as the mechanicals had actually all been signed off on the back by the personnel beneath him, in his Company. Mr Sherwood refused to pay for any of the work and once again the legality of the Contact Report was brought into question. On this occasion the matter ended up in Court and it was reiterated that in their lawyer's opinion this was not a legally binding document. As it had not been signed off and dated by the Head of the Company there was no certainty that this said individual client had in fact ever seen it – which of course he hadn't! What was particularly galling for Christoph was that the lawyer even went as far as to suggest that there was no evidence that anyone at the client end had ever received the Contact Report, nor that there was any acceptance of its content, or that the content was in fact a true reflection of the meeting or the decisions taken at that time. In his opinion, there was no proof at all that this paper was an accurate reflection of the meeting it allegedly was reporting on. This effectively suggested that Christoph was either a liar or a fantasist or had produced the paper at a subsequent time defending the agency's position and stance, effectively making him dishonest.

In defence, the argument was made, for and on behalf of the agency, that there was proof that the meeting had definitely taken place and what the purpose of that meeting had been. Witnesses could confirm, and they did, that the decisions were arrived at, captured in the report. The Contact Report had been issued within 24 hours of the said meeting, and this too could be proven, and it had not been objected to, as the artwork and mechanicals had been signed off at that same juncture, by a known person with status in the client company. The judge however, found in favour of James Sherwood, as he personally should have been involved in the final approval of the decision making process. What actually saved the agency's reputation was that the artwork and mechanicals had been signed off by a Client representative. The ruling was that the client did not have to pay for the materials produced, to date, but that the agency had to be given the opportunity to reshoot and produce new layouts and mechanicals to the specification and revised brief provided by James Sherwood himself, at the agency's cost.

This was how the matter was concluded and the agency was able to persuade a photographer, often used by them, to do the work for a 'knock down' (read - highly competitive) price. For Christoph it left a bitter feeling in his mouth as he felt he had done everything right and yet had ended up on the losing side. This was simply due to circumstances way beyond his pay grade never mind his control. Trust had been the issue and the loser here. But as Christoph would later remark 'Trust does not necessarily pay the bills!'

Budget Meetings, on Thomas Healey, was another area where the outcome was often unpredictable and frequently beyond the control of the Agency. Christoph appreciated that here one was often in the lap of the gods. However, it was absolutely vital, as Christoph knew, to maintain self-control and concentration throughout. Be in command of the facts and hold one's nerve. Being a smart arse, or wise guy, was never advisable. Keeping the answers short and precise was essential. That didn't mean these annual events did not have their humorous moments, as has been written about earlier. In addition to those already cited Christoph was always highly amused by the poor young female Account Manager who had to present a new storyboard, for a proposed new commercial, on a soap bar that Thomas Healey, sold around the world. Hardly unsurprisingly she was extremely nervous presenting for the first time, in such a large and important forum, with senior management being present from both her agency and the client alike. She started her run through of the story board by stating "We open on a clitoris…" instead of 'chrysalis' (an insect pupa form between larva and adult – at the stage prior to becoming a beautiful butterfly!). As soon as the word had come out of her mouth she realised what she had said and nearly died of red faced embarrassment. Christoph often wondered what on earth she was thinking of to have made that faux pas – though he did concede that he had been to some meetings that were dull, pedestrian and simply plain boring so much so that his mind had wandered and as he put it 'he had run out of sexual fantasies!'

Another Budget Meeting occasion that had amused him was when his opposite number at another major agency, on the Thomas Healey business, had stepped in to assist his team. He felt obliged to do so, given his senior position, after his agency had been on the ropes for some time, and on the receiving end of a lecture from the Advertising Manager. Clearing his throat he had everyone on tenterhooks as he was undoubtedly going to throw new light onto the argument but instead stated quite simply, "Uncharacteristically, for me, I am going to step out of line and really stick my neck out, and in this instance, I am going to agree with the client!" The battle was over and the day was lost - but not without a little style, humour and panache!

In the entire span of his career there was only one occasion when Christoph experienced a case of industrial sabotage. It was however highly significant as it nearly cost him his career, before it had even really got off the ground. In late 1975 Christoph had been briefed by Protac Industrial to produce a typeset advertisement for a number of industrial and technical publications. The content was to be a congratulatory message praising the number of years' co-operation and working association between Protac and another European industrial company. For Christoph, this was a very simple job and in fact he wrote the body copy and head-line himself. He then had it art directed by his Creative Director and friend, Jim. When it had been set he carefully proof read the mechanical before getting a copy of it approved by the client. Once the basic mechanical had been sorted and approved the advertisement was sent off to the various publications on the media schedule. Once released Christoph thought no more about it and moved on to his next project. Job done - or so Christoph believed!

A fortnight later Christoph had to have major dental work done, by a dentist in South Kensington, after he had suffered for some time with a broken tooth, and where the nerve needed to be killed and the remaining tooth area cleaned out thoroughly from potential infection before being capped. The work was long and complex and had to be done under anaesthetic that didn't totally knock him out, but made him feel very woozy. As he gradually came round he still felt a little spacey, distinctly battered, and bruised and the dentist wouldn't let him leave until he showed significant improvement and was more 'compos mentis'. He was strongly advised to be accompanied home and not to return to the office that day. Though still numb and not fully all there (not an irregular occurrence for him!) he decided he felt sufficiently well to go back to work.

He was certainly made to question that decision as when he got back to the office he was immediately confronted by the receptionist, on the front desk, at Gris Advertising. She informed him that everyone had been searching all over for him as the Managing Director needed to see him urgently. Arriving outside the MD's office he sat outside until he was called in to the inner sanctum. Here he became immediately enveloped in a blue smoke haze, caused by the large cigar, the MD was to be found puffing on, as he lent back in his large recliner, black leather, chair. This gentleman was very much old school advertising with his thick pin stripe suit, laced up brogues, 'Brylcreemed' hair and thick bifocal tortoise shell glasses, through which he peered at Christoph with something close to disdain. Indeed, Christoph felt like a contemptible small prawn or shrimp on the end of a skewer. In a slightly sneering voice the MD opened his innings with, "Christoph, your job is on the line." Chris was somewhat taken aback as he was quite oblivious of his having done anything wrong. Before he could react the MD went on, "There has been a major typographical mistake in an advertisement for our client, Protac. This has caused no end of embarrassment to them, as an entity, and also to their associate company in Europe." Pausing only to draw again on his cigar he continued through the choking smoke in front of him, "I am afraid if this is correct, which I am sorry to say seems most likely, we will lose the account and with that this will be the end of any job for you in this agency. Do I make myself clear?" Christoph had quickly assessed which ad he must be referring to and despite realising the stakes were very high felt reasonably confident there would be some feasible explanation, though what that might be, at that stage he had no idea. He replied to the MD, "I shall get right on it. And I shall report back to you, or via John, whatever we discover and the full facts of this case, as a matter of urgency. Naturally, if I am at fault I can only apologise and I totally understand the consequences as far as my future is concerned." With that the MD nodded sagely and he was dismissed with a wave of the MD's hand. Christoph was generally and genuinely relieved to escape that smoke filled torture chamber. He had certainly never before come round so quickly from a dentist's sedation!

In investigating what had actually transpired he discovered that the advertisement instead of reading '…this anniversary marked the successful *conclusion* of co-operation…' now read in a French publication '….this anniversary marked the successful *confusion* of co-operation…' He did not wait for his boss, John, to return to the agency, but having discovered precisely, from the junior client, which publication was involved and the nature of the problem he began to consider the likelihood that the agency and more especially himself was at fault. He was prepared to take total responsibility and accept full blame, if indeed, it was wrong. As he reflected back on the proof reading of the advertisement he realised that it was unlikely to be the Agency or his screw up. This conclusion was reached because he realised it would require that he, as an experienced proof reader, had missed one word with two letters difference i.e. 'f' for 'cl' - when 99 times out of 100 any reasonable proof reader would only overlook one letter for another (generally speaking only someone who was not attentive or had not bothered to check the wordings would make this kind of careless omission or mistake). This gave him cause for real hope.

When John arrived back he was able to brief him on what had been discovered up to this point. John, with his well-schooled Oxbridge mind, shared Christoph's viewpoint and knowing the care that the latter gave to proof reading felt fairly confident that the likelihood was remote that such an error could have occurred. John then asked Christoph if there was anything he could recall that might help identify this advertisement in that particular publication. In fact, Christoph remembered that the key line that went round the text had had a small break in it and he had decided to let that go as it was barely discernible. To have filled this in would only have raised the cost of the production for the client and delayed getting it to the publication. The other interesting point of difference could be the typeface, as it was Corina Bold, which, at that time, few people used and was seldom if ever employed in Europe. This seemed to provide a couple of opportunities to avert a disaster. John contacted the publication in France directly, using his more than acceptable French, to establish if they could confirm if the typeface was Corina Bold and if there was a break in the key line. On the first question they stated the font was as it had been presented and on the second yes there was a small gap in the border line. These depressingly were not the answers Christoph was hoping for as they scuppered his initial line of defence. However, John asked them to send, by emergency and registered post, a copy of the magazine, dated the 18th December 1975, in which the ad had appeared, to the agency in London.

The magazine arrived, the next day, and it was immediately apparent that the font had been changed, within the broken key line, and it most definitely looked nothing like the Corina Bold typeface that the publisher had been supplied with. However, this was not necessarily the conclusive proof or clearance that Christoph needed. It could still be claimed or argued by the publication that they had had to produce the advertisement over the telephone and so had had to use their chosen typeface. They could also have claimed that this was what was supplied to them. John rang the publication once he was convinced the font had been changed and asked for the mechanical to be sent directly to Protac's office in London. He had this addressed for the attention of the Advertising Director. Protac was then contacted and John explained to the Advertising Director what had been uncovered to date and that he had insisted that the mechanical was sent directly, to him, at his office. He went on to ask them not to open the package until the Agency was present, but to notify them as soon as it arrived. He confirmed that both he and Christoph would make themselves immediately available. A couple of days later the mechanical arrived and the client, as requested, informed the agency.

Christoph and John went down together to Protac's Head Office and Christoph took a scalpel knife with him. When they got there the parcel was un-wrapped in front of the Advertising Director and his PR and Marketing team, and John took out the mechanical. Christoph then explained how the typeface was different to the one used on all their other communication material. He then, very delicately, with use of the scalpel, lifted the new typeface to reveal the correct type version lying underneath. The publication had simply overlaid their version on top of that provided to them by the agency. And, of course, on the original submitted, the spelling of 'conclusion' was correct.

The Senior Client was both angered by what had been done but also relieved as they and their agency were now completely in the clear. He went on to say how disappointed he was that this type of industrial sabotage could have taken place. He also expressed sadness as this kind of behaviour and activity could have resulted in people losing their jobs and contracts being lost. Then he went on to ask that the situation be contained and handled with discretion and sensitivity as it was potentially dynamite if it ever got out into the media or industry. The noise and embarrassment that this would result in would almost certainly necessitate a full enquiry to discover who was behind this mischief. It was agreed that he would discreetly seek to uncover the truth from his end and the agency would remain totally silent on the matter. The Advertising Director did say, by way of apology, for the doubt that had been cast upon Christoph, as an individual, that he should have the right, with his media personnel, to come to some kind of negotiation over a settlement with the publication directly, as they had clearly been compliant in this tawdry affair. The result was 15 free pages of advertising and a full and unqualified verbal apology.

This situation could have ended so very badly for Christoph but in the end turned out to be a major turning point. The relationship between Protac Industrial and Gris Advertising strengthened, through a new found trust and respect, and this in turn led to some exciting new advertising over the next three years. Christoph reported back to the Agency's Managing Director who claimed to have never had any doubt in him – though Chris knew differently. John and Christoph celebrated a thoroughly professional job and outcome, where they had never panicked, but had methodically taken each step to get the perfect end result, with a long liquid lunch. This took place at Silks, a restaurant, situated in those days just off St. James's Square. John had taught Christoph the nuances of a sound strategy. Unquestionably the decision to have the mechanical sent to the client to show they had nothing to hide was both diplomatically astute and dramatically ingenious.

Fairly early on in Christoph's career he had learnt that working with pets, celebrities, and children should be avoided, at all costs, whenever and wherever possible. Despite this advice and knowledge there would be many times when circumstances would dictate that this golden rule would have to be broken. It was almost inevitable for Christoph as he worked on three categories where at least one of these, in each case, was difficult to avoid – toys, confectionery and pet food. Toys and confectionery had a definite appeal to children. Petcare and pet food spoke for themselves – be that cats, dogs, budgerigars or horses and ponies.

Making commercials with children was nearly always a nightmare as they were often precocious, spoilt, and over indulged and shooting them in a different sense was often the desired action! Productions often over ran due to a failure to remember, let alone deliver, their lines and then there were the endless 'necessary' breaks. When on camera the crew were subject to the mood and disposition of the child, as well as their behaviour and stamina, problems that all too often could equally be applied to their guardians/custodians/agents.

Much later in his career Christoph encountered the vagaries of working with animals. These, of course, were unpredictable and a conversation with the pet was normally futile. Often the creatives' expectations of what an animal could do, or perform, were totally unrealistic. Yet because the idea had been sold, on a storyboard, to the client the promise, idea and action depicted there was expected to be achieved on camera. Christoph could well recall the time an exasperated shooting director completely lost it after the fifty-eighth take. He exploded at the cat trainer stating, "Listen cat lady if your god-damn cat doesn't walk on set as requested, I will make it my mission to see that neither you nor your precious moggy will ever work again in this town. Do I make myself clear?" Believe it or not the very next take was perfection - so clearly something had worked in his method of approach, or perhaps the cat reckoned his 9 lives were decidedly numbered!

Inevitably working with celebrities and personalities was always fraught with danger as has been cited before. Christoph knew just how precarious this avenue was. On one occasion a well-known radio presenter, who was also, at that time, the front for a particular

A life above the line – just!

confectionery brand, lost his job for using foul and abusive language on air. This was deemed not to be the right association for this brand and the commercials featuring him had to be pulled off air immediately. On another occasion three of the four athletes, in the Great British relay squad, were either injured or not selected, which marginalised the impact of the television spot featuring them in action! Fortunately, for Christoph, none of the celebrities he was involved with fell afoul of any money laundering scams, or sexual deviances, or political scandals, though a couple of recognisable voice over actors did sadly die on him. Two in particular of note were John Arlott (of cricket commentating fame with his wonderful deep slow burr 1914-1991) and John Laurie (with a wonderful rich Scottish accent, famously employed as Dads Army Private Frazer 1897-1980). A number of personalities, that had been used under his tenure ship, did fall out of favour, but by then their use had expired, and their value had been fully capitalised upon.

On the subject of death, Christoph learnt that this did not need to be that of a celebrity, a spokesperson, or a voice over, but this certain yet unpredictable event could be way outside the brand's let alone his or the agency's control. In 1995/1996 Christoph was involved with a sugar confectionery product whose claim was that it 'gave a real fruit flavour hit'. This had led to the creatives developing an idea akin to Alan Parker's memorable film, 'Bugsy Malone,' which featured children dressed as gangsters with splurge guns. In the treatment, the creatives devised, the brand's gang of kids were seen getting 'juiced' with different colours representing the flavours available. It was not dissimilar to paint balling though the executions were done in a cartoon animated style and not as real life. This idea had taken all of Christoph's masterful selling skills and techniques to get it sold to the client, who initially thought it was 'way too edgy'. However, backed up by astonishingly positive research results, on an animatic film version, produced by the agency, it was agreed to proceed to seek Copy Clearance. This Christoph had known from the outset would be difficult as he was only too well aware of their attitudes concerning the depiction of violence and the featuring of weapons such as firearms. However, he was confident that he could win the argument as clearly no children were seen to be hurt, as a result of the 'fruit flavour hit' from the machine gun juicing weaponry. In fact all the children were shown alive and well at the end with big smiles all over their faces. This was undeniable and the script and story board, with the demonstrated animatic, were approved for production. The commercial was made and finally went on air at the beginning of March. However, timing is everything. On Wednesday, March 13th, 1996, there was the tragic 'Dunblane Massacre' in which sixteen school children, fifteen aged 5 and one aged 6, attending Dunblane Primary School and a 45 year old teacher, Gwen Mayor, were gunned down by Thomas Watt Hamilton, before he took his own life. The weapons used were two Brownings and two Smith & Wesson Magnum revolvers. Apart from those killed there were at least fourteen other people injured, all mainly taking class, in the gymnasium. Hamilton, a 43 year old man had been accused of various dubious dealings with children, and most notably with young boys, and had been barred from becoming a Scout Leader. The rumours and reports had led to the closure of his shop and he became an isolated and disgruntled individual seeking retribution. The Cullen Enquiry and Report that followed led to the outlawing of private ownership of handguns in the United Kingdom. Naturally in the light of this tragedy as soon as Christoph heard the news he had the commercial taken off air.

As an aside to this story one of the pupils at the school on that fateful day in Dunblane, a small town situated close to Stirling, was one, Andy Murray, who for a short time was ranked No 1 tennis player in the world. Possibly or arguably, the most successful British tennis player, or at the very least good enough to be compared to, and mentioned alongside, the legendary Fred Perry from the 1930s (who won a 'Career Grand Slam' - winning at the Australian, French, Wimbledon and US Opens with 8 victories in total (between 1932 and 1936 when he turned professional) and 55 career titles, compared to Murray's 46 and 3 Grand Slams). To this day Dunblane is not a subject Andy Murray finds easy to talk about but he has done an immense amount to support this area and aid its recovery. Fittingly, it was exactly 20 years later, he became the World No 1, on November 5th, 2016.

Simply no one could have predicted this event which went way beyond the control of anyone. The commercial never ran in the UK again but it did run in other European countries including Italy, where the reputation and association of mafia gangs endured. The cost of the film's production was therefore not entirely wasted or written off.

Unquestionably one of the regrets and a great sadness in Christoph's life was the unintended announcement of his departure from Premium White. This once again was due to circumstances largely beyond his control. Certainly it was never his intention for his time at Premium White to end the way it turned out. Christoph had realised fairly soon after arriving at Premium White that this was not the style of agency, or a culture, that he felt suited to. It did not really play to his maverick manner and way of operating, being too confining at one level and too 'attritional' at another. There were far too many, more powerful, egos to contend with than his own and they were more senior than him! Nevertheless, he had been determined to make it work and to try to make a real contribution to this agency, even though he recognised he could never fundamentally change their ethos. Part of their 'raison d'etre' and point of difference had been based on not having an Account Management department. His hiring to develop such a department therefore seemed somewhat bizarre and contradictory. Deep down however the Agency Management was still determined to remain Creative led and so it would remain. Christoph realised that he could try to make it a more enjoyable place to work and not a place of fear, of failure, or of running scared of the owners of the business. He therefore worked particularly constructively with the younger members of account management and this finally led to the Training Manual detailed earlier. It was on that self-same day 7th June 1985, when Christoph presented the manual that he had also handed in his letter of resignation and gave three months' notice with an intended departure date sometime in September.

The Premium White initial response had been one of surprise and disappointment. When it became obvious that they would not be able to change Christoph's mind they asked him to remain quiet about his departure. This was so as to avoid any possible demoralisation amongst the Account Management personnel. They had seen that some looked up to Christoph as a leader, guide and even in some cases as a source of inspiration (though heaven only knew why? - as he most definitely didn't!). In the ensuing weeks Christoph set about finding the next move in his advertising career. He had decided that this would certainly be to a big International Agency, even if he only worked on their UK domestic accounts (which as it happened he did for the first two years!). Christoph had offers from three of these major names in the International sphere, but in the end chose to go to McKillans. His decision was predicated on the fact that he knew, from his time serving on the IPA Training Committee, their Director of Human Resources (Personnel Director), who was a most impressive individual. He even headed up the training programme in his agency. They had got to know each other well and there was mutual respect. In fact he had been sufficiently impressed by Christoph's thinking, sense of theatre and presentation skills when these senior players had gone on an IPA 'guinea pig' training programme trial that he had asked Christoph to contact him directly, if he ever thought of leaving his current agency. Christoph had got in touch and through him had met many of the young management that had been put in place, for the future, to try to turn around the fortunes of the agency. He had liked the proposed direction they sought to go in and he could see a real role for him, as did they, in the difficult period of transition that they were facing. The notion of breathing new life into an old work horse (not himself) appealed enormously to him. Eventually, there was only the small matter of agreeing terms and a proposed title, with Board status, that would needed to be approved by the old existing crusty Board, on his arrival.

Unfortunately, in their enthusiasm at the likelihood of signing Christoph and possibly even to force his hand the McKillans' PR team had leaked the prospect and potential of his joining McKillans. This they had made known to the trade press, even despite their assurances to him that this would not happen after he strongly requested that this did not occur, as he wanted to inform his current management ahead of any announcement. Knowledge is a powerful instrument. And this was a positive story that McKillans evidently, given the poor year they had had, did not want to miss out on.

The first that Christoph knew about this leak was when the story appeared on the front page of the leading trade magazine. It caused him massive heartache, consternation, concern and embarrassment. This was directly contrary to what he had promised the Premium White Management and it was not how he wanted his fellow workers and colleagues to hear about his departure or indeed his clients, with whom he still had strong working relationships. Most, if indeed any of them, had no idea, not even an inkling, of his desire and intent to leave Premium White, let alone his pending departure.

Regrettably, his problem was compounded by the fact that Christoph was actually ill in bed at home with an abscess, sinusitis, burst eardrum and acute tonsillitis. Furthermore, some days before the story broke, Christoph had been contacted by the trade press to inform him that they had heard a rumour from 'a reliable source' that he was planning to leave Premium White, which at the time he had totally denied. Indeed, when this had happened he had tried to contact the Senior Management at Premium White to inform them of this rumour in the trade press but they were not available. In hindsight he realised he probably should have left them a note concerning this possible leak (in today's techno world it would have been far simpler as he would have sent them an e-mail or text). But then he had simply left the agency without being able to warn them and had gone to an emergency doctor's appointment, from whence he had been promptly sent home to bed, with a heavy dose of Amoxicillin antibiotics. Christoph had been told he needed complete rest to prevent his symptoms developing into something far more serious. This instruction he had followed and had been laid up for the next few days.

To Christoph's eternal regret when the news broke in the press the Premium White Senior Management took the disclosure and announcement of his departure particularly badly. The Deputy Managing Director wrote him a card stating, 'I took it personally that you did not inform me.' The Managing Director wrote even more sternly, 'In my eyes there's no excuse for your behaviour....I had always regarded you as a gentleman and an honest broker. I'm sad that your recent behaviour has destroyed that image once and for all.' Things were made worse by the wording in the press that implied that Christoph's reason for leaving was based on an 'absence of teamwork', which, while he felt this most definitely was the case, he had never expressed this view to the media or indeed his future agency. This had majorly vexed the MD and he took issue with Christoph over this. Christoph felt that in his sick state he was in no position to defend or to do anything other than to deny having ever said this.

There were subsequent meetings with both these gentlemen and Christoph was able to convince the Deputy MD that he was not wholly to blame and that things had been largely out of his control. Indeed, he had said nothing to the media at all other than a denial of the rumour – hence he had not been quoted. They at least would part as friends. A year later he too left Premium White having cashed in his share options and returned to the US, where he had spent much of his early life, and there he set up a business totally unrelated to advertising. The Managing Director never forgave Christoph and seemed extremely annoyed that he had elected to leave his fine-tuned, sleek, modern yacht of an agency to go to work for a behemoth, or leaky old oil tanker, such as he viewed McKillans. For some incomprehensible reason he took this as a personal slight as well as being insulting to his agency. He was sufficiently upset with Christoph that he refused to speak to him in person again even after a clear the air and explanatory meeting, which Christoph had initiated. Worse still, on the MD's instigation, the whole of the Management team were instructed to ostracise Christoph, effectively putting him 'into Coventry', as they ignored and avoided talking to him. Not surprisingly Chris found himself taken off all his accounts except for two minor pieces of business. And so this was how things remained for the last two months of his contract notice period which he was made to serve out fully. It was a sorry situation, unfortunate and truly neither of Christoph's making or desire. He honestly would have preferred to have left with dignity, his head held high and with good feelings between him and his colleagues. Sadly this was not to be the case.

During his time in advertising Christoph had built a reputation for being an extremely hard worker. His hours alone were exhaustive. He would start at 7am and seldom left before 7pm and often later while most weekends involved at least one day at work. As one Creative Director, Marty, a US citizen, living and working in England, said to him, at Gris Advertising, when he rang him at home, at 8am, "Christoph do you know what time this is? And if you're already at work – you're deranged!" before putting the phone down on him! Holidays did not figure in his itinerary. By and large he avoided time-off or being away with the exception of major flat racehorse meetings. At all the agencies he worked in Christoph would be forced to go away on holiday - possibly just to get rid of him for a while (under the pretence it was to give him a break and a rest)! The most notable time occurred at Gris Advertising. Having been viewed, as being worn-out, fractious and difficult to deal with, and more uncontrollable and unreasonable than normal, Christoph was called into the Chief Executive's office. It was September 1983 and he pointed out that apart from his excursions to 'Glorious' Goodwood and prior to that Royal Ascot he had not been away all year. He was ordered to go on holiday.

As it happened this coincided with, his good friend and house mate, Charlene, who had booked to go, for a few days, to the Algarve, with her fiancé and a group of friends, largely with the intention of playing tennis and then wining and dining well. This seemed ideal and they were only too happy to include him, especially as he was more than a passable tennis player. Christoph had always been far too restless to be a 'sun or beach bunny' so imagine his frustration when it turned out to be far too hot to play tennis after 11am and then the sun went down too quickly to accommodate a late afternoon game, when it got cooler. On Day 1 Chris got sunstroke something he had only ever experienced twice before. This had happened both times at The Epsom Derby when he was unable to move, due to the size of the crowd, on blazing hot days, with the sun beating down on him. This time, in Portugal, he suffered dire nausea and a splitting headache and had to retire to a darkened room. By Day 3 the result of playing tennis in the blazing heat had led to acute sunburn, which then turned into open sores. This combined with a snoring bedroom companion made sleeping well-nigh impossible. By now Christoph had rightly earned the nickname 'Lobby the lobster' due to his boiled pink countenance. On Day 4 they went 'en masse' to the fishing port of Lagos (fortunately in Portugal and not in Nigeria!). Here they lunched from an exotic fish menu and somehow Christoph managed to contract fish poisoning from the fried squid. This kept him laid–up feeling ghastly and excreting from both ends of his anatomy for the next two days. Finally on Day 7 it was to be the return to temperate climes and home, but not before a woman on the plane sitting behind him, distinctly inebriated, chose Christoph to be her victim, vomiting all over him. That brought to an end the perfect holiday! The next day, the CEO, Jeremy Clyde, caught up with Christoph and promptly, not having been forewarned by people who already knew better, enquired how his holiday had been. Christoph grimaced for a second or two, narrowed his green eyes, and then simply told him that if he was ever ordered to go on vacation again he would simply respond, 'Fuck Off and no fucking way'. With that he turned around and walked in the opposite direction. It wasn't long before the holiday experience was doing the rounds and jibes about his adventures overseas were being made to Christoph, which he took all in good heart and humour. Looking back on it one really couldn't have made it up! It needed no exaggeration to be highly entertaining. But he was relieved to say that he was not instructed to go on any breaks for the remainder of his time at Gris Advertising.

With regard to illness and food poisoning by far Christoph's worst experience came in France in 1997. During the build-up to the final attempt to salvage 'Reigning Cats and Dogs' core cat food brand Christoph initiated a week away at a 'Relais & Chateaux' hotel, with a number of creative teams, to produce work to his proposed strategic direction. After the welcoming session and initial briefing and discussion they broke for a late lunch. This was a sit down affair as

A life above the line – just!

Christoph saw this as an opportunity for everyone to get to know each other better and to hopefully relax and realise they were not under any real pressure. Nowadays, they would call this a 'team bonding exercise'. The first course was presented in small soup bowls and was a mixture of different mushrooms in an olive oil based dressing. One of the mushrooms must have been off or could have been an errant toadstool that had found its way into the mix. Christoph became extremely sick fairly quickly and had to leave his colleagues and make speedily for his bedroom and easy reach of the bathroom. During the afternoon he started to hallucinate and his temperature fluctuated alarmingly from being very high with Chris burning up in a muck sweat and then suddenly plummeting very low so that he was left icy cold and shivering like a wreck, before going back to him feeling excessively hot and perspiring. In the middle of the night he finally decided to call reception and asked for an emergency doctor. However, while the staff expressed concern they were clearly anxious about their reputation and as such the best they could come up with were some aspirin. The next day still feeling ghastly Christoph got up and dressed and went down to assess the progress to date on the work and to answer any questions that might have arisen on reflection from his briefing. Satisfying their questions and concerns and feeding their desire for further information he then retired back to his room for the rest of the day. And so he continued for the next day until eventually one of the French Creative teams appreciated that Christoph was clearly unwell and insisted he went to see a doctor. They very kindly sought out a local doctor in a neighbouring town and one of them, as a French speaker, accompanied Christoph there. The doctor examined him but his diagnosis was that Christoph was merely suffering from a virulent virus. Because Chris was still being sick and feeling nauseous this also meant that he couldn't prescribe anything that could be taken by mouth. His belief was that the cure would be time and rest. If only, Christoph thought! Despite no progress Christoph returned to the hotel and battled through the next days and on the Friday morning he reviewed all the work and identified the particular directions he felt best met the brief and seemed to have the most potential.

There followed a 'thank you' lunch, at which he ate nothing and simply sipped water but found the stamina to express in words his deep and heartfelt appreciation for all their efforts and creativity. After that and much relieved that the venture had been a success and that he had got through it and was now able to go home he left the hotel and headed for Orly Airport. He was accompanied by a Canadian writer, Will, working out of the Warsaw office, that he had become friendly with while working on the Neptune account together. After the long road journey, when they arrived at the airport Christoph realised that he physically was not going to make it on to the plane, despite this being his major ambition from the time he had got up that morning. He asked his colleague, Will, if he could locate the Medical Centre and then once found and delivered there he bade him farewell. By now he was only semi-conscious and it wasn't brain surgery for the staff in the Medical Centre to realise that they had a serious problem on their hands. When they had taken both his blood pressure and temperature they informed Christoph that they were going to have to call an ambulance as he needed to be taken straight to hospital as an emergency case. When the ambulance arrived they insisted on payment up front before they would take him to the hospital. And so Christoph was wheeled on their trolley to a cash point, where, even despite his semi-comatose state, he remembered his pin number and was thus able to withdraw sufficient funds in French Francs to satisfy his bearers. Only then could they head for the Central Hospital of the University of Bicetre, Paris-Sud, in the Leclerc-Kremlin area. Arriving there he was somewhat unceremoniously dumped in the corridor of the Accident and Emergency Department, as this was a private ambulance company, not associated with the hospital.

There were no seats in the place where he arrived and so as he could no longer walk he propped himself up against the wall before sliding down onto the floor. Here he waited slipping in and out of consciousness. No one seemed to be there, let alone take any notice of him. Eventually, after nearly four hours, a sympathetic nurse asked him what he was doing there in broken English. When he explained he had been brought there as an emergency she was instantly on her bleeper phone. Things then suddenly seemed to happen rapidly as everyone sprang into action. Christoph found himself being moved, by wheelchair, from room to room, for different tests, measurements and examinations so that a full assessment of his state could be made. Concern was expressed on the faces of these specialists, doctors and experts as they sought to comprehend his symptoms, the erratic changes in his body temperature and his overall condition. They were clearly anxious to alleviate his discomfort and get him back on the road to recovery. After all this activity it was getting late and there was a realisation that they were not going to get back the test results, from the blood samples they had taken, before morning. They attached Christoph to a heart monitor and fixed a saline drip into his arm and had him taken down into the basement where he was allocated the only spare bed available, for that night, which just happened to be in the geriatrics ward!

Back home people were becoming somewhat concerned as Christoph had not returned. Will, the Canadian creative had carried out Chris's instruction to call Fiona Sole and tell her what had occurred, but could shed no light on what might have happened to him, or where he might have been taken, after Orly Airport. Fiona rang all the hospitals in Paris searching for him but without success. Her problems had been inexorably complicated by the fact that he had been entered onto the hospital system as 'Aitkin Christoph' and not the other way around, thereby making his Christian name his surname. However, with her customary persistence, determination and diligence Fiona finally located where Christoph was. The following morning she got put through to him in the geriatric ward. Christoph was able to reassure her that he was getting the right and proper medical attention and supervision, and asked her to pass this onto his immediate family, to allay any concerns they might have had.

That same day Christoph was transferred out of the basement dungeon of the hospital - literally six feet under- and its slightly depressing geriatric wing. From here he was taken up to the lofty heights of the Renal and Stomach Unit overlooking Paris and the Ring Road – the 'periphery'- on the top floor of the hospital. When the diagnosis came back it turned out that he had E-Coli 7, an apparently serious food poisoning condition, a state which lesser mortals can die from. As it was, it would take Christoph a very long time to fully recover from this illness.

Nevertheless he knew work wise time was not on his side. As soon as he practically could he had to get out of the hospital, Paris and France. By the following Wednesday he felt sufficiently on the mend and certainly strong enough to want to leave and get off home to 'good ole blighty'. Here, however he encountered a number of problems and hurdles that had to be overcome. Few of the staff spoke any English and the consultant that did was adamant that Christoph was far too ill to travel and he would have to stay in the hospital for at least another two weeks. Christoph realised that the French tend to be slightly more neurotic than the English and evidently suffer from hypochondria when it comes to hospitals. It seems they have to be virtually pulled out of their beds and then kicked out of the hospitals to make them leave, as otherwise they would reside there indefinitely. Given this encountered mentality, it was incomprehensible, to the clinical team, in charge of Christoph, to fathom his continuous attitude and desire to leave. In the end they simply put it down to his being just 'another strange 'Engleeshman'. After much badgering he finally got the reluctant specialist to relent and to let him leave on the Friday, exactly a week after his arrival. But then there was still the matter of payment, which became quite farcical when it transpired that the hospital credit card system was broken making the use of his credit card redundant. Unfortunately, Christoph had not travelled with any details of his Medical and Travel Insurance. Only after lengthy persuasion did the hospital management agree to take his Bank of Scotland cheque with proof of his identity being the details on his passport, and his address details, which he also wrote on the back of the cheque. On the front of the cheque Christoph crossed out the sterling sign and substituted the French Francs symbol and then wrote in the amount of F.Fcs14,378 (circa F.Fcs 8 to £1 making the bill some £1,797.25) in the box and then wrote out the full amount in words. This subsequently took some explaining to the bank on the following Monday morning. Despite being totally bewildered by

A life above the line – just!

his actions they agreed to honour the cheque and to make the payment to the hospital once it was submitted by them. Better still the Medical Insurance Company reimbursed Christoph in full for the ambulance, hospital and his travel costs back to England, including the taxi to Orly and the flight to Gatwick Airport as well as the train fare from there to Victoria. This had certainly been an unforgettable experience and one that had been totally unwanted and definitely way beyond his control in pretty well every regard from beginning to end!

Christoph finally left advertising and McKillans, in 2001. It was a time when the agency itself was struggling with take-overs, mergers and acquisitions. A general downturn in the agency's fortunes meant many good people lost their jobs, insensitively referred to in the trade as 'downsizing'. Realising, in contrast to so many, he had been truly fortunate to leave on his own terms, he set up a group called 'The Recoveries'. Initially he contacted seven people with whom he had either worked or respected and whom he knew had been made redundant. He asked them to join him one Tuesday morning at Esquires Coffee Shop in Gloucester Road Tube Station Arcade. The sole purpose was to find out how they were and if there was anything that they thought he might be able to do for them. From this initial meeting the group grew to number fourteen and they met every Tuesday morning, at 10 am, at the same place. There were, however, three rules Christoph insisted upon. Firstly, he bought the first round, of coffees or teas, recognising that many of them would be struggling financially and should not feel the need to buy a round, especially as the group expanded. Secondly, there was to be no bad mouthing of the 'old firm' as this was simply non-constructive, demoralising, frustrating and counterproductive. It would not help these individuals to move on. Finally, each person attending was expected to come up with six names or six ideas, or a combination of these, that could be discussed, considered and where possible employed. This was true networking at its best.

'The Recoveries' continued to meet for the next six months until all but one of the fourteen members had got themselves back into employment. There was even one amusing instance where Christoph had been offered a job by an old associate, which he turned down – so much for his old 'work ethic'! - but was able to get the offer transferred to one of 'The Recoveries'. This person was a much more suitable candidate, and this bought the individual a year in which he could determine and find what he really wanted to do longer term.

Much to Christoph's surprise and delight even when the initial objective, behind the formation of 'The Recoveries', had been met the group decided they wanted to continue to meet up. However, now they would meet on the first Tuesday evening, of every month. This meant that coffee and tea could now be substituted by beer, wine and spirits a reflection of the more relaxed tenor of the meeting. The rules were abandoned except for the initial one where Christoph continued to insist on paying for the first round of drinks. The purpose was to have a good chinwag, touch base, to further network, and to see if others needed help or if everyone was content. News of this gathering got around and gradually it expanded where once it had been just 7 people then 14 it mushroomed to as many as 54 names. Christoph was amazed by how many people he had worked with were so pleasant to socialise with! To be fair many of these people saw this forum and group as their only way of really keeping in touch with old colleagues. Some also saw the benefits of this group as a networking facility. In time the encounters were reduced to just four a year, with three evenings of drinks in February, June and October and a year-end dinner in early December.

Nearly twenty years later this network continues and pleasingly a few show up for a regular quarterly drink, while as many as twenty-five people make the annual dinner. The nice thing from Christoph's standpoint is that they are all friends, like-minded people, and colleagues he feels privileged to know and to have worked alongside. In his wildest dreams he could never have hoped or expected that what was a small practical idea, to help people find employment, could have evolved into such a longstanding network. So even after his departure from the advertising stage it appeared that some matters, actions and consequences still remained truly far beyond his control!

―――― CHAPTER 11 ――――

The Final Curtain Call?

A curtain call (walk down or final bow) occurs at the end of a performance when individuals return to the stage to be recognised by the audience for their performance.

Christoph had always believed that advertising, especially in the ageist UK, was really a young person's industry. Indeed, he had often remarked half-jokingly that 'people should retire at 39 before they are kicked out at 40'. And now here he was at 50. So when his number came up he was fairly relaxed about it, even if, in truth, he would have liked to have squeezed another four to five years out of the industry. This would have enabled him to take 'honourable' retirement at 55 – oh and, of course, full pension rights. He would also then have been proud to have served McKillans for over 20 years. Christoph felt he still had the passion and desire to give more, that he was still at the top of his game and therefore had something to offer, and that he was possibly doing some of his best work when 'time out' was called. But you know the rowings over when you hear the Tannoy system, broadcasted from the boathouse, calling, 'Come in Number 50 your time is up!'

Christoph had realised too that 'times they were a-changing'. It was a new millennium and the industry needed to adapt quickly, or it would be left for dead. It was truly the era of New Media and technologically driven business with different communication answers. The control of the agencies now lay with the money men – 'the bean counters' and not anymore with people wedded and rooted in the Advertising itself. In Christoph's judgement it really had become a financial business and the bottom line was deemed to be the only thing that seemed to matter. The prospect of making money quickly through mergers, takeovers, acquisitions, shares and share options had become the primary interest and focus – sadly, in his view, at the expense of the products and brands the agencies were commissioned, hired and retained to sell through communication. Share price and financial sector approval and rating became the key drivers for the publicly quoted agencies. This, in turn, meant cost cutting measures and capping of salaries became all too commonplace to protect the bottom line profitability. Small and specialist boutique agencies emerged with their over–riding desire to be acquired by the bigger agency groups, so that their founders could land large financial 'jackpots'. The management of the major agencies often appeared to reward themselves seemingly largely at the expense of the lower and more junior members of staff, on whom they depended. Christoph perceived that short-termism was the order of the day- the quick buck today mentality!

Clearly the advances in technology meant a heightening of interest in 'new media' and social sites. The traditional vehicles of communication were constantly under threat and most definitely open to heavily negotiated pricing. This all meant that the media world became increasingly fragmented and the target audience had to be approached very differently and specifically, by media vehicle and message content. The media men had become the 'power brokers' not only in their area of expertise but also in dictating the terms of the messages delivered. Within the agency structure this was now their day in the sun. The media agencies and independents gradually turned their former agencies into simply becoming suppliers of the message – the advertisement, the banner, the intros etc.

Technological advancements had also occurred in the production field, where shooting on 35mm film became a rarity while video and digital filming was becoming ever more sophisticated and of improved quality. The danger, as Christoph had witnessed and observed, was that all too often the message got lost in the 'gizmo' and the splendiferous techno-effects achievable. The lack of a big idea, a big picture, a point of difference, even a selling idea, let alone a powerful one, was sacrificed at the altar of technological techniques and refinements.

What Christoph also noticed, as the new millennium started, was a changing of the guard. The bravado, business knowledge, marketing thinking, supreme confidence and assurance, led by strong personalities of proven record, so much a feature of the 1970's, '80s and even into the '90s, had disappeared seemingly forever. The standing and currency of the agencies had become distilled, dissipated, demeaned and debased. Clients had become ever more demanding, better informed and instructive over the years. Many of these clients commanded and dictated to their agencies, rather than seeing them as business partners, who could offer a point of difference, opinions, advice and a sense of challenge. This seemed to a somewhat naïve Christoph to coincide with the agencies being run by ever younger, arrogant, expectant, ambitious personnel. All too often, in his opinion, these people appeared to lack sufficient gravitas, depth of knowledge, experience, or even proper training, making, as a result, their views far less valid or justified.

As Christoph looked back on his career he remembered that when he had got to the Board at Gris Advertising, he had just turned 30 and that made him one of the youngest members on any major agency board in London. He already had seven years under his belt, having worked his way up the ladder on both sides of the Atlantic. Now it seemed to him people at 26 with less than 4 years background were wondering why they weren't already Chairman or CEO, never mind being on the Board! The problem Christoph noticed was that these people tended to be highly political, financially incentivised and motivated, fiercely ambitious, but then spent an inordinate amount of time looking over their shoulders and seeking to remove any possible threats from their battlefield. As in history insecurity leads to inadequacy. These people, seemed to Christoph, to surround themselves with sycophants and 'yes' men and women, all hoping to ride their luck on their coat-tails. The problem with this philosophy and approach was that with an entourage offering no points of difference, no opposition and no contrary opinions, the management were in danger of believing their own publicity, and that only their directions and views were valid. As Christoph, in mild amusement, would remark, this was reminiscent of two Prime Ministers, Margaret Thatcher and Tony Blair, who began to believe their own PR, and felt that they were infallible, after long tenure ships (Baroness Thatcher ('The Iron Woman') 1979-1990; Tony Blair ('B-liar') 1997-2007, both winning three consecutive elections before losing out to leadership challenges).

Christoph reflected, with some disbelief, at the rapid changes taking place in the industry he had given nearly 30 years to. He recognised that the business had truly altered in format, style, structure and importance. It would never again reach those heady days of the 1970s and 1980s. Even the people had changed and a 'laddish' culture had emerged intolerant of softly spoken conservative or public school educated people, dismissed as being 'upper class toffs'. And to think that Christoph had spent years refining his voice to sound 'right' only to discover in time it would be deemed 'wrong'! A class war was seemingly bubbling under this veneer. The age that had welcomed people irrespective of sex, colour, creed, education or background had long passed. And yet at the same time people were talking about 'equal opportunities' (be that sex, race/ethnicity, beliefs); 'political correctness' (in how people were addressed and talked to and about) and 'non-stereotypes' (this could be regarding sexuality or origins or race). But it truly wasn't. Now it was an industry seemingly run by people reasonably fresh out of university usually with unrelated degrees, some from institutions, that had, until John Major's Premiership (1990-1997), been Polytechnics and Colleges. No born salesmen. No street fighters. No mavericks. Not even many great thinkers or challenging intellectuals. There appeared to Christoph to be an inability to tell the truth, to be held to account, to take responsibility, or even to apologise and simply say sorry. These values were seen to show weakness. People seemed to be afraid of being accused or blamed or sued. This, Christoph surmised, over the first 20 years of this millennium, seems to have even pervaded the very top of major corporations, companies, organisations and even Government itself.

Specifically, for Christoph, this was an alien world, as his track record and way of doing things and his knowledge now appeared to pose a massive threat for both client and agency alike. His outspoken, maverick, fearless behaviour and forthright manner and honesty were uncontrollable to this new style of management. He made them feel intimidated and deeply uncomfortable.

The beginning of his demise actually came from the client side when the new European Marketing Director, Fran Shilling at 'Reigning Cats and Dogs' had been determined to have Christoph removed from the account. His depth of knowledge of the business and his vehemently strong opposition to her plan to advertise small dogs and cats together made him a genuine and fearsome opponent. Her belief, based on no comprehension, was that both animals had a similar profile, needs and owners. Everything he had learnt over the years working with both species of pets told him this was fundamentally flawed thinking and plain wrong. Following on from a review meeting with Fran Shilling where the Management had sought her feedback on the team, led by Christoph, they reported back to him her views. Her analysis was summed up in these words, "George has neither style nor substance; Roger has style and no substance and Christoph has substance but I don't like his style." Christoph was highly amused and his response was, "Well that was a brief, blunt and succinct annihilation of the team. Can I just ask when Fran was referring to my substance was she talking about my waistline and mid-riff or my thinking abilities and brain power?" No answer was forthcoming as they failed even to see the humour or irony in what he was asking. He realised that his relationship with 'Reigning Cats and Dogs' was at an end!

Christoph knew that his own management were in an impossible position, as their once star player, on the account, was now not liked by the new Client manager, who saw him as an articulate impediment to the new style of play she wanted to implement! In a bold attempt to assist them he wrote a paper for the Senior Management in the United

States. He then flew to New York to deliver this in person – never one to shirk his responsibility. This paper pointed out why the agency was potentially in a perilous position, with the 'Reigning Cats and Dogs' client in Europe and the very real threat Fran Shilling posed. As he put it quite succinctly to them 'never underestimate the power of a woman especially when they are holding all the cards!' He was sufficiently concerned that he even told them, much to their astonishment, that they should take him off the business as in the current climate he was contributing to the problem by opposing this woman, Fran, so openly. Indeed, he recommended, based on his understanding of her that they should either team her up with a woman or a young, good-looking, modern, fashionable man. The game had truly changed and it was a case, just like in horse racing, of horses for courses. In hindsight Christoph appreciated that while they found his presentations on both the future of the business and on the specific issue of 'Small dogs and cats are the same' interesting they did not want to go to the Senior Management of the company in the US as they viewed this could be political suicide. The relationship was already in such jeopardy that they were almost fearful of doing anything - somewhat reminiscent of frightened rabbits caught in the car headlamps.

After a long meeting, with much discussion, the Head of International finally turned to Christoph and challenged him saying, "Christoph, frankly I am disappointed in you. In all the time I have known you I have never known you to duck a fight or to turn down a challenge. Yet here you are proposing to walk away from a contest and resign off the business. What has happened to you?" Christoph looked him straight in the eye, nodded his head, smiled and then replied softly, "Sometimes it is good to know when you are beaten, when the enemy is overpowering and when your general ship may be leading to greater loss of life by your very presence. Sometimes too the ammunition simply runs out and like at The Battle of The Alamo (Jim Bowie, William B Travis and Davy Crockett with around 182-257 Texians, defended the Mission Church and hospital at Alamo, near San Antonio de Bexer, against the Mexican Army, numbering initially 1,500, but increased to 3,100, with advanced cannons, led by President /General Santa

Anna, between 23rd February and 6th March, 1836. All the Texians lost their lives either in defence or in the massacre afterwards) you find yourself fighting with little or no support, against impossible odds! In those circumstances a tactical withdrawal is advisable, acceptable and strategically sound and correct. With the right information fed back, in a tactical withdrawal, the forces can be regrouped, rearmed and the best artillery can be employed that wins the war in the long run even if the battle on the day may seemingly be lost. Heroes die too - often in futile situations. Look at 'Custer's Last Stand' (Battle of The Little Big Horn, where Lieutenant Colonel George Armstrong Custer against the Cheyenne and Arapaho Indians lost his life in the 2 day battle June 25/26th 1876) or Gordon at Khartoum (Major General Charles George Gordon lost his life defending the town against the Mahdist, led by the Mahdi, himself. The siege lasted from 3rd March 1884 until overrun and his death on 26th January 1885)." No more was said in response to Christoph's considered answer. They said they would sleep on it and get back to him the next day.

At the reconvened meeting the Senior Management again praised the work that had been done under Christoph's leadership on the 'Reigning Cats and Dogs' business. It was accepted that a change of personnel –at least as far as the UK and Europe was concerned – was deemed appropriate. Nevertheless, they were still anxious to retain Chris's services, for the time being, on the broader International front, on 'Reigning Cats and Dogs'. Longer term they asked him to consider their offer of becoming McKillans Head of Operations for Australasia, based out of either Melbourne or Sydney. With regard to the job offer in Australasia, Christoph responded stating, "That while I am flattered by your belief in me and recognise the importance and significance of this opportunity you are offering, it is regrettably impossible for me to take this up. I have an 80 year old mother, whom is going slowly blind, and an 8 year old daughter – both who need me back home." (Little did he know that his mother would live on until aged 97 while his daughter would end up going to a private boarding school!).

Interestingly after this encounter and his rejection of the job Christoph never heard from the International Management again. He would carry on working for McKillans for another 9 months. He made a number of attempts to contact them but his calls were never taken and his messages simply ignored. Refusal was evidently tantamount to dismissal!

Christoph returned from New York pragmatically relieved. He had tried, not for himself, but for the agency and he had failed. Once again he had raised his head over the parapet, fired the warning shots, talked himself out of a job, but had still not been heeded. In time he knew deep down he would be proven right – and indeed he was. He was also savvy enough to know that with his refusal of the Australasian job his days were almost certainly numbered, but in truth that really didn't much concern him. There was still a job to do until the clock stopped!

Shortly after he got back from the States he found himself part of a reshaping programme. The UK management decided that the 'International' people should share an office even though they were working on different accounts. It seemed to Christoph that everything had come full circle and that local management had a strongly negative view of 'internationalism'. They appeared to consider this part of the business to be a handicap to producing 'famous advertising'. It seemed like the international business was a necessary evil that had to be tolerated, as these accounts were, after all, the bread and butter of the agency – being the biggest billing clients. It was these clients that paid the bills and met the overheads. Christoph, much to the amusement of many, but also to the irritation of some 'guests/travellers,' referred to this room as 'The International Departure Lounge'. And it proved to be just that as a number of 'roomies'/ roommates/travellers found the exit door, of the agency, via this crammed space. Five members would leave within months of the creation of this workplace. The situation was not helped by the fact that the European Heads of the agency felt it needed to balance the books by moving brands between offices. New hubs or centres were created to use the manpower available and to shore up certain European offices and as compensation for the loss of other brands often on a different client. In one instance two of the brands that moved from the UK to France were not even marketed in the country they were moved to whilst a third brand had actually been lost in this market sometime previously. In Christoph's view a curious decision and not one he was party to.

When it finally came to Christoph's turn to leave the 'International Departure Lounge' it took a while due to the 'paperwork' and travel documents not being in order! The process started on American Independence Day, July 4th 2001, but it was almost a month later before he was granted an exit visa! It was left to the UK Financial Director to finally wield the axe that Christoph had expected to come at any time over the previous 9 months. He was ready and fully prepared. The stated reason for his being made redundant unsurprisingly was that as Christoph had turned down the offer of the Australasian post and as the agency had been unable to find him another position within the group that they had no option but to make Christoph redundant, with immediate effect. Indeed, he went on to state that Christoph should leave by five thirty that same day, which given it was already four o'clock, when the meeting began, was indeed fairly short notice and definitely immediate! The Financial Director went on to say that if he continued to come into the agency and work he would not get paid for so doing. Any time thinking, or doing work, subsequently, would be at Christoph's own cost. A lot of pressure was then put on Christoph to sign a termination agreement that meant he would forego his contract and his entitlements which naturally Christoph point blank refused to sign or negotiate over. The only concession he made was to sign a resignation letter to the Pension Trustees stating that he would no longer be in a position to be a Staff Representative, because even though they had elected him, he was as from today not going to be a member of staff. For the rest he told the Financial Director that he would be seeking legal advice and would therefore sign nothing without his legal representative's say-so. Furthermore, he informed them that as they had chosen to have this meeting without his legal representation being present and had chosen not to honour his contract in full they would be liable for any and all his legal costs. The Financial Director found Christoph's stance deeply offensive and it seemed to frustrate him as there would now not be a clean break. He had seemingly agreed with the management what position to take and to try to hold this ground. The tools at his disposal were to try to bamboozle Christoph with legalise and mild threats of changing and withdrawing the offer if he did not sign there and then. Naturally, as Christoph respected and recognised he was relying on his negotiating skills for the best result and outcome for the Agency. Above all he needed Christoph's verbal agreement and ideally his signature. Instead he found Christoph calmness personified, lacking any hurt or emotion and frustratingly well versed and prepared. Despite the threats of less favourable terms being the possible result and outcome of his intransigence Christoph was immovable. Christoph had expected this meeting and had done all his homework as well as having taken legal advice and had an Employment Lawyer lined up. In exasperation Christoph was informed that as he had chosen to take this position, and as nothing around his termination/separation had been agreed, he was sworn to secrecy and that this meant he would not even be allowed to say farewell openly to his colleagues upon leaving the agency.

Unlike the Agency, whose management appeared to show a total disregard for his clients, Christoph, did not leave that same day but stayed on for another 3 weeks at his own cost. This was simply so that he could complete the work he was involved in, notify the clients as each job was completed, and cover for his intended replacement, who had co-incidentally gone on holiday the same day as Christoph was made redundant! Even after this gentleman returned from holiday Christoph stayed on to ensure there was a proper handover and so that any questions the new person might have could be properly answered. He subsequently was asked if he would agree to attend two meetings, in early September, where the client and, somewhat begrudgingly, the agency recognised his input could be a factor in getting the work through. Christoph actually chaired these meetings as well as being the key presenter. Both fortunately were successful and once completed he was warmly shaken by the hand and his well-meaning successor, said smilingly "Thank you Christoph; you have behaved as an honourable man among scurrilous rogues – one of which you may deem to be me!" He didn't but it was an amusing moment to end on!

When the actual day of his departure came, not only from

A life above the line – just!

McKillans, but from the industry as a whole, some 28 years had elapsed since he had first turned up at Gris Advertising. He didn't leave with gratitude, appreciation, acknowledgement or fond farewells ringing in his ears. Contractually forbidden to say goodbye publicly, because his severance still remained subject to protracted legal debates and on-going discussions, he left quietly - or as he rather theatrically put it later -'as though he was a fugitive fleeing in the dark of night!' Nevertheless, it was not exactly how he would have liked his leaving to be. But at least he believed he had run a true race right up to the finishing line and indeed as it happened beyond! There were no feelings of bitterness, or any recriminations, but just a quiet sense of pride in his behaviour, achievements and his performance right up to his very last day.

Indeed in his very final days he had helped the PR Company in the Group to secure a piece of Thomas Healey business. This was achieved by working with their front line team giving them an understanding into the prospect and an insight in the way they thought and behaved. Additionally, he was able to help them develop their presentation crafting its style, format and content. Separately, he also worked with the Sales Promotion arm of McKillans to help them become a roster agency on 'Reigning Cats and Dogs', with a publicly declared budget of around £1million of business. News of this victory co-incidentally only came out on the morning of the very day that Christoph left McKillans and advertising for good. He received a note of sincere gratitude and deep appreciation just before his PA closed down his computer for the last time. Christoph was thrilled and delighted as he had always wanted to get out at the top and whilst he was still respected and regarded. He did not want to leave as a dead-beat, has-been or 'yesterday's man' burnt out and on the scrap heap of advertising. He had seen over the years too many of those sad characters.

At lunchtime on that final day Christoph bought two bottles of good champagne, some snacks, a cake and sandwiches to celebrate his PA, Morag's birthday. Being a beautiful late summer's day they chose to sit on the lawn in Holland Park and 'chew the cud' (hypothetically!).

It was a stylish way to celebrate and the amusing anecdotes and reminiscences flooded back from their time together. They reflected on past annual Christmas Lunches that Christoph would arrange for all the team members however lowly and where everyone would be given a present, relevant and pertinent to them. In Morag's case this had been a series of alarm clocks that got ever bigger, as she was famed for being unable to get up in the mornings and get to work on time. Then there were the characters they had encountered together and the nicknames Christoph had given them, and the fun they had all had often at each other's expense. The Chauffeur, Bertrand, was one such person, whom had a habit of getting lost, refused Sat-Nav, and so at Christmas always received an atlas, an A-Z or road maps, as his gift, from Santa. On one occasion Bertrand had actually turned up at Christoph's home to collect him to go to the airport; the only problem being that he arrived at 5am instead of 5pm and a week early. Another time he nearly killed Christoph and two guests on the way back from Cheltenham Races. It was a grey, damp, misty evening and he misjudged the distance crossing over a main road and failing to see a car travelling, admittedly too fast, around a bend that ploughed into the side of his car. One of the guests had to go to Cheltenham Hospital with a suspected broken nose, while Bertrand and Christoph took a lift back to London from the AA as the car was not driveable. The stories just flowed along with the champagne, until, at 4pm, it was time to pack up and for Christoph to collect his final belongings and leave the McKillans building for the very last time.

As there could be no goodbyes or fond farewells only very few people knew that he had left until sometime later. One of the Creative Directors whom he had been assisting and advising over his pension did say to him as they parted, "Thank God for a terrier amongst all those poodles." They had it was true fought many good battles together. So for Christoph, the man of theatre, there was to be no final curtain call; no ovations; no bows and no thanks or appreciation. The lights went out on his stage and there was barely enough noise or light, in the dimmed auditorium, for him to find the exit door. The show

A life above the line – just!

was truly over and ended with barely a whimper – but oh what a show it had been!

With just a box containing his table top possessions he kissed the receptionist goodbye and thanked her for having been ever present and a constant throughout his time at the agency. He headed down to the car park put his things in the boot of Fiona Sole's car and then got into the passenger seat alongside her. Christoph smiled warmly at her and she hugged him tight, with moisture in her eyes. Christoph was far more relaxed about it all and quite sanguine and simply retorted, "Hey, it's time to move on," which he most certainly did! They drove out of the car park and left McKillans behind, heading for dinner at Sarastro, in Drury Lane. His day was finally done!

The negotiations with McKillans would continue for another three months and in the end Christoph won all his entitlements except for holiday pay and the 6 week sabbatical entitlement, after 10 years' service. He even got his legal fees paid for and the receipted expenses incurred, during the time he continued to work, post redundancy. By his reckoning it was a fair and reasonable result, though by no means anymore then he believed he deserved. A portion of the redundancy payment was withheld for fifteen months to ensure Christoph did not take another agency job, or bad-mouthed his old firm, over this time period. It was paid in full at the appropriate time.

Despite the settlement Christoph realised that he didn't have sufficient readies/funds to keep his two girls clothed, fed and watered, let alone one privately educated. Certainly he did not have enough to maintain his flamboyant lifestyle over the next 4 years plus before his pension kicked in. The pension had been crucial to hold on to as it was a Final Salary Scheme. He had been approached a number of times and actually offered other jobs prior to ending his days at McKillans but none could match this pension deal. It had been a calculated risk by Christoph but one that would pay off handsomely in the future. When it had been offered to him on joining McKillans he had appreciated immediately that this was a real benefit and potentially a long term asset. Twenty years at McKillans would have given him effectively two-thirds of his final salary (though, some years later, this offer had been capped at a salary level of £100k). No more than two years after he had joined McKillans he had been offered a large cash sum to switch to a Money Purchase Scheme Pension, with a purchased annuity at pensionable retirement age. Christoph could see that rates were high at the time but he could also envisage a situation when they could be significantly lower and in which case the annuity rate would be adversely affected. Besides, he thought, no one offers money unless there is something in it for them. As he said at the time, "No thanks I am absolutely fine with my current pension arrangements and besides, in my experience, there is no such thing as a free lunch! If you are offering me cash to change there must be something in it for you!" Boy was he proven right on that! Guaranteed 5 year Annuity Rates hit a high at around 16% (circa 1984) but then plummeted to around 4% and never picked up again. (Eventually, The Government, when George Osborne, was Chancellor of the Exchequer, scrapped the requirement for people having to purchase annuities, in April 2015). The pension might have stopped Christoph taking other jobs, as he didn't want to forego his pension rights, but in retirement it would most definitely help secure his exuberant way of life!

Apart from the fact that he was banned from taking another job in advertising for over a year Christoph really didn't want to stay in advertising. He truly felt he had done pretty well everything he had ever wanted to do in the industry and it was time to let younger brains have their turn and take their chances. In the initial months post-redundancy Christoph was approached by a number of head-hunters, but the only jobs he was even prepared to consider were not in their remit to offer, or they deemed insufficiently rewarding, in compensation terms, for them. What Christoph proposed was that he would like to offer his services to agencies as a trouble shooter, who could work to secure and lockdown businesses that might be vulnerable or in danger of leaving. He would offer his experience, know-how and creativity to find insights that could lead to potential brand growth through braver, more challenging and hopefully more effective communication. As a secondary offer Christoph proposed that he could go into an agency

A life above the line – just!

and work on new business projects to help convert contacts into real business. This he believed could be achieved through detailed market analysis, strong consumer insights and dramatic presentations putting these findings into advertising and other communication vehicles and media. His most recent victories in PR and Sales Promotion had demonstrated how this could be done effectively. He definitely was in no way blinkered or limited to above-the-line, traditional advertising. Unfortunately Christoph was too far ahead of his time and no one was certain how to channel or market this type of resource to and within the Agencies. In years to come these sort of players would emerge under a variety of guises be that consultants, aides, agents, spin doctors, specialist boutique operations and alternative media outlets.

At the same time Christoph signed up on the dole, which entitled him to Job Seekers Allowance, for some six months. This really took him back to how it all began. It was while he was on the books of the Job Centre in Hammersmith that he had got his initial break in advertising, though not through them. Now here he was nearly three decades later making weekly visits to the Job Centre, filling in a booklet that recorded what he had done over the previous week to engineer conversations, meetings and interviews. What goes around comes around! In this new era everyone had to have a progress discussion with one of the Job Centre Managers, before they could collect any financial support and entitlements. Needless to say they were somewhat surprised by Christoph when he stated, somewhat audaciously with tongue in cheek, that 'what he was really seeking was a job with a £100k plus annual salary in the communications industry'. Needless to say there weren't too many of these flying around the Job Centre; in fact – none! Luckily the man interviewing him had spent his working life, before he went into the Civil Service, in business, so he could relate to Christoph. He was far more interested in talking about his own career and the time he had spent in the telecommunications industry in Germany, then worrying about finding a job for Christoph (which in any case he possibly or even probably thought was a lost cause or a hopeless endeavour!). Eventually he even asked if Christoph could help his daughter prepare for interviews and construct distinctive letters of approach, as well as an arresting/attention grabbing Curriculum Vitae. Christoph was only too happy to oblige and duly did, for which his Manager was definitely most appreciative.

The environment in the Job Centre situated close to the Nightingale Hospital in Lisson Grove, Marylebone, was always 'interesting' - tense, hot, uncomfortable and menacing. Emotions ran high and at times there was a high level of frustration that would bubble away and had the potential to boil over at any moment. Abusive language was common place and aggressive behaviour, with threatening action, was not uncommon, which occasionally led to brawls and fisticuffs. In time, the Government of the day opened up another operation entitled Job Search where carefully selected people were sent and here they were allocated a 'Minder'. Christoph was chosen to attend this office situated in Marylebone Lane, which was a very different set-up, comfortable chairs in nicely decorated offices where entry could only be achieved with an identity clearance. From here Christoph was sent off to many office jobs and call centres all seeking sales personnel. Christoph managed to persuade them all, seemingly without much difficulty, that he was unsuitable to meet their requirements. He certainly didn't relish such a job and besides he had no experience in this field of selling. Fortunately, for him, his 'Minder' was a charming, well educated, very bright, young woman, whose family had originally come from India, who was very conversant and clearly very ambitious. In the end she asked Christoph, even despite his limited exposure to her, and with the details she provided, to craft her Personal Statement, as well as comment on her CV and to work with her at developing letters of application, as she was seeking employment - elsewhere! Christoph was never too sure what the effect was that he had on these operatives that made them seek his assistance. He wondered if it was just the gift of the gab or perhaps it was the realisation that they could do little if anything for him! In her case shortly afterwards she found a job she really wanted and left. It was then that Christoph decided that he too had had enough of Job Search.

One thing that came out of the Job Centre experience, other

than the small weekly remittances, was training! One day the 'telecommunications man' said to Christoph, "You have done so much for me and my daughter is there anything you can think of that we can do for you?" Christoph informed him that he had never learnt to type or how to use a computer. Indeed, he could honestly describe himself as computer illiterate! This he acknowledged was the result of having a full-time Secretary/Personal Assistant. It was immediately organised for him to attend Westminster College for two Pitman Courses – one for Typing and the other for Word Processing. Initially it proved to be a total disaster, as Christoph sat in a class with mainly 18-25 year old women, who were far more savvy with the technology, more adept at typing and distinctly more adroit and skilled on the computer than him. His problems were exacerbated by the fact that he did not own a computer to practice on at home. At one stage his delightful, cheery, middle aged and long suffering teacher, from the West Indies, said to him, in her lovely, lyrical, deep accented voice "Oh Christoph you are so amusing, but absolutely useless. You seem to have forgotten even more than I have taught you!" This accurate reflection of his lack of progress served as a wake-up call and Christoph was prepared to stop playing the fool and get serious. He bought a computer and printer and practiced endlessly on his 'Dell –boy' at home. The improvement was almost instantaneous and astounded Gloria his teacher. Much to his amazement when it came to the Pitman exams he passed both with Distinction – but he would never say 'practice made perfect'. He would always remain a technological Neanderthal and a typist with few fingers working while his eyes were always looking at the key board! It did however change his life as now he could easily keep in regular contact with many colleagues, both in the UK and abroad, via e-mail. He was able to type presentations and letters and he was able to uncover facts and data from the World Wide Web.

All the experiences he had had since leaving advertising whether it was with Job Search, Job Seekers and the Job Centre confirmed to Christoph that he really didn't want a conventional job anymore. He did separately try Marketing Consultancy. While this sphere of operation proved no problem to him and he found he could do this naturally and easily enough, he hated being brought in as the 'outsider'. Nevertheless he felt confident and comfortable enough with the notion that he could add value by coming up with ideas and showing how these could be marketed and communicated. He worked with organisations in the financial sector, in engineering and traditional fast moving consumer goods, but he always felt distanced from the brands, products and even the companies themselves. Chris believed he was there out of necessity and sufferance and not out of desire. There would be sizeable and often totally unrealistic expectations and the paymasters could be rude, disparaging and dismissive, almost as though they resented outside consultants, even though they were there to help them.

Some of Christoph's forays into this field of consultancy included working for a major engineering company, who desperately needed repositioning after a wave of adverse publicity about them had virtually brought them to their knees with a sharp drop in City confidence and a declining share standing. Their turnaround was achieved with a bullish stance on their plans and investments for the future and a strong positive and forward looking slogan. Another had been a major tea brand who was seeking to capture hearts and minds at a time when they were losing out to a trend towards smaller more niche 'country of origin' brands and products in the sector. Here the proposal was for a tie-up with the then emerging 20/20 cricket format, thereby making the brand more topical and of today. Bedsides everything stops for tea, especially in the sport of cricket! In the financial sector Christoph worked on a programme seeking to gain the support and endorsement of the FSA (Financial Standards Authority). The idea was based on the identified need to produce a way of training and making people better informed about their financial options through life. The notion was that this could even become part of the Schools' National Curriculum Programme. Importantly there was an approach to help companies make their staff better financially aware and informed. At the time Christoph was working to win the support of the FSA he had won over a key member, but when it went higher up the line it was rejected as being too costly to administer, implement and control. Less than 10 years later this whole area became a much bigger issue. This was following the Financial/Banking crisis of 2008/2010 in which the FSA were seen, by some people, to have been implicated and like many auditors were criticised in some quarters for not perhaps not having been tough enough in their capacity as financial controllers. Another area that Christoph got involved in was seeking new media opportunities. One of these was potentially quite exciting and novel and that was to create a new visible opportunity, for a small advertiser, by utilising concrete mixer vehicles, as a billboard, for their message. There was a lot of talk with a major concrete supplier but it never finally happened.

Doing the research, solving problems, developing the arguments and routes forward, as well as producing and constructing the visual representations was the fun part, as was writing and making the actual presentations. But it was often the lack of respect, from people Christoph would have expected to know better, and the inability in many cases to take action, or even make decisions that made it all deeply frustrating for a person as decisive as Christoph. It was lucrative and in some ways quite stimulating but being the shit on somebody's shoe was never a good feeling! Sometimes the people didn't even bother to give feedback or response. He really didn't feel the need to do this kind of work. In the end he only offered his services and advice to friends, colleagues and people referred to him by people known to him. From these he refused payment and therefore he never felt 'hired'. He would say to them that if they took his advice and it was successful great and if it didn't work out the advice had cost them nothing – so they should treat it as just another perspective and a learning experience!

It was after these various ventures that the realisation dawned on Christoph that he was ignoring the obvious that was staring him in the face. What he had really wanted to do all along was to write, first and foremost, for his own enjoyment. He didn't want to write for money, but to have a new chapter in his life, and possibly, where relevant, to share with friends, family and associates his output. He had been writing many letters to papers like the Evening Standard, The Sun and even The Times with some success, on a range of different subjects and issues. He had started a local quarterly Newsletter for a neighbourhood, seeking to bring the community together. This had led to Summer Parties in July and Fireworks evenings in November. People seemed to enjoy the newsletter finding it informative and helpful.

Writing was in Christoph's blood. Right at the start of his advertising career he had wanted to be a copywriter. Indeed, he had some success working in this capacity even after he had moved into Account Management. But he had not been allowed to put his name on any of his copy work as he was not a member of the hallowed 'Creative Department' but just a lowly regarded 'Suit'. He had loved writing body copy, pamphlets, leaflets, headlines, banners and posters. Now he was free to write whatever he wanted and better still he had the time to do it!

However, to fully gain this release he needed to be financially secure. And so once again Christoph came full circle. Before he had gone into advertising he had spent an enjoyable period taking his dole money and 'investing' it at the local bookmaker on the horses. It had been a fairly lucrative and profitable pastime. Chris had made money and survived and had even found the time to create his own system to beat the odds. He had also enjoyed his time at the Southern race courses and White City dog track (only on a Saturday evening!) and would bet on the photo finishes with the on-course bookies. All through his advertising career he had continued to enjoy punting on horses, especially at weekends and on the big meetings. So it was not really surprising that he would turn to gambling now to make his freedom from 'gainful employment' a reality.

But what was really surprising was that this time he did not return to the turf and to betting on racehorses. No, instead he looked at the financial sector and decided to plump for the Currency Exchange Markets. Here there was great volatility, and the chance to make a significant gain quickly without losing all of his investment. Christoph carefully weighed up the chances and realised that if it didn't come off he would, on the downside, have lost some money and he would have to go back to work. On the plus side, if he could pull it off, the upside potential was that he would make sufficient gains that he would never have to be in anyone's employment again. A fair set of options and better than horse racing where it was a straight win or loss and where recovery was far more circumspect. Not familiar with this kind of speculation he tried it out a few times with minor amounts traded to assess how immediate the trade was and how much time it would take him to instruct and execute the deal. Once he had these answers and had set up the funds, ready to make the exchange, he then waited for the optimum moment when a big announcement or result would cause a significant shift. One day, in 2010, with just 10 minutes to spare before the market closed he made the trade. He had bided his time, sweated it out and got it absolutely right. He made the money he needed. He smiled philosophically knowing that luck of that nature seldom strikes twice and swore he would never make another currency exchange trade again – and indeed he never did! That night over a couple of bottles of champagne in an old fashioned wine bar, amid much revelry, he toasted his soul mate, Fiona Sole, and declared laughingly, "I truly have now joined the ranks of the 'unemployable'!"

As Christoph looked back and reflected on his time in advertising it truly had been a long, tough, draining and sometimes arduous journey. Nevertheless, in his final analysis, he had loved the business and it had rewarded him well. He had given it everything he had and it had graciously, generously and gratefully provided him with a lifetime of stories, unbelievable experiences and great friendships that would all live long into the future. Advertising had provided him with a great career. It truly had emanated from the humblest of beginnings and allowed him to reach the pinnacle of the profession. He had often swum against the tide and nearly drowned under the pull of some of the currents. He had been prepared to take risks, gamble against the odds and take some chances. Perhaps that's why he had had so many strange and even bizarre encounters, not always of his own making. He had been given opportunities to see the world, develop new territories, and to make an impact and arguably at times even the odd contribution. His time from the 1970s until the new millennium had seen unexpected changes. There had been the best of times for the industry and then there were the hardships that would follow – in a sense it moved from feast to famine. He had got out at the right time when he was still at the top of his game, still challenging, still a threat and a factor that posed problems for a changing style of management and an altered environment. He finished his race as he had begun it full of running, and not as a tired old nag, holding on for dear life, desperate to reach the finishing line.

But it was definitely time to move on. He had survived his time in advertising, nearly always sailing as close to the wind as he dared and he truly had lived 'his life above the line – just!' Now it was time for another chapter in his life. This was the chance to write; be that letters, articles, short stories, and maybe even books. As Christoph succinctly, optimistically and cheekily put it, "Where one yarn finishes another tale begins!"

CPSIA information can be obtained
at www.ICGtesting.com
Printed in the USA
BVHW031210031120
592422BV00007B/17